The Culinary Caper

Books by Nick Greenberg

By Cook or By Crook: Trilogy
Book 1: The Culinary Caper

Coming Soon!
Book 2: The Caterer
Book 3: The Epicurean Ambassador

For more information
visit: <u>SpeakingVolumes.us</u>

The Culinary Caper

Nick Greenberg

SPEAKING VOLUMES, LLC
NAPLES, FLORIDA
2025

The Culinary Caper

Copyright © 2025 by Nick Greenberg

All rights reserved. No part of this book may be reproduced or transmitted in any form or by any means without written permission.

ISBN 979-8-89022-303-6

As always, for Rebecca

Acknowledgments

I would like to thank my agent, Nancy Rosenfeld, for believing in me, and leading me across that elusive finish line. I will always be indebted to you. Additional thanks to my editor, Dylan Garity, for cleaning up my grammatical messes. Thanks also to Charlie Goering for answering my art-related questions. My gratitude also goes out to Kurt and Erica at Speaking Volumes for shining the light of day on the string of words that some might call a novel.

Speaking of words, there aren't enough of them to describe how much I appreciate the warm embrace of the Queen City Fiction Writers. This book would not exist without their insight, guidance and most importantly, love.

Speaking of love, I send buckets of the stuff to my family for not declaring me legally insane when I started fancying myself as a writer.

Chapter One

Are We Really Doing this?

"Are we really doing this?" I stopped the van in front of a tall, wrought iron gate, behind which stood a colossal faux Victorian, lit up like a Disney Palace.

"Can't turn back now," Enrique replied.

I punched the buzzer on the intercom, set into one of the high stone columns.

"Yeah?" answered a brusque voice.

"Caterer," I replied. A few seconds later, the gate rumbled open. "Did you remember everything?"

Pivoting in his seat, Enrique surveyed the back of the van. "I think so." A smile played across his face. "Let's go make us some money."

After we passed through the gate onto a cobblestone drive, a stocky man in a fitted gray suit motioned for us to stop. "You the caterers?"

"Yep," I said.

A year ago, I'd bought a beat-up white cargo van for my catering jobs. I'd meant to have a name stenciled on the side but kept putting it off for lack of funds. In the meantime, it would continue to compete for "Vehicle Most Likely to Be Involved in a Crime."

"Mind opening up the back of the van?"

After exchanging a nervous look with Enrique, I pressed a button on the dash, and the side door slid open.

Gray Suit executed a cursory exam of the coolers and the insulated food carrier, then pointed a thick finger toward one end of the large house. "Head around the corner. There'll be someone there to show you where to set up."

I followed his directions, parking outside a pair of French doors that opened into a spacious, brightly lit kitchen. I took a deep breath, exhaled slowly, and climbed out of the van.

"Evening, gentlemen. I'm Stephanie, the event planner," said a slender, peroxided blond in a too-tight black dress. "Which one of you is Chef Anton?"

"Please, just call me Anton." I'd never been one for labels.

"Okay, Anton. We're so excited to have you here this evening. Sorry about the late hour."

"No worries." Having spent almost two decades in the food business, I was used to late nights—though 11 p.m. did seem a tad late to start a party.

"Grab your stuff and follow me."

Stephanie—like most event planners— was clearly used to being obeyed. We obeyed.

"I'll let you get set up. I've got to go check on the musicians. Let me know if you need anything." She scurried off before we could make any requests, not that I had any. I made a point of bringing everything I needed to the events I catered.

The kitchen was almost as large as my entire apartment. Granite countertops and tile floors gleamed like a show room floor. All the appliances were cutting-edge, high-end brands.

I lifted stacks of plastic containers out of the cooler and removed several stainless pans from the insulated carrier, setting them on the counter. Enrique stacked cocktail napkins, then draped black cloths over the serving trays.

This was an easy gig—which, after a rough evening on the food truck, I was grateful for. Aside from adding garnishes and arranging appetizers artfully on the trays, there was little for me to do. The heavy lifting would fall on Enrique, who would be serving late-night snacks to a mob of Major League Baseball players.

"Obviously, you're a great painter," I said, "but it's a good thing you learned the other essential skill required of fine art majors."

Enrique shot me a pained look. "And what is that?"

"Waiting tables."

"Ha, ha. Hundreds of comedians out of work, and you're cracking jokes? But seriously, Anton, if you hadn't dropped out of art school, you might have become an amazing sculptor."

"As if," I snorted. Unlike Enrique, I hadn't been a naturally gifted artist. Nor had I received any scholarships. I'd put myself through art school working in restaurants, a skill I'd picked up during high school, climbing my way up from busser to dishwasher to line cook.

Not that I didn't occasionally wonder if I'd made the right career choice. Food, typically, was a more in-demand product than random shapes carved out of inanimate objects.

I'd prepared a total of six appetizers. On the first tray, I placed a trio of lamb empanadas, smoked lake trout with capers, and scallion pancakes, making sure each item was well-spaced and properly composed.

"Take these three out first," I said. "We'll rotate them with the other three, keep 'em wanting more."

"Yes, Chef." Enrique paused at the door; his expression unreadable.

"We could always just serve the food and go home," I said.

"We could. But what about the greater good?"

"The greater good? Really?"

"Yes, really," Enrique said. "The one-percenters shouldn't be allowed to get away with whatever shit they want. Even if they aren't aware that it's illegal."

"There is that." I glanced around the immaculate, state-of-the-art kitchen, trying to imagine what it'd be like to even be a forty-percenter.

"I'll do the initial reconnaissance and scope out the situation."

I shifted a couple of empanadas to avoid crowding the pancakes. "Sounds like a plan. But remember, there's no hurry. We've got two hours."

"Except, the sooner we do it," Enrique said, "the sooner we can chill."

"Speaking of which, if you could snag me a drink, I'd greatly appreciate it. My heart's racing faster than an Olympic sprinter."

"I got ya," he said before disappearing through the door.

I was setting up the next tray of appetizers when Stephanie came back into the kitchen.

"Everything okay?" she asked, grabbing a prosciutto-wrapped fig and popping it into her mouth.

"All good." I wondered if her heavy lipstick paired well with the saltiness of the prosciutto.

Stephanie pointed at the small ramekins on the tray. "What are those?"

"Seared butter plums with goat cheese."

"Ooh. You're the guy with the food truck, right? What's it called?"

"EpicCure."

"Epic Cure?" she repeated. "I don't get it."

I shrugged. People either got the name or didn't. I rarely felt compelled to explain.

Stephanie, still hovering, spotted the *gougères*. She quickly devoured one and then a second. "That is sooo yummy! We've been hearing such fabulous things about you. That's why Mannie insisted on hiring you."

Mannie Ortega, when he wasn't hosting elaborate late-night parties, was a pitcher for the Cincinnati Reds—and this was my first big-league catering gig.

"We're excited to be here." Excited for reasons I couldn't share.

"Well, I'll be flitting about." She smiled flirtatiously. "Don't hesitate to grab me if you need anything at all."

"Okay," I said. She was gorgeous, but I made a strict rule of steering clear of event planners. Once bitten . . . yada, yada.

Enrique, with an empty tray in one hand and a tumbler filled with a couple inches of amber liquid in the other, nearly collided with Stephanie as she was leaving the kitchen.

"Oh, I'm sorry," he said.

Glaring at him, she sidled past. I hoped she hadn't seen the booze.

"Mrow," he hissed, handing me the glass. "What's her problem?"

"She's an event planner. Stay away from her." I sampled the bourbon. It was easily the best I'd ever tasted. "So, what'd you find out? Is our intel reliable?"

"Look at you and your spy jargon," Enrique purred, grinning mischievously. "Well, what I did find out was that these boys are absolutely gorgeous."

"Focus, Enrique. Focus."

"Yeah, yeah." He picked up the loaded tray. "The painting is exactly where it's supposed to be. The plan is a go."

"Alright, then. Here's to the plan," I said, raising my glass and downing its contents in a single swallow.

Chapter Two

Go Time

"Go-time," Enrique said, entering the kitchen with an empty tray and another glass of bourbon—which he handed to me. "Everyone's heading back to the music room."

"And Stephanie?" I asked.

"She's herding the band and the guests better than a well-trained border collie."

After downing the bourbon, I removed the false bottom of the cooler and pulled out the cardboard tube containing the fake Vermeer painting. Before popping off the end cap, I slipped my hands into a pair of disposable latex gloves, then eased out the canvas, gently unrolling it on the empty serving tray. The painting was a somber portrait of a woman seated at a harpsichord, peering up at a young girl playing a lute, their faces deeply shadowed. Neither of them seemed to be enjoying their little Baroque jam session.

In spite of, or perhaps because of the melancholy mood, the painting spoke to me in some undefinable way. Probably because it reflected my, as of late, current disposition.

Enrique's reproduction didn't need to fool an expert. It just needed to pass muster long enough for us to become a distant memory. But it was very good. So good, in fact, that I wondered why, with talent like that, he would want to get involved in the craziness we were about to embark on. Oh yeah; we were both broke and in debt up to our eyeballs.

"Did you make me a copy?"

Ignoring me, Enrique, already gloved, laid a thick cloth over the painting, and then set the appetizer-laden tray on top of it. "You ready?"

I stared at him, wondering what the hell I'd gotten myself into. "Umm . . . no."

Enrique hoisted the tray and headed out of the kitchen. Following reluctantly, I peered into each of the immense, high-ceilinged rooms, making sure there was no one lingering behind. The rooms had surprisingly little furniture, which gave the house an after-hours museum-like feeling.

"There," whispered Enrique, pointing down an oak-paneled hallway lined with paintings. "It's the one all lit up."

"Great," I muttered. Nothing like a well-lit stage for committing larceny.

"I'll work as fast as I can," he said. "But let me know if you hear anyone coming."

Without waiting for a response, he headed down the hall. Standing guard, I watched as he placed the tray of appetizers on the floor, lifted the Vermeer from the wall, and set it next to the tray.

Muffled sounds of someone singing, accompanied by a piano, drifted from a far-off room. No doubt some A-list musicians flown in for the occasion. I wished I'd had another shot of bourbon. Instead, I attempted to slow my breathing before I hyperventilated.

Years ago, I'd attended a yoga retreat with several other cooks. The hope had been that we could learn to cope with the intense stress of our jobs. I'd managed to lower my blood pressure by breathing properly, but otherwise, the weekend had been a bust. Mainly because, instead of going to bed when it got dark, like the rest of the attendees, we snuck into the woods every evening to drink and get high, which greatly impacted our ability to get up with the sun.

Enrique lifted off the top tray—without spilling any of the appetizers—then removed the cloth covering and slid out the reproduction. After releasing the real Vermeer from its frame, he worked his way around the canvas, pulling out the tacks that secured it to the stretcher bar.

Somewhere, I heard a voice say, "I'll go find him." A couple of seconds later, Stephanie came out of a room at the far end of the wide corridor.

"Shit," I muttered. Realizing there was no time to warn Enrique, I hurried toward the event planner, hoping to steer her in another direction.

"There you are," Stephanie said. "Where've you been? They're almost ready for dessert."

"We went to find the . . . rest room, but . . . got lost," I said. "This house is huge."

She seemed to buy it. "Where's your partner in crime?"

My heart skipped three beats, and I also nearly swallowed my tongue. "My . . . what?"

"Your server."

She either hadn't registered the alarm in my voice or just assumed I was stressed from my struggle to find the bathroom.

"Oh . . . he's still in the—"

"Ready for dessert?" asked Enrique, appearing at my side. The disposable gloves were stuffed in his back pocket, and the serving tray was tucked under his arm.

I stared at him, wondering what he'd done with the appetizers.

"Yes!" Stephanie barked. "Concert's almost over."

Having mostly regained my composure, I asked, "Where would you like dessert served?"

"The Great Room. Make sure it's there before everyone comes in." There was a note of testiness in her command.

"No problem."

She clattered off in her high heels.

"What'd you do with the apps?" I asked once she was out of range.

"Ate 'em," Enrique said, brushing crumbs off the front of his shirt.

"All of them?"

"I heard you say we went to the loo. I didn't want her thinking I took a full tray of appetizers in with me."

"You've got prosciutto in your teeth," I said.

"I've got a stolen Vermeer under my arm, and you're worried about my dental hygiene?"

Chapter Three

Asymmetrical Hipster

I glanced over at Rollie, who had dozed off, as I pulled into line behind the convoy of food trucks vying for prime parking spots. Rollie and I had done plenty of rallies, so neither of us was concerned about our pierogi holding their own against the competition. I was still getting used to the word "pierogi" being both singular and plural.

I was also majorly stoked up over the previous evening's adventure. All day, I'd fought against the uneasy feeling that a team of FBI agents was about to pound on my apartment door, guns drawn, and haul me off to some dark dungeon.

Did one theft a criminal make? I played keyboard in Remoulade, a band made up of other cooks, but I didn't consider myself a real musician. Unlike the occasional Remoulade gig, I had no intention of repeating my criminal dalliance.

The only other time I'd stolen something was when I was eight, and I'd pocketed Donny Peterson's Aston Martin Matchbox car. After a week of stomach-gnawing guilt, I slipped the silver Aston back into Donny's nifty carrying case.

Part-time musician or one-and-done thief, wasn't I—regardless of what I got up to in my off hours—still just a cook? I gazed in the rearview mirror, hoping for clarification. But instead of clarity, I began wondering who this guy was and why he looked like a late-period Picasso self-portrait. Did the rest of the world see me as this asymmetrical hipster?

I ran a hand across my face. It felt like a normal face, all the correct features in all the correct places. I glanced back at the mirror. Did adding thief to my resume change my appearance, or simply how I perceived myself?

The sound of the crash was far louder than the force of the impact.

"What the hell, dude?" Rollie screamed. "It's a food truck rally, not a demolition derby."

"Sorry," I said.

Reversing Prudence, our food truck, a couple of feet, I jammed her into park and peered in the back. Aside from a box of aluminum foil and a dish towel lying on the floor, everything was still securely stowed.

In the nautical tradition, Rollie, an avid sailor, had named the truck Prudence. More as a reference to the sunny outlook of the woman in the Beatles song than the dictionary definition. It'd also been the name of one of his former girlfriends. I wasn't in the habit of christening motor vehicles, but I'd agreed to the appellation.

"I don't think you did any damage, but Jiro's going to be pissed. You know how he gets," Rollie said. Rollie, who'd spent his life in the restaurant trenches, was my partner in this crazy world of mobile cuisine.

As if on cue, Jiro opened the back door of his truck, knife in hand. Inspecting his bumper, he glared at me.

Shrugging apologetically, I stuck my head out the window. "Sorry, Chef." I seemed to be apologizing a lot lately.

"You're such a klutz, Anton!" Jiro shouted. "That's probably why you couldn't handle a real kitchen."

"That, coming from a guy who's been fired more often than the previous administration's staff," Rollie quipped.

Years ago, Jiro, Rollie and I had worked together at Plank, a trendy farm-to-table bistro. Jiro was fired for stealing boxes of Wagyu. Rollie and I had left because the head chef was a petty despot, and nothing less than a full-on coup would have resulted in a regime change.

I climbed out of my seat, tied on an apron, and fired up the stove. "Show time."

Chapter Four

Picasso or Pierogi

"Dammit!" I shouted.

"What now?" Rollie asked.

"Another burner just quit working." I handed a trio of goetta pierogi to a uniformed police officer, whose appearance at the window had nearly given me an aneurysm.

"I guess now's not the time to tell you that one of the fryers is out, too?"

I sighed, wondering what else could go wrong. Prudence had lived through various culinary incarnations, and the miles on her odometer were beginning to take their toll. On hot days, the greasy aroma of fried poultry still permeated the tiny kitchen.

Having spent most of my career working in large restaurant kitchens, I'd been claustrophobic in the truck's narrow confines at first. But since a kitchen was just a kitchen, regardless of size, I gradually came to appreciate the close proximity of the appliances and stock shelves.

I still, however, occasionally missed the cacophony of sounds and aromas that kept a commercial kitchen humming—not to mention the accompanying high-octane camaraderie. And, in those kitchens, as a cook, not an owner, I could walk away at the end of shift with no concerns about repairs and budget.

"Probably just the igniters," Rollie said. "I'll pick one up tomorrow."

"Buy a couple. Unless you think we should just toss this piece of shit into the dumpster."

"Take a breath, Ant Man. You know we can't afford a new stove."

He was right about our financial situation, one of the reasons for last night's larcenous escapade.

After plating the last lamb and shitake pierogi, I passed it through the window into the hands of a stocky, heavily tattooed woman with spiky blond hair.

"Thanks, Anton. Smells amazing." She smiled broadly.

"Enjoy." I slammed the service window and began shutting off burners. I had no idea who she was or how she knew my name.

"You could be a dash more polite," Rollie said, wiping down the prep counter.

"I thought I was." I turned off the oven and the one working fryer. Was I growing into a grumpy old man? Was thirty-five the new sixty-five?

"Just try to be nicer to our comrades-in-arms. CeeCee's a loyal customer. She works at Tina's Tacos but prefers our food."

I covered the remaining garnishes with plastic wrap and stuck them on the top shelf of the fridge.

"You okay?" Rollie asked. "You seemed a bit off tonight."

"Peachy, as always."

"And the crash?"

"What crash?"

"Really?" Holding a sauté pan, Rollie studied me for a minute. "I saw you staring in the mirror just before you hit the Jiro mobile."

Grabbing a water bottle out of the fridge, I twisted off the top and took a long swig. "Do you think I'm weird? I mean, weird looking?"

"What's with the self-reflection all of a sudden?"

It wasn't all of a sudden. "Do you think I look like a late-period Picasso?"

"Picasso?" He stared at me for a couple of seconds, then shook his head. "I don't really know much of his work, but I don't think so."

I gazed at my reflection on the door of the refrigerator. Maybe I looked more like the eerie figure from "The Scream." "Guess I was just trying to figure out who I really was."

Rollie exhaled sharply. "Hey man, that's some deep shit. Way above my pay grade. But I can tell you this: There were several hot young ladies out there tonight who were quite smitten with you, and not just your cooking."

"Really?"

"You were too busy searing scallops to notice." Rollie began filling the sink with hot water. "But the red-headed twins in the matching sundresses—who I'm sure even you noticed—asked if you were single. I told them if you were any more single, you'd be nonexistent."

Unsure what that meant, I went with the less confusing topic. "Twins?"

"I knew that'd get your attention. Maybe they weren't technically twins. Anyway, to answer your earlier question, you are *definitely* weird, but apparently not too weird looking."

"Good to know," I said, though I was still skeptical.

My phone buzzed. Sliding it out of my pocket, I glanced at it and tapped a response. "Would you mind if I bounce a little early?"

"No problem," Rollie said. "Hot date?"

"I wish, but no."

My recent relationships had been with talented, brilliant, and gorgeous women. But I went through them quicker than disposable razors. Mostly, they vanished because I was working every time they wanted to do normal things, like go out to dinner, hear a band, or watch a movie. There were probably other reasons as well, but I wasn't astute enough to figure out what they were.

"So, what's up?" Rollie asked.

"Grabbing a drink with a guy I went to art school with. He's in town for a couple of days. I'd ask you to join us, but you'd be bored stiff listening to us reminisce."

I'd been a fair-to-middling sculptor and a below average art history major at the University of Cincinnati. At the end of my sophomore year, after realizing that I preferred brushing puff pastry with egg wash than I did analyzing the brush strokes of Flemish painters, I dropped out and began cooking full-time. Or, to put it another way, I preferred making tempura to reading about tempera, a thirteenth-century painting technique.

After a couple of years of working crazy hours in a series of restaurants, I realized that I loved the intensity of the kitchen lifestyle. But I also realized that I lacked the finer skills required to move to the next level. That was when I decided to apply to culinary school.

"No problem," Rollie said. "But I need to finish doing inventory before I drop you off." Grabbing a note pad, he opened the fridge and began tallying its contents.

"Actually, Enrique's picking me up."

Someone rapped on the door.

"That's probably him," I said. Slipping past Rollie, I opened the door.

Standing at the foot of the stairs, Enrique, his jet-black hair pulled back into a tight ponytail, was dressed completely in black, even his sneakers.

"Everything okay?" I whispered.

"Why wouldn't it be? And why are we whispering?"

"Just don't say anything about last night. Be discreet."

Enrique glared at me. "Discreet? You really think I'd tell him we just committed a felony?"

"Of course not. But he doesn't know about my side hustle as a caterer."

"Why not?"

"I don't want to get into that right now," I said, ushering Enrique into Prudence. "It's all right, Rollie won't bite."

I shoved him forward. "Rollie, Enrique. Enrique, Rollie."

"Call me Ricky," Enrique said, surveying the kitchen. "Cool truck."

He'd been Enrique for as long as I'd known him. Was this name change a dig at me because I'd told him to be discreet, or was he hiding something else I didn't know about?

"Wish we could offer you something to eat," Rollie said. "But we just put everything away."

"No worries."

"There might be a slice of key lime pie in the back of the fridge," I said.

"I'm good," Enrique/Ricky said. "We should probably get going."

"You kids have fun now," Rollie said.

Chapter Five

Monet's First Fingerpainting

Fortified with a couple of Manhattans, Enrique and I grabbed a small table at the back of Wiseguy Lounge on Main. The bar was not extremely busy, but the music was loud enough to have a conversation without being overheard.

"Just so we're clear," I said, "last night was exciting, but it was an anomaly. I'm a cook, not a burglar. So, if you're going to ask me to do it again, the answer is *absolutely not*."

He smiled, gave an almost imperceptible nod, and then sipped his cocktail.

"Am I supposed to call you Ricky now?" I asked.

"I'm trying to make some changes in my life," he said. "Enrique sounds a tad pretentious."

I wondered if I, too, should consider rebranding.

"So, remind me again, why don't we just call the cops and let them repossess these stolen paintings?"

"Really, Anton?" Ricky shook his head. "Because that would be like throwing the reward money in the dumpster. And, if my memory serves me correctly, that's cash you desperately need."

He had a point. "And how much is that reward money?"

"Ten percent of the value of the painting." Ricky said, sampling his cocktail. "But Vincent gets a cut."

After doing the math, I raised my glass and followed suit. "Is Vincent the guy from the insurance company?"

"Actually, Vincent works for a private investigator, who also gets a cut. And the private investigator works for the insurance company."

Maybe it was the potent Manhattan, but I was having trouble following the line of succession. "Huh?"

"When a work of art gets stolen, the insurance company, Lloyds of London for example, puts out a finder's-fee notice to the handful of private investigators they've vetted. These private investigators then reach out to their slightly dodgier contacts."

I was going to have to start taking notes. "Does that mean the insurance company doesn't want to know the particulars about how a piece gets returned?"

"Exactly," Ricky said.

"And does that mean Vincent is a dodgy character?"

"You could say that. I met him at the gallery I worked for in New York. He was looking for a stolen Calder, but he was also trying to find the Vermeer that my friend William had told me about."

"Okay, now that we got that all sorted out, when will we get paid?" I glanced around at the bar's other occupants, wondering if they were as consumed by debt as I was.

"Vincent caught the red-eye," Ricky said. "I met him at the airport first thing this morning with the painting. He gave me a check and then flew back to New York."

"Does that mean you have a little something for me?"

"Yes, a check, but it's a personal one." Ricky reached into his jacket pocket, pulled out a folded check, and handed it to me. "So please don't cash it for a few days."

Receiving a check for illicit activities didn't seem like the wisest plan, but unless he had written *burglary* on the memo line, I wasn't about to turn it down. I flattened out the check and read the amount: $8,100. "Not bad for a night's work. Should cover the cost of a new stove and fryer, with a little left over."

Ricky stared at me over his drink.

"What?" I asked.

"Wanna go again?"

It was my turn to stare. "What did I just tell you?"

"There's another painting that needs to be repatriated."

I scowled at him. The only way Enrique—I mean Ricky—had managed to convince me to participate in last night's little escapade was by assuring me that the Vermeer had been previously stolen. And that Mannie Ortega, the painting's owner, hadn't known it was stolen.

"Did you know I used to date a Reds outfielder?"

"I did not." Not having kept up to date on his courting history, I revisited my cocktail.

"Almost nobody did," Ricky said. "William hadn't come out yet. So, everything had to be tres discreet."

"I would imagine."

"Actually, you can't, but I'm sure you don't want to hear the sordid details of my love life."

I didn't. My own love life was sordid enough.

"The point is, William played for the Reds, and although he wasn't out, he partied with the rest of the team." Ricky sipped his cocktail. "Sadly, he tore his ACL and had to retire early. Now he plays guitar, runs some kind of charity, and coaches up-and-coming ball players."

I wondered where this was going.

Ricky raised his glass but didn't take a drink. "About a month ago, William called to tell me that a bunch of the team had started collecting art. They had tons of dough and wanted to invest in something, but didn't know exactly what."

"Once you have a Lamborghini and a house in Aspen, what else do you spend your money on?" Lambos aside, I was happy to just make rent and chip away at the mammoth iceberg that was my monthly expenses.

"Anyway," Ricky continued, "I figured William was going to ask me to steer them in the right direction—point them to some up-and-coming artist, like myself. But I was wrong; they already had a broker. He was just super excited because he'd bought a Chagall. And since he knew, as an artist, I'd be interested, he wanted me to see what the team was buying."

"That's pretty cool," I said. If I had that kind of cash, I'd open a brick-and-mortar restaurant and start building my culinary empire.

"When I asked William who the broker was, he told me it was some guy who knew how to find obscure works by famous artists."

"Like Monet's first finger-painting?" I asked. My mom still had a framed painting I'd done in first grade. She'd made me sign it, saying someday I'd be a famous artist.

"Don't laugh—that might go for a quarter million."

"Seriously?"

"No," Ricky said. "Anyway, I asked William about his Chagall. After some digging, I discovered it'd been stolen from a German collector a number of years ago. I told William, but he didn't believe me. He was a talented ballplayer, but kind of naïve. That's one of the things I loved about him."

"Interesting," I said. "But why are you telling me this? Are you planning on stealing his Chagall?"

"William is off-limits. But hear me out," Ricky said. "I'm getting to the good part."

"Can't wait." I knew he was trying to reel me in like a trophy walleye, but I was intrigued by the story.

"I had William take pictures of the paintings the other players had bought. I explained that I was just curious. Then I sent them to Vincent. A couple of days later, he called and said that every one of them was stolen."

"And none of the Reds knew?"

"They assumed the dealer was legit," Ricky said. "Why wouldn't they? But that wasn't the only issue. Most of these pieces had been stolen from collectors who'd also acquired them in slightly shady transactions. Naturally, they didn't want to make too much of a fuss when they went missing."

"So, you're saying the paintings have already been stolen, what's one more time?"

This reasoning, when extended to matters such as imperialism, murder, or that last drink at closing time, didn't really hold up.

Ricky, unaware of my internal extrapolations, said, "I guess you could say that. Anyway, it got me thinking."

"Wait," I said, rising from my chair. "I'm going to need another drink."

"Make that two."

I returned to the table a few minutes later.

"Where was I?" Ricky asked after we'd taken time to appraise the fresh Manhattans.

"You were thinking," I prompted.

"Yeah, thanks," Ricky said. "I was thinking that there's a lot of stolen art right here in Cincinnati."

"And?"

"And, given the paintings' somewhat dubious history, and William's connection with the Reds, we could have quite a lucrative opportunity here."

"We?" I asked. "To reiterate, I'm just a food truck jockey."

"Look, Anton, I've been painting my ass off ever since I got out of school and can barely get a show, much less sell anything for a decent price. I'm the very definition of 'struggling artist.' That's why I started painting these reproductions, as an exercise to hone my skills. But then I realized they were pretty damn good. Which gave me an idea."

"About art heists?" I asked.

"Not exactly." Ricky plucked the maraschino cherry out of his cocktail, popped it in his mouth, and then set the stem on the table. "There are several reasons why artists might turn to forgery: pride, revenge, fame, money. For me, it's mostly about validation of my craft. And, of course, the satisfaction of returning the art to its rightful owners."

"Of course," I echoed. Wasn't everyone on the planet looking for respect and validation? At what cost, though? "Wasn't it Picasso who said 'good artists borrow, great artists steal?' I guess that makes you a great artist."

"I guess it does. Although I don't think Pablo was referring to burglary." Ricky ran a finger around the rim of his glass. "And if the team ever discover they're fakes, they'll probably just think they got swindled by the dealer."

After taking a long pull of my cocktail, I let the previous evening replay in my head. It'd been an easy gig. Aside from some minor aiding and abetting, it was like the dozens of other catering jobs I'd done. It was Enrique . . . Ricky, who'd gotten us hired for the event, planned the whole affair, painted the reproduction, swapped out the original, and handed it off to some dude at the airport. I'd mostly just stayed in the kitchen. Mostly.

I'd only agreed to get involved because it sounded like a simple way to make some quick cash, something I desperately needed—and because it was a one-off foray into the dark side. But now he was asking me to wade back in. With both feet.

Ricky rapped his knuckles on the table. "Well?"

"Well, what?" I said, still trying to wrap my mind around his proposal.

He pointed at the check in front of me. "Does that solve all of your financial problems?"

I glanced at the check, hoping it had grown a zero or two. It hadn't. Then I got to thinking about the fridge on the truck. It'd been acting up lately. "No."

"Carl Beavers has an early Edward Hopper. It was stolen last June while on loan to a gallery in Nyack."

"Who is Carl Beavers?" I asked. "And what was a Hopper doing in Nyack?"

"If you read the sports page, you would know that Beavers is a catcher for the Reds," Ricky said. "And if you'd paid more attention in art history, you'd be aware that Nyack, New York was Edward Hopper's birthplace."

I didn't read the sports page. I also hadn't paid attention in art history—one of the many reasons I dropped out.

"Anyway, Beavers is throwing a party and happens to be looking for an extremely talented chef to cater his little soiree."

"I might be able to recommend one or two," I said.

"He was at the party last night. He wants you."

"Maybe I could just get hired as a personal chef to one of the Reds. That'd be an easier and safer gig." I imagined myself serving salmon Wellington on a private jet at forty thousand feet.

"You'd hate being a personal chef, working for the man. Not cooking what you want to cook. Whipping up frittatas at three in the morning for drunk girlfriends."

I sighed. "When you put it that way."

"The Hopper's estimated value is about $350,000," Ricky said. "Do the math."

I did the math. Almost without realizing it, I began nodding my head.

Chapter Six

Steady as She Goes

"Hey Anton, whatcha up to?" Rollie asked, stepping onto Prudence. I was sitting on the floor, wrench in hand, the toolbox beside me.

"Check it out." I pointed at the shiny new stove and fryer.

"What the . . ." Rollie's eyes went wide. He held up the bag he was holding. "I just bought new igniters."

"Sorry, meant to call you."

"Is this a good idea? You know how broke we are. And did you forget the transmission's been acting up?"

Being broke was not something I needed to be reminded about. It was the dark cloud that hovered over me from the moment I climbed out of bed until the second my head dropped back on the pillow.

Standing up, I brushed myself off, turned on the sink, and started scrubbing the dirt off my hands.

"I didn't forget, but I thought the stove and the fryer were more important than the transmission." I didn't mention that I wouldn't have the funds from Ricky's check for several days and that my credit card was now totally maxed out. Which was the reason I hadn't also bought a new fridge.

"But if the transmission goes out, we won't be able to work at all." Rollie sighed. "You haven't been betting on the ponies again, have you?"

"Definitely not." A couple of months back, hoping to settle some debts, I doubled down on the trifecta. Things hadn't gone exactly as planned. "I just received a bit of a windfall. Might be more on the way." I probably shouldn't have said the last part.

"Want to tell me about it?"

"No." Actually, I kind of did.

"I hope you're not dealing drugs," Rollie said. "Remember what happened to Zeke?"

A fellow food truck cook had gotten busted for putting hallucinogenic mushrooms on his wood-fired pizzas. They'd been a huge hit, but the police had showed up after several of his customers had stripped naked and started dancing down the middle of Vine Street.

"I am not dealing drugs," I said. We'd eliminated gambling and narcotics. I hoped he wouldn't move on to larceny. I was not a gifted liar.

"Anton, we're doing fine. Our food is great, sales are up, and the buzz on social media is blowing up. Don't do anything that might jeopardize that, okay?"

"Steady as she goes." When in doubt, go nautical. I slipped off my dirty sweatshirt and pulled on one of our black EpicCure-logoed tee shirts.

Rollie glared at me.

"All is well, my friend." I tied on an apron, then powered up the new fryer.

"One more thing," Rollie said, wringing his hands. "Can we talk about the menu?"

"What about it?" I was anxious to start cooking, but Rollie's fidgety hands were a clear sign that there was trouble in paradise.

"You know," Rollie twisted the cap off a water bottle and took a swig, "when we first started, we were like, 'Go pierogi!' But we agreed that if we got bored, we'd think about branching out."

I didn't like where this was going. "Are you bored?"

"No. I mean, I love what we're doing. Our pierogi are the bomb. But maybe we could add a couple of new menu items."

"Such as?" I wasn't ready to admit I'd been thinking the same thing. As much as I loved the challenge of cooking on a food truck, there were days that I questioned my decision to leave the luxury of a restaurant kitchen, where you weren't constrained by limited space or the culinary niche you had to carve out in order to be successful.

"Everyone loves tacos," Rollie said.

"Yeah, but that's a crowded field."

"Not if we go full-on gourmet." Rollie's excitement was palpable. "I've got a bunch of great ideas I'd love to share with you."

"Okay." I paused, considering the idea. Perhaps his gourmet tacos had legs. "It wouldn't hurt to liven things up a bit."

Rollie threw his arms around me. "Thanks, dude. I knew you'd get it."

Chapter Seven

Trina

"Trina's going to meet us there." Ricky opened the rear door of the catering van.

"Trina?"

"Our extra help," he said. "Did you forget?"

More focused on prepping food for the event, I hadn't given much thought to staffing issues. "Is she going to be a problem?"

I eyed the poster tube Ricky had tucked under his arm.

"No. She's very discreet. And I'll make sure she stays occupied while we make the switch."

I opened the cooler and pulled out the false bottom. "Are you sure the cold isn't going to hurt the painting?"

"You worry too much." Ricky placed the tube in the cooler and then fit the false bottom over it. "Relax. Just do your chefy thing and leave the rest to me. FYI, always remember to roll the canvas paint side out. If you don't, the painting might crack. Also, don't roll the canvases too tightly before you stick them in the poster tubes."

"Roger that," I said. "Is this going to take a lot longer than last time?" The Hopper was twice the size of the previous one we liberated.

"Dude, everything's under control. Take a Valium."

"Do you have one?"

Ricky glared at me. "I was kidding."

"So was I." At least, I was pretty sure I had been.

Burglary aside, I was happy to be working. The food truck usually stayed idle on Mondays and Tuesdays, and catered events at the beginning of the week were few and far between. I'd done the majority of the prep in the kitchen of Price Hill Creamery and Café in the Incline District, where, for seventy-five dollars a month, we rented a space to park, as well as plug Prudence into an electrical outlet. The evening's event would mostly just be warming and plating.

Tonight's gig was a surprise birthday party for the daughter of Reds catcher Carl Beavers. Beavers was taking advantage of a rare evening off that he was actually in town.

"Can't wait to feed a bunch of screaming ten-year-olds." Having had little experience with the younger set, I tried to feign excitement. I understood the definition of "catering" and always gave 100 percent, regardless of the clientele.

"Ten-year-olds don't scream, unless they're riding a roller coaster or watching horror movies," Ricky said. "My niece is ten. She and her friends mostly surf TikTok and listen to whatever latest pop band is trending."

I set four trays of sushi in the cooler and closed the back hatch. "I'm surprised Carl Beavers wanted an all-Asian menu."

"I don't know if my niece is typical," Ricky said. "But her crew is into all things anime."

"If you say so." I climbed into the van. "Maybe Beavers should have hired a real Asian cook."

Twenty minutes later, GPS informed me that we'd reached our destination. I could just make out a colossal brick mansion at the end of a long, curvy driveway. "That must be it."

"There's Trina." Ricky pointed at a slender woman, dressed in black, leaning up against an aging Honda parked on the side of the road. He lowered his window. "Hey girl, how come you're parked out here?"

"Didn't think Richie Rich would appreciate my piece of crap parked next to his Bentley?"

Ricky grinned. "Trina, this is the famous and talented Chef Anton."

"Hi Anton," Trina said, her green eyes lighting up as she gave me a wide smile. She had a slight accent that I couldn't quite place.

"Nice to meet you, Trina," I said.

Her warm smile, sparkling eyes, and shiny black hair made it difficult not to stare. After a few awkward seconds, I regained my ability to speak. "If you don't mind squeezing in next to Ricky, we can give you a lift."

"I bet she'd love to squeeze in beside you," Ricky whispered. I jabbed him in the ribs.

"Sure, thanks." Trina hopped in and perched on the edge of the passenger seat. "Ricky tells me you play in a band. What kind of music do you do?"

For lack of a better answer, I repeated my usual response. "French jazz."

"And what exactly is that?" Trina prodded. "And don't say jazz sung in French."

"Well, our lead singer is French, so . . . yeah," I said. Until recently, we'd called it Gypsy jazz. That was before we learned that "gypsy" was a racial slur, which in itself was a long, complicated story.

Ricky leaned into Trina. "I warned you."

Trina was not deterred. "What instrument do you play?"

"Keyboard, but I've been learning accordion."

"Oh," Trina said, turning to look out the window.

That was the typical reaction when I mentioned accordion.

"Trina sings in a band," Ricky said.

"What kind of stuff do you sing?" I was increasingly intrigued by our new addition.

"Definitely not French jazz." She laughed. "More Indie. Think Edie Brickell."

Carl Beavers had been adamant about the van staying out of sight, so I drove around and parked at the rear of the house. He'd also said that no one would be home, but the kitchen door would be unlocked.

"We don't have a lot of time to prep." I switched off the engine. "Let's hustle."

We piled out of the van and started hauling food and equipment into the restaurant-size kitchen. Without waiting for instructions, Trina began unpacking boxes of plates and glasses and stacking them on one end of the mile-long granite island. Clearly not her first rodeo. Which was a relief, because I had enough to do without having to spell out every detail of her job.

I wheeled the hotbox into the gleaming, probably rarely used kitchen and then opened the door to check the temperature of the appetizers—still toasty. I'd wait until the guests started arriving before taking them out.

Ricky grabbed a handful of tablecloths and tapped Trina on the back. "Walk with me."

After they left, I pulled the trays of sushi out of the cooler and set them on the counter. I was wiping my hands on a dish towel when my phone rang. I fished it out of my pocket.

"Hello?"

"Hey Anton, it's Carl Beavers. Just wanted to let you know we're running a little ahead of schedule."

Shit! "How much ahead?" My heart started racing.

"Probably be there in about twenty, if traffic's not too bad. You going to be ready?"

"No problem." That was my standard response to a customer. And, if we hadn't been about to steal a half-million-dollar painting, it wouldn't have been a big deal. The food was under control, but the other matter . . . "I should probably get back to work."

"Of course. Brianna's going to be so thrilled."

Brianna was the birthday girl.

"Has the DJ arrived yet?" he added.

"What?" Panic set in. The last thing we needed was another person to worry about while Ricky and I engaged in our extracurricular activities.

"Spinmaster Slinky."

"Slinky?" I repeated, desperately wanting to get off the phone.

"Yeah, remind him to set up in the media room. Should be obvious. It's the room with the 219-inch flat screen."

"I'll let him know." I barely registered the obscene size of his TV.

As soon as he hung up, I dashed out of the kitchen in search of Ricky.

I found him and Trina coming out of the room Beavers had described. In the far corner, Spinmaster Slinky himself was placing speakers onto tripods and raising them up to full height.

Ricky gave me a look before saying, "Trina, head back to the kitchen. I'll meet you there in a minute."

"Yes, boss." She smiled at me, then turned and left.

"Guests are arriving in twenty," I said.

"Shit!" Ricky exclaimed.

"I know. Should we abort?"

He stared at the floor. A solid sixty seconds passed before he spoke. "I'm still in if you are."

On the drive over, I'd told myself that if there was the slightest complication, I'd bail. Did an unexpected DJ count as a complication?

"The painting's at the other end of the house. Captain Slinky over there shouldn't be a problem," Ricky said. "I'll give Trina something to do. And then, if you'll be the lookout, we can knock this out in no time."

I was surprised to find myself nodding once again.

Chapter Eight

Spinmaster Slinky

In the kitchen, Ricky loaded up a tray of panda-shaped cookies, handed them to Trina, and then sent her off to the media room. After she left, Ricky and I gloved up—we didn't want to leave our fingerprints on the forgeries. I opened the cooler and lifted out the false bottom. Twisting my head, owl-like, I checked the two doorways that opened into the kitchen, then removed the cardboard tube, slid out the faux Hopper, and gave it to Ricky. He tucked the painting into the lining he'd sewn on the inside of his apron. The apron, slightly wider and longer than usual, hopefully wouldn't be noticeable.

I placed the empty tube back in the cooler and degloved. "I don't have much to do until everyone arrives. So, I can hang out in the hall and text you if I hear anyone coming."

"Sweet," Ricky said.

Heading out of the kitchen, we ran into Spinmaster Slinky.

"Hey, you're the caterers, aren't you?"

Given that Ricky was dressed in black with a black apron and I was clad in hound's-tooth pants with a white chef's jacket, and the minor fact we were just leaving the kitchen, the answer seemed obvious. But it was clear Slinky was waiting for it anyway.

"We are," I said, glancing past him toward our intended destination.

He peered into the kitchen. "Sure would love a beer, if you could manage that."

"Sorry," I said. "All I've got is Ramune."

"What's that?"

"A Japanese soft drink."

DJ Slinky narrowed his eyes at me. "Are you sure you can't find me a brew somewhere?"

"You do know this is a children's birthday party?"

"Come on, dude."

"Check with Mr. Beavers," I said. "He'll be here soon."

Slinky glared at me, then slunk out of the kitchen. Ricky and I waited a few seconds before hustling down the hall.

"This is it." Ricky was pointing at a spacious, sunlit room with a high ceiling and a polished wood floor. The Hopper was hanging on the far wall, in between a portrait of Elvis and a vintage Reds jersey.

"You ready?" I asked.

Ricky nodded. "I was born ready."

Why were people always saying that? The only thing you were born ready to do was scream and poop.

"Hey guys, what should I do now?" Trina called from the far end of the hall. "What's in there?"

"Um . . ." My mind raced. "We were trying to . . . ah . . . figure out where they want the cake served. Why don't you grab the drinks and take them to the media room?"

"Okay." She lingered a little too long, eyeing me suspiciously, then turned toward Ricky. "Why are you wearing gloves?"

"More hygienic," Ricky said.

I glanced at my watch. Almost ten minutes had passed since Beavers had called.

"Ricky . . ." I prodded.

"I know, I know" he said, slipping into the room.

As I stood in the hall, the world seemed to slow to a glacial pace. I tried resisting the urge to check the time. When I finally broke down, I discovered that twenty minutes had elapsed.

Time's running out, I texted Ricky.

The Culinary Caper

No response. I texted again. Somewhere in the house, a door slammed. Soon, excited voices filled the house.

I shot off another text. *They're here*

The reply came a few seconds later: *I'm hurrying*

A trio of young girls, laughing hysterically, came barreling down the hall. They were followed by a larger group, equally boisterous, racing toward the media room. In the distance, adult voices grew louder.

Ricky!!! I texted.

"What?" He hurried out of the room, pushing me down the hall.

"Well?"

When he patted his apron and grinned, my heart began to slow to a less frantic beat.

"You must be Anton," boomed a tall, muscular man in khakis and polo, flanked by equally large and similarly attired giants.

I froze, figuring he and his pals were about to pound us senseless for stealing his precious painting.

"Everything's good to go." Ricky placed a hand on my shoulder. "Right, Chef?"

"Uh . . . yeah. Good to . . . go," I parroted.

"Excellent!" Beavers boomed.

"I'm going to start with the sushi," I said, my voice still shaky. "Is that okay?"

"The girls will love that!" Beavers shouted—or perhaps that was the default decibel level of his voice. "They've been babbling about seafood the whole ride home from the aquarium, arguing about which of those fish would make the best sushi."

He laughed. A laugh that would have caused an avalanche at higher altitudes.

Ricky and I stood, waiting to be dismissed.

"I better let you get to it, then," Beavers said.

We sidled past the Major League blockade.

"Wait!" Beavers hollered before we could reach the safety of the kitchen.

I glanced at Ricky, wondering whether we should make a run for it or just pretend we hadn't heard. Which, given his thunder-like roar, would have been impossible.

"Hold up," he blared.

I pushed Ricky into the kitchen and then turned slowly toward Beavers.

He lumbered down the hall, stopping a few steps away, towering over me like an angry T-Rex. "Do you happen to know the lyrics to Destiny's Child's birthday song?"

It was several heart-racing seconds before I was able to shape my mouth into words. "Sorry, no."

Beavers chuckled. "No worries. Maybe Slinky can dial it up."

I managed an awkward smile and pointed toward the kitchen.

"Of course," Beavers said. "Didn't mean to keep you."

Grateful to survive unscathed, I dove into the kitchen. Ricky, standing next to the cooler, was tapping his fingers anxiously on the granite counter. Trina was leaning up against the fridge.

"What do you want us to serve next?" she asked.

Now that I was back in the kitchen—my natural habitat—time shifted to an almost slow-motion pace, allowing me to mentally expedite everything that needed to be done.

"Ricky, grab the sushi. I'm going to set up the tempura and spring rolls," I said, finding my groove. "Trina, set a couple of those silver trays on the counter."

She slid a tray onto the counter, bumping an open bottle of orange-flavored Ramune, which tipped over and painted the front of Ricky's apron in a neon sheen. Worried about the precious contents tucked behind the apron, he and I gasped.

"So sorry!" she exclaimed. "I am such a klutz. Let me get you a clean apron." She started untying his apron strings.

"No." Ricky pushed her away. "We got to get the food out. I'll change later."

"I promise I'll be more careful," she moaned.

"That's okay." I began loading one of the serving trays with an assortment of sushi. "Accidents happen. Go ahead and take these out."

I filled a second tray with shrimp and vegetable tempura, intermingled with the spring rolls for balance.

As soon as she was gone, Ricky yanked off the apron and slipped the Hopper out of the inner lining. It was dry. We both breathed a sigh of relief.

Opening the cooler, I lifted the false bottom, grabbed the packing tube, and handed it to Ricky. He kissed the back of the painting, slid it into the tube, and then placed it in the cooler. I was fitting the false bottom back in the cooler when Spinmaster Slinky sauntered into the kitchen.

"Is that where you keep your private stash?" Slinky asked.

"What? No," I said. "Just making sure we didn't miss any sushi."

"That's Anton's motto," Ricky said. "No sushi left behind."

"That's not what it looked like," Slinky said.

The three of us traded stares.

"What can I do for you?" I said, hoping to steer the conversation in a different direction.

"Nothing." Slinky headed to the fridge. "Carl said I could help myself to a beer."

"Nice," I said.

The DJ opened the fridge, grabbed a Rhinegeist Truth, and flipped the tab. After taking a prodigious swig, he wiped his mouth on his sleeve. "Guess I better get back to work. Thanks a lot for the beer." Smirking, he stole another glance at the cooler, then vacated the kitchen.

Ricky and I breathed a second sigh of relief.

"Chef Anton," Beavers bellowed. He had entered the kitchen from the dining room. "Do you have a minute?"

I eyed the ramen stock, bubbling away on the stove. "Uh . . . sure."

Ricky grabbed the second tray of apps and started out of the kitchen.

"Let me have some of those." Beavers palmed a couple of shrimp tempura. "Can I get your unbiased opinion on something?"

"Okay," I said, apprehensive about what that might mean.

He popped both tempura into his mouth and then set the shrimp tails on the counter, the fried batter crumbling down the front of his shirt. "What do you know about art?"

"What?" I gasped, trying to mask the terror in my voice, instead focusing on the trickle of oil glistening on his chin.

"Art. You know, the stuff they put in museums."

"Uh . . . nothing." I glanced at Ricky, still holding the tray of appetizers, frozen in the doorway, his face frozen with fear.

"Perfect," Beavers said. "I want you to look at the painting I just bought. I'm kind of nervous about showing it to the guys. I'd like your honest opinion."

Shaking my head, I said, "I should probably finish up the ramen. Besides, I'm no art critic."

"Nonsense." He placed a huge paw on my shoulder. "The ramen can wait. Smells great, by the way."

Beavers steered me out of the kitchen and down the long hall.

"What do you think?" the catcher asked when we were standing in front of the Hopper.

The painting, a rural landscape, with a melancholic barn nestled amongst a sea of rolling hills, was a contrast of shadows and light combined with the vivid colors typical of realism. Not a style that appealed to me. But, given what Hopper's paintings sold for, it appealed to plenty of avid collectors—and Ricky had absolutely nailed it.

"Alphonso bought a Pollock, and Devon bought a de Kooning," Beavers said. "I'm worried this is too boring. But I just didn't get those paintings. This one reminds me of the farm I grew up on in Kentucky."

Talk about first-world problems.

Beavers stepped closer to the painting. "That's weird. The frame's crooked."

Chapter Nine

So, There's This Rothko

"That was a fantastic party!" Trina exclaimed. "Carl tipped me three hundred dollars. I don't understand why you guys were so stressed."

Ricky and I exchanged glances. Trina caught it.

"What?" she probed.

"Nothing," Ricky said. "But you owe me half the tip."

Trina frowned. "He gave it to me. Said I deserved it."

"Just kidding," Ricky said. "You were great today. But he only gave me two hundred."

I'd have been lying if I said I wasn't jealous. Cooks rarely got tipped. True, I was banking the majority of the cash, but I'd put in many hours of prep time. All told, I probably made less per hour than they did.

"So, what *was* going on back there?" Trina asked.

"Your chariot awaits." I pulled up alongside her beat-up Honda and shifted into park.

Trina opened her door but didn't get out. "Anyone feel like grabbing a drink?"

"I'm bushed," Ricky said, faking a yawn.

I gestured toward the back of the van. "I would, but I've still got to unload all of this stuff."

"You could leave it until tomorrow. Food's all gone," Trina said.

Avoiding eye contact, Ricky stiffened in his seat.

Trina was right. Besides, I could use a strong drink. Also, there was something— I couldn't quite put my finger on what—intriguing about her. If I declined the invitation, I might never discover what that was, and I knew I'd regret it.

"Okay. How 'bout I drop off the van and meet you somewhere?"

Trina's face brightened as she climbed out of the van. "That's the spirit."

Maybe it was my recent bout of celibacy, but even in her server's uniform, she exuded a sensuality I'd been too busy, until now, to notice.

Trina pulled out her car keys. "See you at the Comet in a half hour."

"It's a date then," I said.

Ricky poked me in the arm. "Glad we got that settled."

After giving me the same smile and eye twinkle as she had when we first met, Trina waved and headed toward her car.

Ricky jabbed me again. "Way to go, Romeo. Now, let's get this painting to a safe location."

"Are you meeting up with Vincent again?"

"No. He's sending a courier. Didn't want to risk TSA confiscating it."

"Does that mean we have to hold on to it for a few days?" I wondered where in my apartment I could hide it.

"No, I'll take it with me. I already texted Vincent. He said the courier will be here first thing in the morning."

"When will we get paid?" I pictured the shiny new fridge I could now afford to buy.

"As soon as the painting gets returned to its rightful owner," Ricky said. "They're going to Venmo me. Then I'll Venmo you. Could be tomorrow."

"How much?"

"Not sure. After Vincent's cut, maybe ten grand?"

That would more than cover the cost of a new fridge and several beers at the Comet. But probably not a new transmission. And it definitely wouldn't be enough to dig me out of my other ongoing money woes, which meant my days as a thief were far from over.

Reading my mind, Ricky said, "So, there's this Rothko . . ."

Chapter Ten

A Cook, Not a Thief

Monday was open jam night at the Comet, which meant it was either packed to the rafters or crickets. Tonight tilted more towards insects.

"Wasn't sure you'd come." Trina was already outfitted with a pint of beer.

I dropped onto the stool next to her. "Why would you think that?"

"I don't know. You and Ricky were being kind of weird. Thought maybe you didn't like girls."

I laughed. "Girls are okay. I like them way better now than I did in third grade."

Had Trina seen Ricky pulling the rolled-up painting out of the poster tube? We'd been extra cautious, but maybe she'd been spying on us. "We were just stressed because we'd heard that Carl Beavers could be difficult. Turns out he was a super nice guy."

"He was," Trina agreed.

The bartender, a bearded, tattooed, Northsider, leaned over the bar. "Get you something?"

"Can I have an Entropic Theory?"

"Coming right up."

"What's Entropic Theory?" Trina asked.

"Some kind of sciencey thing. But it's also an IPA." I'd come to the Comet not to engage in small talk, but in hope of finding out more about this beautiful, enigmatic woman. "Is Trina your full name, or is it short for something?"

"Katrina," she said with a more pronounced accent. Eastern European, perhaps.

"Pretty. May I ask your last name?"

"Depends. Are you going to deport me?"

"What? No."

"My full name is Katrina Viera Danielovitch. I was born in Moscow, but we moved to the States when I was twelve. And, by the way, I'm distantly related to Kirk Douglas."

"The actor?" She'd lost me.

"Like many Jewish performers, back in the day, Kirk Douglas Americanized his name. My father, on the other hand, was adamant about keeping ours. We're Russian. Just like you."

"I'm as American as . . . uh . . . Facebook."

"Maybe so," Trina said, "but your father, or maybe grandfather, wasn't."

"Grandfather. And Ukrainian, actually. How'd you know?" Beyond the basic knowledge that both sets of my grandparents had emigrated from Ukraine, I knew few details of their previous life. I imagined their departure from the Old Country was due to less than pleasant circumstances.

"I googled you, Antonovich Cherny."

"It's just Anton. My parents named me after Anton Chekhov." I wasn't sure what naming me after a Russian playwright said about them, nor if I'd lived up to the name.

"Maybe, but if you'd been born in Ukraine, you'd be Antonovich." Trina sipped her beer. "Did you know that Cherny comes from the Russian word for 'black' or 'black dark'?"

"I did not." Given my hair color and my usual mood, it didn't surprise me.

"So, Antonovich, what do you do for fun?"

Would she think I was joking if I said burglary? That was less hobby and more about dire circumstances. "Drink beer with talented servers?"

"Fair enough. But I'm not just a server," she said, twitching an eyebrow.

"Enjoy." The bartender placed the beer in front of me. "Want to start a tab?"

I handed him my credit card, unsure how much I intended to drink.

"What I meant was," Trina continued, "aside from being a server and a singer, I'm also studying botany. And no, I don't mean weed."

"What a coincidence," I said. "I'm looking for a source for locally grown herbs. And I also don't mean weed."

She laughed. A musical laugh. "I just built a small greenhouse in my backyard and started growing microgreens and herbs. Mostly as a side hustle."

"Maybe you can hook me up."

She bumped my knee with hers. "Oh, I'll hook you up."

I could feel my face heat up a few degrees. "I mean . . ."

"Let's check out the band." Rising from the stool, Trina grabbed her beer.

She led me to a table about halfway back from the stage. The band, a quartet of hipsters, was playing a reggae version of the Beatles tune "Julia." Surprisingly, it worked. Although given that Julia was the name of one of my exes, it stirred some unpleasant emotions.

"So, how do you know Ricky?" Trina asked once we were seated.

"We went to art school together."

"Wait, what?" She grabbed my forearm. "You're a chef, a musician, and an artist? Quite the Renaissance man."

"Not exactly," I said. I didn't know what it meant to be a Renaissance man, but I'd always wanted to be one. "I dropped out halfway through art school. And I'm not really a musician either. My band only plays one or two gigs a month. We're all in the restaurant business and work crazy hours."

"Don't be modest. I'm sure you're good at whatever you do."

I was tempted to say, *Steal paintings?* Instead, I went with, "How do *you* know Ricky?"

"We've catered a lot of events together. Also, I went to high school with his sister, Isabella. Known her forever."

A few years back, Isabella and I had dated. She was super-smart, funny and gorgeous, but the relationship only lasted about six months because I was working all the time and she was looking for long-term commitment, something I was allergic to. To say things ended badly would be like calling a tornado a slight breeze. Ricky had not been pleased. Hopefully Trina, if she knew, wouldn't hold that against me.

The song ended. There was a smattering of applause. Trina and I clapped the loudest.

"Thanks, everyone," said the lead singer, the most bearded of the group. "And thanks for being here tonight. We're Kafka's Umbrella. Hope you enjoyed that last tune."

The bass player, a lanky, long-haired dude in a satin smoking jacket, whispered something in the guitarist's ear. The guitarist leaned into the mic and pointed at our table. "Hey Trina, now that you're finally here, wanna come up and sing a tune?"

"Sure." Trina downed the rest of her beer. Before getting up from the table, she tapped the back of my hand. "Don't run off now."

"And miss hearing you sing?"

After a brief huddle to choose a tune, the drummer launched into the intro, and then Trina jumped in with "Try (Just a Little Bit Harder)." Instead of copying Janis Joplin's trademark rasp, Trina delivered a soulful, yet equally powerful rendition. I was well beyond floored.

The Culinary Caper

When she finished, the meager crowd went wild, and I was the most enthusiastic. She gave a slight curtsy, thanked the bearded quartet, and bounded off the stage.

"Wow!" I exclaimed. "That was fantastic!"

"You should see my microgreens."

This girl sure knew how to make me blush. "You know these guys?"

"It's my band."

"Wait, what?" I glanced at the band, who were still eying her expectantly. "Why did you—"

"Because serving pays better than singing. And I made a three-hundred-dollar tip. Believe it or not, Monday nights at the Comet are not that lucrative." She pointed at my glass. "Buy me another beer. I'm parched."

I returned several minutes later with fresh beers and a pending burrito order. Drinking made me hungry.

Fixing me with a fierce stare, Trina asked, "Were you guys stealing stuff?"

I almost spit out a mouthful of beer. "What?"

"At Beavers's house. Is that what you were doing in the solarium? Stealing his stamp collection?"

"W . . . why would you think that?" I stuttered. "I'm a cook, not a thief."

Trina laughed. "Of course you are."

"Hey, piano guy, want to play a tune?" asked the retro-clad bass player, pointing at me.

I don't sit in on open jam nights—too intimidated by the real musicians in the room. But, needing some distance from Trina's line of inquiry, I headed to the stage.

"Go, Anton!" she shouted.

The bassist extended a hand. "Hey man, I'm Chaz. Do you know 'Little Wing'?"

"Are you kidding?" I said, surprised the song would be in the band's repertoire.

"Of course," Chaz said. "We're all about the classics."

Maybe classics with a twist. An earlier tune, which I'd heard from our seat at the bar, was a funk version of "Every Breath You Take."

"Want to count us in?" asked the singer.

"About here," I said, clicking my fingers to indicate the beat.

If it hadn't been for the nearly empty room, I would've been extremely nervous. Instead, playing with these guys felt almost like I was just jamming with a bunch of pals in someone's living room.

Chapter Eleven

Chain of Command

Why was my phone ringing at the crack of dawn? Had someone died? Was my landlord calling to remind me I was two months behind?

Picking up the offending device, I saw it was Rollie, and that it wasn't dawn—it was ten thirty.

My "Morning, Rollie" sounded like the phlegmy rasp of a chronic smoker.

"Dude, you okay?" Rollie asked.

I considered the question. In spite of being hungover, I was still exhilarated from the previous evening. I'd had a blast sitting in with the band—I ended up playing three tunes. And Trina and I stayed at the Comet until nearly two, drinking and talking, almost like we were making up for lost time. After last call, we exchanged an awkward kiss, lingering on the sidewalk before heading to our separate cars.

"Yeah, I'm good," I said. "Late night."

"Cool. So, what time are you getting to the truck?"

"Uh . . . remind me, where we going tonight?" Checking the calendar required juggling my phone, something I wasn't quite capable of at the moment.

"Washington Park. I'll text you the details. I can prep today."

"That'd be cool, thanks." I dragged myself up to a sitting position.

We usually took turns prepping for the truck. Occasionally, if we were doing a huge party, we'd share the duties. Today, I didn't have anything terribly important to do, other than sober up, but it was my turn, so Rollie's offer was greatly appreciated.

"Now, go get yourself some coffee." Rollie disconnected.

Before I could heed his advice, the phone rang again.

"I handed our little . . . package . . . off to the courier a couple of hours ago," Ricky said. "He's already on his way back to New York. I was thinking, next time, maybe we could bypass Vincent."

"What do you mean?"

"Do you remember me telling you that Vincent works for a private investigator, and the PI works for the insurance company?"

"Vaguely." I was still confused by the chain of command.

"The PI receives the reward money from the insurance company, and then he pays Vincent, the guy who supposedly actually finds the paintings. That means the total amount has been cut twice before any of it comes to us. What I'm saying is, why should we share the finder's fee with Vincent when we're doing all the work? Especially since William already told us where the paintings are?"

Now, I was even more confused. But I was afraid if I asked Ricky for a better explanation, things would just get murkier. "I could certainly use the extra cash. But is Vincent going to be happy getting cut out?"

"No, but who cares? He kind of creeps me out anyway. I think he used to be a gangster or something."

"Great. A pissed-off ex-gangster." As I ran the idea around in my head, cartoon-like bags of money began dancing across the inside of my eyelids. "So, hypothetically, if we do this, and Vincent doesn't encase us in concrete and dump us in the Ohio River, how do we return the paintings to their rightful owners?"

"We'll deal directly with the PI," Ricky said. "Glad you're in."

"I said, hypothetically."

"Of course. I'll text you later about the Rothko. Oh . . . and we should get paid later today."

"Ricky —" I was going to tell him we should reconsider firing Vincent, but he'd already disconnected.

Here I was on the cusp of a relationship with Trina, and instead of being thrilled about having someone new in my life—if I didn't screw it up too quickly—I felt an impending sense of doom about my latest career choice.

In my previous, carefree life, I had the tendency to see something that I wanted and go for it: art school, CIA—not the clandestine agency, but the Harvard of culinary schools, the Culinary Institute of America. Then there was the Porsche. Yes, it was used, with high mileage, but the insurance had been astronomical and the fuel efficiency obscenely low. And, like James Dean, I'd totaled the car. Unlike Mr. Dean, I survived, leaving me to contend with a stack of medical bills.

Those weren't my only bills.

After graduating from the CIA, I moved back to Cincinnati. Thanks to a recommendation from one of my instructors, I landed a job at Orchids, an upscale restaurant at a downtown Art Deco hotel. A year in, I began butting heads with the executive chef, Mark "Bananas" Foster. Partly because I was a cocky little shit with an oversized culinary school ego, but also because Bananas, as his nickname implied, was batshit crazy.

When an opportunity arose for an up-and-coming chef to partner with a local restaurant consortium, Foster suggested me for the position. I guess he thought I had the necessary skills, but primarily, he wanted me gone. I was thrilled about it for the same reasons. Also, I saw this as the perfect chance to make a name for myself.

There was one small catch, though. I had to invest thirty thousand of my own money. Since I had slightly more than zero in my bank account, some major soul-searching was required before making this once-in-a-lifetime leap.

After being turned down by several banks—I had a poor credit rating and no collateral—I was given the name of a private lender by the cousin of a friend of a friend. At the time, I hadn't realized that "private lender" meant loan shark. Thrilled to get the cash, however, I signed away the soul I'd just finished searching.

I should have heard the alarm bells going off. Starry-eyed and hyper-focused on the explosive launch of my culinary career, I didn't.

Less than a year later, I realized the horrible mistake I'd made. The consortium—four rich button-down types—hadn't actually been interested in my impressive cooking skills or my innovative gastronomic ideas. They were just looking for a foot soldier to follow their prescribed agenda—an agenda that was just as bland and pedestrian as they were.

Had I hired an attorney to read the contract, or even perused every page, I would have discovered that if I bailed before the one-year anniversary, I forfeited my initial investment. But again, I didn't—leaving me thirty thousand dollars in debt to a loan shark, with nothing to show for it.

Debt aside, though, what was really preventing me from getting ahead was the other deep dark secret that no one in my present orbit knew about.

Chapter Twelve

Prudence Gets a Present

I'd just swallowed the last bite of my five-way chili at Skyline when my phone lit up, indicating a Venmo payment. Opening the app, I saw that Ricky had deposited $12,480 into my account.

I texted Ricky: *That was fast!!!*

He responded with five smiling emojis.

I saw his five and raised him two. Twenty minutes later, I was at Restaurant Depot, swiping my credit card for a new fridge. Shortly thereafter, after a couple of store employees slid the new fridge into the back of my catering van, I texted Rollie: *You at the truck?*

Prepping, he replied. *When r u coming?*

Soon. Feeling strong?

A pair of question marks followed.

Got a surprise 4 u, I added.

I hate surprises!

Too bad, I thought. After thanking the store guys, I closed the back door and climbed into the driver's seat. I stuck the key in the ignition, but I didn't turn it.

Did etiquette dictate that I call Trina and thank her for an enjoyable evening? Or better to wait a couple of days and invite her out for lunch? I was usually working dinners. And was a text acceptable for this sort of communication? I was never good at these kinds of decisions.

Undecided, I turned the key in the ignition and headed to the truck.

Chapter Thirteen

Define Stupid

It was a short drive to the back lot of Price Hill Creamery. I had worked together with the owner, a former chef and now cheesemonger, as line-cooks at various restaurants around town. In exchange for my occasional help in his cafe, he allowed me the use of his kitchen to prep for my catering gigs.

"Well?" Rollie said, after I climbed aboard Prudence. He was standing at the prep table, a flotilla of pierogi spread out across the counter.

"Come out and see." I imagined this was what parents felt like on Christmas morning.

"You didn't do something stupid, did you?"

"Define stupid," I said.

Rollie followed me down the stairs. I pointed at the rear doors of my van. "Open it."

He did. "What the hell, dude?" he exclaimed. "This is amazing! Wait, how did you pay for this?"

For months, I'd managed to keep my catering side hustle a secret, but now I realized there was no way, short of telling him about my newest, even more clandestine enterprise, that I could explain the sudden influx of cash.

"I had a very lucrative catering gig last night."

He glanced at the fridge and then back at me. "What are you talking about?"

Initially, the catering had been a one-off thing for a friend who was throwing a party. She knew my cooking and had given me carte blanche to make whatever I wanted. The freedom of designing the menu and preparing all the dishes was exhilarating and rewarding. That night, one of her guests asked if I could do a party for her as well. I accepted. And then it had taken on a life of its own. A life I didn't want to share with Rollie or anyone else.

"I catered an event for a Reds pitcher."

"Reds, as in the ball team?" Rollie asked.

"The very same."

Rollie studied Prudence for a minute, as if to reaffirm her presence. "I didn't know you catered?"

"Look, dude, it's just an occasional thing. And last night was a small event, just me and a couple of servers. In no way does it take away from what we've got going on." I had no intention of telling him that my catering business was taking off. Or how much I liked it.

Instead of calling me out on my disloyalty, he turned his attention back to the shiny new appliance. "I know we need this. But shouldn't we be paying down some debts? Like what we still owe on Prudence's renovation?"

"Next time, I will. I promise." That was what I'd told Ilya—the single-named emissary of the loan shark—the most recent time he called.

Rollie eyed me skeptically, then ran his hand up the side of the stainless appliance. "If you get any more Reds gigs, can you bring me in on it?"

"If it's a two-man job, absolutely. Grab the dolly." I pointed at the two-wheeler strapped to the inside of the van.

After emptying the contents of the old fridge into several large coolers, we hauled it out of the truck and set it next to my van. Then we loaded the new one in and powered it up. We stuffed the old fridge in the back of the van to take to the recyclers. It would be an hour or so before the new one would be cold enough. Hopefully, before the start of service, we'd be able to transfer the food out of the coolers.

"Everything's prepped." Rollie patted Prudence's fender. "Let's motor, bro!"

Chapter Fourteen

Dude's a Wide Receiver

The moment we opened for business we were slammed. Washington Park, when we were lucky enough to get a spot, was like that. Thanks to a fully functional kitchen—new stove, fryers and fridge—and the added assistance of Ricky to take orders, we were mostly able to keep up.

"Beer time," Rollie announced.

I glanced at the clock. Forty-five minutes remaining. After sliding a basket of duck fat fries—one of Rollie's new menu items—through the window, I opened the fridge, pulled out a couple of beers, and tipped the contents into three glasses, handing one to Rollie and one to Ricky. "Cheers."

Then we were back at it, Ricky passing back orders and Rollie and I—in spite of the 100-plus-degree temperature of the truck—ripping through them like thoroughbreds on the final stretch.

"When's your next catering gig?" Rollie asked, as I slid a trio of lentil pierogi into a sauté pan.

"Not till next month. Some kind of ladies' tea party. Scones and everything." Not wanting to rile Rollie up with thoughts of disloyalty or jealousy, I realized I probably needed to change the subject.

Rollie began assembling a duck Reuben taco—duck was the night's featured protein. "Didn't know you baked." He was like a dog with a bone.

"I don't. Figured it was time to learn."

"I could make the scones for you," Rollie said. "I did a stint as a baker. Scones were kind of my thing."

"That'd be awesome," I said. It seemed I wasn't the only one with secrets.

"Where do you prep?" Rollie asked.

"The Creamery." I wasn't about to tell Rollie that I occasionally used Prudence. "Jarrod lets me have kitchen privileges in exchange for helping him out when he's short-staffed."

Rollie gave me an odd sideways look. "Makes sense."

I slid the final order out the window to a tall muscular man in a tight T-shirt and downed the rest of my beer.

"You Anton Cherny?" the man asked.

I nodded, hoping he wasn't an FBI agent.

"Love your food! I was at Brianna's party yesterday. My daughter goes to school with her."

"Thanks, man. Appreciate that. Enjoy your tacos."

"No doubt. Hey, I'm having a party in a couple of weeks and was wondering if you'd be interested in catering it. I'm Alphonso, by the way. Alphonso Johnson."

I looked at Rollie. He shrugged.

"Give me the date and I'll check my schedule."

"Dude's a Bengal's wide receiver," Rollie whispered.

I didn't follow football.

"Give me your number and I'll text you the date," Alphonso said. "We'd love to have you. We'll do whatever we can to make it work."

Chapter Fifteen

Is it Too Abstract?

Rollie and I had worked every night for the past two weeks. Although exhausted, I was looking forward to catering the event at Alphonso Johnson's sprawling Montgomery house. It would be the largest party I'd ever catered, but not so big I couldn't handle the cooking duties myself. It was also a relief to be taking a break from the claustrophobic mobile kitchen, as well as from Rollie.

"Ready for our first Bengals party?" Ricky asked. We were standing on a newly refinished redwood deck, overlooking a stone patio and a well-manicured English garden.

"I hope so." I wondered if I'd made enough food to fill the substantial stomachs of these gridiron titans.

Ricky had hired, in addition to Trina, three other servers. They were busy setting up tables on the immense stone patio. There were also two bartenders stocking stations at either end.

I brushed a finger across Ricky's cheek. "How do you do that?"

"Do what?"

"Always manage to have the perfect two-day stubble," I said. My facial hair went from clean-shaven, to scrubby, to full-on beard in rapid succession.

Ricky laughed. "It's a Latino thing."

I eyed him skeptically.

"Just fucking with you, dude," Ricky said. "It's called personal grooming. You might want to look into it. Anyway, the guests are mostly going to be outside, so we should have free run of the house."

I considered defending my shaving skills, but I knew they were sorely lacking. Besides, there was a more pressing matter that had been bothering me. "Are you sure William was right about this? I thought he was just connected with the Reds."

"The Bengals and the Reds hang out. You know, professional athletes with tons of dough. Lots in common. And yes, William has seen the painting."

"Well, if things start to look squirrely," I said, "I'm going to bail."

"Fair enough."

I had full access to the restaurant-quality kitchen, which was great for my catering needs, as well as for serving as a staging ground for less legit activities. "Guess I better get busy, then."

Ricky grabbed the sleeve of my chef's jacket. "Tell me again how great my Pollock is."

"Did you pan fry or poach them?"

He snorted. "You know I'm talking about the painting. Besides, you know I can barely heat a can of soup."

Back in college, he'd forgotten to remove the cardboard from a frozen pizza, and it had caught on fire. "Even Jackson Pollock himself couldn't have done as good of a job as you. Especially when he was off his meds."

"Oh, shit!" Ricky exclaimed. "Does that mean Alphonso will know it's a reproduction?"

"Relax, dude. Just means that only an expert will know. And it's not likely a Pollock scholar will be attending a Bengals party." Sometimes, even I could be an optimist.

Ricky grinned. "FYI, we're doing this on our own this time."

"What do you mean?"

"No more Vincent."

"Ricky . . ."

The Culinary Caper

"I got this. I've already talked to the PI. This'll give us a nice bump in pay."

"I don't know." Our little side hustle was stressful enough without adding in a pissed-off thug.

"Look, Anton. We . . . well, William found the painting, I did the forgery—but let's not call it that because it's so good—and you got us in the door with your fab cooking. What do we need Vincent for?"

"Hey, boys," Trina said, coming up behind us. "Planning your next caper?"

A slight pause followed before Ricky and I forced a laugh.

"Just the capers that are going on the smoked salmon," I quipped. "Which I better attend to before some three-hundred-pound lineman starts gnawing my arm off."

"Give me a hand with the linens." Ricky took Trina's elbow and guided her toward the patio stairs. Trina winked conspiratorially at me before following Ricky down the steps.

Shaking off the unsettling feeling that she knew more than she should, I made my way back to the kitchen.

I'd done a large part of the prep earlier in the day. Most of what I'd be doing during the party was reheating, quick searing, and last-minute garnishes—all tasks I could do in my sleep. That left me with plenty of headspace for burglary.

I was doing the second fry on a batch of tostones when I sensed someone behind me. Assuming it was Ricky, I pulled the tostones out of the fryer, shook off the extra oil, and then tossed them into the herb mixture.

"Almost done," I said. "Then we can get to the real fun."

"Fun?" asked a voice I didn't recognize.

Panicked, I spun around. Alphonso Johnson was looming over me. He seemed much larger than he'd appeared through the food truck window.

"Yeah... nothing more fun than, uh... bison sliders," I stammered. "They're locally sourced. Everyone will love 'em."

"That does sound great," Alphonso said. "Do you have a minute?"

"Um, sure. Just let me set these in the oven."

"I know you're super busy, but I just have to show you something. I don't usually get so excited about my investments, but this is so cool. I'm going to be showing everyone later."

I wasn't sure I liked the sound of this, but I could hardly refuse the man who, at the end of the evening, would be writing me an extremely large check.

I set the tray of tostones in the warming oven and followed Alphonso out of the kitchen, down a long hallway and into a massive game room.

"This probably isn't the best place for it, but I needed to hang something here." Alphonso pointed at the Pollock hanging on the far wall next to a freighter-size pool table.

Standing in front of the painting were two refrigerator-sized men, sipping cocktails.

"I get what you're saying about how the tendrils of black play against the splashes of lavender," said Fridge One. "But for me, it's more about the intersection of lines and the way Pollock uses contrasting colors to create depth."

Had I stumbled into some alternate universe where football players, like Upper East Side art critics, spent their days pontificating on the nuances of abstract impressionism?

"Fair enough," said Fridge Two. "But I'd argue that Pollock's wife, Lee Krasner, was the better artist."

"Hey guys," Alphonso said, "can you give Chef Anton and I the room?"

"Dude," Fridge One boomed, "your samosas are the bomb. I could eat a million of 'em."

Judging by his size, I was sure he was more than capable.

The Appliance Pair drifted out of the room, discussing Miro's influence on the New York School.

"What do you think?" Alphonso asked, gesturing at the painting. "It's a late-period Jackson Pollock."

Why did these ballplayers care what some hash slinger thought about their newest acquisition? Did even successful athletes seek validation?

"Is it too . . . abstract?" Alphonso queried, when I didn't respond.

I wanted to say, *That's the whole point.* Instead, I said, "Love it." Tempting as it was to launch into the kind of rhetoric the Fridge duo had been engaged in minutes before—a vestigial remnant of my art school days—I didn't want to show my hand. "Very cool."

"Right?" Alphonso grinned. "I had to have it the moment I saw it."

"Where *did* you see it?" I was curious how these stolen works were being marketed.

It was Alphonso's turn to remain silent.

"Sorry, none of my business."

"No, fair question," Alphonso said. "It's just that I can't really talk about that."

Most collectors loved to talk about their finds and the amazing deals they got. His reticence to share this information only confirmed the shadiness of the purchase.

"I better let you get back to work," Alphonso said, turning away from the painting.

"Yeah, I should probably start slicing the Kobe."

Chapter Sixteen

Can't Wait to Sample Your Wares

"Ricky wanted to know when we should start circulating with appetizers," Trina said.

"Are the guests here already?" I asked. This was not great news. They weren't supposed to arrive for another thirty minutes.

"Starting to drift in."

"You can start with these." Sliding a baking sheet out of the oven, I off-loaded triangles of spanakopita onto a silver serving tray, then rearranged them for a better sense of proportion. Even though art school was miles behind me, the main principles of creating art, which had been drilled into me, were present every time I plated a dish.

"Yes, boss."

"Hey, I'm sorry about the last couple of weeks. The truck's been crazy busy."

I hadn't seen her since the Comet. We'd exchanged texts and chatted on the phone a couple of times, but when I wasn't working or sleeping, she was working or sleeping.

"No worries. I've got other things to do too." There was a salty tone to her voice.

"How about tonight?" I asked. "After we get done?"

"Might be late," Trina said. "We might be too tired."

"I won't." That was a lie. After a day of prepping and cooking, I'd be exhausted. But, in the interest of budding romance, I'd suck it up and find a second wind.

Trina smiled. "Okay, you're on. That is"—she paused— "if you don't get arrested first."

The Culinary Caper

"Is my food really that bad?" I was getting better at responding to her odd remarks, but there was still a moment of panic as I tried to convince myself that she was just kidding.

In lieu of a response, she redoubled her smile, grabbed the silver tray, and scurried out of the kitchen.

There was no time to dwell on her increasingly worrying comments, since the early arrival of guests meant I needed to start cranking out some food.

I was loading up two trays of sliders—one bison, the other goetta and gorgonzola—when a quartet of dreadlocked dudes came into the kitchen, followed by the unmistakable bouquet of reefer.

"Hey mon, you the chef?" asked the tallest and skinniest of the bunch.

"That'd be me," I admitted, detecting the lilt of a Caribbean accent. "What can I do for you?"

"Alphonso said we could eat before we start jammin'."

"We the band," said the guy with the longest dreads.

"Cool," I said. "Yeah, I'll take care of you. When would you like to eat?"

"We don't start for an hour, but we have to finish setting up," Tall Man said. "Alphonso told us to wait in the game room after that."

That would put a slight wrinkle in my thievery.

"I got you." I pulled a handful of dinner dishes out of one of the cabinets. "Shouldn't take me long to put something together. I'll bring it to the game room."

"That's perfect, mon. Can't wait to sample your wares," Long Dreads said. "Maybe later, you can sample some of ours."

The quartet left the kitchen, chuckling.

Chapter Seventeen

Let's Do Some Crime

Ricky burst into the kitchen with an armful of empty serving trays. "The band just started playing, there's plenty of food on the buffet table, and the guests are outside, eating and drinking. We should do this. Now!"

The past hour had been a blur of plating, slicing, and handing off loaded trays to the servers. Things had just begun to ease up, giving me a moment or two to catch my breath.

"What if one of the servers comes looking for us?" I asked.

"They won't," Ricky said. "I told them to take a break. The last thing they're going to do is come looking for more work."

"And Trina?"

"I asked her to keep an eye on things."

"What about art-loving Bengals?" Was that an oxymoron?

"Swilling cocktails on the veranda."

"All righty, then. Glove up," I said, having run out of ways to stall. "Let's do some crime."

Ricky spread his reproduction out on a collapsed folding table and then tacked two thick tablecloths around the edges. The Pollock was the largest painting we'd done so far, and since it wouldn't fit into a poster tube, this was the only way we could think of to smuggle it out to the van.

I glanced around the kitchen, making sure I hadn't left a burner on or forgotten something that needed to be refrigerated. Satisfied that all was well, I grabbed an end of the table and followed Ricky out of the kitchen.

The Culinary Caper

Reggae music drifted in through the open windows—the band sounded fantastic. Alphonso, wanting the real deal, had flown them in from Jamaica.

We passed a couple of lost souls looking for the bathroom, which made me apprehensive, but otherwise the house was empty.

The door to the game room was closed, perhaps to discourage guests from hanging out in the house when they should have been enjoying the outdoor festivities. This made our venture a tad easier.

By now, we'd established our routine. I was the lookout, and Ricky would do the down and dirty. Without turning the lights on—there was plenty of light coming through the floor-to-ceiling windows—we strode over to the painting and set the table on the floor. Ricky promptly got down to business.

Before taking up my position on the other side of the door, I watched as he lifted the Pollock off the wall, unscrewed the stretcher bar from the frame, and then began pulling out the staples that held the canvas to the stretch bar. I was amazed at how skillful he was. Kind of made me wonder if this was just a skill he'd learned in school or he'd been engaging in other off-road ventures.

"You need to learn how to do this," Ricky said. "Just remember, sometimes the paintings are attached to the stretcher bar with tacks. So, you need to be prepared with both staples and tacks—and, of course, the right tools."

"Why do I have to know?" I asked. "I'm the cook, not the artist."

Ricky laughed. "Just in case."

"In case what?"

"Shit happens," he said, dropping the staples into a neat pile on the floor. "You might need to step in sometime. Who knows?"

"Who does know?" I rubbed my chin like the Thinker, then left him to it.

No sooner had I stepped out of the room than a pair of supermodels came breezing down the hall. Okay, they probably weren't technically supermodels, but they certainly could have passed.

"Hi there," said the one who could have been a stand-in for Beyoncé. "Is that where the Pollock is?"

I was speechless in the face of such beauty.

"You know, the abstract impressionist painter?" said the other, a Gisele Bundchen clone, complete with accent.

Apparently, even quasi-supermodels were versed in the stylistic nuance of artistic genres.

"I do know," I said, finding my voice. "But Alphonso wants everyone to wait until later before he does the big reveal." I had no idea if this was true.

"Typical Alphonso. Always the showman," Beyoncé said.

"So, who are you and what were you doing in there?" Gisele asked.

"I'm the caterer." Doubling down on my story, I added, "We'll be serving dessert in the game room."

"Ooh, I love your food," Beyoncé purred. "I can't wait to taste your desserts."

The feeling's mutual, I thought. But what I said was, "Come back in about an hour. That's when Alphonso wants to have his little art show." And that was when the Pollock would be safely in my possession.

"Oh, we'll be here," Gisele said, flashing me her supermodel smile. "Come on, Tanya, let's get another one of those super delicious cocktails." Instead of sashaying off, she paused. "Wait, what's that noise?"

I could hear Ricky gently pounding the tacks back into the stretcher bar. "Squirrels."

"Hmm. How do you feel about Warhol?" Beyoncé asked her companion, escorting her down the hall.

I took several calming breaths—the one thing I'd learned at the otherwise failure of a yoga retreat—and not because I didn't want to discuss the merits of Andy Warhol's oeuvre.

A few minutes later, Ricky slipped out of the room with the folding table, retacked with the two heavy tablecloths. "Sorry it took so long. I had a hell of a time getting some of those staples out."

"But we're good?" I asked, grabbing one end of the table.

"Yeah, man."

"Let's skedaddle, then," I said, not wanting to encounter another pair of art-loving cover girls.

At the far end of the kitchen, a door led out to a side patio. The catering van was parked just beyond that. We were almost to the door when Trina came into the kitchen with another server, a young guy with a goatee and multiple piercings.

"Hey guys," Trina called out. "Can we use that tablecloth? Some idiot just spilled a glass of red wine." She tapped Goatee on his gym-toned stomach. "Anton, this is Sparrow by the way."

"Hey, dude." Sparrow waved.

"Uh... this one's dirty," Ricky said, tapping the tablecloth but ogling Sparrow.

I nudged him. "Easy there, buckaroo."

Trina came closer. "Looks fine to me. No wine stains. Wait, why is the cloth tacked onto the table?"

"Easier to carry," I said.

"It smells a little funky. Anton doesn't want it in the kitchen," Ricky said, handing the table off to me. "I'll show you where the clean ones are."

Taking my cue, I exited stage right.

I was sliding the table with the concealed Pollock into the back of the van when I felt a tap on my shoulder. Spinning around, I found myself facing a bulldozer of a man with a cigar the size of a small submarine clamped between his teeth.

"What ya doin'?" He exhaled a leafy puff of smoke and peeked inside the van.

Instead of the booming bass I'd expected, his voice was a high tenor. This only slightly lessened the anxiety produced by his close proximity.

"Just . . . ah . . . putting away stuff."

Extending a palm-frond-sized hand, he stroked the tablecloth, causing my heart rate to soar to precarious heights.

"I can't believe you use such nice material," Bulldozer said. "What's the thread count on these?"

"I have no idea." But I *was* counting the seconds before my ticker exploded.

"Most caterers use cheap linens, so they won't have to worry about stains and tears."

"True," I said, trying to slow my breath. "I inherited these from a caterer who just retired. She bought the best of everything. From linens to silverware."

"I get that. When I retired from the Bengals, I started a design company. Our motto is 'Always the best for the best.'"

Maybe Ricky and I needed a motto. But what would it be? Stolen art, stolen by artists?

"I better get back to the kitchen." I closed the rear door of the van. I wanted to click the lock button, but I was worried that might seem suspicious, given that we were in one of Cincinnati's wealthiest neighborhoods.

He clapped me on the back, nearly snapping my vertebrae. "Right on bro. Love your food."

"Thanks, man."

"Hey, before you go." Bulldozer clasped a gigantic hand on the back of my neck.

I slipped my hand into my front pocket, fingering the key fob, wondering if I could wrench free and make a run for it. Feeling the immense pressure of his grip, I realized that wouldn't be possible.

"If you ever need any design ideas, you should call me. I mostly do interior, but my partner specializes in logos, social media, and websites. And, if you want to update your catering uniforms, we do custom tailoring. Here's my card." After adjusting the collar of my jacket, he produced a vibrantly colored business card and slipped it into my jacket pocket.

"Thanks. I'll keep that in mind." More concerned about making a quick getaway than the fit of my jacket, or the ineptness of my social media presence, I took the opportunity to dash back to the kitchen.

Chapter Eighteen

Did You Steal It?

As the steady stream of appetizers and entrees were carted off by the team of servers, I fell into my usual groove. I was no stranger to working at a frenetic pace, and the intense focus of the work kept me from worrying about the Pollock hidden in the back of the van.

"They're ready for dessert," Ricky said, sticking his head into the kitchen.

"I'm about to start plating. Just give me a few minutes. Why don't you grab a couple of servers to carry them out?"

"Roger that, boss. You doing all right?"

"Peachy." The hard part was over, and my heart rate had almost returned to normal.

Ricky paused at the door. "Tell me again why we're serving dessert in the game room."

"Because I told Beyoncé that's why we were there, and then she mentioned it to Alphonso, who thought it'd be a brilliant way of showing off his new painting."

"Beyoncé?"

"Well, not really," I said. "But the point is, it'll take suspicion off of us—if he ever finds out what you did."

"Me?" Ricky snarled. "What about you? You're in this as deep as I am."

"Sorry, I didn't mean—"

"No worries. I'll corral a couple of the guys." He darted out of the kitchen.

The thought of being close to the finish line pushed me into high gear, slicing and plating Key lime cheesecake and then squeezing on tentacles of raspberry sauce. I'd finished about a dozen slices when Alphonso's wife, Monica, rushed into the kitchen.

"You haven't seen a diamond tennis bracelet, have you?" She was out of breath. "Maybe it came back here on a serving tray or something."

"No, sorry," I said, completing another five plates. "Check with the servers. They might have picked it up."

"Al's going to kill me if I can't find it."

"Al?"

"Alphonso," Monica said. "He gave it to me on our last anniversary, when we were in Paris."

With dozens of desserts to get out, I didn't have time to chat, but not wishing to be rude to the woman throwing the party, I asked, "Did the clasp break?"

"No. I took it off to play cornhole, and kind of forgot about it. I swear I set it on a table, but now it's not there."

"I wish I could help you look for it, but I have to finish these desserts." I squeezed on more raspberry sauce. "Ask Ricky, he's good at finding stuff. He's the guy dressed in black with a ponytail. I'm sure the bracelet will turn up. Somebody probably moved it somewhere safe."

"I hope you're right." Monica shook her head and stared at the floor.

How could I refuse to help a woman in distress? "Tell you what, as soon as I get the rest of these plated, I'll come help you look."

"That'd be great. Just don't tell Al."

"I promise."

"Those ready to go?" Ricky set a tray of empty wine glasses on the counter and tilted his head toward the cheesecake slices.

"Ricky, Monica needs your help. She lost her diamond tennis bracelet."

"That's terrible," he said, eliciting a round of tears from the woman.

"Can you help her find it?" I asked. "Trina and the other servers can handle dessert."

"Of course." Ricky took Monica's hand. "Come on, sweetie, I'm sure it'll turn up."

Trina and Sparrow arrived a few minutes later and started loading the cheesecake slices onto the serving trays.

"Hold off taking those out," I said. "Just for a few minutes. Why don't you clear the dirty dishes first?"

"Go ahead, Sparrow. I'll be right behind you," Trina said.

Sparrow headed out of the kitchen.

"So," Trina said, "I hear someone lost a valuable bracelet. Did you steal it?"

"What? No, of course not. I'm kind of busy here." To prove my point, I sliced and plated another dozen pieces of cheesecake.

Trina smiled. "Just messing with you. Maybe I stole it."

"Are you still messing with me?"

"Possibly."

"Mess with me later." I set up another round of plates. "I got work to do."

"Yes, Chef." Trina said. "Does that mean you want to grab a drink later?"

"Sure, if I'm still standing."

Trina paused at the door; a coy smile painted on her lips. "Who says you'll need to stand?"

Ricky rushed back into the kitchen. "Alphonso wants everyone outside. Now."

Trina's smile vanished. "Why?"

"Maybe he's going to search everyone. I don't know."

"I thought she wanted to keep it a secret," I said.

"Alphonso found out she was upset and insisted on knowing why."

"Fine." I wiped my hands on the dish towel draped over my shoulder.

"Not you, Anton," Ricky said. "Just the servers. Apparently, he trusts you."

Trina nudged my arm. "Maybe he shouldn't."

"Let's go." Ricky clasped her elbow and escorted her from the room.

I liked Trina, but the way she talked was making me increasingly nervous. Did I need to remove the Pollock from the van and stash it in the bushes? Could I do that without being seen?

"How well do you vet your employees?" Alphonso's massive form filled the doorway, his thick arms crossed.

"I . . . well . . . Ricky hires the servers," I stammered. "But I'm responsible for any damage they might cause."

"Including theft?"

"Maybe your wife misplaced the bracelet."

"Monica. Doesn't. Misplace things," Alphonso grumbled. "And I know it wasn't one of my guests. They don't need to steal a bracelet."

Ahh, to be a one-percenter.

"And it's not the bartenders. They're coaches' sons."

Maybe coaches' sons were like preachers' kids, prone to mischief. There was always the band. But I was hesitant to point a finger at them. Musicians get a bad enough rap without adding burglary to their faults.

"Do you think it might be that hipster kid with the pierced nose?"

"Sparrow? I'm sorry, but I only just met him today." With a name like Sparrow, it was hard not to be a bit distrustful.

"Ricky seems like a good guy," Alphonso said. "How about that Russian girl? What do you know about her?"

It was a valid question. How well did you know someone after working together twice and going on a single date? All I knew, aside from her being a server, was that she was a great singer, and that she raised microgreens. We hadn't talked politics or religion—my two least favorite subjects.

"I can't imagine her stealing anything." I hoped that was true.

Alphonso eyed me skeptically. "Hmm. Well, hold off on dessert for the time being. I need to get this sorted."

"Of course. And if there's anything I can do . . ."

He seemed to consider this. "You didn't steal it, did you?"

I managed an awkward chuckle. "Yeah, I got bored juggling pots and pans and needed some real excitement."

Alphonso's laugh shook the kitchen like a 7.0-magnitude earthquake. "Well, let me know if the bracelet turns up in a half-eaten bison slider."

"You got it."

Twenty minutes later, Ricky, Trina and the three other servers came into the kitchen.

"Alphonso's ready for dessert," Ricky said.

"Does that mean someone found the bracelet?" I asked.

"No, but he's adamant about the party not dying."

I squirted a dollop of whipped cream on each slice and then zested some lime on top. "These are good to go."

Chapter Nineteen

I Should Have Said "Check, Please"

I handed Trina a pint of Bubbles and sat down next to her with an IPA. We were on the rooftop at Rhinegeist. It was late, so it wasn't too crowded or too hot.

"That was some party," I said, clinking her glass and then taking a long pull of my beer.

"Indeed," Trina concurred.

Peering out over the nearby buildings, we sipped our beers, savoring the post-work calm.

"Anton."

I waited for her to continue. She didn't. "Yes?"

"I need to tell you about my family."

"Okay," I said. Did this mean we'd reached the next stage of our relationship?

"They're Russian."

"You told me that at the Comet. And . . .?"

"My father's kind of old school."

"Does that mean he drinks vodka, listens to Tchaikovsky, and eats borscht? I make a mean borscht, by the way."

"He does love vodka and borscht, but Papa's more of a Shostakovich guy."

"Okay. Vodka and Shostakovich. Got it. What about your mom? What's her jam?"

"Let's just say my family is less like characters in a Chekhov play and more like supporting actors in *Scarface*."

"Wait. You just went from Russian immigrants to Latin drug runners? Are you saying your family's a bunch of dope peddlers?"

"No. Papa abhors drugs."

"Glad to hear that." This was not the conversation I'd been expecting.

"But they might engage in illegal activities." Trina drained her glass and then wiped her mouth with the back of her hand.

"You're just messing with me again, right?" Sometimes, I could be a bit slow on the uptake. I was hoping this was one of those times.

"Nyet."

"So, you're saying that your dad is Russian Mafia?" And I was just starting to really like Trina.

"We don't really care for that word, *mafia*. Besides, there isn't just one mafia in Russia. There are different organizations. But, if you have to put a label on it, I guess you could say he's a Cincinnati Russian Jewish . . . entrepreneur."

I ran a hand through my hair, trying to process this new information. "I had no idea there was mafia in Cincinnati. Much less a Russian one. Much less a Russian Jewish mafia. I've never seen or heard any mention of such a thing."

Trina glared at me. "What did I just say about that word?"

I hung my head. "Sorry."

"But semantics aside, just because you don't know about something doesn't mean it doesn't exist."

"So, there is a—"

Trina silenced me with an index finger across my lips.

I eyed the row of taps, wondering which beer was the strongest. "And how does your mom feel about your dad's line of work?"

Trina gazed into her empty glass. "She's dead."

"Oh shit, Trina." I reached for her hand and gave it a squeeze. "I'm so sorry."

She pushed my hand away. "It was a long time ago." Trina studied the table for a minute, then looked up at me. "Does that scare you?"

"Does what scare me?"

"What I told you about my family."

Mobster father, dead mother—yeah, that was frightening. But Trina was smart and funny and beautiful. A compelling trio. "Why *are* you telling me this?"

"You're about to find out," Trina said.

That was when I should have asked for the check and high-tailed it out of Rhinegeist.

Chapter Twenty

I've Said Too Much; Now I Must Kill You

Against my better judgment, I hadn't bolted from the brewery. Maybe it was abject curiosity. Or maybe I'd just forgotten what happened to the proverbial cat. Not that I ever really knew the details of his demise.

"And what about you?" I asked, hoping Trina would tell me she wasn't part of the family business. "Are you a card-carrying gangster?"

"Papa didn't want me following in his footsteps," Trina said. "He was adamant about me having a 'normal American life.' It was hard not to be aware of what was really going on."

"Should I ask what that might be?"

"No, but . . ." Trina reached into her purse.

For a moment, I thought she was going to whip out a gun and say, *I've said too much. Now I must kill you.* But instead, she pulled out a diamond tennis bracelet and set it on the table.

"Trina, what the hell?!" I exclaimed, shoving the bracelet back into her purse.

"I know."

"Why did you show me that?" I glanced anxiously around the bar. "Now I'm an accessory."

Trina poked me in the arm. "You watch too much TV. But unless you tell me what you and Ricky are up to, I'm going to say I found the bracelet in your van."

It felt like someone had grabbed my throat and was squeezing the life out of me.

"Relax, Chef. I'm not going to call the cops. I just want in."

I took several deep breaths, trying to quell the panic bubbling up inside of me. "You just told me you weren't in the family business."

"It's complicated," Trina said.

I waited for her to elaborate.

She rapped the table with her knuckles. "I suppose you want some backstory?"

My preference was any story with a happy ending. Sensing that wasn't an option, I shrugged.

"Well, you already know about my microgreens and the band I sing with. But I guess that's not enough."

I drank some beer, considering how much more I wanted to know about her family. Eventually, I came to the conclusion that it was best to be well-informed on the subject. "Not quite."

Trina sighed. "Okay, fine. Here goes. My senior year in high school, I won a full scholarship to study opera at CCM."

"Wow!" I exclaimed, grateful for the change of topic. The Cincinnati Conservatory of Music was world-renowned for its opera program. "I knew you were a great singer, but I had no idea you were classically trained."

"La-di-dah, right? Anyway, after my sophomore year, I realized that I preferred singing pop and jazz. So, I switched my major to the Commercial Music Program."

I wasn't sure what this had to do with the stolen tennis bracelet, but I much preferred hearing about her conservatory days to discussing her family's larcenous tendencies.

"Of course," Trina continued, "that killed my opera scholarship. And when Papa, musical snob that he is, found out, he cut me off, forcing me to load up on student loans to finish my degree. I'm still paying them off. Not to mention, I desperately need a new car."

"That explains why, in addition to singing, and selling microgreens, you're working as a server. But why would you . . ." I didn't finish the sentence, because talk about pot calling the kettle.

She must have read my mind. "Seriously, Anton? You're judging me?" Trina patted her purse. "This thing's easily worth twenty grand. Of course, that's retail. Papa's fence would probably only give me seven. But that would help ease some of my debt. Besides, it's probably insured. And your buddy Alphonso can easily go out and buy a new one."

"Trina . . ."

"But I'll make sure he gets it back—if you deal me in on whatever it is you and Ricky are up to."

I glared at her, wondering if I had a choice in the matter. If I refused, would her father send over a couple of thugs to break my legs? "I have no idea what you're talking about."

"Discuss it with your accomplice," Trina said, standing up. "I'm going to run to the loo."

I gazed out over the rooftops from my brewery perch, considering whether to bolt before she came back—not that that would solve anything. Instead, I downed the rest of my beer, hoping it would wash away the fear coating my insides, and punched in Ricky's number.

He answered immediately. "S'up bruh?"

"We got a problem," I said as calmly as I could.

"No, we don't. The night was a success, and all is safe and sound."

"Trina."

"Come on, man, it's too late at night to be cryptic," Ricky said. "What about her?"

"She knows. Well, she doesn't *know* know, but she knows enough. And she wants in."

"What the hell are you talking about?"

The Culinary Caper

I barely understood what I'd just said, but I relayed the ultimatum Trina had delivered. "I thought you knew her."

"I do," Ricky said. "We worked together at Peacock."

"She was probably stealing there, too," I said. Peacock was a catering company that specialized in large corporate events. Squads of CEOs and their spouses, all dressed to the nines, spreading their largesse like billionaire Johnny Appleseeds.

"Tell her we were thinking of stealing the bracelet, but she beat us to it. Then she's got nothing on us."

I considered Ricky's solution. "Okay, that could work. But what if she doesn't buy it? I mean, her family's mobbed up. We don't need that kind of trouble."

"Wait. What do you mean 'mobbed up'?"

I glanced toward the restrooms. No sign of Trina. "Her father is a straight-up Russian OG."

"Are you shitting me?"

"I wish I was."

"Fuck!" Ricky exclaimed. "So, letting her in is like letting the Russian mob in."

"There's not *a* Russian mob. There are many independent factions."

"Okay, professor," Ricky said. "Just tell her what I said and see if she buys it."

Trina returned with fresh beers. She handed me one. "You looked thirsty."

I took a sip. The beer was strong. Very strong. Just what the doctor ordered.

"It's a double IPA. Thought you might need it," Trina said, sampling her own. "So, what'd you all decide?"

"Well, I probably shouldn't tell you this. But we were planning on stealing the bracelet, only you beat us to it."

She set her beer on the table and fixed me with her fierce green eyes. "I call bullshit."

"No, it's true. Like you said, it's worth at least twenty grand. That would go a long way to paying down some debt."

"There's no way you knew about the bracelet before the party. For me, it was just a crime of opportunity."

"Trina . . ."

"I'm guessing it was the painting," she said.

And there it was. How long could I continue to deny? "What painting?"

"The Pollock."

"A fish painting?"

"Ha, ha. I know you were an art major."

"I was a sculptor. I never painted fish." I studied the bar's other denizens, wondering if their conversations were equally as stressful. From their cheery conversation and easy laughter, I doubted it.

"Really, Anton!" Trina exclaimed. "Do I have to spell it out? Jackson Pollock. The painting Alphonso was so pumped about."

"I think I remember it. And I'm pretty sure it was still hanging on the wall when we left."

"I bet you and Ricky are going back in the middle of the night to abscond with it."

"Abscond?"

"Bring me along," Trina said. "Or . . . should I tell Papa and let him relieve you of it?"

I exhaled a long slow breath. "Okay, say you're right—and I'm just indulging you here—the only reason that we would be taking the painting is to return it to its rightful owner."

Trina eyed me skeptically. "What the hell are you talking about?"

"The Pollock was stolen from a private collector in Chicago, about seven months ago. Although Alphonso didn't know." I guzzled some of the potent ale, wondering how many glasses it would take to render me unconscious. "We are simply returning the painting to the collector. In exchange, we get a small reward from the insurance company. Hypothetically, of course."

Trina didn't need to know the minor details, like that Ricky was a master forger and his former boyfriend was our connection.

"Interesting little story. Do you really expect me to believe it?"

"Uh . . . yeah," I said. "If Vincent doesn't get the painting by tomorrow, he won't be very happy. And he's not the kind of guy you want to piss off."

"Vincent?"

Trina also didn't need to know that Vincent was no longer part of the equation.

"He kind of works for the insurance company. Probably an ex-gangster from New Jersey," I said. At least I hoped it was "ex."

"So, you're telling me that you and Ricky, great altruists that you are, are not thieves, but simply art liberators. And that I should back off because some semiretired gangster is breathing down your neck."

"Exactly. Of course, like I said, this is all hypothetical."

"Of course." Trina nodded, then drank some more beer.

I followed suit, hoping my explanation would scare her off.

"Sounds like you don't really need this Vincent guy. Besides, he can be dealt with," Trina said.

"Wait, what does that mean? Dealt with?" I didn't like where this was going.

"Don't worry. My family's not a bunch of ruthless assassins."

"Glad to hear that."

"Nah, they usually subcontract that out."

Instead of showering Trina with a mouthful of IPA, I managed to just dribble some down the front of my shirt.

Trina laughed. "Dude, just messing with you. You should have seen the look on your face."

My phone chimed with a text. Ricky. Grateful for the distraction, I read it.

Did she buy it?

I replied with a frowning face.

Shit!!!!

I tried convincing her that Vincent was still in the picture. She started joking about hit men.

It was Ricky's turn for an emoji, this one a face of horror. *I guess we have to tell her.*

"Let Ricky know that I'm your new partner," Trina said.

"And how would this work?" I asked. "Our partnership."

"I would get a percentage—Vincent's, perhaps. In return, I don't just steal it myself, eliminate the competition, and fence it through Papa's guy."

Alarmed, I stared into my glass, trying to think of another solution. Nothing came to me. I drank more beer. Still nothing. "We already have the Pollock."

"What? How?"

"Replaced it with a forgery."

"You mean you bought a print at the Art Museum and switched it with the original?"

"It's not a print. Ricky painted it. He's very good."

"That's crazy. I mean, that's amazing. What a perfect scam. How many times have you done this?"

"This was the first."

"Bullshit. I remember how squirrely you two were at the last party."

"Okay," I conceded, "that was the first time."

Speaking of first times, this was the first time I'd ever wanted to leave Rhinegeist while there was still beer in my glass.

"Lie if you need to. Doesn't matter. So, what happens now? Do we meet Vincent at an abandoned warehouse at dawn?"

I sighed. "Vincent's out of the picture."

"You lied about him, too? Is this forgery thing also a lie?"

"Yeah, I lied. We didn't steal anything. We're just caterers."

"Nice try," Trina said. "Just tell me the truth. It'll be much easier."

The evening's truth-telling, so far, had been the exact opposite of easy. "Fine. Ricky decided to bypass Vincent. From now on, we're going to deal directly with the private investigator."

"I bet Vinnie's not going to be too thrilled with that."

"Probably not," I said, not wishing to dwell on that thought.

"No worries. So how do you collect the reward money?"

She was asking too many questions. Was she trying to work out how to take over our side hustle? "Not exactly sure. Ricky's handling that."

"Do you trust him?"

"Absolutely."

"Hmm." Trina didn't sound so sure.

Chapter Twenty-One

Junior Miss Don Corleone

"Just our luck that your girlfriend turns out to be Junior Miss Don Corleone," Ricky said.

We were seated at a small table at Deeper Roots, drinking coffee and contemplating our pastries.

"I'm not sure she's officially my girlfriend. We only went out twice. And last night didn't exactly turn out as planned. At least not for me."

I'd recently weathered a string of short-term relationships, all of which had ended poorly. Trina, it seemed, possessed those not-quite-identifiable qualities that pointed toward a more promising and possibly lengthier association. Until the night before. "Besides, you're the one who brought her on board."

"Let's not play the blame game, alright?"

"Sorry," I said. "So, when do we get paid? And how much should we give Trina?"

"I handed the package off to the courier just before I came over here. Should be in Chicago in about five hours. We'll get paid shortly after that." Ricky sipped his latte. "Trina doesn't need to know how much our cut is. We can just make up a reasonable amount."

"If she finds out we lied, she might have us killed." I hoped I was joking.

"How's she going to find out? I'm not about to tell her, and there's no way the insurance company is either."

Ricky was right, but it still made me nervous. When my phone rang, I assumed it was Trina—that somehow, she knew we were talking about her. After glancing at the number, I realized it was Julia, my ex. Someone I wanted to talk to even less than the Godfather's daughter. I hit ignore.

The phone chimed with a text from Rollie. *Morning, bro. Here's the itinerary.*

It chimed three more times, each with some bit of food truck minutiae that Rollie deemed critical. Lately, every morning, he'd been sending me reams of texts about our upcoming jobs. I wasn't sure whether it was because I'd been forgetting stuff, or he was just off his meds.

"My, you are a popular boy." Ricky sampled his latte. "Anyway, there's the other question."

"You mean which is best, bear claw or croissant?" Food was my go-to solution for navigating life's persistent quandaries. Was that why I became a cook? Or was it because I had no other discernible skills?

Ricky shook his head. "Apple fritter, obviously. But also, whether we should we call it quits or let Trina hone in on our gig?"

I peered into my mug, seeking an answer. There was only coffee, and that too was vanishing. "Well, I still need the money. So, my vote is to cut her in."

"I was hoping you'd say that." Ricky clinked his mug with mine.

Chapter Twenty-Two

You Have a *Tell*

It was my day to prep. I was looking forward to the tunnel vision that that type of work required. No unpleasant distractions from complicated Russians or worrying about stolen art that needed relocating. The instant I lined up my *mise en place* on the counter and unwrapped my knives, I was swept away into a universe where nothing else existed.

Two hours later, when Rollie stepped onto the truck, everything was ready for the night's service.

"How was your catering gig?" Rollie asked.

"Stressful." But not because of the food.

"That's why I like this," Rollie said, gesturing around the kitchen. "It's only as stressful as we make it. And you and I don't make it stressful."

"Amen, bro." If he only knew about my intimate relationship with "stress."

"Remind me again, which brewery are we going to?"

"Brink," I said. "The one where everyone loved our scallop tacos. By the way, I got a great deal on some amazing scallops this morning."

Rollie's taco concept was going gangbusters. Every day, we'd discuss adding a couple of new items to the roster. And surprisingly, the pierogi hadn't suffered from the self-imposed competition.

"Cool. Did you see that Russian chick again?"

I nodded, trying to summon some degree of enthusiasm.

"What does that mean? Did she dump you already?"

"No, it's complicated." That was going to be my new catchphrase. Everyone needed one, right?

"That's what I've been trying to tell you." Rollie peered into the fryers. "It's always complicated."

"So, you're an expert now?"

Rollie's relationships were as fleeting as mine. To his credit, he'd been in his current one for almost four months—a new record.

He patted my shoulder. "Listen, my friend, everything in life that is important is complicated. You've just got to be willing to work at it. And that work, when it's meaningful, is well worth the effort."

"Thank you, Buddha." He clearly didn't know Trina. "We better get going. You mind driving?"

"Por supuesto, mi amigo." Ever since we'd rolled out our taco line-up, Rollie had begun dusting off his four semesters of high school Spanish.

My phone rang as Rollie pulled out of the lot and headed down Mt. Hope Avenue. I didn't recognize the number, but I answered anyway.

"What kind of crap are you shitwads trying to pull?" the caller barked.

"Um . . . I think you have the wrong number?" I racked my brain, trying to remember who I'd pissed off lately.

"Your buddy Ricky is ignoring my calls." He paused. "This is Anton, right?"

Not sure I wanted to admit to being me, I remained silent.

"This is Vincent Corelli. The guy that's been putting money in your pocket. And the guy who doesn't appreciate getting stabbed in the back."

"I don't really—"

"Shut the fuck up and listen," Vincent snapped.

"Is that her?" Rollie whispered.

I shook my head. In spite of my new insight into Trina's hobbies, I'd still rather have been talking to her than Vincent.

"I talked to James. I know what's going on," Vincent growled.

"Who?" I hoped James wasn't another pissed-off gangster.

"James Troggert, the private investigator who works for the insurance company. I know he paid Ricky for the Pollock. So, here's what's going to happen. In the next half hour, either you or Ricky—I don't give a shit who—is going to Venmo me my cut of the reward."

"You should probably talk to Ricky," I said. Sorry, Ricky.

"I'm talking to you. And if I don't get my money in half an hour . . . you *stronzos* are not going to like the consequences."

"Look, Vincent," I pleaded, but he'd already hung up.

"Who's Vincent?" Rollie asked, turning onto the I-75 ramp.

"He's . . . It's . . ."

"Complicated, I know," Rollie said. "Does this have anything to do with your recent influx of cash?"

"No." I'd fessed up to my catering gigs, but I wasn't ready to confess to my more nefarious moonlighting ventures.

"Bullshit. I know when you're lying. You have a *tell*."

"I do not!" If Rollie was right, maybe it'd behoove me to know. "What is it?"

He ignored my question. "Is this Vincent guy your bookie or what?"

"Rollie, I love you man, but believe me, it's better you don't know." I'd sure have liked to know what my "tell" was.

"What did I say about not getting mixed up in crazy get-rich-quick schemes?"

My phone rang again. Ricky. I debated not answering, but after a few rings, I gave in. "One word. Vincent." There was a lot more I wanted to say, but with Rollie sitting next to me, that would have to suffice.

"I know. But it's too late. I already got paid," Ricky said. "I'm about to Venmo you."

"We can still send Vincent his share."

"Maybe Trina can help," Ricky suggested.

"I don't think that's a great idea."

"Do you have a better one?"

"Already told you," I said, frustrated by this exchange and increasingly worried about what Vincent might do if he didn't get his cut.

"What's going on?" Rollie accelerated around a convoy of slow-moving trucks.

I glanced at him and shook my head.

"I'm texting her about our situation," Ricky said.

"Ricky . . ."

Seconds later, he said, "I just texted Trina Vincent's full name and who he works for."

"I gotta go. I can't deal with this right now." I hung up.

"Anything I can do to help?" Rollie asked.

"Cook the shit out of this thing tonight."

"I got you, bro."

Chapter Twenty-Three

I Want What He's Having

"Damn, dude, we're killing it tonight!" Rollie shouted. "Till's clankin' with coin."

There was no actual till or coins, but the money was definite flowing in.

I pirouetted around him, grabbed a squeeze bottle off the counter, and scribbled some mole sauce onto an order of lobster-caviar tacos. "I just hope the food lasts another hour."

"Doesn't matter," Rollie said. "That'll just mean we can knock off early."

He was right. If we ran out of food, then none was wasted. Besides, the insanely hot temperature on Prudence was starting to take its toll.

I slid the tacos out the window to a large dude with a braided beard who was dressed in a monk's robe. "Enjoy."

"Bless you, my son," he replied, doing some kind of surfer-priest hand gesture.

"I want what he's having," Trina said, coming into view after the bearded friar stepped aside.

Rollie typed her order into the tablet and swiped her credit card.

"What are you doing here, Trina?" I asked. "Kind of busy right now."

"And I'm kind of hungry. Whip me up some tacos, chef boy."

"Is that her?" Rollie stuck his head out the window to get a better look. "She is muy caliente!"

"And dangerous," I added, lining up three corn tortillas on the counter, spooning in a generous portion of lobster, and topping it off with lumpfish caviar and a dollop of sour cream.

Rollie grabbed a plate off the stack and set it next to the tacos. "You, my friend, are a true artiste."

After transferring the trio of tacos to the plate, I sprinkled them with a handful of cilantro leaves.

"So, when are you going to introduce me?" Rollie asked.

I loaded the tacos onto a plate and then finished them with a handful of crumbled cotija. "We'll see."

"I dealt with your little problem," Trina said. "And you're welcome."

"Problem?"

"How do you solve a problem like Vincent?" Trina sang, apparently a fan of *The Sound of Music*.

I handed her the tacos, anxious to return my focus to plating food rather than whatever drama she might have in mind.

"I'm going to grab a seat and chow down on this delicious food," Trina said. "Come find me when you're done."

"Damn, dude!" Rollie exclaimed. "Don't let her get away."

Until the previous evening, I would have agreed with him. Now, I was torn between infatuation and abject fear. Extremely confusing.

Thirty minutes later, we sold the last taco and began cleaning up.

After the countertops were cleared and wiped down, and the remaining food items refrigerated, I dabbed the sweat off my brow with a dish towel. "I guess I should see if Trina's still here."

"Go," Rollie said. "I can drive Prudence back if you wanna hang out a while."

I threw the dish towel into the laundry hamper, along with my apron, and headed into the brewery. Trina was sitting at the bar, chatting with the bartender, a heavily inked woman of Amazonian proportions.

"You look like you need a beer," Trina said. "Hey, Charlie, grab my friend here a pint of your strongest ale."

"Coming right up." Charlie moved off toward the row of taps.

"The lobster-caviar tacos were pure ecstasy!" Trina exclaimed. "I almost came."

If I'd been holding a beer, I probably would have done a classic spit-take.

Trina patted the empty stool next to her. "Sit already."

I eyed the door, not sure I wanted to stay, but when Charlie placed a beer on the bar, I dropped into the seat.

Trina clinked her glass to mine. "Vashe zdorov'ye."

Assuming that what she'd said meant cheers, I attempted to repeat it.

Trina laughed. "We'll have to work on your Russian. So, you guys must have made bank tonight. Does that mean you're going to retire early from your side hustle?"

"Yeah, we did well tonight. And yes, my days of thieving are now behind me." I hoped she didn't know my tell.

"Good one. Shall we talk about Vincent Corelli?"

I sampled the ale. Lethal. I took a second sip. Then, I noticed she was waiting for an answer. "Whatever you did, I don't want to know."

Trina grabbed my hand. "I didn't do anything. But my cousin Vlad might have had a 'conversation' with him."

"Conversation?"

"Vlad can be very persuasive," Trina said. "Don't worry, he rarely resorts to violence."

"That's reassuring." No doubt my tell was redlining.

"The main thing is that Vincent won't be bothering you guys anymore. Which means more money for all of us. Ricky paid me, by the way." Trina traced a line down my arm with her index finger. "I know you're thinking, since I'm taking Vincent's share, that you boys are still making the same. But, trust me, I'm bringing a lot more to the table than Vincent ever did."

Rather than inquire as to what exactly she meant, I dove back into my beer.

"For example." Placing a hand on my knee, she leaned in for a kiss.

Chapter Twenty-Four

Still a Bachelor

Peeling my eyes open, I realized I was sprawled out naked on a bed. A bed that wasn't my own. Usually, that was a good thing. But given that Trina was the party involved, the jury was still out.

On the one hand, Trina was smart, gorgeous, and a blast to hang out with. On the other, why the hell had I gone home with a mobster's daughter/thief who was now meddling in my own illicit activities?

After running a hand through my hair, I dragged myself up to a sitting position and collected my clothes. I was mostly dressed when Trina came into the bedroom in short-shorts and a sheer white T-shirt. She was holding a cup of black coffee.

"Don't get dressed on my account."

I managed an indecipherable grunt. She laughed—a laugh that almost made me forget her back story. When she handed me the cup, I took an eager sip.

"What should we do today?" Trina asked. "Grab some breakfast, steal a Monet, get married?"

I nearly choked on my coffee.

"Kidding. I was only serious about one of those." I hoped it was the breakfast option. I was starving.

"Justice of the peace, okay?"

"What's next?" Trina asked. We were eating chocolate croissants and downing copious amounts of coffee in the back room at French Crust. And I was still a bachelor.

"I've got to buy groceries for the truck."

Trina nudged me with an elbow. "I meant, as if you didn't know, whose painting are we going to steal next?"

"Not so loud," I pleaded. I took another bite of the flaky, buttery croissant, amazed at the perfection of French Crust's offerings. Especially since my pastry skills were sorely lacking. "Ricky hasn't mentioned anything about another . . . project, yet."

"Maybe I should talk to him."

"Be my guest." I shouldn't have said that. Trina's involvement wasn't Ricky's fault. Or maybe it was. Sure, I'd slept with her, but he was the one who'd originally hired her. "None of my upcoming catering gigs are for the Reds or Bengals."

"Too bad. Those are the only ones I'm interested in."

My phone erupted with a series of chimes. Rollie, no doubt. I did a cursory read, replied with a thumbs-up, and then set the phone back on the table. "When are you going to return the bracelet?"

"Aww, do I have to?" Trina pouted.

"That was the agreement."

"Even after last night?" When I didn't respond, she added, "Fine. I'll do it tonight. Unless you want to come back to my place and pick up where we left off."

"Wish I could, but I've got to get my shopping done." As tempting as her offer was, I had numerous food-truck-related errands to run. Also, I needed time to process our . . . complicated relationship, or whatever this was.

"What are you buying?"

"Mostly produce, shrimp, some cooking oil . . . I don't remember everything. Rollie just texted a new list."

"You should come check out my greenhouse," Trina said. "I might be able to hook you up with some fresh produce. What do you need?"

Lately, Rollie and I had been dissatisfied with the quality of purchases from our current supplier. Maybe it was time to look elsewhere. Nepotism wasn't necessarily a bad thing, right? "Cilantro, green onions, maybe some arugula."

"Arugula, I don't have, but I do have kale. Would that work?"

"Possibly. But don't get mad if I don't buy anything. Rollie's very picky about produce. Actually, he's picky about everything." I wondered why he put up with me.

Trina tore off an end of her croissant and stuffed it into her mouth. "I won't get mad, because my stuff is amazing. If you don't believe me, I can give you the names of half a dozen chefs who swear it's the best in town."

"Easy there, buckaroo. I believe you."

"Then let's go right now."

"Can I finish my breakfast first?"

Chapter Twenty-Five

The Kitchen, She Never Sleeps

I placed the last pierogi on the sheet pan and dusted a thin coating of flour off of my apron. My hands were stiff from the four hundred or so I'd just finished making. I definitely needed a break before starting on the taco fillings. The floor of the truck, looking like it had just snowed, was going to require a thorough sweeping before I got back to work.

I had slipped the pan into the fridge and was washing my hands when the phone rang.

"Hey Phillipe, long time no," I said.

"The kitchen, she never sleeps," Phillipe said, exaggerating his French accent.

Phillipe, a former Parisian, and graduate of Le Cordon Bleu, was also the lead singer in Remoulade, the band—all cooks—that I played in. His accent, authentic as it was, came and went according to the situation at hand. He could just as easily mimic a New Yorker.

"We should grab a drink one of these nights," I said, knowing his propensity toward excellent wine.

"Mais oui, mon ami. But I'm actually calling to tell you about a band gig."

"If I'm free, I'd love to do it." It wasn't often, given our crazy schedules, that we were all available for a gig.

"Don't worry. It's on a Monday night," Phillipe said.

"Cool." Except for the occasional private party, Prudence didn't go out on Monday. It was also rare to have a catering gig that early in the week. The rest of the band worked restaurant jobs, but they were mostly off on Mondays.

"Troy Bradington, one of the Reds, is throwing a French-themed party for Bastille Day. His wife is French. *Vive la France*!"

"Reds, as in the baseball team?" I had a reputation for not being particularly well-informed about sports-related matters. A reputation I strived to maintain.

"No, the Cincinnati Communist Party," Phillipe retorted. "They're doing a recruitment drive."

"Are you joining?"

Phillipe laughed his guttural French laugh. "Anton, comrade, did you know that the word 'gullible' is not in the dictionary?"

This could go on all day. "I'm just surprised a bunch of ballers would want to go all French."

"What are you saying about my beloved country? Our food and wine is the best in the known universe."

Never debate a Frenchman about the above topics. "I love your country. You guys make great fries. So, tell me about the gig."

He told me about the gig.

"Do they need a caterer?" I asked, tapping the date into my calendar. After setting my phone on the counter and switching it to speaker, I grabbed a broom from the storage closet and swept the spilled flour into the dustpan.

"Yes. Me, of course."

"You're going to sing and cater?"

"And play guitar. I'm very talented, non?"

Talented, yes. Humble, not so much. "Do you need help cooking?" I knew the answer, but I couldn't help myself.

"Are you French?" Phillipe asked. He responded for me. *"Non."*

"How are you going to play guitar and cater?" Outside of the kitchen, I wasn't much of a multi-tasker.

"Did I not just say how talented I was? But seriously, Anton, you've worked in real kitchens. You know you have to trust your staff. And I do, with my life. But then again, as we've established, you're not French. So, you may never understand."

He was right. I wasn't French. Wait. Reds? Party? Might there be a stolen painting hanging in the man cave?

"Do you need servers?" I asked.

"You really want to do that?"

I laughed. "No. I'd be terrible at it, but I've been using some good people."

"On your little truck?"

"I do a bit of catering myself." Around Phillipe, I constantly felt the need to defend my career choice. "Actually, I've been working quite a bit for the Reds and Bengals."

"That is fantastique! I knew you were a fine chef. It's a pity your skills are being wasted cooking in an RV."

I glanced around Prudence, admiring her compactness. Everything a cook needed was no more than two steps away—a luxury no restaurant kitchen offered. Phillipe would never understand the thrill of working in such an environment. "Would you like my server's contact info?"

"Yes, please."

After sharing Ricky's details with Phillipe, I called Ricky.

"What's up, Anton?"

"Party. July 14. Troy Bradington's house."

"Are you asking me out on a date? And who is Troy Bradington? Are we having a ménage a trois?"

"To answer your first and third questions, no," I said. "It's a catering gig. And Troy plays for the Reds. Find out if he has any stolen . . . cookies."

"I'll check with William. How many servers do you need?"

"I don't know. Phillipe Rameau is doing the catering, but our band is playing."

"Ooh, la la. The famous French chef."

I'd never get famous being a food truck cook. Not that I cared. Really.

"Should I see if Trina is available?"

"If we must," I grumbled. Opening the fridge, I began pulling out ingredients for the night's taco offerings and lining them up on the stainless counter.

"William just texted back. Troy has a Rodin."

"Seriously? Even professional athletes can't afford a Rodin. Can they?"

"It's just a maquette, but it's still pretty valuable."

"Very cool," I said. A maquette was a small preliminary model of an artist's sculpture. A kind of rough draft. Kind of like the way I'd been feeling lately—rough, and a fraction of the value of the real deal.

"What's the medium?"

"Terracotta."

"Too bad you're not a sculptor," I said. "At least you'll get some catering work out of it."

"But you are," Ricky said.

"I'm what?"

"You were an extremely talented sculptor. Before you got all chefy."

"A million years ago. And I wasn't that talented. That's why I dropped out." After seeing the art my classmates had been creating, I realized I was way out of my depths.

My phone chimed. I opened the text. Ricky had sent a photo of a sculpture depicting a muscular man who'd just bowled his game-winning strike. Or maybe not.

"Above my pay grade," I said, admiring Rodin's work.

"Give it a shot. You've got nothing to lose."

"I don't own any tools."

"Did I tell you I was renting a studio on Central?" Ricky asked.

"Central Parkway?"

"No, Central Avenue. The building used to be a warehouse or something, but now it's divided up into studios. Anyway, Alfie, the guy in the space across from me, is a sculptor. He might let you use his stuff. He's nice. Cute too."

Central Avenue was Central Parkway's black sheep uncle, or redheaded stepchild, depending on your color preference.

"Ricky," I pleaded, but he'd already hung up.

After grabbing a bottle of water, I dropped into the truck's driver's seat, twisted the cap, and took a swig. I tapped the phone again and studied the picture Ricky'd sent. It wasn't a life-sized sculpture, but it was still a work of art. And I hadn't done art in close to a decade.

"Looking at porn?" Rollie asked as he stepped onto the truck.

He was wearing a button-down shirt and a sport coat. For as long as I'd known him, he'd been extremely neat and clean-cut—not just his clothing and hair, but his character and his outlook on life. Everything well-defined. My character, on the other hand, was well represented by my flour-speckled clothes and riot of dark hair.

I stuffed the phone into my pocket. "Nah, just pictures of your sister. But check this out," I said, pulling out several bags of produce I'd bought from Trina.

Rollie peeked into the bags, giving each one a thorough sniff. "Damn, these look nice. Obviously not Marcello's. Where'd you get 'em?"

"Trina. Did I tell you she had a greenhouse?"

"You did not." Rollie removed his jacket and shirt and slipped into an EpicCure tee. "She's full of surprises, isn't she?"

He had no idea.

Chapter Twenty-Six

Rodin, You Crazy Nut!

"Dammit!" I screamed, flinging the carving knife across the room.

I'd been at Alfie's—Ricky's newest crush—studio every morning for the past week, attempting to scrape out a Rodin clone. Alfie was spending the month in Maine and had offered me the use of his space while he was gone. I still wasn't sure how Ricky had talked me into this latest madness.

The good news was that the sculpture was only thirty-six inches high. The bad news was that my artistic skills were rustier than a '63 Chevy.

Every time I got close to perfecting Bowling Dude, something would crumble off. I guess breaking down whole chickens wasn't the best way to keep one's hand in as a sculptor. Although, my hands were equally as gnarly.

Ricky appeared in the doorway. "Everything okay?"

"The party is less than a week away, and I still don't have a serviceable reproduction. So, no, everything is not okay."

"Chill, dude. You got this. You just need to relax."

I grabbed a sculpting rake off the workbench and waved it at Ricky. "Don't tell me to relax! You think this is like riding a fucking bike?"

"Let's go get a coffee, or—I know it's early—a drink."

The last thing I needed was more caffeine. And 10 a.m. was a trifle premature to have a cocktail, except under extenuating circumstances. Maybe this was the definition of extenuating.

Standing in a puddle of wet clay, I studied the enlarged photo I'd tacked to the wall. "Wait." I stepped closer to the picture. After staring at it for a couple of seconds, I scrutinized the rake I was holding.

"I'm waiting," Ricky said.

"Rodin, you crazy nut!" I shouted, grabbing a different knife. "Why didn't you tell me I was using the wrong tool?"

Rodin, still dead, didn't answer.

"Guess I'll leave you to it, then," Ricky said, backing out of the studio.

Chapter Twenty-Seven

The Girl Had Skills

"It's done," Trina said after I answered the phone.

"What?" I rasped, disappointed she'd interrupted my dream about dancing truffles, complete with pink tutus.

Slipping on sweats and a T-shirt, I stepped to the window and lifted the shade. The sun, apparently having been up for hours, showed no mercy on my sleep-encrusted eyelids. In protest, I lowered the shade to a more benign position.

"The bracelet. I left it under a chair on the patio."

"Weren't you worried about security cameras?"

"Nah. It was a new moon, and I was dressed in black."

The girl had skills. "Do you think they'll find it?"

"The missus already did."

"How do you know?"

"I hid in the bushes to make sure."

"Wow. Okay. Great." I sat back down on the edge of the bed, reminding myself to never underestimate the thoroughness of this woman.

"Wanna grab some breakfast?"

"Can't. Too much to do." I was planning on grabbing a quick bite and then heading to the studio to put the finishing touches on the sculpture.

"I'm downstairs," Trina said. "I have bagels with lox and cream cheese."

It's best not to work on an empty stomach. And she did mention lox.

***

"Are you going to play that at the Bastille Day party?" Trina was pointing at the accordion sitting on the sofa.

I wiped a dab of cream cheese off my chin, glad she hadn't pointed out my lack of housekeeping skills. I had, at least managed to make a pot of coffee. "It's my first all-accordion gig." And the reason I'd been practicing like a fiend.

"Cool." Trina sipped her coffee, then lowered her voice to a whisper. "Can I see it?"

"That?" I pointed at the accordion. No one had ever asked to see it before.

"No, silly, your sculpture."

"I don't think so."

Trina knew about the plan, but that didn't mean she needed to know how and where the reproductions were being made.

Ricky was the only one who'd seen the sculpture. I hadn't even wanted to show him, but I needed to know whether it would pass muster. To my relief, he loved it. His main complaint was that it was too pretty. That was my morning's task. Rough it up a bit. Put some scratches on it. Make it look like it had some miles on it.

"Aww, you're no fun," Trina pouted. "Guess I'll have to wait until tomorrow. Have you figured how you're going to make the switch?"

"You're going to smuggle it in in a hollowed-out, five-tiered cake."

"Seriously?"

"No. You'll find out tomorrow."

My phone pinged twice. I glanced at the ID.

"Rollie?" Trina asked.

"Yep."

"If you're not doing anything tonight," Trina said, "you should come hear my band at Fret Board."

I checked my calendar. "I'm working until at least ten. What time is your show?"

"Eight to ten." Trina tossed a napkin at me. "You're always working."

"Sorry." I was happy to be busy, though, because that meant the greenbacks were flowing in the right direction. "Let me know the next time you're performing somewhere."

"Actually, my band's playing down the street from your apartment on Sunday, at MOTR. Nine to midnight. We'll be doing all original tunes. Some by yours truly. So, you better come."

"That sounds great." I scrolled to Sunday. "I'll be there. Probably not until after ten, though."

That earned me a big hug.

Chapter Twenty-Eight

Vive Le France

Remoulade—not the name I would have chosen—wasn't a band that required truckloads of equipment, a sound engineer, and a posse of roadies. Troy Bradington didn't care. He'd spared no expense, renting a huge PA system, stage lighting, and a fog machine. Overkill, definitely, but with the armada of anvil cases full of gear, it'd been a piece of cake—not a literal one—to smuggle in a small case carrying the ersatz sculpture.

Not having any kitchen duties to attend to, I played a few scales and attempted to find my way through The Beatle's "Something." Arthur, the drummer, was setting up his kit center stage, and the rest of the band was drifting in, tuning up and going in search of drinks. We were, aside from Phillipe, cooks with a night off.

"Just because you can play 'Purple Haze' on the accordion doesn't mean you should," Ricky said, appearing in front of me in server's garb.

"'Purple Haze' is Hendrix. 'Something' is the Beatles." I rested the accordion in my lap.

"You're missing the point."

"Anyway, what's the haps, brah?" I was trying for laid-back LA cool. But the accordion and my Midwestern inflection exposed me as a mere poser.

Guests, drinks in hand, were trickling out from the house onto the vast patio. Since the patio was surrounded on three sides by glass-walled rooms, each with their own porch, perhaps "courtyard" was a more accurate term.

"Apparently you hadn't noticed, but there's a slight problem," Ricky said.

I waited for him to explain. I didn't like "slight problems."

"Troy moved the Rodin outdoors." Ricky pointed toward the fountain in the middle of the courtyard. Just beyond the fountain's mist, the sculpture sat on a marble pedestal.

"Shit!"

"Exactly," Ricky said.

"Enrique!" Chef Phillipe shouted from the porch. "I need those galettes to go out *maintenant*."

"Yes, Chef," Ricky replied, snapping to attention. "Got to go, bro. Talk later. In the meantime, figure out a plan."

I stared dejectedly at the Rodin. "I'll try."

Phillipe, sporting a crisp white toque and pristine chef's jacket, ambled toward the small stage at the end of the patio. "Everyone set?"

Fredo, the bassist, recinched his ponytail and nodded.

"You're not wearing that?" asked Kiko, a former Cincinnati Symphony violinist, now chef/owner of the city's hippest Japanese bistro. She was dressed in a black leather miniskirt and lace top.

"No worries." Phillipe, grinning impishly, lifted up his chef's jacket, revealing a black tee shirt that read *Vive Le France*. "Ready to rock and roll?"

In response, I played the opening bars of "La Marseillaise."

Phillipe stood a little straighter, placed a hand on his heart, and glanced at his watch. "Back in ten. Got to check my Alsatian tarts."

"You're always checking on your tarts," Kiko quipped, then began lathering her bow with rosin.

Needing to take advantage of those ten minutes to do some reconnaissance, I set the accordion on a chair and strode to the fountain. Pretending to watch the water cascade over the dolphins and mermaids that adorned the fountain's many tiers—no accounting for taste—I studied the Rodin and the layout of the courtyard, trying to think of a way to make it vanish into thin air, or at least into the back of my van.

The good news was that the sculpture was at the far corner of the patio, next to one of the hedges bordering the porches. The bad news was, even though the Rodin was only thirty-six inches tall, the hedge looked too dense to push the sculpture through.

"That's not good." Trina had appeared behind me with a tray of champagne flutes. "Bubbly?"

"No, it's not," I said. "Any ideas?"

She handed me a glass. "Deus ex machina?"

"Perfect." Sighing, I took a glass and downed it in a single swallow, the bubbles tickling my nose. "Alien abduction, perhaps?"

Trina smiled. "You're a brilliant chef and a talented musician—you'll figure something out. I gotta get back to work. Miles to go . . . yada, yada."

She flitted away before I could ask how the aforementioned occupations might provide me with the skill set for the problem at hand. I could have used a little more support from my Latin-speaking, Frost-quoting partner. But maybe she was right, and the solution would appear out of nowhere right when I needed it the most. Unlike in the rest of my life.

"Let's hit it," Phillipe said, relieving me of the empty champagne glass.

Chapter Twenty-Nine

I'm Here Just to Play Accordion

Halfway through the third set, the sun vanished in an impressionistic blaze of color. But I still hadn't figured out a way to vanish the Rodin off the patio. Would all the time and effort I'd put into replicating the sculpture be for naught? Could I sell it on Etsy?

Phillipe started his vaguely French-sounding arrangement of the Rolling Stones' "Wild Horses." A few bars into my accordion solo—yes, accordion solo—a thick mist began creeping across the courtyard. At first, I thought it was a combination of the humidity and falling temperatures. Then I remembered the fog machine.

By the time we started "My Girl," the fog was so dense I could barely see my fingers on the instrument. Apparently, someone hadn't bothered to read the instruction manual. The guests however, properly inebriated, were laughing and joking about the thick haze. I wondered, if things grew worse, whether they might start to panic.

The next tune, an original by Phillipe, was very melancholic and very French. It was also just him singing and playing guitar. Taking advantage of the break, as well as the poor visibility, I unstrapped the accordion, set it on my chair, and then slipped behind the stage. After opening the case containing the faux Rodin, and making sure no one was watching—pointless, since I could barely see a thing myself—I grabbed the cloth-covered maquette and made my way over to the real sculpture.

The party-goers—whom I kept bumping into—were dancing like it was midnight on Mardi Gras. Making my way through the festive gathering and past the fountain, I had the eerie sensation that I was wearing an invisibility cloak.

It took me less than a minute to switch out the sculptures and wipe off my fingerprints, and then another couple to carry the real Rodin backstage and secure it in the case. Picking up the accordion, I hoped, in my rush, that I hadn't mixed up the pair.

"Where'd you disappear to?" Phillipe asked when his solo performance ended.

"Had to pee. Couldn't wait." I hoped he didn't know, or couldn't see, my tell.

Phillipe glared at me. "If I find out that you set foot in my kitchen, I will cut your heart out, sauté it with garlic and onions, and then firebomb your food truck."

"Wouldn't dream of it, Chef." I could have pointed out that it wasn't technically his kitchen, but that would have only fueled his culinary anxieties. "I'm just here to play accordion."

Phillipe retuned his guitar, then counted out the next tune.

Halfway through "Make You Feel My Love," the fog began to abate.

Trina sidled up to my side of the stage. "You're welcome."

"What are you talking about?" I asked.

She grinned. "The fog. That was all me."

"Huh?" Was Trina the Goddess of Weather?

"I cranked the fog machine up to eleven to give you the cover you needed."

"Wow! Nice." This woman was constantly surprising me. I gave the accordion an appreciative squeeze. "The case is behind the stage—it's the one with the Grateful Dead stickers on the top. Grab it and stash it in my car."

"You got it," Trina said, slipping into the shadows.

Chapter Thirty

Make Good Choices

"That thing with the fog," Ricky was saying. "Brilliant."

"Adapt or die," Trina declared.

"Sounds very Russian," I said.

Trina responded with a Russian shrug.

Ricky and Trina were leaning up against the side of my car, sipping from a flask. After setting the accordion in the trunk, next to the Rodin, I closed the lid. Ricky handed me the flask, and I took a long pull.

"Doesn't that make you feel all warm and fuzzy?" Trina pulled out her scrunchy and shook out her long black hair.

"Are you talking about the whiskey?" Ricky asked.

"No," Trina said. "I'm talking about returning great works of art to their rightful owners."

"I don't know about warm and fuzzy, but it does make my bank account healthier." I handed the flask back to Ricky, then did a quick calculation of my bank account. Still teetering on the edge of negative numbers. "And that helps me sleep at night."

"I thought I helped you sleep at night," Trina purred.

"And that's my cue to leave." Ricky slipped the flask into his back pocket.

I tapped the trunk of my car. "What should I do with the Rodin?"

"Call you tomorrow, after I talk with James."

"James?" Trina asked.

"With Vincent out of the picture, we've been dealing with the private investigator who works for the insurance company. His name is James," Ricky explained.

"Sounds complicated." A mischievous smile played across Trina's face. "Perhaps we should eliminate James."

Earsplitting alarms went off in my head. "Trina, I don't think . . ."

Trina burst into laughter. "Just kidding, Anton. You always take everything so seriously."

Only where she was concerned . . . or my recent career choices . . . or my current fiscal situation. Okay, maybe she was right.

"Goodnight, kids," Ricky said. "Make good choices."

I watched him disappear into the darkness, pondering the recent choices I'd been making. Then I pondered my not-so-recent choices, many of which were also suspect. Choices, it appeared, didn't always come with a side order of good judgment.

"Penny for your thoughts," Trina said, interrupting my existential musings.

"Guess I better leave before someone starts suspecting the accordion player."

"Wanna grab a drink somewhere, or"—Trina paused—"come back to my place?"

Good judgment—there were those two pesky words again—told me I should decline, but still amped up from the gig, and the thrill of knowing there was a Rodin in the trunk of my car, I said, "Sure, but can we make it my place? I need to stash the sculpture somewhere safe."

Not that my apartment was all that safe. But it was definitely more secure than it'd be sitting in my car outside some bar, or in the house of a mobster's daughter.

Chapter Thirty-One

Sometimes I Don't Know Who You Are

"I hate these things," Rollie moaned. "Why did we agree to do this?"

Steering Prudence onto the northbound ramp of I-75, I merged into the heavy Friday-afternoon traffic. "Food truck rallies can be very lucrative," I reminded him. "Besides, we didn't have anything better going on."

Rollie glared at me. "But West Chester?"

He had a thing about the suburbs. Rollie believed—although he'd grown up in one—that suburbia was the source of all of societies ills. My theory was that he never got picked for dodgeball or perhaps was still bitter about having to play trombone when he really wanted to play clarinet.

"It'll be fun. The gang'll all be there." I slid a CD into the player. *Led Zeppelin IV*. "We'll party after."

Rollie's scowl morphed into a semi-grin. "I wonder if Iris will be there."

"Wait, what happened to Helga?" I asked, cranking up the AC in anticipation of a scorching night in the truck. I don't know if it was a subconscious thing, but Rollie had been dating alphabetically for the last couple of years.

"Iris makes incredible doughnuts."

"Doughnuts? That's why you broke up with Helga? I liked her."

"She's all yours," Rollie said. "But you'll have to move to Omaha."

Time to change the subject. "I hope the lobster pierogi sell well tonight."

"What's with you and lobster?" Rollie pinched his fingers together and grabbed the sleeve of my shirt. "We could have just stuck with the scallop tacos. One seafood item on the menu is plenty."

"The price was right, and they looked fresh. Besides, who doesn't like lobster?"

"Last week you were on a sea bass rampage. Sometimes I don't know who you are."

Join the club, I thought.

"I mean, how long was it before I even knew you played accordion?"

"A gentleman doesn't share his deepest, darkest secrets," I said. Secrets which were growing deeper and darker every day.

"What else don't I know about you?"

"I hate beets." As a cook, I was reluctant to mention this—given how trendy the root vegetable had become. But I needed to share some tidbit with him to quell his current line of questioning.

Rollie glared at me, aghast at this revelation. "I'll pretend I didn't hear that."

Would he be equally appalled at my recently acquired larcenous tendencies? Knowing his infallible sense of right and wrong, I had no doubt.

My phone rang. Needing to put an end to Rollie's game of Truth or Dare, I answered.

"Anton, my man, what cha up to?"

"Hey, Arthur. Heading up to West Chester for a food truck rally. What's up, yourself?"

"The other band I play in, Knife Rack? Well, we're talking about adding a synth. I know you used to play a Moog and was wondering if you might be interested in joining up."

Arthur, the drummer in Remoulade, dabbled in several bands. How he had time between cooking full-time, I had no idea.

"Thanks for thinking of me, dude, but I kind of have a lot on my plate at the moment." Between the truck, catering and thievery, this was true, but I also had no interest in playing in a metal band.

"Well, at least consider the idea," Arthur said. "We've got a bunch of gigs lined up. And you'd like the guys—they like to party."

"Okay, Arthur, I'll consider it." This was my go-to response to most of Arthur's propositions: karaoke, skydiving, heroin.

"Cool. Talk soon." He disconnected.

Arthur was a talented drummer, and I appreciated his offer, but outside of Remoulade, we didn't have much in common.

My phone rang again. I figured it was Arthur, not ready to give up on his recruitment drive. But it wasn't his name that appeared, it was the Jaws emoji that I'd assigned to Ilya. Like Prince and Cher, Ilya went by a single name and worked as an emissary for the private lender, aka loan shark, from whom I'd borrowed 30K. As per usual, I hit ignore.

"We need to come up with a mission statement," Rollie said, drumming on the dashboard. He always got slightly manic on the way to a job, a mania that was funneled into cooking once we opened for business.

"What do you mean by 'mission statement?'" I was afraid this would send him off on some new tangent.

"You know, like where do we see ourselves in one year, five years, ten years?"

Given that the Rodin was stashed under a basket of dirty clothes in my closet and that the last check I'd written was overdrawn, ideally I'd be debt free and not in jail. Unable to share that, I took a minute to consider his question. I had, as of late, uncharacteristically given some thought to what the future might look like. Like a lot of cooks I knew,

I imagined myself opening a brick-and-mortar establishment. One where every detail represented my cooking philosophy. The only problem was I hadn't yet defined this philosophy.

Rather than share the true details of my future dreams, I altered it slightly. "I don't know about one year, probably more of the same. But five years, perhaps Anton and Rollie's Bounteous Bistro, famous for its innovative dishes and craft cocktails."

"You don't know how happy that makes me." Rollie beamed. "I always figured you'd go your own way, leaving me in a wake of food truck exhaust. Slight edit, though, my name should come first and 'Bounteous' sucks."

"Done," I said. Five years was a lifetime, and Rollie had never been one for long-term commitments.

For the time being, I was happy enough serving up tacos and pierogi. And glad I didn't have to answer to a corporate drone from some soul-sucking restaurant conglomerate. Been there, done that. The only downside was Prudence's space limitations and the inevitable compromise of a partnership.

I loved Rollie like a brother, but when my culinary vision finally unveiled itself, the way forward would have to be all mine. From kitchen to front-of-house, it needed to be a reflection of me. For now, however, I had little vision and even less money.

Chapter Thirty-Two

What's the Plan, Rodin?

I'd agreed to meet Ricky at his studio but was running late because I'd spent the previous evening carousing with Rollie and a bunch of food truck cooks after the rally. Which meant I was nursing a killer hangover.

It wasn't only the hangover contributing to my lethargic state; it was the building itself. Not that there was anything wrong with the neighborhood or the individual studios. Mostly that I still harbored a slight aversion to any place populated by an encampment of artists. Reminded me too much of art school.

One of the reasons I'd dropped out—aside from my growing obsession with food—was because I never felt like I fit in. Especially when my classmates began discussing French art films and the vast footnotes of *Infinite Jest*. I was more into the oeuvres of George Lucas and Douglas Adams. An intellectual, I was not.

"Looks like you've been rode hard and put up wet," Ricky said as I darkened the doorway. "Come in. I'll make you an espresso."

"Yes, please." I was too much in need of caffeine to make a wry comment about his quaint Texan colloquialism.

While he set about making coffee, I locked the door, opened my backpack, unwrapped the sculpture, and set it on one of the workbenches. The studio was a large industrial space, consisting of a small living area, a tiny kitchenette at one end, and a bank of tall windows showering the room with an abundance of natural light.

"I hope you've been practicing," Ricky said.

"The accordion?" I queried. "Was I that bad?"

"No. Although it is an accordion, so . . . what I meant was, removing paintings from frames."

Ricky, adamant that if circumstances dictated, I'd be able to step into his job, had given me a bunch of frames to practice on. After a few disasters—one where I ripped an edge of the canvas, another where I jabbed a hole through the painting, both thrift store finds—I was getting faster and less prone to total destruction. But, there was no way I was ready to attempt the real deal. Maybe after another fifty repetitions.

"What a hottie," Ricky said over his shoulder.

I assumed he was referring to Bowling Dude, Rodin's sculpture. Which reminded me of a question I'd been meaning to ask. "Was the Rodin from the same broker who sold the paintings?"

"Of course," Ricky replied. "It was the last piece he sold."

"Why is that? He didn't like the medium?"

"Did I ever tell you how this whole thing got started?" Ricky handed me a blue and white demitasse, the rich aroma of espresso wafting upward.

"My savior." I took a sip, savoring the strong brew, but wishing he had poured me a Big Gulp-sized portion. "You told me that some guy was selling not-so-famous paintings by famous artists."

Ricky gestured toward a pair of upholstered chairs that looked like they might have been salvaged from a condemned frat house. "I can only repeat what William told me. You remember William, right?"

"Your ex. Former Reds player. Our source for art." I dug my phone out of my pocket, placed it on the coffee table, and settled on one of the chairs, resting the demitasse on its slightly chewed-up arm.

"You get an A-plus. Anyway, according to William, one of the Reds pitchers had this less-than-reputable cousin. Supposedly an artist. I heard he got kicked out of some East Coast art school for stealing paintings from galleries and claiming them as his own, which is usually

The Culinary Caper

frowned upon." Ricky brushed a handful of crumbs off the cushion of the other chair and then dropped into it. "Aside from being a thief, this guy was also a dealer. Drugs as well as art."

"Important to diversify," I said. We certainly had.

"Anyway, this dealer, let's call him Tim, finds a de Kooning for his cousin, the pitcher."

"I never thought of de Kooning as a gateway drug."

"Right? And," Ricky continued, "the next painting Tim brokered was a Duveneck."

"Wait, a de Kooning and a Duveneck?" I did a quick tally. "We haven't rescued either of those."

"I'll get to that. Don't you want to hear the rest of the story?"

"Of course." I leaned back in the chair, which produced a frightening moan, and nodded for Ricky to continue.

"As soon as the pitcher, let's call him Devon, bought his de Kooning, he began showing it off to his teammates. And suddenly the whole team gets bitten by the art bug. That's when Crazy Cousin Tim realized he was looking at a serious cash cow."

"But none of this explains how . . ." I was going to have to start taking notes. "How Tim got these paintings in the first place."

"I'll get to that," Ricky said. "So, Tim—good job keeping the names straight—sees that these ballplayers, even though they know nothing about art, are dying to spend some cash on something that makes them appear more refined than your typical pro athlete. And that they have a shit-ton of money. That's also when Tim decides to set up an Amway-type scheme to market his products. Kind of a show-and-tell for the jet set."

"Wait a sec." I was definitely going to need more coffee to follow this saga. "They were having Tupperware parties, but instead of plastic storage containers they were selling fine art?"

"Bingo. Unlike Amway, however, they couldn't just invite anybody. Only professional athletes, and no rookies."

"That makes no sense," I said.

Ricky shrugged. "But there it is. Want another espresso?"

"Yes, but make it a triple this time," I said.

Ricky headed back to the kitchen, where he ground another batch of coffee beans and then loaded them into a sleek Italian espresso machine.

"Are you going to explain how Tim got hold of these works of art?"

"Don't know exactly, but rumor has it that he was involved with some of the guys who pulled the Gardner heist."

"No way!" I exclaimed. The heist at the Gardner Museum in Boston was probably one of the most infamous and unsolved art thefts in the United States. The artwork still hadn't been recovered.

"I know, right?"

"So, is Tim connected to the Boston mafia?" Trina was gangster-adjacent enough for me.

"Only loosely," Ricky said. "He was mostly just a petty thief."

"And where is Tim now, if that's even his real name?" I asked, only slightly relieved by his wannabe-ness.

"No one knows. He disappeared after selling the Rodin."

My phone vibrated on the coffee table. I ignored it.

"Don't you want to see who it is?"

I didn't.

Ricky picked it up. "Who is Julia?"

"Don't answer it!" The last thing I wanted was to make polite small talk with my ex. Not that it would be "polite" or "small."

"Well, who is she?"

"I don't want to talk about it."

"Fine. Keep your little secrets."

The Culinary Caper

"Anyway," I said, trying to steer the conversation back to the matter at hand, "where is this Duveneck you mentioned?"

"You'll find out shortly."

"Okay." I pointed at the sculpture. "What's the plan, Rodin?"

Ricky laughed. "I talked to James. He's sending a courier to pick it up."

If I were an insurance company, I wouldn't hire a PI who called himself James. Jim, Jimbo, or Jimmie, definitely. But James, I didn't think so.

"What are those?" I pointed at the row of easels at the far end of the studio, each holding a painting.

"I've got a show coming up. My first in years."

"Dude, why didn't you tell me?" I pushed myself out of the chair and strode over to the paintings.

The first painting, extraordinarily lifelike, was of five elderly gentlemen seated around a rustic wooden table on a stone patio, glasses of red wine in their hands. "I had no idea you were so good at Realism."

Ricky chuckled. "Only on canvas, not in real life."

"These are seriously good. Who are these guys?"

"My great uncles," Ricky said. "I didn't tell you about the show because I'm extremely nervous about it. That's why I asked you to come. To let me know if they're any good."

"Are you kidding? They're fucking amazing." I stood back to get a better view. He'd done more than just copy the photograph that was taped to the bottom of the frame. I'd never met his uncles, but looking at the painting made me want to grab a glass of wine, join them at the table, and hear their life stories.

"Thanks, Anton."

"What's that?" I pointed at a canvas in the far corner with a white sheet draped over it.

Ricky grinned. "Our next project."

I headed over to the easel. "Can I look?"

"It's not finished, but sure."

I slipped the sheet off and took a couple of steps back. "Is this the Duveneck?"

"Glad you could tell," Ricky said. "I guess that means it doesn't totally suck."

In spite of being unfinished, Ricky had captured the very essence of Frank Duveneck. The colors, the lighting, the brushstrokes, even the somber-looking woman in high collar and sun hat seemed to jump off the canvas and shout, *I'm the real deal!*

"This is fantastic!" I lacked the vocabulary to better describe the skill it took to create a painting like this. "You should be making a living doing this."

Ricky sipped his coffee and smiled. "You mean as a forger?"

"No, you idiot, painting." Ricky going legit would force me to wrestle with my debts in other ways. Which would take a lot longer, but would definitely be less stressful.

"I tried that. Couldn't sell enough paintings to pay the rent."

"That's 'cause you were in New York," I said. "Rent's cheaper here, and you can sell your paintings anywhere."

"I know," Ricky said. "Anyway, pack up Bowling Dude, we got to get going."

"Where?" I asked. "I thought we were meeting the courier."

"Not here," Ricky said. "I just wanted to see the Rodin one last time. And show you the paintings for the show. I don't want anyone else knowing about this place."

"Okay. Where then?"

"Home Depot."

Chapter Thirty-Three

Let's Rescue Some Art

"How will we recognize him?" I asked. We were sitting in my car at the far corner of the Home Depot parking lot, waiting for the courier. I'd been steadfastly ignoring the daily barrage of texts from Rollie.

"We won't," Ricky said. "But he'll recognize us. I texted him a picture of your car."

"How did you know we'd take my car?"

"You always drive."

It was true, I always seemed to be sitting behind the wheel. Was that by chance or by choice? Somewhat ironic, given my lack of direction.

"That must be him." Ricky pointed at a black SUV with tinted windows, creeping across the parking lot.

As the SUV pulled up alongside my car, the front window descended, and a thirtyish man with a two-day beard and a man-bun stuck his head out. "You Ricky?"

"That'd be me." Ricky leaned toward my open window.

"Cool," the man said, bobbing his head. "I'm Dave. I work for Hawkes Fine Art Insurance. Let's rescue some art."

Dave and his man-bun didn't exactly instill the confidence I would have preferred in a courier about to transport a priceless work of art across the country. But I guess if the insurance company trusted him—and more importantly, we got paid—then appearances didn't matter. I mean, by all accounts, one would assume I was a relatively docile food truck cook and not an experienced art thief.

Dave climbed out of his car and popped his trunk. We did the same.

"I've got some paperwork for you to sign." Dave opened a sturdy black case, lined with thick foam. "But let's get the sculpture safely stowed first."

I grabbed the backpack from my trunk and pulled out the Rodin, aka Bowling Dude. As I was unwrapping it from the folds of the heavy cloth, a bright red Dodge Charger screamed toward us, squealing to a stop inches away from Dave's rear bumper.

"Vincent, what are you doing here?" Dave asked when the car's occupant climbed out.

"I'll take that, if you don't mind." Vincent extended a hand toward the Rodin.

Clutching it to my chest, I considered tucking it under my arm and running into Home Depot.

"Not cool, dude," Dave said. "You shouldn't be here."

Vincent shook a finger at me. "Did you really think that some Russian goon was going to scare me off?"

Ricky and I exchanged glances. Apparently, Cousin Vlad hadn't managed to convince Vincent to walk away.

"This is *my* business," Vincent continued. "And I don't appreciate a couple of punks cutting me out."

"It wasn't personal," Ricky said. "It just seemed like it'd be easier to deal directly with James. Save you the hassle of being the go-between."

"Oh, it's personal. And you're going to find out just how personal it is."

Ignoring Vincent, Dave motioned for me to hand him the Rodin. I did. Vincent scowled as the man leaned into the trunk, set the sculpture in the case, and secured the latches.

"Sorry about this, Dave." Vincent bashed him in the face with a vicious right cross.

The Culinary Caper

After hitting his head on the lid of the trunk, Dave collapsed unconscious onto the pavement. Vincent grabbed the case and headed toward his car.

Unaccustomed to real-life violence—as opposed to watching Captain Kirk duke it out with some four-armed alien—my feet remained glued to the ground. Which seemed odd given that every neuron in my body was firing on hyperdrive. Apparently, the whole concept of fight-or-flight response didn't apply to me, since I was doing neither.

Ricky, apparently made of stronger stuff, went after Vincent, but paused when the man spun around, arm cocked.

"You want some too, pretty boy?" Vincent barked. "I'd be more than happy to rearrange your face."

Ricky, who appeared more pissed-off than afraid, declined to engage. After sliding the case into the trunk of his car, Vincent turned around holding a tire iron. "Want to see personal?"

Ricky and I backed away. But instead of coming after us, Vincent began smashing the windshield of my car, with each swing shouting, "This personal enough for you?"

When all that was left of my windshield was a gaping maw, he tossed the tire iron into his trunk and slammed it shut.

It wasn't that I was emotionally attached to my aging Toyota, but I had racked up almost a quarter million miles on it. Animate or not, it was a lot of time spent together, and seeing it pounded like a veal cutlet elicited a queasiness deep in the pit of my stomach.

"Next time, asswipes, it'll be your heads!"

Vincent climbed back in his car and sped off.

"What happened?" Dave moaned. His lip was swollen, and there was a bloody gash on his forehead.

"Vincent clocked you." I rubbed my own lip out of sympathy, relieved that I only felt the way he looked.

"Crazy motherfucker!" Dave wiped a dollop of blood off his right eye. "I've been doing this for seven years and never been assaulted. And I thought driving Uber and substitute teaching were bad gigs."

"Sorry." I didn't know what else to say.

"Where's the Rodin?"

Ricky helped ease Dave up to a sitting position, his back against the car.

"Gone," I said. "But I have no idea whether Vincent's going to take it to James or try and sell it on his own. Either way, there goes our money."

"Shit!" Dave winced as he rubbed his chin.

"We better get you to the hospital," Ricky said.

"Fuck that." Dave climbed to his feet and pulled out his cell phone. "I got to call this in. See what my boss wants me to do."

I peered into my newly ventilated Toyota. The dashboard and front seat were covered with tiny shards of glass, and the floor mats twinkled like the Milky Way.

"Now what?" I asked no one in particular.

"Call Trina," Ricky said.

I glared at him. "Why would I do that?"

"First, she's our new partner. Second, she may be able to get the Rodin back."

"And how exactly would she do that?" I asked, already afraid of the answer.

"You said yourself that her cousin had a 'conversation' with Vincent. That means he knows how to find him."

"Apparently that 'conversation' didn't take hold." I eyed my car, hoping it had regrown a new windshield. It hadn't. "Look, Ricky, you know I want the reward money as much as you do. But if it means more of this . . . that's not what I signed up for."

"I get that, Anton. I really do. I'm just saying we shouldn't give up on the Rodin. At least, not yet."

"Hey guys, I'm out of here." Dave shuffled over to where Ricky and I were standing. "My boss might call you to confirm what I just told them, make sure that it wasn't me that absconded with the Rodin."

"Should we call the cops?" I felt like I needed to take some kind of action.

"Don't do that," Dave said. "Management wants to handle it in-house. They don't like bad publicity."

Did insurance companies hire bigger, meaner thugs to deal with the lesser, naughtier ones? Was there some kind of hierarchical thuggery that dealt with ex-gangsters on the payroll?

"Sorry about all this, Dave," I said, giving Ricky a look. "This is our fault. We shouldn't have let this happen."

"Thanks for saying that." Dave, still wobbly from the punch, braced himself against the hood of his car. "But Vincent always was a time bomb. It was only a matter of time before he detonated."

It was Ricky's turn to give me a look.

Dave closed his trunk and climbed into his driver's seat. "Later, dudes."

Chapter Thirty-Four

Why the Long Face?

Ricky grabbed an Uber. I spent the next couple hours aimlessly browsing the aisles of Home Depot, waiting for my windshield to get replaced, and then rushed off to my next errand.

The events of the morning had put me behind, which meant I couldn't dawdle at Chef's Warehouse, checking out new products, like I usually did when I bought supplies. At the register, I felt the sting of the bill, already missing the thwarted reward money. Naturally, I was late getting to the truck.

Trying to ignore the morning's events as they played on a continuous loop in my head, I sliced the ahi tuna that would be the star of the evening's fish tacos and then began measuring out flour for a second batch of pierogi dough. With every slap of the dough on the counter, I heard the sickening thud of Dave's head hitting the trunk of his car, followed by the disturbing vision of Vincent engaging in batting practice with the windshield of my poor, defenseless Toyota.

"Why the long face?" Rollie asked, after he climbed aboard Prudence.

"Just tired." I could have lied about some random dude breaking my windshield, but that might have required further explanation. Something I didn't have the energy for.

"You need to start replying to my texts. If you don't, how will I know that you read them?"

"Sorry." I thought my lack of response would have highlighted that very point.

The Culinary Caper

Rollie leaned back against the counter, watching me knead the dough. "Did you have another catering gig?"

"No, a Remoulade gig." I was relieved I didn't have to lie about that. "One of the Reds was throwing a Bastille Day party. Phillipe catered it."

"Of course he did," Rollie said. "No one can compete with Monsieur Rameau and his epicurean empire."

Rollie was still bitter that Phillipe had never hired him at any of his restaurants. Not that Rollie didn't have the skills, but Rollie had learned those skills on the job. Phillipe, food snob that he was, only hired culinary school grads.

"Chef Rameau will never be able to compete with us, Titans of the Food Truck Galaxy." I smacked the dough onto the counter and began shaping it into a tight ball. Satisfied the texture was good, I tossed it into a bowl and covered it with plastic wrap. "Sorry I got a late start. The dough can rest while we drive."

My phone rang. After rinsing the flour off my hands, I picked up. "Hey Arthur, what's going on?"

"Thought I'd check back in with you about what I asked you the other day."

My mind drew a blank. Had I asked him to sub for me on the truck? "Sorry, about what?"

"Dude, really? This is important. The synth gig."

I'd totally forgotten about his offer to play synthesizer in his metal band. Probably because I had exactly zero desire to sign on with a bunch of testosterone-driven, multi-tattooed head-bangers. "Yeah, that's not going to work for me. Too much going on. Thanks for asking, though."

"Your loss," Arthur muttered, and then hung up.

That was easier than expected, but he'd probably give me the cold shoulder the next time I saw him, which I was okay with.

Rollie climbed into the driver's seat, started the engine, and selected a playlist. I tossed my dish towel in the hamper, shrugged out of my apron, and dropped into the passenger seat.

I pointed out the front window. "Vamonos, muchacho!"

Rollie put Prudence into gear, but nothing happened.

"Wiggle it," I said. "Sometimes it doesn't engage right away."

He wiggled the shifter, then stepped on the accelerator. Nothing.

"Fuck!" Rollie shouted, slapping the steering wheel.

"Take a breath, dude," I said. "Put it in park and shut the engine off."

Rebooting was the extent of my mechanical, technological, and emotional aptitude.

Rollie did as I suggested. The engine started, but Prudence still wouldn't move.

"I told you it was only a matter of time before the transmission gave out," Rollie snarled. "But no, you had to spend all your money on new appliances."

"Give it a minute." I wanted to believe that our current predicament wasn't all my fault, even though, deep down, I knew that it was.

"A minute's not going to rebuild the fucking transmission. We need to figure out a plan, or tonight's going to be a total bust."

Not working tonight would mean a loss of income that we couldn't afford. There was also the issue of having to throw out expensive ingredients, like the tuna.

"I'll call around." I pulled out my phone. "Maybe someone's not using their truck tonight."

Burying his face in his hands, Rollie shook his head. "This isn't like borrowing your neighbor's lawnmower."

Every food truck had the same basic amenities: stove, refrigerators, possibly fryers. But each truck was equipped for the specific needs of its particular cuisine. Using someone else's truck would mean bringing in all of the additional items required for our menu. Not impossible, but very time consuming.

"Let me see what I can come up with," I said.

Rollie and I spent the next hour with our phones glued to our ears, him calling mechanics, me attempting to find an idle food truck.

"Fuck!" Rollie screamed when we both gave up.

"Maybe I can sell the ahi." I was trying to sound optimistic, but the tone of my voice belied my words.

When my phone rang, I hoped it was good news.

"Hello?" I answered without looking at the caller ID.

"Bonjour," Phillipe said, annoyingly chipper. "How are you this fine afternoon?"

"What's up, Phillipe?" I wasn't in the mood for pleasantries.

"Ooh, someone is grumpy today. Run out of butter?"

Leave it to a Frenchman to think that that was the worst thing that could happen.

"Kind of busy at the moment. Do you need something?"

"Just you, my friend," Phillipe said. "I might have a job for you."

Was he about to offer me an executive chef job at one of his latest restaurant ventures? I'd turned down past offers, wanting to do my own thing, but maybe the transmission kicking the bucket was a sign from the universe.

My heart palpitated with anticipation. "What kind of job?"

"You know my bistro, Ferme?"

"Yeah," I could feel my excitement ebb. Ferme, a small farm-to-table eatery, wasn't quite the vision I had for myself. To be honest, my vision, as of late, was a trifle blurry.

"How would you like to play accordion a couple of nights a week for my dinner guests?"

Maybe I should have been flattered by his opinion of my musical prowess, but when an acclaimed French chef would rather hire you to play accordion than whip up duck confit . . . well, talk about ego deflating.

"Can we talk about this later? I gotta run." I hung up before he could reply.

Chapter Thirty-Five

Dinner's On Me

Jiro's shiny red food truck pulled up alongside Prudence. Painted on the side was *META*, with a single gold chopstick under it. What the hell was the lone chopstick supposed to represent? Apparently too meta for a less enlightened guy like me.

I was sitting on the bottom step of Prudence, browsing aimlessly—was there any other way? —on Instagram. Rollie, in a dark mood, had vanished, leaving me to deal with the truck and the food.

"Hey, Anton." Jiro dismounted his truck, wearing a META T-shirt, as unapologetically red as his truck. "Guess you won't be banking any Benjamins tonight."

For a guy who insisted he was in this business solely for the love of cooking, cash always seemed to be foremost on his mind. Not that I could pretend it wasn't a concern for me. I just chose not to broadcast it.

"On the bright side," I said, "while you're sweating in the back of a hot truck, I'll be enjoying a night off."

In reality, I'd be too upset about the lost income to have a good time.

"So, is your truck in as bad of shape as it looks?" Jiro asked.

"Do you want to buy some product or not?" I refused to rise to his usual competitive bullshit.

"Depends on if it's any good," Jiro said.

I motioned him into the truck. Onboard, Jiro surveyed the interior and whistled. "Man, this kitchen is great. I wasn't expecting—"

"What, you thought the décor would be post-apocalyptic?"

When Rollie and I bought the truck, we gutted the interior and rebuilt it to our specifications. We'd spent a ton of money on the renovation but had considered it a worthwhile investment. The added expense, however, only augmented the debt from my failed restaurant venture.

I opened the fridge and pulled out the things I thought Jiro might want to buy. Jiro inspected the ahi tuna and the fresh veggies, deemed them acceptable, and agreed to take them off my hands for a ridiculously low sum. After some minor haggling, we settled on a price. Or to put it another way, I caved. I did, however, hang on to several pounds of locally raised organic lamb, hoping Prudence would be back on the road in a day or so.

"Pleasure doing business with you, Anton. Stop by tonight and I'll give you a great deal on some of my sushi masterpieces."

"Wow, thanks, Jiro!" I made no attempt to hide my sarcasm. "How generous of you."

Fortunately, a large tow truck arrived then, ending any pretense of further conversation. The driver, a burly, grease-covered man, hooked up Prudence and hauled her away in less than ten minutes. Hopefully the repair would be equally as timely.

Seated behind the wheel of my newly windshielded car, I contemplated how to spend the rest of the day. Grabbing Indian take-out and a six-pack and heading home seemed to make the most sense. My phone, apparently having other plans, rang.

"Working tonight?" Trina asked.

"I should have been." I told her about the demise of the transmission, which just made me more depressed.

"That's awful," Trina said. "Let's go out. Dinner's on me."

"I don't know." I'd been looking forward to a night of self-pity and copious alcohol consumption.

"Ricky told me what happened with Vincent. And now the truck dying. You deserve a night on the town."

Those were the very reasons I wouldn't be good company. "Trina—"

"I won't take no for an answer. Where are you right now?"

Summoning my brief yoga training, I took several long breaths. "Still at the Creamery."

"Come to my place. I know a way to make you feel better."

That I didn't doubt. "Okay." I'd always been easy.

"Oh, almost forgot, I'm looking into the Vincent problem."

"Trina, please don't—" She hung up before I could finish the sentence.

Chapter Thirty-Six

You Don't Know Me

"Pretend like you don't know him," Ricky whispered, jutting his chin in the direction of a tall Black dude in a tight black T-shirt, heading our way.

"I don't," I said.

"That's William."

We were standing in the doorway of Reds second baseman Malcom Duriki's cavernous all-white kitchen, peering out at the two dozen or so people milling about on the slate-floored living room, Blake Sheldon playing softly on a hidden sound system.

"*The* William, as in your ex, who thrust us into a life of crime?"

"The very same," Ricky said. "Although to be clear, we chose this path. He had nothing to do with it."

Sporting a neatly trimmed beard and an athletic physique that made a mockery of my own, Ricky's ex set his empty champagne glass on an end table and moseyed up to Ricky.

"Enrique," William said, kissing Ricky on the cheek, "you're looking well."

"You don't look too bad either," Ricky said, unabashedly giving his ex a thorough head-to-toe perusal.

"And this must be the famous Chef Anton." William grasped my hand in a bone-crushing grip. "I've been hearing a lot about you."

Glancing anxiously at Ricky, I rubbed my hand back to life.

"I understand you're really into art," William said.

Not sure if that was a question or a statement, I stared at him, hoping that it was simply a non sequitur.

The Culinary Caper

"Enrique tells me you're a very talented sculptor."

"A million years ago." I wondered what had become of the Rodin maquette that Vincent had stolen. "Whether I was talented or not remained to be seen."

"I hear you've been checking out the paintings of my former teammates." William folded his well-toned arms across his chest, reminding me that I needed to visit the gym. Of course, that would require joining one. In my defense, it's not easy to stay in shape when you're working crazy hours and constantly knee-deep in gourmet chow.

Again, I wasn't sure whether he was asking a question. Was this some new form of discourse where neither inquiries nor responses required confirmation? Was I supposed to retaliate with another question? Regardless of the rules, it was a conversation I didn't want to have. However, sensing the need to say something, I said, "When I'm not flipping burgers, I do enjoy looking at art."

"A chef like you, flipping burgers?" William laughed. "That's about as likely as you browsing for Monet prints at Walmart."

I was tempted to say, *You don't know me.* But he was right.

"Anyway," William said, "you gotta check out Malcolm's Hockney. It's to die for."

Ricky clasped William's elbow, ushering him out of the kitchen. "I didn't realize you were going to be here tonight."

"Relax, Enrique. I'm here with my partner. Everyone knows. Come upstairs and see the Hockney."

Ricky and I traded looks.

William laughed. "It's okay, Malcolm loves to have people to look at his painting."

"That'd be fantastic," Ricky said, recovering quickly. "But we better let Chef get back to work."

"Of course." William put a hand on my shoulder. "Nice to meet you, Anton." Then, leaning close to Ricky's ear, he added, "The Hockney's in the master bedroom."

"Okay, then," I said after William and Ricky had sauntered off.

Not having time to worry about William's unexpected presence, I checked on the short ribs braising in the oven. They appeared content, so I peeked at the garlic mashed potatoes and then began slicing a mound of collard greens.

"The bedroom is huge." Ricky grabbed a bottle of water from the fridge.

"Just the bedroom?" I asked.

He slapped me on the shoulder with the water bottle.

"Please tell me that you and William didn't . . ."

"I never kiss and tell," Ricky said. "But no. William's here with someone."

"And the Hockney?" I asked.

"Hanging on the wall above the bed," Ricky answered. "With the Hockney in the bedroom and it being on the second floor, smuggling out the painting might be a bit tricky."

"No shit, Sherlock." Not in the mood for "a bit tricky," I pulled the short ribs out of the oven, gave them a gentle shake, and then added another half cup of red wine. "I still think we should have waited until we figured out what happened to Vincent and the Rodin."

Ricky laughed. "Sounds like a band name."

Still holding the bottle of wine, I was tempted to take a medicinal swig. Instead, I slid the pan of ribs back into the oven. Their rich aroma wafting through the kitchen.

"Trina's cousin told her that no one has seen or heard from Vincent since he busted my windshield." I wiped my hands on a dish towel. "If he's not going to return the sculpture to the insurance company, then what's he going to do with it?"

"I talked to James, the PI," Ricky said. "He thinks Vincent's probably looking for a fence. In which case, he'll soon discover that Rodins aren't as easy to move as diamond earrings. The good news is, with Vincent in hiding, its back to business as usual."

Outside of the kitchen, I didn't know what "business as usual" meant. But I did comprehend the dangers of the unknowable. "What happens if the Rodin turns up at some auction and one of the Reds hears about it?"

"You worry too much," Ricky said, like I'd just told him I'd misplaced my phone charger. "Anyway, I'll try and find out when our host's daughter is going to give her little dance recital."

"Wow, a dance recital!" I exclaimed, feigning excitement. "I bet the guests will be thrilled with the Junior Miss America's Got Talent performance."

"She has some big competition coming up and wants to practice in front of an audience. If you had kids, maybe you'd understand what it means to be a proud parent," Ricky said.

Ricky was right, I didn't understand. Maybe I needed to. "This coming from a confirmed bachelor."

"My singleness is not by design," Ricky said. "Anyway, do you want to hear the plan or not?"

"If you insist."

Ricky sketched out his strategy.

An hour later, the host, Malcolm Duriki, clinked a spoon against his wine glass. "Can I have everyone's attention, please?"

When that didn't work, he shut off the music and clapped his hands three times. I half expected the lights to go out. Instead, silence reigned.

"Thank you," Malcolm said. "And thanks for coming out tonight. Sheri and I are so excited to welcome you to our new house. It should have been finished a year ago, but you all know how those things go."

A smattering of first-world laughter.

Leaning against the super-tanker-sized granite counter, I surveyed the abundant square footage and the décor—generic and slightly tacky. Money doesn't, apparently, buy you good taste. But aesthetics aside, I imagined the expense of building a house this size would probably eclipse that of the future bistro I someday hoped to open.

Thoughts of my own place had been popping into my head more frequently lately. Which made no sense, given that Rollie and I could barely keep up with the truck expenses. It was, however, probably that ultimate dream that kept driving me forward through mountains of debt, grueling hours on Prudence, and Grand Theft Art.

"Before we sit down to dinner," Malcolm—unaware of my occupational daydreams— continued, "my daughter, Melody, has graciously agreed to demonstrate her newest dance routine with us."

Amazingly, there were no audible groans. If I hadn't needed the distraction that Melody's performance provided, I would have taken the opportunity to step outside, or at the very least down several shots of the high-end bourbon I'd discovered on the top shelf of the pantry.

Malcolm motioned to Ricky, who was doling out appetizers at the far end of the hangar-sized living room, and Ricky threaded his way toward him.

"Can you make sure everyone has a drink or whatever they need?" Malcolm asked. "I don't want any interruptions once Melody gets started."

"Of course," Ricky said.

Once the guests were equipped with the necessary victuals, Ricky returned to the kitchen.

"You ready?" I asked.

"You betcha. Where's the . . . *candy*?"

I started to slide the poster tube out from under the linens on the bottom of the service cart.

"Hey Ricky," William said, appearing in the kitchen. "Come sit with me and my partner. Malcolm doesn't want you bustling about during the recital, so you may as well join us."

"Better not," Ricky said. "I'm just the help."

"Nonsense. Malcolm won't care, and Greg wants to meet you."

"I can't," Ricky protested.

"Sure, you can," William said. "You can handle things. Can't you, Anton?"

I took turns staring at Ricky and William. "Uh . . ."

"Won't take no for an answer. Besides, if you sit with me, I'll try and convince Malcolm to buy one of your paintings." William grabbed Ricky's arm and dragged him from the kitchen.

The recital was the only safe opportunity we had to sneak upstairs and nab the Hockney. With Ricky benched, this meant either bailing on the heist or me doing the heavy lifting.

Malcolm grabbed a remote off the coffee table and stabbed a couple of buttons. Loud, bass-heavy EDM erupted over the sound system. Seconds later, a young girl in a gold-sequined leotard bounded into the room, did a double somersault, dialed up a beauty-contestant smile, and launched into a no-holds-barred dance routine.

Instead of the cringeworthy performance I'd expected, the high-energy number had every guest—even me—fully captivated. This girl had serious skills.

After gloving up, I slid the PVC tube—with the Hockney reproduction stashed inside— under my apron, grabbed the kit containing the staples, tacks, staple-puller, pliers, and screwdriver, and sidled out of the kitchen toward the stairs. Not a single head turned in my direction.

Upstairs, in the warren of rooms, it took me a minute to find the master suite, which spread across the entire back of the house and featured a kind of atrium overlooking the heavily wooded backyard. I couldn't help thinking a whole fleet of food trucks would fit quite comfortably in here. Admiring the view through the vast array of windows would have been preferable to the task at hand but needs must prevail.

In art school, I'd learned to paint, although I was never very good at it. Part of that training also involved learning how to stretch a canvas. Since that was the last time I'd done that, Ricky had given me a refresher course, just in case an occasion like this arose. I wasn't as quick as he was, mainly because I didn't want to be the guy who shredded a million-dollar masterpiece, but I got the job done.

The Hockney, by definition a masterpiece, was of a technicolor Yorkshire landscape. The big bright colors were playful, yet compelling. Kind of like Edward Hopper on acid. The very essence of the artist's style.

The heavy bass throbbed through the house as I worked my way around the stretcher bar, removing the tacks. I wasn't a fan of EDM but hearing that driving beat helped ease the tension that increased with every passing second. Ricky's reproduction was already spread out on the bed, waiting to be installed.

I was about three quarters finished when I heard voices in the hallway. *Dive under the arena-sized bed or put the pedal to the metal*? I asked myself. The voices—not the ones inside my head—didn't appear to be getting louder, so I chose the latter option. I should have known that this was a task that lent itself better to the tortoise than the hare, because yanking out a particularly stubborn tack, I managed to gouge

The Culinary Caper

my index finger through the glove, which began producing a steady flow of blood.

I wanted to scream, *Fuck*, but I also didn't want to alert whoever was in the hallway to my presence. Not wanting to spray blood all over the Hockney, I dashed to the en-suite master bath in search of a bandage, hoping to stop the bleeding and finish the job before someone came in.

Under the granite his-and-hers sinks, I found a first aid kit worthy of a neurosurgeon and pulled out a roll of thick gauze and some adhesive tape. I slid off the ripped glove, not bothering to disinfect the wound, tore off a length of gauze, wrapped it around my finger, and then layered the adhesive tape over that. When you work with knives for a living, you're no stranger to dealing with deep cuts.

After dashing back to the bedroom, I launched once more into the job at hand. When the last tack popped out, I removed the painting, rolled it paint-side out, and eased it into the cardboard tube. I then tacked the faux Hockney onto the stretcher, attached it to the frame, and hung it back on the wall. Way faster than the removal.

That was when I heard the door open.

Luckily, the Hockney was at the far end of the bedroom, not visible from the door. Again, I considered diving under the bed, but seeing an open window, another option occurred to me. After peeking out, and taking notice of the shrubbery below, I dropped the PVC tube out the window.

"What are you doing in here?" asked a tall blonde woman, flanked by two other tall blondes.

"I just . . . well, I wanted . . . um . . . to see the . . . uh . . . Hockney," I stuttered.

"I know, right?" Tall Blonde Number One said. "I just had to show the girls."

The girls, six-two by the looks of them, nodded enthusiastically.

"What were you doing at the window?" Tall Blonde Number Two asked. "I thought you said you came to see the painting."

"Admiring the view," I said. Which was true, because the back yard with its thick screen of trees and Olympic-sized pool was way more calming than the current quarters.

"What happened to your hand?" Blonde Three pointed at the blood seeping out under my bandaged finger.

"Sliced myself while trimming the short ribs." My hands, like those of most cooks, sported a collection of scars.

"Ooh, you're the chef, aren't you?" Three said. "Loved the appetizers. Can't wait for dinner."

"I want one of these." Blonde One, hands on her hips, seemed to be appraising the painting. "I wonder if Malcolm and Sheri would be willing to part with it."

The blondes all turned their attention to the painting. Dismissed, I took the opportunity to vamoose.

Chapter Thirty-Seven

Aren't We Testy?

"Where is it?" Ricky whispered. "And what happened to your hand?"

I'd managed to get back to the kitchen just as the young dancer was taking her final bows. Ricky had broken free from William and his partner and was ushering me to a far corner.

I pointed out the window. "Painting's in the bushes. And my hand is fine."

Ricky glared. I glared back.

"That's what happens when we switch jobs." Something I hoped wouldn't happen again.

"First of all," Ricky said, "I've yet to lay a finger on any of your precious pots and pans. Second, what do you mean by 'in the bushes?'"

"I threw the Hockney out the window. Speaking of, I need to get back to those pots and pans."

Ricky followed me to the stove—my preferred milieu—where I turned off the oven, pulled out the ribs, and stuck a fork in the potatoes.

"How do you intend on rescuing it?"

"I'll leave that to you," I said. "I've got stuff to do. Stuff I would have been doing if you hadn't been flirting with your ex and enjoying the floor show."

"Ouch! Aren't we testy?"

"Sorry," I apologized. "It's just that things upstairs got a little dicey. And my hand hurts."

"Aww. Do you want me to kiss your little booboo?"

When Ricky reached for my hand, I batted him away. I wasn't looking for sympathy, just wanted him to realize we had different skill sets. "No, I want you to serve food and drinks and then retrieve the Hockney in the bushes."

"Yes, my liege."

"But first, taste this." I fished out a couple of ribs and tossed them onto a small plate.

"Damn, boy!" Ricky shouted. "That's what I'm talking about."

For the next half hour, I plated, and Ricky served. The guests ate and drank, asking for more of everything. When I sensed a lull in the culinary onslaught, I crooked a bandaged finger at Ricky and motioned for him to follow me out the kitchen door.

"Are you going to tell me how you cut your finger?"

"No." I was embarrassed by my clumsiness. "But I will tell you that this is probably a good time to retrieve the package."

"Now? You sure?"

I glanced through the window. The guests seemed content, and dessert was probably thirty minutes off. "All's quiet. I can handle anyone who comes into the kitchen." I pointed toward the back of the house. "The Hockney is in the second shrub from the left. If anyone asks, just say you were having a quiet smoke."

"Do you have a cigarette?" Ricky asked.

"Smoking's bad for your health." Tightening my apron, I reached for the door.

"Thank you, Surgeon General," Ricky said. "And, for the record, it was William who was doing the flirting. He always was shameless. One of the reasons I broke up with him."

"What was the other reason?"

Ricky studied the festive tableau through the living room window. "He was a wealthy professional athlete, and I was a starving artist. Our worlds weren't compatible."

Back in the kitchen, as I sliced the flourless chocolate tortes, I contemplated the concept of compatibility. Were Trina and I compatible? How about Rollie and I?

Trina and I had a lot in common. We both loved food and music, not to mention our proclivity for crime. Also, our families came from neighboring countries. At least, Ukraine, my land of origin, wasn't ruled by a paranoid megalomaniac. Did these similarities make us compatible?

Like Trina, Rollie and I had similar interests, at least in gastronomic matters. And we also weren't afraid to get into it when we had differences in opinion. Lately, Rollie had been getting prickly about my catering, accusing me of putting those gigs before the truck. I was careful to send a competent sub, but working on a food truck required an almost intuitive choreography that only came from working hundreds of hours side by side in extremely close quarters. Last week, after a less-than-stellar performance by my replacement, I had to reassure Rollie that I had no intention of leaving our partnership.

Then there was Ricky. This was a compatibility born of adrenaline and highly illegal activities. Activities that hopefully had an expiration date.

I scooped a couple of tablespoons of raspberry sauce onto each torte slice and then added a dollop of whipped cream.

"Done!" Ricky exclaimed, entering through the kitchen door. "The candy is in the van."

I assumed he was referring to the Hockney. "That wasn't so hard now, was it?"

"It wouldn't have been if you hadn't thrown it into a holly bush." Ricky showed me the scratches on the back of his hand.

"I didn't throw it. But we're even," I said, offering up my injured finger in solidarity.

"Hey cook, what'd you do to your finger?" Malcolm asked.

"One of the perks of the job," I replied.

Ricky took the opportunity to vacate the kitchen.

"Dessert looks amazing," Malcolm added.

"You want me to send it out now?"

"In a couple of minutes." Instead of moseying back to his guests, he peeked into one of my coolers, then lifted the lid of the pan I'd used to braise the ribs. "I understand you were upstairs."

Concentrating on putting the finishing touches on the desserts, I pretended I hadn't heard him. It was harder to pretend that I wasn't about to have a panic attack.

"Did you like the Hockney?"

How long could I continue to ignore him? "What?"

"You know what I'm talking about," Malcolm said. "The painting. Did you like it?"

"Oh . . . that. Yeah, it's great." I squeezed more whipped cream on the torte slices, hoping he wouldn't notice my hand shaking.

Malcolm pointed at my finger. "Was it you who dripped blood onto my carpet?"

I studied the bandage. A spot of red was showing through, but nothing was oozing out—at the moment. "Geez, I sure hope not."

"What were you doing on the bed?"

Alarmed by Malcolm's question, I almost painted the entire length of the counter with whipped cream. "Your . . . what?"

"There's blood on the bedspread and the carpet." Malcolm no longer sounded like the previously congenial host. "How do you explain that?"

His question left me mortified and speechless. My finger must have started bleeding again while I was replacing the frame. Where was Ricky when I needed him the most? He always had an answer.

"Well?" Malcolm was still staring at me, his anger making him seem larger.

"I am so . . . sorry," I stuttered. Would Malcolm know my tell? "I must have bumped my hand on the bedpost when I was trying to get a better look at the Hockney."

"Hmm." Malcolm studied me distrustfully. "You're covering the cleaning costs."

"Of course." I tried to steady my heartbeat. "Send me a bill, or you can deduct it from what you owe me for tonight. I'm terribly sorry."

"So am I," Malcolm said. "It's going to be hard to recommend you to my buddies when you go around destroying people's property."

"I'm . . ." How many times could I apologize? At least I wasn't apologizing for repossessing his painting. Not yet, anyway.

"Just stay in the kitchen where you belong." After spitting out that scornful edict, Malcom spun on his Gucci loafers and departed.

If staying in the kitchen meant not having to confront tire-iron-wielding gangsters or entitled professional athletes, I was more than happy to confine myself thusly.

Chapter Thirty-Eight

If I Buy You a Shot, Will You Shut the Fuck Up?

MOTR was packed with the usual mix of music lovers and locals in search of a refreshing beverage. My apartment was only a couple of blocks up, just off of Main Street, so on any given day, I could fit into either of those categories.

Like many establishments in the Over the Rhine neighborhood, MOTR, a cozy, slightly bohemian bar, was situated on the first floor of a nineteenth-century building, probably looking much like it had when it was constructed. I preferred that vibe to the glitzier downtown bars.

After snagging the last empty stool at the bar, I ordered a citrus IPA and then spun around to watch Trina sing. In black leather and fish nets, she was belting out a powerful anthem-like song, and the audience was clearly along for the ride. The tune, filled with the usual mixture of love and loss, sounded like something Amy Winehouse might have sung.

The decibel level was high, but Trina and the band sounded great. I studied the audience, riveted by Trina's performance, wondering what it'd be like playing music as a day job, rather than cooking. Would I be happier? Did I have the skills? Why did I always have more questions than answers?

"I don't see how you can drink that wacky shit," croaked the grizzly-looking guy, reeking of Camel Straights, on the stool next to me.

I'd seen him here before. Apparently, we were both semi-regulars, but this was the first time I'd ended up on a neighboring stool. His stringy gray hair and four-day stubble contributed little to his curbside appeal.

Dug in at the bar, with his unironic can of Pabst Blue Ribbon and shot of whiskey, he resembled any number of aging bar flies. The OTR neighborhood was filled with guys just like him. Someday, I'd probably be just like him.

I shrugged. "Just wanted something cold and refreshing."

Having just slogged through three hours of slinging tacos and pierogi on the hundred-plus-degree food truck, I was grateful—after an invigorating shower—for the short walk to the bar.

"Can't beat a PBR for that." Grizzly tapped the rim of his Pabst.

I trusted that would be the end of our conversation.

The song ended, the applause that followed deafening.

"Hot, isn't she?" Grizzly said. "I mean, obviously she can sing, but holy shit she is smokin'!"

He was right on both counts, but his leer, and the way he said it, came off as pervy. Either that, or it was just a reflection of his general appearance. Choosing to ignore him, I took a healthy swallow of beer and leaned back on the stool.

Trina waved at me and, after taking a swig of water, stepped back to the mic. "That was a song I wrote called 'Polar Opposites.' Our next tune was written by Chaz, our bassist. Hope you like it."

Chaz started snapping his fingers. A few seconds later, the drummer began a heavy backbeat, and the rest of the band eased into the groove. When Trina came in, her voice was high and breathy, a striking contrast to the hard, driving intensity of the previous tune. In fact, it was the polar opposite.

Grizzly grabbed my arm. "You know her?"

Not wishing to further engage with the guy, I shrugged his hand off. Besides, Trina's voice was mesmerizing, and it was easy just to let the music seep into my pores and transport me somewhere where everything was peaceful.

Grizzly downed the rest of his whiskey and poked me on the shoulder. "I asked you a question."

"Yep." Pulled from my reverie, I mentally returned to the crowded bar. "I do know her. She happens to be my girlfriend. Now, can I just drink my beer and enjoy the music?"

"Yeah, right." Grizzly chuckled, then guzzled more PBR. "She's probably just your sister or something. I mean, she's sizzling and you're . . . you."

Fair point, but ouch.

Grizzly wasn't quite done. "Besides, never seen you here with a woman before. Figured you were gay or something."

Or something? Why did this guy care about my sexual orientation? I came to MOTR to catch a band or have a quiet drink, not to discuss my dating habits.

I wasn't sure if Grizzly was looking for a fight or just failed to comprehend the art of conversation. Not desiring either, I considered how to deal with the dude. Assuming subtlety wasn't something he'd understand, I said, "If I buy you a shot, will you shut the fuck up?"

He downed half his beer and glared at me, probably trying to decide if that was a worthy trade. "Make it a double and I'll consider it."

After making good on my end of the deal, I was tempted to vacate my seat and wedge myself in between a couple of high tops. But I'd been standing all evening on the truck, and my feet were tired. I wasn't about to let some drunk bozo run me off.

Thankfully, Grizzly turned his attention to the generous pour of whiskey the bartender had placed in front of him, and I turned my mind back to the music.

Aside from saying hello to a couple of neighbors and friends that drifted by, I ignored Grizzly and focused on the music. Mostly on Trina.

On stage, she was a different person, and not just in how she dressed. Her face glowed from some kind of internal furnace, and the customary twinkle in her eyes had grown to supernova luminosity. It was almost as if she'd metamorphosed from a human into an otherworldly entity. Was this transformation a byproduct of doing what you truly loved, what you were meant to do? Had I ever transformed? As far as I knew, the only time I glowed was when the temperature in the truck equaled that of the sun's surface.

The band were all extremely accomplished musicians, with a unique and compelling sound, and the original tunes were truly original, but Trina was the real star. Or maybe I was just biased. Regardless, why was she wasting her time serving jalapeno poppers and stealing anything that wasn't nailed down instead of focusing on her singing career? Given my recent and pending activities, who was I to judge?

"We're going to take a short break and then come back for one more set," Trina was saying. "Hope you can stick around. We're Kafka's Umbrella. Please follow us on your favorite social media platform."

A few minutes later, after debriefing with her band, and accepting the adulations of some enthusiastic fans, she made her way to the bar, greeting me with a kiss.

"Thanks for coming out," she said. "You look exhausted."

"I'm fine, but you were amazing." Amazing didn't quite describe what I'd thought of her performance, but I'd never been the articulate sort.

Grizzly, pivoting on his stool, glanced unapologetically at her chest before asking, "You really with this guy?"

Accustomed to dealing with all manner of cretins, Trina smiled, put her arms around me and anointed me with a second noisy smooch. "You better believe it, buster."

I pointed at a table that had just opened up. "Let's move over there."

"Let's," Trina agreed. Before following me, she turned toward Grizzly, narrowing her eyes. "The next time you stare at my tits, it will be the last thing you ever see."

Trina motioned to the bartender. "Sally, can you get Anton another beer? And I'll have the same."

"What'd ya think?" Trina asked as we threaded our way to the high top, leaving Grizzly, mouth agape.

"About Grizzly Adams over there?"

"No, silly. The band?"

I smiled at her. "If what you're *really* asking is what I thought about your singing, I'd have to say you were spectacular. You should be on American Idol. Without you, they'd just be a bunch of talented hipsters on a rudderless ship."

"Not sure about the nautical reference, but thanks. Do you really watch that show?"

"No, but I'd watch if you were on it." Lately, I'd been thinking about breaking up with Trina. Mostly because I was super-stressed that her father was a Russian mob boss, but also because every time I hung out with her, those feelings escalated a couple of notches. After hearing her sing, however, I had the sense that this was the true Trina. Not just a mobster's daughter.

"You're just saying that because you want to sleep with me," Trina teased. "That was going to happen anyway."

I lobbed a gloat across the bar at Grizzly. He returned it with a sneer.

"I'm serious," I said. "I don't know if it's because of your opera training or what, but there's a quality to your voice that goes far beyond the typical pop singer. You should be thinking bigger than singing in bars. Just my two cents."

Trina threw her arms around me and gave me a tight squeeze. "You are so sweet, Anton. Although I don't consider myself a pop singer." After releasing me, she took a sip of beer and then grabbed my hand, the hand not holding my beer. "We should collaborate."

Unsure what type of collaboration she was referring to, I twitched an eyebrow. "I thought we had been."

"Not that way, you naughty boy. I meant musically. We could do some duo gigs. Just piano and vocals."

"Not accordion?"

She tilted her head and fixed me with a look. "No."

I'd grown used to accordion discrimination. In fact, I used to be in the anti-accordion camp. That was before I started hearing all these amazing accordionists playing everything from Led Zeppelin to Charlie Parker.

"Trina, my musical skills are nowhere near your level. If you want to do duets, you should find yourself a serious pianist. One who actually knows what they're doing."

Playing in a five-piece band, I could mostly blend into the background. In a duo, there was no hiding.

"Stop it, Anton. I've heard you play. You play piano almost as well as you cook."

"No wonder I'm just a struggling food truck cook."

Trina batted me on my shoulder, the shoulder attached to the hand that was holding a beer. Luckily, the glass was slightly depleted, and the damage minimal.

"You gotta stop underestimating yourself," Trina said. "That's one of the things holding you back."

"One of the things?"

"You need to start thinking more positively." She slid my glass away from the spill. "Can't you see how talented you are?"

"Uh . . ." Thinking positively, I reached for my beer.

One of Trina's bandmates approached the table, possibly the drummer. Between the plaid shirts and beards, they were nearly indistinguishable.

He stopped next to Trina, jutting a chin in my direction. "Did you ask him yet?"

Trina shook her head. Beard continued staring at Trina, as if afraid to make eye contact with me.

Intrigued, I asked, "Ask me what?"

"Gordon is moving to LA." Beard shot a glance in my direction, then quickly looked away.

"Okay," I said. I had no idea who Gordon was.

Trina, also avoiding eye contact, didn't offer an explanation, so Beard jumped back in. "Wanna join the band?"

Assuming he was joking, I laughed. His frown, however, suggested otherwise.

"Trina," I said, "didn't you tell him I had a day job?"

Beard nodded. "Oh, she did. But she mentioned that you were super unhappy at your job. And with Gordon leaving . . ." He shrugged.

I never would have expected Trina to go around broadcasting my occupational grievances. Setting my beer down, I glared at her.

Trina reached for my hand. "I can explain."

Beard gestured toward the stage. "Anyway, we're back on."

"Ronald, gimme a minute."

Ronald, nee Beard, studied me for a second. "Cool."

"Off you go, Ronald." Trina shooed him off.

"What the fuck, Trina?"

"I know. It was just a thought," Trina said. "But maybe the change of scenery would do you some good."

"Wait." I pulled my hand away from hers. "Is that why you asked me to do a duo gig? Because your regular pianist is flying off to California to seek his fame and fortune?"

"No," Trina sighed. "I mean yes, but no."

Should I have felt hurt that I was her second-choice piano player, or flattered that she thought I was good enough to play in her band and accompany her on a duo gig? Uncertain of the answer, I downed the remainder of my beer.

"I just want you to be happy." Trina slid off her stool and put her arms around me. "Join the band, don't join the band. Just do what's right for you."

"Trina!" One of the other plaid-shirted beards was waving her over.

"I better go." She ended the hug but grabbed my hand. "Look, Anton, as I've told you before, you're a great chef, a talented pianist, a fine sculptor, and a blossoming thief. Not to mention . . . a sensitive lover. Quite the Renaissance man. So, quit fucking around and take charge of your life."

Talk about rallying the troops. I was half tempted to start running around the bar shouting, *Go me!* She should have been a motivational speaker or a football coach.

"Okay." I wasn't sure whether my positive response was to playing music with her or taking charge of my life. But either way, I was ready to do something.

"I've already talked to a couple of venues about the duo thing. Gave them my demo," Trina said. "Ghost Baby is interested. Offered me a couple of dates."

"Wait." I set my glass down a bit too hard. "Slow down. You're already booking gigs?"

"I'm about to. Unlike you, when I get an idea, I actually act on it."

Like stealing diamond tennis bracelets? I pulled out my phone and opened the calendar. Maybe I could derail this speeding train with a work conflict. "What's the date?"

"Three weeks from now, on a Thursday night. It's just one set. I won't take no for an answer. You can call a sub for the truck."

I looked at the date. I was free. Normally I'd have been working, but Prudence was getting a tune-up and new tires, and Rollie was heading down to Louisville to visit his parents.

Trina, crossing her arms, fixed her green eyes on mine. "So, what do you say? Wanna collaborate?"

I glanced toward the stage where the band was reassembling, then at my beer, and finally, in spite of the anxiety I was already feeling about the gig, said, "Sure, why not?"

Chapter Thirty-Nine

Legacy Was Pretty Far Down on My To-do List

"Hey man, hand me another rag." Lying on my back, I was trying to reach the far corner under the stove.

"Gimme a sec," Rollie said, giving the prep counter a final polish. "Ain't that purty?" Stepping over me, he reached into the bundle and tossed me a clean rag.

"You do excellent work. Want to come over and clean my kitchen?"

Rollie stood back, admiring his work. "You couldn't afford me. Besides you know I hate doing these deep cleans."

"We were long overdue," I said. "If the Health Department had boarded us, they would definitely have shut us down."

"Yeah. Thanks to the transmission shop, Prudence still reeks of grease and mechanic sweat."

"Do you mind starting on the fryers next?" I asked. We'd lost six days of work, plus the cost of a new transmission. I didn't even want to think about how long it'd take to make up the lost income.

"Your turn to do the fryers," Rollie said. "I'll work on the fridge."

"Fine." Contorting myself like a seasoned Cirque de Soleil performer, I scrubbed around the back legs of the stove.

I'd spent the morning hunched over the piano, plodding my way through the tunes Trina wanted to sing at Ghost Baby. Tunes I'd never played before. They weren't difficult songs—I could get through them okay—but doing something interesting with them would take time. Cleaning the truck was a useful distraction from the hours of practice.

"Be nice if you'd hire me for one of your fancy catering gigs." Rollie began pulling out the shelves and setting them in the sink. "Sure could use the extra money."

"I told you, dude. You're my first call if I need help with the food." Unknotting myself, I slid out from under the stove and stretched my limbs. "I had a couple jobs, and they were both pretty small. Just me and a couple of servers."

"Maybe I should start a catering business, too," Rollie said. "Something to fall back on if you quit the truck."

"Come on, Rollie. It's not like that." Doing a deep clean was bad enough without having to cope with his crockpot full of insecurities. "You know I love working with you."

"Hmm." Rollie stuck his head in the fridge, running a damp cloth down the inner walls.

"I'm going to get some air." I grabbed a water bottle and stepped out of the truck.

"You got a call," Rollie shouted, waving my phone as I strolled back across the parking lot. After enjoying a breath of disinfectant-free air, I'd used the bathroom at the Creamery. A perk of our parking agreement. "Julia."

Fuck. A call from my ex-girlfriend was rarely a pleasant one. "You answered it?"

"I saw that it was a weird number. Thought it might be a catering job."

"You were going to steal the job?" I yanked the phone out of his hand. The day was not off to a stellar start.

"Chill, dude. I just didn't want you to lose the gig by not picking up."

A reasonable assertion, but one that made me uneasy. I didn't know if the trail of blood I'd left on Malcolm Duriki's bedspread would scuttle any future catering gigs with the Reds. And if so, would that affect the little art project Ricky and I were involved in? "What'd she say?"

Rollie fixed me with a hard stare and began shaking his head. Which, in itself, was an answer.

Julia and I had dated in culinary school—she was a talented pastry chef. Coincidentally, she was from Cincinnati. And, like me, she wanted to get away from where she grew up. After graduating and not having jobs lined up at any Michelin-starred restaurants, Julia and I had moved back to Cincinnati.

With the skills we'd acquired at school, we quickly found jobs— her working as a pastry chef for Phillipe, and me as a sous chef at Orchids, an upscale downtown restaurant.

The jobs were great at first, and I was reasonably happy. She, apparently, had other plans. Six months later, she flew off to Paris to work in her grandparents' bistro, leaving me in a blizzard of bread flour. I was uncharacteristically heartbroken. So much for eternal love.

"I don't know what she told you," I said, trying to preempt the pending line of questioning. Rollie had never met Julia, but when he and I had started working together, I still waxed poetic about her charms. "But it probably wasn't true."

"What the fuck, dude?" Rollie exclaimed. "Why do you keep secrets from me? And I'm not talking about hustling catering gigs. No, this is major life-event shit."

I glanced longingly at Prudence, realizing this was the first time I'd rather have been scouring the fryer than having a conversation with my business partner. But, on the off-chance Julia had called to chat about some new Parisian restaurant or even just the weather, I wasn't going to be the one who brought up the inevitable elephant in the . . . parking lot. "Are you going to tell me what she said?"

Rollie continued glaring at me. "You're behind on child support."

And there it was. After years of keeping my deep, dark secret, secret—which, in itself, was impressive—the proverbial feline was out of the bag. Damn cat!

"How could you not tell me that Julia and you had a kid?"

"It's complicated."

"Really?" Rollie gave me one of those you-expect-me-to-believe-the-neighbor's-dog-ate-your-homework looks. "You abandoned your kid on the other side of the planet, and that's all you got?"

I wiped a trickle of perspiration off my forehead. "Do you mind if we go in the truck? I'm baking out here."

Onboard, in an attempt to delay the inescapable, I reached into the cooler, pulled out a couple of beers, and handed one to Rollie. Not sure where to start, I pulled the tab and guzzled a third of its contents. Rollie tapped his foot impatiently.

"Julia and I didn't keep in touch much after she moved to Paris. She was super busy with her new job, and I'd just started working at Roberto's."

Rollie nodded. "And?"

"She came back for Christmas every year to see her parents and would usually find time to see me. Those were some intense evenings." I could still picture the nights we spent holed up in my apartment with carry-out and cocktails, leaving only to replenish supplies.

"And?" Rollie repeated.

"And then, one time, she didn't come back to Cincinnati for the holidays. But I got a call. A call that would forever change my life."

"Are you sure the kid's yours?" Rollie asked.

"She insisted it was. But I asked myself that same question." The memory of that phone call still triggered my already high level of anxiety.

It wasn't like we hadn't taken precautions. I mean, we weren't completely clueless on the birds and the bees, nor were we religious zealots. Maybe for some reason she'd stopped taking the pill. If she'd been looking for a sperm donor, she might have aimed a little higher.

"Did you do a paternity test?" Rollie asked.

"Julia actually insisted on that."

"Why would she do that?"

"Because," I replied, "she was asking for money. A lot of money."

"You mean your share of raising a child?" Rollie set his beer on the counter and opened a bag of pretzels.

I dropped into the driver's seat, unsure whether I wanted to give him the unabridged edition. I hadn't balked at supporting my unexpected progeny; I did have some degree of moral compass. My hesitation, aside from the sheer terror of finding out there was a mini me running around, was the magnitude of Julia's financial request.

"Well?" Rollie prodded.

I sighed and then downed another mouthful of the hoppy ale. "A couple of months after the birth, the baby started having serious heart issues. Julia told me that the national health care wouldn't cover all the expenses, and her medical bills were piling up."

"Hang on," Rollie said. "I know you were really into her. But you believed everything she told you?"

"I didn't start sending money until after we did the paternity test. By which time she'd sent me copies of the medical records."

"Maybe they faked the results."

Had Rollie suddenly become a conspiracy theorist? "You can't fake a paternity test."

"You sure about that?" Rollie asked. "What about the medical records? Maybe she downloaded those off the internet."

"Anyway," I continued, not wanting to feed his paranoia. "I told Julia I was going to hop on a plane to Paris as soon as I could get time off, but she was adamant that I not come. She didn't want me disrupting her new life."

I'd been devastated when she'd said that. Not that I was ready to embrace the role of father—it was more that I still missed Julia. Besides, who wouldn't want an excuse to move to Paris?

"That sucks, dude." Rollie put a hand on my shoulder and gave it a squeeze. "So, how old is this kid?"

"About six and a half." Feigning a cough, I fought back a wave of tears.

"That's okay, brother. Let it all out." Rollie pulled me into a man-hug, which nearly opened the floodgates.

After a minute or two, I pushed him away and blew my nose on one of the cleaning rags.

"So, you've still never met the kid?" Rollie asked. "Doesn't she come back to visit her parents?"

That was a question that weighed heavily on me and almost brought on another round of tears. Maybe it was time to ignore Julia's decree and show up unannounced on her doorstep with Play-Doh and a box of Legos.

"Apparently not. Or, if she did, she didn't tell me. I've got a picture." Like a proud parent, I reached into my back pocket and extracted my wallet. "Want to see it?"

The first photos she'd sent looked like every other baby—a baldish, scrunch-faced alien. Gradually, the ET began to take the shape of an actual human, one with characteristics resembling a curious amalgam of Julia and me.

Rollie squinted at the photo. "Cute kid. He's got your nose."

"Thanks. I guess."

"So, how much?" Rollie asked.

"How much what?" I grabbed another beer out of the cooler.

"How much are you sending her every month?"

"I'd rather not tell you. Let's just say, after I pay the rent, I barely break even."

"Shit, dude. I'm really sorry. I promise I'll stop bugging you about the catering gigs."

"Thanks, man." I patted his back, then opened the beer.

"On the bright side, you're a daddy. Mazel tov!" Rollie clinked his beer against mine. "What's the little rug rat's name?"

"Francois. Her grandfather's name." Did I secretly wish Julia had named him Anton Junior? Absolutely not. Juniors were all about legacy. And legacy was pretty far down on my to-do list.

"Are you going to call her back?" Rollie asked.

"Probably just text her and let her know the check's in the mail." With the high cost of international calls, the last thing I wanted was to listen to her berate me for my tardiness.

"Is it?"

"It will be." As soon as there were sufficient funds in my account.

Chapter Forty

Are You a Serial Killer?

My admission to Rollie was both a relief and a source of anxiety. On one hand, it was nice to finally share the deep, dark secret that had been haunting me for the past few years. On the other, it wasn't something I was ready to disclose to anyone else—namely Trina and Ricky.

Rollie's awareness of my situation, given his propensity for inebriated confessions, only made my secret that much more tenuous. At least for the most part, my worlds didn't collide. If only I could keep it that way.

Having a free morning, and since Ricky was spending the day with his sister, I took advantage of his offer to use the studio. Making the Rodin knock-off had sparked a renewed interest in sculpting. Not that I had any delusions about pursuing a career as an artist, especially since most of my recent efforts resembled creatures that might have crawled out of some primordial swamp. Getting my hands dirty was more of a solitary, almost Zen-like outlet. One that didn't involve the seismic stress of my income-producing revenue schemes. However, figuring out how to work his high-tech Italian espresso machine had caused minor heart palpitations.

Fully caffeinated and covered in clay, with Miles Davis's dulcet tones emanating from the stereo, I didn't hear Ricky enter the studio until he was standing right beside me. I didn't scream, really, but I did almost jump out of my socks.

"You always this skittish?" Ricky asked.

"Only when a serial killer is about to dismember me." I wiped my hands on the front of my apron, set the chisel on the work bench, and dialed down the music. "Are you a serial killer?"

Ricky pointed at my current attempt at Art. "This is fantastic! Who is this? Brahms?"

I'd hoped to have the morning to myself. The last thing I wanted was for anyone, even Ricky, to see my pathetic dabblings. In fact, I had every intention of destroying any completed efforts, which would be equally as rewarding. "It's supposed to be one of your uncles. From your painting."

"Dude! That's totally Tio Arturo. How could I have missed that? Everyone used to tell him he looked like Brahms."

"What are you doing here?"

Ricky glared at me. "Excuse me, it is my studio."

"Sorry, I meant . . ." Why was I always saying the wrong thing?

"Just messing with you." Ricky tied on an apron splattered with every imaginable color and began lining up tubes of paint on a wooden tray. "Isabella's son got sick. She had to take him to the doctor. Figured I'd do a little painting. Thought you wouldn't mind some company."

"Sorry to hear about her kid. Hope it's nothing serious." Better to express sympathy than to tell him I preferred to be alone.

"Nah. Just some kind of rash."

I imagined that rashes and all manner of childhood maladies were common, and that one simply took them in stride. Part of being a parent—a part I would never experience.

Ricky's phone rang. He put it on speaker. "Hey, James, what's up?"

"What's up is the Rodin maquette. I just retrieved it from a fence in New Jersey. Which is lucky for me, because I get to keep all the reward money. Not so lucky for you."

"Fuck!" I shouted, and then poked Ricky. "Can he do that?"

Ricky shushed me. "James—"

"This whole thing with Vincent never should have happened. I don't like messy, and neither does the insurance company," James said.

"My job is to recover art. And I want to do that without drama. If you can't do that, then I'll find someone who can."

"Not without our help," I whispered.

"Look, James," Ricky said. "We got this. Everything's under control. You just received the Hockney, right?"

"Yeah," James muttered.

"Okay, then. All's good. We'll be in touch." Ricky disconnected.

"Not how I would have handled that."

Ricky glared at me. Second glare of the day. More to follow?

If James worked for the insurance company, and we worked for James, didn't that, technically speaking, make him our boss? And, no matter what you actually thought of them, weren't you supposed to be deferential to your boss? When I cooked in restaurant kitchens, I always pretended to worship the head chefs as if they were all-seeing, all-powerful deities. Any time you screwed up, they did seem to have eyes in the backs of their heads, so maybe that was partially true.

I cleaned my knives and chisels, then placed them in the cabinet Ricky had allotted me. I considered returning Tio Arturo to the mound of clay he'd risen from but realized Ricky might not be thrilled seeing his uncle slaughtered before his eyes. Instead, I wrapped him in plastic, to keep from drying out, then removed my apron and washed my hands.

"You do the cooking," Ricky said. "I'll handle James. Or, better yet, we could bypass James and work directly with Hawkes Fine Art Insurance."

"Ricky . . ." That was exactly what he'd said about Vincent. And, aside from getting a new windshield, that hadn't turned out so well.

"Think about it," Ricky continued. "Dealing directly with Hawkes means more money in our pockets. More money means less debt."

Both valid points. But putting us on the insurance company's radar probably meant greater scrutiny, and scrutiny was not something we desired.

My phone began chiming with Rollie's morning fusillade of texts. As per his request, instead of totally ignoring them, I replied to each with a smiley face. Hearing the ringtone instead of the text chime, I assumed it was Rollie, unhappy with my snarky replies, but it wasn't. It was Ilya, the loan shark. When I didn't answer, a text chimed.

Your last payment was light. Again. Next time I call you better answer.

I jammed the phone into my back pocket.

"Knock, knock. Can I come in?" William stood framed in the studio's doorway.

"What are you doing here?" Ricky immediately slipped out of his apron and draped it on a corner of the easel.

"Thought I might buy a painting." After taking a couple of tentative steps, William spotted me. "Oh hey, Anton. Do you share the studio with Enrique?"

"For heaven's sake, come in already." Ricky piloted William toward the kitchen area. "Want some coffee? Or something stronger?"

"No, Enrique. I'm good. Just wanted to see what you've been working on?"

Seeing my cue to leave, I began collecting my things. Feeling mischievous, I said, "Should I tell William your new name?"

Ricky glared at me. "Anton—"

"What new name?" William asked.

"Enrique is now officially known as Ricky." I grabbed a bottle of water from the fridge and twisted off the cap.

William studied Ricky for a minute and then started laughing. "I totally get it. We all need to reinvent ourselves once in a while. It's how we move forward. Shows growth. Maybe I should start calling myself Billy. Billy sounds way more fun than William."

I wasn't sure I would call the illicit activities that Ricky and I had been engaged in "moving forward" or "growth," but we'd definitely been reinventing ourselves.

Ricky gestured to the far end of the studio, where his finished paintings rested against the wall. "Do you want to talk about personal development, or do you want to see art?"

"I want to see your paintings," William said. "Oh, Anton, almost forgot. Walter Owens is throwing a little shindig next week; he plays for the Reds. I hear he's looking for a caterer. I know it's kind of last minute, and you're probably already booked, but I'm sure he'd be thrilled if you could do it."

My schedule was usually set weeks in advance, but since catering gigs tended to pay more than what I made on the food truck, I was reluctant to turn them down, especially if it was for the Reds or Bengals. I just needed to check my calendar and find a competent sub to work with Rollie on the truck.

"Did I mention that Walter owns a Frank Duveneck?" William added.

I stole a glance toward the cloth-covered canvas at the far corner of the room—Ricky's latest reproduction. How had Ricky known that the Duveneck was going to be our next project?

Before we'd launched into our larcenous enterprise, William had given Ricky a list of art purchased by the Reds players. But how would William, or Ricky, know who was going to throw a party?

William reached into his back pocket and pulled out a phone. "Give me your number. I'll text you Walter's contact info."

I did as instructed, and seconds later my phone chimed.

Chapter Forty-One

It's Complicated

The only thing worse than being woken up by a ringing phone is being jarred awake by the buzzing of a doorbell. At least, since my apartment was on the third floor, the meddlesome cretin couldn't pound on the door or peek in the windows.

The persistence of the bellringer eventually pulled me out of bed.

"Yeah," I croaked. I'd had a series of late nights on the truck. The later the nights, the longer the decompression times. Typically, that necessitated alcohol.

"It's me. Ricky. Let me in."

"Can't you come back later?" I whined. "Like tomorrow?"

"No. And don't forget you're catering a party tonight."

I'd been dreading the evening's event for the past week. Not because of a demanding client or a difficult menu—those I knew how to deal with. The problem was, instead of my usual catering gig, the client had opted to rent the food truck. Which, if it hadn't been for the Duveneck Ricky and I needed to repatriate, wouldn't have been an issue. But since it meant Rollie would be there, it was an issue. A huge issue. I'd tried to convince Ricky that we should wait for a better opportunity to present itself, but he was adamant about "seizing the day." Thanks a lot, Horace. Or, more likely, *Dead Poet's Society*. Sighing heavily, I buzzed him in and waited at the apartment door.

"What's so important that it couldn't wait until tonight?" I asked when Ricky appeared in the hallway.

He slid past me, closing the door behind him. "I can't believe you're still here."

"You thought I'd be dead?" Did I look that awful?

Ricky laughed. "No. I meant this apartment."

Not wanting to discuss the emotional, not to mention physical, stasis that kept me from moving, and desperately needing coffee, I started the proceedings. "Well?"

"I'll wait," Ricky said, tapping his fingers on the kitchen counter and then pacing about the room.

With each lap, he made me more anxious. After grinding the coffee and turning on the water kettle, I grabbed his arm. "What the hell's going on?"

"The Rodin maquette is a fake."

"Of course it is. I made it."

Ricky dropped onto the couch. "The Rodin that Vincent stole from us, and that James reclaimed from the New Jersey fence, was examined by an expert appraiser and discovered to be a forgery."

"Wait . . . what?"

"You heard me. Vincent, or the fence, might have swapped out the real maquette with some museum gift shop clone. Or . . . maybe you mixed up the Rodins at the party."

"That's not possible," I said. "There's no way I could have . . ."

Flashbacks from the night in question began replaying in my head. I'd been rocking out on the accordion—quite well, if I said so myself—and then the fog machine had gone crazy, blanketing the entire patio in a nearly impenetrable cloud, during which time I'd switched out my Rodin replica with the original. Or had I? Confused by the dense fog, had I forgotten which hand held the real sculpture?

"Exactly," Ricky said, finishing my internal thought. "The good news is that the insurance company doesn't know who to blame. The bad news is that James is super pissed off and is looking for someone to blame."

"Well at least, thanks to Vincent," I said, "we don't have to return any reward money." Which was fortunate, because it would have already been spent.

When the water finished boiling, I poured it into the French press and set the timer on the stove. "If the real maquette is still at Troy Bradington's house, does that mean we have to steal it again? And that I have to make another one?"

Ricky, who a minute ago seemed about to implode, began chuckling; the chuckles soon morphed into a full-blown belly laugh.

I crossed my arms and glared at him. "I fail to see the humor in this." The full ramifications of multiple Rodin maquettes floating around washed over me. "What happens if Bradington hears about this?"

"He won't." Ricky replied. "It's not likely that a Reds player would have any ties to Hawkes Insurance or the original owner."

"But what if he does?" I'd always been a worst-case scenario kind of guy.

"If he does, we'll figure it out."

I wasn't sure I believed him. "So, what happens now?"

"For now, we concentrate on stealing the Duveneck."

"About that," I said. "We could put off pilfering the painting, and I could just do my food truck thing. Maybe it's time to quit, anyway."

"What are you talking about? This is our window of opportunity. We need to climb through it."

"I prefer doors." Ever since last week, when William had shown up at the studio, I'd been mulling over the timing of Ricky's Duveneck forgery, and the last-minute party being thrown by Red's outfielder Walter Owens.

From the very beginning, I'd accepted Ricky's explanation about the list of stolen art owned by the baseball players. William had shared that list, along with photos, with his ex because Ricky was an artist, and as such, would appreciate seeing these great works. Which made sense. But what if William had been the catalyst for our nefarious ventures? Which didn't make sense. I mean, why would a seemingly successful, retired ballplayer want to dupe his former teammates, and possibly call attention to his equally misbegotten Chagall?

I pulled a couple of chipped mugs out of the cupboard and set them on the counter. "How did William know where the studio was?"

"What?"

"Last week, when William showed up wanting to buy one of your paintings, how did he know where your studio was? I thought we were trying to keep it a secret." I studied Ricky's face, looking for signs of deceit.

"I'm a painter who needs a place to work, and occasionally, if I'm lucky, a location for selling my stuff." Ricky said. "What are you implying?"

At the very beginning, Ricky had told me that like me, he had financial woes, but he'd also made it clear that our illicit venture was just as much about artistic validation as it was about money. Seeing a way out of my own economic slump, it hadn't mattered to me that our goals were slightly dissimilar. "Is there something you're not telling me about William's role in all of this?"

Ricky stared at me. The stove timer beeped. I plunged the coffee press, waiting for his response. When he still didn't reply, I filled both mugs and handed him the Skyline Chili one.

He blew steam from the cup and took a cautious sip. "It's complicated."

That was my go-to answer for anything I didn't feel like explaining. To hear it thrown back at me made me realize what a frustrating response it was. I motioned toward the living room. "I've got time. Enlighten me."

Ricky settled on the sofa, which groaned when he sat. I chose one of the IKEA chairs.

"William never felt like he fit in with his teammates." Ricky sampled the contents of his mug and set it on the coffee table. "When he joined the Reds, no one knew he was gay. He'd played several seasons for the Twins and had a reputation for being a solid outfielder."

Sensing this was going to be a long story, I settled back in the chair, coffee mug cradled in my lap.

"William is a super nice guy, so he had no trouble making friends with the rest of the team. But, as a member of the Reds, he was also well aware of his semi-celebrity status and always did his best to be discrete in public. Me, on the other hand. Well, as you know, I'm not exactly the bashful sort, especially after a couple of drinks, and especially when I'm out with a gorgeous man." Ricky shifted on the couch, which creaked in protest. "Anyway, one night, after a game, William and I were having cocktails at a table in the back of Japp's. I was just about to plant a big smooch on his lips, when a couple of his teammates strolled by our table. They didn't stop, but it was clear they saw us. Everything changed after that."

As a straight man, it was hard to imagine the ramifications of a simple kiss. Although I'd once kissed a woman at a party, at her request, only to find out she was just trying to make her boyfriend jealous, and that he was a former Golden Gloves boxing champion. Which hurt my feelings and broke my nose.

"Don't get me wrong," Ricky continued. "They weren't all mean to William. And when he played well, they cheered him on, but when he had an off night, they could be quite cruel."

"Sorry to hear that." I meant what I said, but I wondered what this had to do with stealing paintings.

"The upside of this was that he finally came out. But he still felt like he had to be discreet about our relationship." Ricky picked up his coffee but didn't take a drink. "That didn't really work for me. So, I broke it off. I felt bad about that, especially since it was my fault he got outed, but I had to do what was right for me."

"Sorry." I knew I was repeating myself, but I didn't know what else to say.

"It was a long time ago. And you're probably wondering what this sad tale has to do with the Duveneck."

I nodded. The backstory, compelling as it was, hadn't connected all the dots.

"Shortly before William got injured, the team started buying art. The pitcher—whose crazy cousin was the broker, probably just a glamorous word for fence—was one of William's worst tormentors. Anyway, this pitcher refused to let William participate in this cultural bonanza. William was only able to acquire the Chagall because one of his friends agreed to buy it and sell it to him. When the pitcher found out, he and a couple of his buddies tried to make William return the painting, even threatened to steal it from him. But William loved that Chagall and refused to give it up."

"Hold on a sec," I said. "If these guys were so nasty, why is he still going to their parties?"

"I'm getting to that."

Having finished my coffee, but still in need of caffeine, I went to the kitchen, topped off my cup, and then offered Ricky a refill. He declined.

The Culinary Caper

"Which brings us to William's injury. He believes his career-ending injury was not entirely accidental." Ricky stared at me, letting that sink in.

Standing at the kitchen counter, I sipped my coffee, trying to imagine what Ricky was about to tell me.

"I don't follow baseball, so I don't really know the lingo, but William was chasing down a fly ball to left field when Cameron, the third baseman—and the biggest, meanest of them all—charged into him, tearing his ACL and breaking his ankle." Ricky set his mug back on the table. "Cameron claimed he'd shouted that it was his ball, but William says it was clearly his. They had to carry William off the field on a stretcher. That was his last professional game."

I'd read somewhere that it wasn't uncommon for soldiers to get hurt or killed by friendly fire. But I imagined those accidents were just that, accidents. In William's case, however, since there'd been a history of intimidation, maybe Ricky was right, and it was intentional. "Did they review the game footage?"

"Of course, but since there weren't any microphones in the outfield it was impossible to know if Cameron had called the ball or not, and none of the team chose to weigh in. It was William's word against Cameron's, which was a moot point given that he'd never play again."

"Damn!" The thought of losing the career you'd worked your whole life for in a single instant was almost unfathomable. If I couldn't cook, what would I do? Would it feel like losing a limb?

"Exactly," Ricky said. "And to answer your earlier question, William is going to continue to go to the parties, pretending to be all nice and friendly, until all the artwork has been replaced by my fabulous forgeries."

"Wait." My jaw dropped. "You mean he knows what we've been doing?"

"Sorry, I should have told you earlier. Didn't want to worry you about William's involvement."

I should have realized that William giving Ricky photos of the stolen art and telling him where they were located was a bit too convenient. Had I been so seduced by the prospect of piles of cash that I didn't bother to question the details of Ricky's plan? I always was the gullible sort.

Aside from Ricky having held back a key piece of the puzzle, did this change anything? Probably not. Perhaps having William on our side made things easier. Still, the fact that Ricky was keeping things from me was more than a trifle disconcerting. "Was this his way of getting back at his teammates? Even the ones that were his friends?"

"Absolutely. The friends, however, were collateral damage." Ricky tilted his head toward the kitchen. "I'm ready for more coffee."

Chapter Forty-Two

Yes, Chef

"Thanks for selling Walter Owens on the food truck concept," Rollie said. "I can't wait to see how these ballers party."

"Happy to do it." That was a lie. It hadn't been my idea. In fact, the last thing I wanted was to mix Rollie up, even peripherally, in the art heists. But Owens, a devoted fan, had insisted on hiring the truck instead of having me cater his party.

Opening the fridge, I pulled out the ingredients for the night's lineup, including the newest addition: Soft-shelled crab with kimchi tacos. After taking a whiff of the kimchi, properly pungent, I sharpened my knife and began slicing a mound of scallions.

Rollie hovered over my shoulder. "Don't cut those so small. They'll get lost on the tacos."

"Yes, Chef," I muttered.

He was right, but I didn't appreciate getting schooled by my partner. We'd agreed, when we first started, to put the quality of our products above our egos. In theory, this was a great idea. In practice, it could be a bit awkward. Especially since lately, Rollie seemed to constantly be calling me out. Maybe my side hustle was starting to take its toll.

Rollie set a sauté pan on the stove and fired up a burner. "Have you heard from Julia about how Anton Junior is doing?"

"His name is Francois. And no." Ever since I'd confessed my youthful indiscretion—okay, maybe not so youthful—Rollie had been quizzing me for more details. Aside from the admission that I was a dad, a word that still terrified me, and that the child was not in great health, and that I owed a mountain of child support, I had no further details. I was beginning to wish I hadn't told him.

"Geez, dude. Excuse me for caring about your family."

Maybe that was the true source of my annoyance. Julia and François were not my family. Family meant having some kind of relationship. I hadn't seen Julia since she left for France, and I'd never met my son. There was no way an emotional bond could exist. Or could it? What if "family" had a far deeper meaning than mere proximity?

"Sorry, Rollie. Every time I think about them, I get twisted up inside. Sometimes I consider driving to the airport and hopping on the next flight to Paris."

"I feel you, bro," Rollie said. "When Chowder, my yellow lab, died, I used to grab a six-pack and go to the dog park. Mostly I'd just sit there, drink beer, watch the other pooches, and cry."

Okay, that's not weird. But this wasn't the time to tell him that his dog park behavior was borderline stalking.

Having shared a sufficient amount of brotherly compassion and realizing that it was time to double down on food prep, we launched into our pre-game routine. A routine that, once I found my groove, required no words, but did require an intricate choreography that was only achieved by years of working side by side in a small space.

It wasn't just the choreography that was dimension-altering. It was almost as if time itself slowed down around me. A sensation that I sometimes experienced playing keyboard with Remoulade, on nights where everything clicked, and we were propelled into another universe. A universe where we became a single living, breathing organism. Of course, due to the bandwidth that our day jobs as cooks required, we were lucky just to get through each song without a minor train wreck.

Chapter Forty-Three

Respect the Pierogi

I parked Prudence on the circular cobblestone drive, in front of what looked like a Tuscan villa situated on the top of a hill overlooking the Ohio River. Or at least, what I imagined said villa would look like.

"So, this is how the other half lives?" Rollie stuck his head out the passenger window and took a deep breath. "It even smells better up here."

"I'm pretty sure way less than half of the population lives like this." I shut off the ignition and climbed past him.

At one end of the villa was a stone carriage house. Above it appeared to be a spacious apartment. I imagined I would be quite content living there. Would living that close to great wealth be far more intimidating than just feeding its denizens?

"Do you think we really needed to hire two extra people?" Rollie asked. "I mean, even when we're crazy busy, we've always been fine with just three of us."

"That's what Owens wanted. So that's what he gets," I said. "He wanted somebody to run food inside if one of the guests didn't feel like coming all the way out here."

"What time are the servers getting here?" Rollie asked.

I glanced at my phone. "Soon."

"And it's going to be your usual guy, Ricky, and your girlfriend?"

"Yep. And her name is Trina," I said. I was still getting used to the idea of her as my girlfriend.

Rollie joined me outside the truck. "Is it awkward having your girlfriend work for you?"

"Not really. I'm not very demanding."

Awkward was having Trina involved in the thefts.

"Are you serious?" Rollie asked. "You're a bloody tyrant. If the temperature in the fryer is three degrees too cool, you practically have a coronary."

"Respect the pierogi." I tilted my head toward the house. "I better check in. Make sure this is where he wants us."

"That should totally be our new motto," Rollie said.

"Huh?" Sometimes it was hard to follow Rollie's non-sequiturs.

"Respect the Pierogi. We should make T-shirts." Rollie pointed at Trina's beat-up Honda rumbling up the drive. "Is that them?"

Trina pulled up behind Prudence, and she and Ricky climbed out of the car. Instead of the usual black server's garb, they were both wearing yellow-and-blue T-shirts with *EpicCure* on the front. The colors of the truck as well as the colors of the Ukrainian flag.

"I like this place the best," Trina said. "The other houses were all big and fancy, but this one seems more real."

With the number of forgeries passing through my hands, I wasn't sure what "real" was anymore.

"You just like it because it reminds you of that opera festival you attended in Italy," Ricky said.

"Sorry to interrupt, guys." I steered Trina away from Ricky. "Rollie, this is Trina."

"Nice to officially meet you." Rollie shook her hand. "I've heard so much about you."

"Oh . . . hope it wasn't all bad." Trina gave me a look.

"I've got to pop inside for a minute and talk to Walter. Ricky, do you mind coming with?"

"Right behind you, boss."

"What about me?" Trina asked. "What should I do?"

Even though Trina was now officially a member of the klepto crew, I didn't want her inside while Ricky and I scoped out the layout of the house and the location of the Duveneck. She might be tempted to steal another diamond bracelet. "If you were a smoker, I'd say smoke 'em if you got 'em. Since you're not, you can just chill till we get back."

"You could help me do a bit of prep," Rollie said.

Trina's pout morphed into a smile. "At least someone appreciates my talents."

On one end of the terracotta-tiled foyer, a sweeping marble staircase descended dramatically to the second floor. Straight ahead, and on both sides, arched doorways led to spacious, sunlit rooms. Voices emanated from somewhere deep in the house, but it was difficult to tell from which direction.

"Let's try this way." I pointed forward, figuring the odds were in my favor.

"The Duveneck is in the parlor," Ricky said.

"Shh." I put a finger to my lips. "With all this stone and tile, sound can really carry."

"Sorry."

"What's the difference between a parlor and a living room?" I asked as we peeked into a couple of rooms.

"Historically"—Ricky cleared his throat—"parlors were a sign of social status. They were used for conducting business as well as entertaining guests. Even funerals. But, to answer your question, they're probably pretty much the same."

"Thanks, professor," I said. We passed several rooms that seemed to fit that description. "Maybe, while I'm discussing logistics with our host, you can sniff out the painting."

"Roger that."

"Is the copy in the trunk of Trina's car?"

"Yep," Ricky replied.

"And you're sure this is going to work?"

"It worked before," Ricky said. "At least this time, we don't have to keep secrets from Trina. Especially since she'll be wearing the apron with the hidden lining. To which, by the way, I added a waterproof layer. Just in case someone spills a glass of wine on it."

"Chef Anton, glad you were able to find our humble abode." Beer in hand, Walter Owens, in a boisterous Hawaiian shirt, filled a doorway at the end of the long hallway. "Can I offer you a beverage?"

Walter and I clearly differed in the definition of "humble." But a cold beer sounded great. Past experience, however, had taught me that drinking too early on the job was not a recipe for success. "Perhaps later. Just wondering where you'd like us to park."

"Of course. Let me show you."

"May I use your restroom?" Ricky asked.

Owens pointed in the direction we'd just come from. "Back down the hall, and to the left."

This was Ricky's chance to initiate the treasure hunt. Under my breath, I whispered, "Good hunting."

Ricky winked at me.

Chapter Forty-Four

Go, Talk to the Mother of Your Child

Under Walter Owen's guidance, I relocated Prudence to the right side of the house, parking a few yards off a multilayered brick patio. Trina moved her car a short distance behind the truck, close enough that it wouldn't appear suspicious when the time came to retrieve a certain item from the trunk.

The rich blend of spices and simmering meats was already emanating from the truck. The guests hadn't arrived yet, but Rollie and I were knee-deep in prep. By the time they showed up, we'd be ready to start pushing tacos and pierogi out at top speed.

To facilitate the proceedings, Ricky and Trina had set up a couple of folding tables just outside. Ricky was tacking on floral tablecloths, and Trina was laying out salsas and other condiments to accompany the tacos and pierogis.

"Going to be a great night," Rollie said. "I still can't believe how much Owens was willing to pay us."

Rollie and I had catered dozens of private events with the food truck. But this was the first one for a mega-wealthy client, and the first one where the client insisted on paying us substantially more than our usual rate. The higher pay came with special dietary requests as well as an agreement to stay as long as there were guests. No matter the hour.

"I hope they like the soft-shell crab." New menu items always made me anxious. Afraid that I'd left out some key ingredient, I couldn't help tweaking the dish up until the minute I passed the first order through the window.

"Dude, they're the bomb!" Rollie enthused. "I'd eat a whole plate of them right now, if I hadn't just devoured a couple of Kobe pierogi."

"Thanks." I stirred a couple of tablespoons of fresh lime juice into the guacamole. "How's the cilantro looking?"

Prying the cover off one of the garnish containers, Rollie peered inside. "Should hold out."

My phone buzzed. I glanced at the ID. Julia. Everything was prepped, and we probably had another twenty minutes before the guests arrived. That didn't mean I wanted to answer. But as much as I preferred to ignore her calls, they weren't going to end, and there would never be a perfect time to talk.

"Rollie, its Julia. I need to take this."

"Of course. Go. Talk to the mother of your child."

Rollie's phrasing wasn't exactly what I needed to hear, but I strode off toward a well-tended rose garden and accepted the call. "Bon soir, Julia."

"Bonjour, Anton. Why the hell don't you answer my calls?"

I'd been practicing my French, but I couldn't even manage the proper greeting. "Didn't you get my texts?"

"I got your texts, but what I didn't get was your check. Do you not care about your son?"

This was the first time she'd referred to Francois as my son. That was a major development. Or was it just a new ploy to endear me to the lad and pry open my wallet? A wallet that was sadly empty.

"I'm on it. Rollie and I have a big food truck gig tonight. I should be pretty flush by tomorrow." Not entirely true. We'd received a fifty percent down payment, but the remainder would probably take several days to process—assuming we had the check at the end of the night. Then there was the other reason I was at this event. A reason that would

The Culinary Caper

provide me with a healthy chunk of change, and that Julia would benefit from, a reason I would never reveal it to her.

"And how is your food truck empire?"

"Fantastic!" I lied. We'd had this conversation before.

"Really? Okay. But that's what you call a big gig? In my world, a banquet for three hundred is a big event."

"I've been doing a lot of catering lately. A bunch of jobs for the Reds. They pay extremely well." It seemed like I was always having to defend my chosen profession with non-food-truckers—and, apparently, bakers.

"The reds?"

"The Cincinnati baseball team."

"Oh," she said, clearly not impressed. "So, when can I expect the money? Or, better yet, Venmo me."

"Soon. I promise." Time to change the subject. "How is he?"

"Who?"

Why did she have to make every conversation an uphill battle? "Francois."

"He's doing fine. Well, not really fine. If he was fine, we wouldn't be having this conversation."

Which would be perfectly "fine" with me.

What happened to us? Before she left for Paris, we'd seemed, to me, like the perfect couple. We used to finish each other's sentences. And when we cooked together, each with a glass of wine in hand, it was almost intuitive. She would dice an onion or pass me the next ingredient even before I asked for it. We even liked the same music and movies.

How could a relationship that felt so comfortable, so right, collapse so suddenly? Had I missed something? I am male, so probably. But why couldn't she have just told me to shape up, or stop being an idiot?

"Julia, I want to help. I am helping. I just can't . . ." Every call from Julia elicited an uninvited trinity of anxiety, frustration, and sadness. One of those emotions, I probably could have dealt with. But together, they left me tongue-tied and exhausted. "I'll send you the money tomorrow."

"Wonderful. You should have led with that."

"Julia—"

She hung up before I could finish my thought—not that I had anything profound to add. Just once, though, during our increasingly sporadic chats, it would have been nice to have a less combative dialog. Perhaps talk about her life in Paris or the trials and tribulations of running a food truck. Normal, everyday stuff.

After stuffing the phone in my back pocket, I wandered back to the truck. Trina, seated on the steps, was browsing on her phone. Standing next to her, Rollie was guzzling from a bottle of water.

"Got to hydrate, bro," Rollie said. "How was your call?"

"Rather not talk about it." I slipped past Trina, who was eyeing me suspiciously, and onto the truck.

"Who'd you call?" she asked.

"No one." I checked the fryer temperatures and did a quick count of the scallops.

"His ex," Rollie said.

Trina glanced up from her phone. "Oh? Do tell."

"Rollie . . ." I warned.

"Now I am intrigued," Trina said. "Are you dumping me for some hot pastry chef?"

How did she know Julia was a pastry chef? Had Rollie spilled the beans about Julia and Francois? Would I get back together with Julia if she asked me? Worried that the look on my face had already confirmed her assessment of the situation, I redirected. "Time to get to work."

Ricky tapped the service window. "Show time."

Chapter Forty-Five

What Little Secret?

After sliding an order of pesto pierogi through the window, I tossed a new batch into a sauté pan and gave them a shake. Traditionally, pierogi were boiled. Rollie and I, however, were anything but traditional. Besides, we liked the crispness that came from pan frying.

"We're killin' it, dude!" Rollie shouted over the high-octane playlist blaring from the kitchen's wireless speakers.

"Did you tell Trina about Julia?" We'd been slammed since we opened for business. This was the first opportunity, where Trina and Ricky weren't hovering nearby, that I had to press Rollie about Julia's pastry chef comment.

Rollie pivoted behind me with a trio of scallop tacos. "What? No."

"Then how'd she know Julia was a pastry chef?" I gave the pan another shake.

"Lucky guess, I guess," Rollie said. "I swear I didn't tell her anything. Especially not about your little secret."

"What little secret?" Ricky, who had just come up the stairs, was glaring at me like I'd just given away our not-so-little secret.

"Anchovy paste. It's the secret ingredient," Rollie replied, deftly covering for me.

"Gross." Ricky looked skeptical but chose not to pursue the matter. "Anton, do you have a sec?"

"Sure. What's up?" I plated the pierogi, then ground some sea salt and black pepper over the top of them.

Ricky gestured toward the door. "Outside?"

"Who has secrets now?" Rollie probed.

Ricky was probably going to tell me it was time to get down to business; the non-food-related kind. Luckily, there were only a couple guests waiting for orders. "Rollie, can you handle things for a few minutes?"

"Fine. Go. Take a break. Leave it to old Rollie to keep the wheels of commerce running."

"Be right back." I followed Ricky to the windowless side of the truck. "Go-time?"

"Looks like things are slowing down. So, yeah." Ricky glanced around nervously. "Just wanted to remind you, since you're going to be kind of busy, Trina's going to act as the lookout. That means you won't see us for a while. You okay with that?"

"That's fine. I'll tell Rollie you guys are doing something inside. Cleaning up, maybe. If you need help, I'll try to slip away."

"I'd be lying if I said I wasn't a bit anxious about this one. Having Rollie here definitely complicates things," Ricky said.

Lying was something I was getting pretty good at, but I still wished I knew what my tell was. "You're the one who wanted to do this tonight. I tried to talk you out of it."

"I know. It'll be fine. I'm just having pregame jitters."

I always had pregame jitters. That was my jam. "Does Trina know the backup plan?"

"What backup plan?"

"Exactly." Very few of our ventures had gone off without at least a minor hitch. But somehow, we'd always found a work-around. I wasn't sure Trina would be as adept at improvising.

"Might I remind you; she is the daughter of a mob boss? I think she'll be fine."

"Good point," I concurred. Must be nice to inherit real-world skills. My parents had shown me the world, introduced me to various cuisines, and stressed the importance of being well-read. Useful qualities all, but I'd had to learn more practical skills like changing my oil and paying off my credit cards. Oh wait, I was still working on that last one.

Ricky headed toward the house, and I climbed back on the truck.

"I guess if you and I have secrets, it's okay that you and Ricky have some too." Rollie grabbed a steel out of the drawer and began sharpening his favorite knife. "If you ever feel like sharing, I'm all ears."

"It was nothing. Really."

Rollie pointed the tip of his knife at me. "I wonder if Trina has any secrets."

That was a can of worms he didn't want to open.

"Customers," I said, nodding toward a half dozen or so guests heading our way.

Dialing up full-service mode, we cooked, assembled, and dished out a battalion of tacos and pierogi in near record time. The last order went to William, who lingered outside the window.

"Hey Anton, how's it going?"

"It's going." I wiped down the counter in preparation for the next assault. "Enjoy your tacos."

Ricky had warned me that William would be at the party, but his presence still made me uncomfortable. I hadn't gotten used to the idea of him being the catalyst for our thievery.

"Have you seen Enrique? I mean, Ricky."

"He's around somewhere," I said. "Salsas are on the table over there."

"Thanks." William glanced at the multicolored array of salsas. "I've been looking for him. Can't seem to find him."

"I asked him to pick up empty plates. He may be in the far end of the house." The Owens' abode had more rooms than a Holiday Inn.

"If you see him, tell him to come find me." William spooned a substantial amount of chipotle salsa on his tacos and carried his plate toward the house.

"What's that guy want with Ricky?" Rollie asked.

"Don't know. They used to be an item."

"Ricky dated a ballplayer?"

"Is that so hard to believe?" Opening the fridge, I did a quick inventory. We still had enough ingredients to last a couple more hours. Hopefully, we wouldn't have to stay that long.

"Yes. I mean no." Rollie lifted two pierogi out of the reject bowl, grated on some parm, and then swallowed them in a couple of bites. "It always amazes me how some people get together. I mean, look at you and Trina."

"What's that supposed to mean?" I wasn't sure I wanted to hear his answer.

"Well, since you asked, she's drop-dead gorgeous, and you—you were the guy who once asked if he looked like a Pablo Picasso self-portrait."

He had a point.

"Speaking of the devil." Rollie jutted an index finger toward the front of the truck.

Through the windshield, I caught a glimpse of Trina, clutching the front of her apron, before she disappeared from view.

"Be right back," I said.

"More secrets?" Rollie queried, but I was already stepping out of Prudence.

"Trina."

"Oh, hey." Trina closed the trunk of her car and turned around, but instead of making eye contact, she focused on something over my shoulder. "Just changing my shirt. Some lady spilled salsa on me."

The Culinary Caper

"Do you have the Duveneck?" Her furtiveness was making me uneasy.

"Not yet." She glanced back at the house. "I was supposed to meet Ricky in the parlor, but he got waylaid by an old boyfriend."

Great. Just when it was Ricky-in-the-parlor-with-the-Duveneck time, William throws a wrench into the mix. Or was it a candlestick? Maybe William was having second thoughts and issuing a cease-and-desist order.

"Maybe you and I could do it," Trina said. "I've been practicing."

"Practicing what?"

"Removing canvases from the stretcher bar. Ricky gave me a pile of thrift store paintings to work on."

The last time I'd swapped jobs with Ricky, I'd bled all over the carpet and nearly gotten busted by a trio of blonde Hockney enthusiasts. Still, I wasn't sure whether to be hurt or grateful that Ricky had sought Trina out for his backup.

"'I'm getting pretty good at it. And fast," she added.

"I don't think Rollie would appreciate being abandoned. When we get swamped, we need at least two people on the truck."

"You really think anyone else is coming?"

"You'd be surprised." On more than a few occasions, Rollie and I'd been about to close up shop, only to have twenty hungry customers storm the window like frat boys after last call.

Trina tightened her apron strings. "Did you make the desserts?"

"No." Baking and I didn't play well together. "Walter hired someone else to do the honors."

Rollie came around the back of the truck. "Hey kids, hope I'm not interrupting. I need to hit the head. Can you man the fort for a few minutes?"

"Of course," I replied. "Trina, go find Ricky."

"Yes, Chef. But remember what we talked about." Trina winked, then headed the other way around the truck.

"What *were* you talking about?" Rollie did a passable Groucho Marx eyebrow wiggle. "Or shouldn't I ask?"

"You shouldn't ask." But not for the reason he suspected.

Rollie laughed. "I knew she was a firecracker. Gotta pee. Back in a minute."

On the truck, I threw together a couple of brisket tacos and ate them in the driver's seat. On busy nights, when Rollie and I got slammed, I usually didn't eat until the mayhem ended. My band gigs were often the same story, with late-night eating binges.

After brushing the taco crumbs off the front of my apron, I tossed the cardboard plate into the trash. Briefly, I considered making a couple more tacos. Why was taking Rollie taking so long?

Just as I was about to abandon my post and launch a search party, Ricky exited out of one of the patio doors, followed by William.

"Where is—" I stopped myself from saying Trina's name, unsure if William knew about her role in the heists.

"Trina?" William asked.

"She's dealing with the object in question," Ricky said. "Everything's cool."

I was still getting used to the idea of William being part of the team. A team that had grown to four. Which was fine for a dinner party, but in the thieving business, it only increased the odds of getting caught.

Then there was the matter of Trina's somewhat dubious family history. And her being alone with the Duveneck. How could everything possibly be cool? I was not one to hyperventilate, but this seemed as good a time as any to start.

Ricky put a hand on my shoulder. "Take a chill pill, Ant Man. All's well."

"Do you trust her?" I tried to take a couple of deep breaths, but failed miserably.

"She's *your* girlfriend," Ricky said.

Of course, he would bring that up.

"Can I be of assistance?" William's voice was as calming as a Zen master. Instantly, I felt my breathing dial back several notches.

"How?"

William, a serene smile painted on his face, put a reassuring hand on my shoulder. "I'll go check on her."

As if on cue, Trina bounded out of the house, trailed by Rollie. My first thought, given the recent revelation about William as a founding member of the League of Pilfering Purveyors, was that Rollie had just become the newest inductee. Who was next?

"Gang's all here," Rollie said. "Too bad there's no one to feed."

Had Trina already stashed the Duveneck in the trunk of her car? If so, the sooner we left, the better.

"I think we can probably call it a night." I was relieved that Rollie didn't appear to have joined the League. "Let me go check with Walter. See if he wants us to stay."

Rollie grabbed my sleeve. "Walter already said we could go ahead and pack up."

"You spoke with him?"

"Yeah. Got lost looking for the bathroom and ran into him. We had a little chat. Super nice guy. Loves our food." Rollie pointed at Prudence. "I'm going to shut down the fryers."

"Cool. Be right in." I wasn't the competitive sort, but if I booked a catering job, I was the one who dealt with the host. Food, logistics, scheduling, cost—that was all me. The food truck, since it was a partnership, was a slightly different animal. Not that I thought Rollie would try and steal catering gigs from me; he'd rather be cooking than coping with the mercurial demands of party planners or hosts, who usually didn't know what they wanted.

So, what was it that worried me about Rollie schmoozing with Walter?

"I better get back inside," William said. "Call me later, Ricky."

Ricky nodded.

"Did you guys get everything *cleaned up*?" I asked.

"Every last thing." Trina winked at me.

I wished she'd be a tad more discreet. Rollie wasn't the most observant sort, but he also wasn't an idiot. "Ricky, help me break down these tables."

"I'll do it," Trina insisted.

"Why don't you pack up the car instead?"

The last thing I wanted was a sharp edge from one of the leg braces to slice through her apron into the painting. Wouldn't want Duveneck coming back to haunt me for destroying one of his paintings.

"Don't forget we're rehearsing tomorrow," Trina said. "I'm rethinking some of the intros and outros."

"I remember, but can we talk about this later? I've got to give Rollie a hand."

Anxiety about the upcoming Ghost Baby gig was bubbling just below the surface of my already addled brain.

Trina and I had selected enough tunes to fill our one-hour time slot. Tunes that required me to do more than just show up. But every time I sat down at the keyboard, I got distracted by something else: doing the dishes, cleaning out the fridge, browsing Instagram. Did this mean I wasn't fully committed to the gig, or was it because apprehension about playing a duo, with me as the sole instrumentalist, was taking its toll?

Commitment and apprehension aside, I needed to get back to the truck before Rollie started complaining about me shirking my present duties.

Chapter Forty-Six

Steal Any Art Today?

"Trina stole a second painting," Ricky said.

"What did you say?" Surely, I'd misheard.

It was two days after the Duveneck caper, and we were sitting in his car at Home Depot, waiting for Dave, the courier. Still uneasy from the previous windshield incident, I'd made Ricky drive.

This was not the way I imagined my day starting. I'd envisioned a stress-free day: a five-mile run, a leisurely lunch, a long nap. True, there was the rehearsal with Trina. But, in the privacy of my apartment, with her singing and me tinkling the ivories, the time would fly by. Unless, of course, I couldn't manage to get my head in the game.

Ricky leaned back in the driver's seat and stared out the front window. "She didn't even try to hide it from me. When she dropped me off at my apartment, she popped the trunk and slid the second painting out of the tube, saying something about it being a well-deserved bonus for all her hard work. I read her the riot act, but she just gave me that crazy inscrutable smile of hers and climbed back in her car."

"She rolled it up with the Duveneck?" I asked, incredulously.

"Yep."

"What the fuck was she thinking?" My easily excitable neurons were now firing on all cylinders. "Without a forgery to take its place, Walter's going to notice its missing. Like right away. What was the painting?"

"A Charlie Goering."

"Don't know him. Nineteenth century?"

"Charlie's a local artist. Young. Very talented." Ricky pulled out his phone, dove into Google, and showed me some of Goering's work. "He mostly does Contemporary still lifes."

"Cool stuff." I took a couple deep breaths, trying to lower my blood pressure. "Do we need to make a copy and sneak it in before Walter discovers its missing?" I wasn't sure Ricky's artistic skill lent itself to Goering's style. But then again, he only had to fool a baseball player.

"Maybe." Ricky shook his head. "If we could find an excuse to go back over there."

"Why'd she steal it?" I asked.

"Said she liked it."

"Seriously?" I liked Lamborghinis, but I didn't go around hotwiring them.

"Let's not get ahead of ourselves," Ricky said. "There were a ton of people at the party that could have lifted the Goering. The guests, a DJ, a couple of bartenders, and whoever delivered the desserts. Maybe Goering himself stole it, looking for publicity. But I'm voting for the baker."

"What do you have against bakers?"

"I don't trust anyone who wakes up before the sun. It's unnatural."

This wasn't the time or place to tell him about Julia. "Let's just lay low for a while. See what shakes out."

"In the meantime, talk to Trina. This can't happen again." Ricky pointed toward a black SUV slinking in our direction. "There's Dave."

My phone rang. Trina. Reluctantly, I answered. "What the hell, Trina?"

"Yeah, sorry. I have impulse problems." She didn't sound sorry.

Didn't everyone have impulse problems? Wasn't that part of being human? Most of us, however, managed to refrain from the morally unacceptable ones. Maybe I needed time to contemplate the nature of our relationship. "Trina—"

"More importantly, what are we going to do about William?"

"What are you talking about?" I knew she was trying to deflect from her . . . indiscretion, but I'd listen to her concerns about William, given that I had some myself.

"How much of a cut is he getting?"

"Don't know." I nudged Ricky. "Trina wants to know about William's cut."

"Put her on speaker," Ricky said. "Hi Trina. Steal any art today?"

"Still early. So, what's your boyfriend's deal?"

"First off, William and I are no longer a 'deal.' Haven't been for some time. Second, he doesn't want a cut. He's just happy to see his buddies burgled."

"Don't bullshit me. I know William is your connection. There's no way he doesn't want a cut. Everyone expects a taste. It's how the world spins."

Wow. She was a bitter little emigre. It might take an experienced therapist to unpack all those issues, but Dave was getting out of his vehicle. "Trina, the courier is here. Gotta go."

Ricky leaned closer to the phone. "You know I love you, doll, but like I told you last night, if you ever steal something on one of our expeditions again, I will cut your hand off and, regardless of the consequences, deliver you to the offended party on a silver platter." He ended the call, handed me my phone, and exited the car.

I'd seen Ricky angry, but there was something more venomous about this version. Not that I should have been surprised. Everyone keeps certain aspects of their personality under wraps. I mean, look at me. Ricky had no idea I was the proud parent of a child I hadn't even met.

"Hey, dudes." Dave, dressed in jeans and a threadbare sport coat, glanced nervously around the parking lot. "Please tell me Vincent isn't joining us today."

"I think we've seen the last of him," Ricky said. "Between the insurance company and James, the PI, he's officially persona non grata."

I wished I was as certain of that as Ricky.

Dave pulled back the left side of his jacket, revealing a holstered gun. "Just in case."

Not what I expected from a reformed hipster. Barely 10 a.m., and the day was full of surprises.

"All righty then, let's get down to business." Ricky clicked his key fob. The trunk popped opened. "Anton, will you do the honors?"

The Duveneck was inside one of the PVC storage tubes we'd started using to give the paintings better protection. I reached into the trunk, pulled it out, and handed it to Dave.

Chapter Forty-Seven

What Was Happiness?

Trina waved down the harried server, who appeared to be the only one working. "Could I get another Spiked Arnold Palmer?"

We were sitting on the patio at Incline Public House, enjoying the view. At least I was trying to; since it'd been a couple of days since I found out about her supplemental art theft and I was still waiting for a better explanation. To be fair, I was enjoying the braised short rib grilled cheese sandwich. Brilliant idea. But I would have substituted smoked Gouda for the Swiss, and I couldn't fathom why they'd used white bread. A travesty! Or, since I'd been practicing my French—just in case—*quelle horreur*!

I was capable of enjoying a meal without giving it a thorough critique. But, always interested in expanding my own repertoire, I was never content to simply steal the recipe—not when I could make it better.

"Have another beer," Trina said. "It'll help you relax."

I was only halfway through my first beer and hadn't planned on having a second one. "Please, Trina, steal whatever you want on your own time. But, for all of our sakes, don't do it while Ricky and I are lifting one of our paintings."

"Do you really trust this William guy?" Trina deflected expertly.

"We wouldn't have known about any of this without him. So, yeah. Besides, we're all making bank, right?" William's involvement was never something I'd had a say in. Which did worry me.

"I suppose." Trina placed her hand on mine and fixed me with a beguiling smile. "What have you got going on after lunch?"

"Uh . . . nothing." I didn't want to admit that my big afternoon plans centered on a long, uninterrupted nap.

She traced a finger, starting at my palm, up to my lips. "Well, you do now."

Dammit! Why was I such a sucker for her feminine wiles? For that matter, why was I always doing what everyone else wanted? Julia, Rollie, Ricky. When was I going to do what I wanted? Okay, the post-lunch plans would most likely be spectacular, but that wasn't the point. The point was . . . I didn't know what the point was.

By all accounts, the food truck, my catering jobs, and playing with a band indicated that my dance card was full. Did that mean I was happy? Were most people happy? What was happiness?

"Penny for your thoughts," Trina said, interrupting my rapidly derailing inner dialog. "Are you picturing me naked, covered with whipped cream?"

Having just taken a sip of beer, I nearly showered her with a mouthful.

Without missing a beat, she added, "I'll take that as a *yes*."

My turn to deflect. "About what we were talking about earlier, just promise me you won't double dip on our future ventures."

Trina sighed dramatically. "Fine. I promise. But you're supplying the whipped cream."

Chapter Forty-Eight

Damn Altruists!

Awakened by the jarring tones of my cell phone, I glanced begrudgingly at the time. A normal person with a normal job would have been up hours ago. But, by any definition, I was not normal.

"I'm still asleep, Ricky," I sputtered.

"And I'm downstairs. Let me in."

I craved another hour or so of shut eye, but I sensed it was not to be. "Can I say no?"

"No."

"Fine." I dragged myself out of bed and buzzed him in. Then I threw on some clothes and waited for him by the door.

"You look like shit." Ricky slipped past me into the apartment. "Late night on the truck?"

"Thanks, and yeah." Rollie and I had dished out food at a succession of breweries, finishing in the wee hours at West Side Brewing. "So, this better be important."

"Would I be here if it wasn't?"

I was not awake enough for rhetorical questions. Afraid I might need to be, to hear whatever Ricky was about to tell me, I started a pot of coffee.

While I performed the necessary tasks, Ricky rifled through an old stack of *Food & Wine* magazines. "Do you remember the Vermeer we appropriated?"

"I don't think I'll forget a single one of the pieces we've stolen. Ever. Especially the Vermeer, since it was our first." At least once a week I woke up in a cold sweat, reliving any number of the close calls that had happened during our capers. "Why?"

"Mannie Ortega is putting the Vermeer up for auction."

"Fuck! Why?"

Ricky tossed the magazines back onto the coffee table. "Ortega is starting up some kind of charitable organization and needs some cash to get it going."

"Damn altruists." I gazed out the window, trying to imagine what it would be like to have more money than you needed.

"He's also building a winter home in Costa Rica. The problem is the painting will have to be authenticated before they put it up for sale."

I collapsed on the couch. "What the hell are we going to do?"

"What *can* we do? Look, Anton, the important thing is that no one can trace the forgery back to us." Ricky shoved my feet aside and joined me on the couch. "Besides, we did what we set out to do—returned the painting to its true owner. Yay us!"

I never understood how Ricky could always be such an optimist. "How can you be so sure that someone won't point a finger at us?"

"First off, neither Mannie Ortega, nor anyone else, will ever know when the painting got switched. Second, it's not as if I sign my masterpieces." Ricky scratched his chin for a minute. "I did consider it, though."

"Funny. So, if everything is peachy, why are you telling me this?"

"Always good to be prepared." Ricky patted my knee. "Just have your go-bag ready if we need to bounce."

"What?"

"Just messing with you," Ricky chortled. "You should have seen your face."

"Asshole." The coffee pot gave a final sputter. I got up and poured a cup.

The Culinary Caper

"You going to offer me one?"

"Do you want some?" I asked.

"No, I've been up for hours. Already had my daily quota."

I took a couple of sips and then turned toward Ricky. "I'm done."

The thought of quitting had been lurking just below the surface for weeks, and actually saying those words felt like a great weight being lifted off me.

"You haven't even finished your first cup."

"I mean the art stuff."

"Art stuff? What are you talking about?"

"I can't do this anymore. I want to go back to just being a cook. There's enough drama in my life without the added risk of prison." I topped off my mug and carried it back to the couch.

"Drama? What are you talking about?" Ricky protested. "We had a few minor setbacks. That's all. Besides we're not finished yet. There are still three more paintings. What about all your money troubles?"

"I'll figure something out. I can probably pick up a couple of shifts somewhere. Maybe Phillipe will hire me." Before Rollie and I had bought Prudence, he had offered me a job. Several, actually. Each time, I'd told him I wanted to do something different. Something that was, at least partially, mine.

Ricky rose from the couch, marched to the kitchen, grabbed a mug from the cabinet, and helped himself to the coffee. "You can't quit."

"Of course I can. It's not like I signed a contract."

"William's counting on you," Ricky said, his back to me. "I'm counting on you. Even Trina is counting on you."

"You guys don't need me."

"Don't be absurd." Ricky spun around, jabbing a finger at me. "The whole premise is based on your catering. Without your food, we'd never get through the front door."

He had me there. "What about William? Can't he get you in? He's the one that got the ball rolling." Which reminded me of a question I'd been meaning to ask Ricky. "And why has he suddenly started showing up at all the parties?"

"Anton, don't you see how important it is that we finish what we started?"

"No." Culinary school was the only thing I'd ever finished, and just barely, at that.

"Don't you realize what's at stake for each of us?"

I didn't. "Enlighten me."

"Gladly." Ricky rejoined me on the sofa. "For William, this is payback for being mistreated on the team. For me, as I've told you several times, it's about validation as a serious artist. For you, obviously the money. And Trina . . . well, who knows. But the point is, none of us can go back to Kansas until we've accomplished our goals."

"I'm not sure that revenge, validation and greed were the main constructs being explored in the Wizard of Oz. And Trina is definitely not Dorothy." I leaned back and closed my eyes.

"Anton." Ricky set his mug down and clasped his hands around mine. "Please, help me steal these last three works of art. After that, you can walk away and never have to see me again."

"How about if I just cater the parties and leave the heavy lifting, no pun intended, to you and Trina?"

"For this to work, we all have to be equally invested." Ricky released his grip. "Not that I don't trust you. But, if you're just cooking, then you don't really have skin in the game."

Ricky was right. If things went south, I could pretend that I had no idea what was going on and, if asked, say that I was just there to cook. Lurking in the shadows like a tenacious prowler was the very reason I signed on to this whole affair. A reason that had only slightly abated. Namely, soul-crushing debt.

Shaking off the image of Debt as a hipster in a black hoodie with a two-day beard, a braided bracelet, and a hookah, I guzzled more coffee. "Answer the question."

"What question was that?"

"William? Parties?"

"Oh, that," Ricky said. "No big deal. William started attending the parties because he wanted the satisfaction of seeing, in person, these remarkable works of art—that the team was so proud of—swapped out with paint-by-the-numbers reproductions."

"Good for William. He gets his revenge. But I'm still quitting."

I didn't quite buy Ricky's answer, especially since his copies were anything but paint-by-the-numbers. I could still picture Ricky's Vermeer, his masterful use of shadows to cast a somber, melancholic mood across the faces of reluctant musicians. A mood that, thankfully, I never felt when playing with my band.

"Maybe this'll help," Ricky said. "I probably should have told you this earlier. But two of the pieces are at the same house. So, there's actually only two more excursions."

I glared at Ricky. "That's supposed to convince me? Stealing two paintings at one party."

"Actually, one of them isn't a painting."

I doubled down on my glare. "Please don't tell me—"

"You guessed it."

Ricky pulled out his phone and showed me the picture on the screen. It was a bronze sculpture of a bull. A piece I knew intimately. "Is this actually 'El Toro'?"

"Indeed, it is. You, my friend, are looking at a genuine Picasso."

Less than two months ago, I'd stared in the food truck's rear-view mirror and asked Rollie if I resembled the illustrious Spanish painter. Now, here I was, staring at a sculpture by that very artist.

Sculpture wasn't what Picasso was best known for, but it was his work in this medium that had influenced my decision—however short-lived—to be a sculptor. And this particular piece was one I'd already copied as a fledgling art student.

"You know I made 'El Toro' in school," I said.

"I remember that. I also remember that Professor Cappucci gave you something like a D on it."

"D-plus, actually." I could still picture Cappucci's smug face. "What a prick."

I shook off the disagreeable image of my least favorite professor, a man who probably contributed to my art school demise. "Anyway, where the hell did this guy get a Picasso?"

Instead of answering, Ricky stared at me like a teacher with a particularly obtuse student.

"Oh, yeah," I said. Like all the pieces we'd recovered, the Picasso no doubt came from the broker who'd acquired it in a less-than-legal fashion.

Ricky, his stern educator's expression morphing into a full-on grin, held out his phone and offered me a second look at the photo.

"Seriously?" I muttered. "That's your enticement? You think that a chance to relive my art school days will convince me to stay the course?"

Even as I asked the question, I felt something stir deep inside of me. Something I hadn't felt in a long time. Okay, I'd felt it briefly when I'd finished the Rodin maquette. But this sensation was much stronger. I could almost feel my fingers twitch with faint muscle memory.

Ricky set his phone on the coffee table, then leaned back and crossed his arms, satisfaction painted on his face. "Yes, I do."

"You realize this is not as small as it looks?" If memory served me correctly, the bull was about eighteen inches in length.

"Yes."

"And that, even if I could make a serviceable copy, switching it out with the original is going to be extremely difficult?"

"Yes."

"And that we're going to need a foundry to cast the bronze."

"Yes."

He was asking for a punch in the arm. I obliged him. "Stop saying 'yes.'"

If the desire to once again try my hand at sculpting hadn't been enough, the need to return the Picasso to its rightful owner was even greater. Damn him! "Fine. I'll make the Picasso. So, what's the painting?"

Ricky grinned. "A de Kooning."

"How can *even* a Reds player afford a Picasso and a de Kooning?" I couldn't begin to imagine the value of these two pieces. A million? Five million? Ten million?

"He was a pitcher. A great pitcher," Ricky said. "You've probably heard of him—Devon Snoot."

"Seriously? His name is Snoot? And I don't follow baseball, so no, I haven't heard of him."

"Doesn't matter," Rollie said. "But he was the guy who started this whole art-buying craze. His cousin was the broker."

"Wow, okay. Full circle." I sighed. "And the third and final piece?"

"Tell you later."

Couldn't I have just fought off those nostalgic twinges? Did my abbreviated years at art school still have such a powerful draw? Apparently, because here I was, once again surrendering to the Greater Good. And I had an uneasy feeling that I was going to regret it.

Chapter Forty-Nine

It's Bad Luck to Murder a Chef

Being alone on Prudence was oddly comforting. Not that I loved doing prep. Mostly it was because every square inch of the kitchen was deeply ingrained in my DNA. Also, I could work at my own pace without distraction, or the choreography required around another cook. Prepping, for me, was an almost Zen-like experience. A state of inner calm that I seldom found in the chaos of the external world. Maybe it was because, except for the occasional appliance failure, there were rarely any surprises. Unlike my side hustle.

I'd just finished mashing a dozen or so avocados when someone pounded on the side of the truck.

"You Antonovich?" A burly man with a thick neck and a pronounced accent stuck his head in the doorway.

Trina was the only person who'd addressed me by that name. Ever. That alone was cause for concern.

"No, I'm Anton." Maybe he had the wrong guy. "Sorry, we're not open yet. We'll be at Sawyer Point tonight, though."

After coming up the steps, he scanned the interior, taking in the bowl of mashed avocados and the stack of corn tortillas next to the stove, and glared at me. He was a large man, probably in his late sixties. "I hate tacos."

His size and close proximity, not to mention his hands, the size of a grizzly bear's paw, were more than a little intimidating. The realization that his accent was probably Russian contributed to my growing sense of discomfort. Also, who doesn't like tacos?

"We make pierogi, too. Kind of what we're famous for." Always wise to appeal to a man's epicurean predispositions. It's a chef's most lethal weapon, after his knives.

His eyes softened and a smile crept across the wide expanse of his face. "*Ya lyublyi pierogi.* I love them."

The man seemed to have a clear idea of his likes and dislikes.

"I haven't started any yet. But there's probably some in the freezer."

"Maybe later," he said. "First, we talk business."

It seemed unlikely, but maybe this scary Russian was just another salesman—a species I knew how to deal with. Salesman or not, though, my earlier Zen-ness had swiftly evaporated. "I'm sorry, but I have a lot of prep to do. Leave me your card, and I'll call you later."

"My name is Pyotr Danielovitch. But you may call me Peter."

"Look Pyo . . . Peter, I don't know what you're selling, but I gotta get to work. Maybe we can set up a meeting with my business partner."

He inched a couple of steps closer, placing a beefy hand on the counter. "I am not selling, Antonovich. I am Katrina's father."

It took me a couple of seconds to understand he was talking about Trina. And a couple more to fully comprehend the ramifications of a brawny Russian mobster looming over me in the confines of the truck. Especially since there was the very real possibility that he was here to defend the honor of his daughter, recently doused with two cans of Reddi-wip. Processing my pending departure from this mortal coil rendered me speechless.

"So, shall we talk business?" Given his epic smirk, it was evident Danielovitch was enjoying my distress. "But don't let me keep you from doing whatever you need to do. I love watching a chef at work."

To avoid hyperventilating and contemplating the manner of my death—beheading, submersion in hot oil, Sweeny Todd-ed into a meat pie—I assembled flour, eggs, butter, and salt for a new batch of pierogi dough.

"Katrina tells me that in addition to being a talented chef, you are also quite the thief." He opened the fridge and freezer, studied their contents, and then grabbed a bottle of water. "No vodka?"

"What can I do for you, Mr. Danielovitch?" The last thing I wanted to discuss with a card-carrying gangster was my less-than-legal activities.

"Right to it. Very good." Danielovitch grinned. "I think I'm going to like you. But if your pierogi are terrible, or . . . you mistreat my daughter. Then I'd have to kill you."

The rolling pin leapt out of my hands, did a double axel, and crashed to the floor.

Danielovitch chortled. "A joke. It's bad luck to murder a chef. Unless of course he tries to poison you first."

Retrieving the rolling pin, I forced a smile.

"I need you to steal something for me. Should be easy for a gifted burglar like yourself. Especially since you won't need to make a forgery."

Had Trina divulged our entire game plan to her father? And why had I just told Ricky that I wasn't quitting the burglary game?

"You are surprised that I know about your little scheme?" Danielovitch's grin resembled that of a hungry hyena. "You shouldn't be. Katrina tells me everything. Well, maybe not everything."

That was some relief. But I would definitely be rethinking any future dairy-related activities with Trina.

"With the proper training, Katrina could have sung at the Met. Which obviously doesn't compare to the Bolshoi, but it's not bad for American opera." Danielovitch gazed wistfully out the window. "Such a pity she threw away an amazing career as a singer. Instead, she grows herbs, sings with a band and works as a server. A server! So sad. Someday, when you have children, you'll understand."

Given my current parental situation, I wasn't so sure that I would. "Mr. Danielovitch—"

"Call me Peter, please."

"Peter, as much as I'd like to help, I'm afraid we're done with all that. We had some debts. We paid them off. Now, we're finished." If only that were the case.

"Do not lie to me, Antonovich. That would be most unwise." He picked up a knife and examined the blade. "Let me tell you what's going to happen."

Did even he know my tell?

Trina had finally revealed to me that when I fibbed, I rubbed my left thumb and index finger together, like I was trying to start a fire. I needed to remember to stuff my hands in my pockets when I talked.

In an attempt not to have a full-on panic attack, I washed off the rolling pin and plunged back into the dough.

"Trevor Anderson. Does that name mean anything to you?"

I shook my head.

Danielovitch set the knife back on the counter. "He plays for the Bengals. I don't follow American sports, but I believe he is a tackle, whatever that is. I'm more of a futbol guy."

After flattening out the dough, I used the three-inch cookie cutter to portion out the pierogi wrappers.

"I had my heart set on a Norman Rockwell painting," Danielovitch said. "I saw it in a gallery in Hyde Park, and it spoke to me. Something about the quintessential American experience. And yet, somehow so Russian."

I nodded, only half listening, and continued cutting out wrappers.

"The owner promised she would hold it for me. But then this Anderson guy comes in with cash and she sells it to him." Danielovitch's ears blossomed bright red. "I almost torched the place, just to teach her a lesson about breaking promises. But Trina talked me out of it."

If he hadn't been a Russian gangster, I might have commented on his choice of a Rockwell. Not that there was anything wrong with the artist's paintings. They were just a bit too sentimental, not quite my cup of tea. But, in the few minutes Danielovitch had been on the truck, he'd already mentioned murder and arson. At this rate, even without offering a critique of the popular American painter, there seemed to be little chance of me leaving with all my extremities attached. If only I could rewind to before he'd stepped in here, while I was still savoring the quiet solitude of prep work.

Danielovitch exhaled deeply, his ears returning to their slightly pinkish hue. "Instead, I will take possession of the painting without having to pay the gallery's bloated price. And you, of course, will be adequately rewarded. You see . . . I don't like to lose."

Losing wasn't so bad, once you got used to it. I scooped a tablespoon of lump crab and ricotta filling onto each of the dough discs. Six other fillings still waited in the fridge to be wrapped.

Danielovitch peered over my shoulder. "Not very traditional. But I do like crab. Perhaps I should come down to Sawyer Point tonight. Bring the family."

By "family," did he mean the wife and kids, or was he referring to his crime family? Given Trina's predilections, maybe they were one and the same. Not wanting to dwell on the matter, I folded the discs in half and pinched the edges.

"You should make blinis," Danielovitch said. "They are the most popular dish in Russia. And one of things I miss the most. Unlike that maniac in the Kremlin."

The Culinary Caper

People were always telling Rollie and me to add their favorite dishes to our line-up. Not wanting to alienate potential customers, we'd usually just say, "That's a great idea." But food trucks, unlike Applebee's, didn't have the versatility of a full kitchen and a cavernous walk-in refrigerator.

"Not much of a talker, are you?" he asked.

"Just concentrating on what I'm doing." And wondering if my will was up to date. Did I even have a will?

"Very good, Antonovich." He patted my back. "A man without focus will never succeed."

Great, just what I needed—an aphorism-spewing Russian. Of course, I'd often pondered the definition of success. I was a partner in a business, played in a band, and moonlighted as an art thief. Did that constitute success?

"Do not worry, my friend. I, too, am a man of focus." Danielovitch rummaged through a couple of drawers, found a spoon, dipped it into the crab filling, swallowed it in one bite, and then tossed the spoon in the sink. "I have worked out all the details. All you have to do is work your culinary magic and retrieve my Rockwell. But I don't want that boy, Enrique, to be part of this. In fact, don't even mention this to him."

I didn't want to be part of this either. But that didn't seem to be an option. "Mr. Danielovitch . . . Peter, if I can't use Ricky, I mean Enrique, would it be okay for Trina to help?"

"I'm not going to risk the safety of my delicate little girl!" Danielovitch roared. "These men, these Bengals, their profession is driven by brute force. Do you have any idea what they might do if they caught her?"

"Delicate" was a not a word I would use to describe Trina. And if he was trying to summon my sense of gallantry, he was doing a poor job. Not that I relished sending her into the lion's . . . Bengal's den.

But, not exactly a titan myself, if I failed, I'd also suffer a disagreeable fate. Danielovitch, I sensed, was not a man to be refused. "I'll do whatever you need me to do." Talk about a pact with the devil.

"Excellent!" He clapped me on the back, nearly severing my spine. "I knew you would do the right thing. I will be in touch. Maybe I'll even see you this evening."

Chapter Fifty

Beholden to a Russian Godfather

After Danielovitch left, I abandoned the pierogi assembly, dug out my secret stash of bourbon, tilted some in a glass, and downed it in a single gulp. The adrenaline racing through my body didn't subside, so I repeated the process several times. When that still didn't help, I dialed Trina.

She answered immediately. "Hey, lover."

"So . . . just met your dad." I let that hang there.

"Oh?" When I didn't say anything, she added, "Ohhh."

"Yeah, 'oh.' Did you know what he was going to ask me to do?" Her father's taste in art notwithstanding, the mere thought of him sent chills up my still intact spine.

"Not the particulars. He just said he had a job for you."

"Why the hell did you tell him about us?" Trying my best not to shout, and failing, I took a deep breath before continuing. "And by *us*, I mean Ricky and me."

"Anton—"

"I thought you said your father cut you off."

"Financially, yes. But he's still my father. Don't you believe in family?"

There was that word again. A word that continued to haunt me. Not wanting to tumble down that particular rabbit hole, I shook it off and began pacing the length of the truck—too short a distance to be effective.

"Why the fuck would you think I'd want to get mixed up with your gangster father? Between stealing paintings with Ricky and trying to cope with Rollie's temperamental bullshit, I've already got enough going on. The last thing I need is one more . . ." I stopped myself before mentioning my Parisian progeny.

"Are you done? Because if you are, I'd like to explain."

"Fine. Explain." I poured another shot of bourbon, collapsed into the driver's seat, and put her on speaker.

"You never told me why you started stealing art," Trina said. "I know, you're in debt. Aren't we all? But that doesn't spur the average citizen to larceny."

"Trina—"

"You agreed to listen."

I sighed. "It's all you."

"Clearly, you have some deep, dark secret compelling you to risk serious jail time. Otherwise, like most enterprising entrepreneurs, you'd be taking out a second mortgage on your business. You don't want to tell me what the secret is, fine. But don't try and pretend that you haven't already crossed a line."

Wow, talk about putting me in my place. Crossed lines aside, this wasn't the time to unveil my crippling loan shark debt or the Julia Situation. Not when the specter of Trina's father was breathing down my neck. "What Ricky and I are trying to—"

"Shh. No talking." Trina paused, making sure I was done interrupting. "So, given that your debts—whatever they might be—are huge and that you've already stepped over that previously mentioned 'line,' it seems to me you'd appreciate the generosity of a man who was trying to help you."

Gag order, or not, I couldn't refrain from responding to this outrageous claim. "You call forcing me to steal 'help'?"

"No one is forcing you. I'm sure he told you that you'd be well paid for your troubles. Cash money that could help ease your financial situation."

"Making me beholden to a Russian Godfather."

Trina laughed. "Beholden? Really? Who uses words like that?"

"A man about to be that word." I contemplated doing another shot but given that I still had a shit-ton of prep to do, managed to refrain. "I gotta get back to work. Can we discuss this later?"

"Of course. What time will you get done?"

"Probably eleven."

"Wanna come to my place?"

What I wanted to do was walk away from all of it: Debt, Trina, her father, robbery, Julia, the food truck. Move to a sparsely populated Caribbean Island, open a tiny bistro, and, in my off-hours, sit on the beach with a rum cocktail. Instead, having to face the reality of my current situation, and because I was easily persuaded, I muttered, "Okay."

As soon as I hung up, I realized that Trina hadn't explained why she'd exposed our whole art liberation scheme to her father. She'd once again distracted me with shiny objects like family, financial gain, and the prospect of sex.

In spite of Trina's questionable family and illicit hobbies, I was still attracted to her. I wasn't sure what that said about me.

Chapter Fifty-One

Never Argue with a Frenchman About Wine

"What's up with you?" Rollie, a kitchen towel draped over his shoulder, paused between stove and sink, studying me like a science experiment gone awry. "Did someone kidnap Anton and replace him with a McDonald's fry cook?"

From the moment we'd opened for business, we'd been teetering on the brink of disaster. Not that it was all my fault. Our customers, usually polite and eager, resembled a pack of *Lord of the Flies* disciples. Maybe it was the fallout from the zombie-anime rock concert they were attending at Sawyer Point. Or maybe it was because I couldn't wrap my mind around the strange amalgam of real-life, neon-colored anime characters and pasty-faced, drooling zombies.

Japanese-horror mashups aside, my game was definitely off. To be honest, I had no game. Nothing felt right. I'd burned several batches of pierogi, which had to be eighty-sixed. Then I accidently tossed a dozen scallops into the fryer. They were supposed to be pan seared—a very expensive mistake. I also kept bumping into Rollie and spilling food. Something that never happened, since we were typically so in tune.

"Sorry, my concentration sucks." Understatement of the year. Apparently, I also hadn't shaken off the unpleasant visit by Trina's father. Being a successful cook, however, meant having the ability to forget the outside world as soon as you stepped inside the kitchen. At least in theory. "I got this now."

"I hope so. You're scaring off the customers." Rollie tossed a handful of chopped red onions and cilantro onto a trio of tacos and then crumbled on some cotija.

The Culinary Caper

I'd screamed, "Fuck" rather loudly when I deep-fried the scallops. But the customer, a shuffling, orange-haired Gen-Zer, insisted on eating them anyway. And she loved them. So, all wasn't lost, and maybe we had a new menu item.

"Look, if this is about Julia, I understand. But remember what we said when we first started all this?" Rollie swept his hand majestically around the truck.

My mind drew a blank. "Was it something Three Musketeer-like?"

Rollie swatted me with the dish towel. "See, that's the problem. When you lose sight of our mission statement, you lose sight of . . . well . . . our mission."

As far as I could recall—despite Rollie's insistence that we have one—we'd never actually drafted a mission statement. I wouldn't rule out the possibility that Rollie, seeing my reticence, had taken the initiative to put pen to paper.

Regardless, I'd never been a "mission" kind of guy. Mission implied direction. And direction implied some sort of destination. Even Google Maps couldn't plot a course for me. "Rollie—"

He plunged ahead. "But don't worry. I'll handle the mission. I'm happy being the mission specialist. And you, you're more the artistic type. You can be the . . . artistic director."

"Great." I'd also never been one for titles. Rollie, most likely somewhere on the spectrum, was a stickler for definitions, quantifications, and coloring between the lines.

"That doesn't mean you can sleepwalk your way through service." Rollie said. "Anton, please tell me you're still a hundred percent in. Because if you're not, this isn't going to work."

Ultimatums, like mission statements, scared me. Always had. Mainly because they required decisions, something I'd never been good at. To hide my tell, I grabbed a water bottle and took a swig. "Of course, I'm one hundred percent in. This is a partnership. I will always have your back."

Rollie folded me into a crushing bear hug. "Love you, man."

"Same." I patted his back, the one I supposedly always had, feeling a trickle of guilt seep out of my pores.

Rollie pushed me away. "All right, enough of this mushy stuff. We have work to do."

I replenished the garnishes and did a quick tortilla count. We were running low, but there was probably enough to get us through the rest of the night.

My phone buzzed. I didn't typically answer when I was working, but after peering out the window and seeing a brief lull, I accepted the call. "Phillipe, shouldn't you be standing over a hot stove?"

He laughed his guttural French laugh. "Shouldn't you?"

Cooks didn't make social calls during the thick of service.

"What's up?" I asked. Rollie was glaring at me, so I knew I better keep it short.

"I thought it might be fun if we had a jam session tonight. Let off a little steam. At my place." Phillipe, Remoulade's lead singer and guitarist, accustomed to being the executive chef, had taken on the de facto role as band leader. The rest of us were happy to indulge him. "The guys are all down for it. How about you? You in?"

This was exactly what I needed. Total decompression from work. Legal and illegal. "Hell yeah! What time?"

"Fantastique! Whenever. We all get off at different times. I should be home by eleven. You don't need to bring a keyboard. I have one. But if you want to bring your accordion, that would be *formidable*."

"Cool. I'll pick up beer and wine." A post-kitchen jam would definitely require alcohol.

"Beer would be okay, but please do not bring wine," Phillipe pleaded. "I will handle that."

Never argue with a Frenchman about wine.

"Ahh, merde!" Phillipe shouted and then hung up. Probably a kitchen emergency.

"You seemed more excited about whatever that call was about than being here on the truck," Rollie grumbled.

He was right. Did that mean I'd lost my love for Prudence? For Rollie? Not ready to admit to waning affections for either, I slipped the phone back in my pocket. "Just the band. We're getting together after work."

Oh shit, I'd told Trina I was coming over. Would she be super pissed off if I canceled on her? We had spent the previous afternoon together. With whipped cream. Maybe I could tell her it was a rehearsal instead of a jam. That might sound more legit. Or I could invite her to come hang out at Phillipe's.

On second thought, that was a bad idea. These late-night get-togethers quickly descended into long-winded jams and nerdy debates about French mother sauces. Trina would be bored senseless. Not to mention the possible Yoko Ono-ness of the situation.

If I was already thinking of excuses, did that mean I'd chosen the band over Trina? Was there some significance in that?

"I played trombone in high school," Rollie said. "Never made All-State, but I was pretty good. Do you think Phillipe would let me audition?"

I loved Rollie, but nearly everything he'd just said was problematic. Playing an instrument in high school—like probably three quarters of the population—didn't necessarily qualify you to play in a band, regardless of whether you made All-State. And, in spite of what your drill-sergeant-like band director might have told you, there was a huge difference between blasting out Sousa marches with a legion of other brass players and playing tasty harmonies under a vocalist.

Not to mention that Phillipe the musician was much like Phillipe the chef. Kind of a snob. But Rollie was a sensitive soul, and I couldn't tell him this. "You should ask him."

"I don't think he likes me." Rollie jutted his chin toward the fresh batch of customers lining up outside the window. "Back to work. Try not to fuck up. Again."

The sudden onslaught of zombie rockers in their post-apocalyptic garb pushed thoughts of jam sessions, Trina, and culinary partnerships aside. For the next hour, it was all we could do just to keep shoving tacos and pierogi out the window. Somehow, I managed to rediscover my inner game of cooking.

Chapter Fifty-Two

If I Can't Cook or Play Music, Who the Hell Am I?

Standing outside Phillipe's swanky apartment building on West Fourth with my accordion and a partially drunk bottle of añejo tequila, I mentally replayed my conversation with Trina. She'd seemed to accept my explanation for bailing on her, even offering me a raincheck. But there was something in her tone that suggested she wasn't thrilled by my choice of post-work activities.

Fortunately, in a few minutes, I'd unpack my accordion and let the music wash away my raft of anxieties: capricious girlfriends, Russian mobsters, and paintings waiting to be stolen.

"Looks like you started without me." Fredo, his gig bag slung over his shoulder, appeared at my side, pointing at the bottle of tequila.

Like me, Fredo was clad in jeans and a T-shirt, but somehow, with the skill that appears to come naturally to Europeans, he looked remarkably stylish. Maybe it was the addition of the scarf and Italian loafers. I was lucky just to have matching socks.

"Thought I shouldn't show up empty-handed." I raised the bottle. "It's the only liquor I had that wasn't half empty."

"Leave it to you to say, 'half empty.' Me, I'm more of an optimist." He showed me his open palms. "But since I didn't get a chance to stop home, tonight I'm just Freddie Freeloader."

When not thumping away on his bass, Fredo was the sous chef at Roberto's, an Italian bistro, several blocks north on Vine Street. The job I had, before joining the ranks of the mobile cook brigade.

"How was work?" I asked. I could tell he was amped up. No matter how exhausting the night is, the second you step out of the kitchen, you're ready to party.

"Busy and insane. But I love busy and insane. Helps the time fly by." Fredo hit the intercom buzzer. "How about you? Where'd you work tonight?"

"Sawyer Point." Being busy was great, but I was getting tired of insane.

"Cool." The door clicked. Fredo pulled it open. "After you, maestro."

"Bon soir, mes amies. Come in, come in." Phillipe, dressed in a tailored button-down and designer jeans, took the añejo from me and escorted us into the living room. Most cooks, once they packed up their knives and tossed their aprons in the laundry basket, threw on faded jeans and logoed tee shirts. Phillipe, on the other hand, was always thinking about his brand.

Kiko, as per usual clad entirely in black, was already installed on the sofa, sipping a glass of red wine, her violin case open beside her.

"Gentlemen," she said, not getting up.

"Hey, Kiko." I gave her a peck on the cheek. "Off early tonight?"

"Perhaps." She fought off a coy smile.

There'd been speculation that Kiko and Phillipe were an item. He'd just come off a messy divorce and was trying to keep a low profile. Which, since he was a local celebrity, tended to be a losing proposition.

Phillipe handed Fredo and me each a glass of red wine and then clinked his to ours. "*Santé!*" He settled on the couch, next to Kiko. "Anton, I have an idea for your little truck. A new menu item. Would you like to hear it?"

"It's not exactly a little truck, but sure." The wine was very good, lessening my inclination to defend the size of my business establishment.

Phillipe fixed me with a frown. "I always wondered why you quit that great job at Roberto's to cook on a truck." He said "truck" like he'd just eaten a bite of rotten fish.

"Long story." Actually, it wasn't a long story. I just didn't want to tell a roomful of cooks that I'd gotten bored and wanted to do something radically different.

Phillipe waited for me to elaborate. I didn't. "Anyway," he said, grinning like a Cheshire cat on oxy. "My idea? Two words. Truffle pierogi. Brilliant, *non*?"

Phillipe's bottomless reservoir of gastronomic innovations was one of the skills that had made him so successful. To ignore free advice from the French chef would be like walking past a hundred-dollar bill on the sidewalk. Besides, anything in a pierogi was delicious, and I was a huge fan of truffles. "It is brilliant. One small problem, though."

"And what is that?"

I set my glass on the kitchen island. "Truffles are cost prohibitive."

"If you believe that, my friend, then you do not understand your customer base." Phillipe splashed more red wine into my glass. "It is kind of like that baseball movie. What was it called . . ."

Customer base, baseball. Did I detect a theme here? Regardless, I would need more to go on than "baseball movie." "Dunno."

"No matter. It is the line from the film that's important: 'If you build it, they will come.'"

"I know the movie, Phillipe, I just don't follow the correlation."

"If a customer wants a pierogi and loves truffles," he explained, "they will happily pay any price for the privilege to eat such a wonderful concoction."

"He's right," Fredo concurred. "For certain items, you can ask almost anything. Roberto once charged sixty bucks for sea bass topped with sea urchin and caviar."

Unlike Chef Roberto, I didn't have an eponymous downtown bistro.

"I'll have to think about it," I said. Determined chefs always found a way to justify their chosen menu items. I'd done that with my scallop pierogi, and they'd been a hit. "Although I have no idea where to buy decent truffles."

Phillipe grinned. "I know a guy."

Of course, he did.

"Hey guys." Phillipe gently swirled the wine in his glass. "I'm looking for a new pastry chef. If any of you know someone, have them contact me. Goes without saying they need to be extremely talented, with a kick-ass resume."

"There's a guy I work with who's looking for a change of scenery," Fredo said. "He makes mostly Italian stuff, but he's a quick learner."

"Hmph," snorted Phillipe. "Anton, is that girlfriend of yours still in Paris?"

Julia had worked at Phillipe's flagship restaurant before shipping off to France. He'd been impressed with her skills and tried to talk her out of leaving. But in the end, it was Paris, and Phillipe understood.

"Julia's not my girlfriend. But yeah, she's still in Paris." I hoped that put an end to any further discussion about my ex.

I wasn't about to admit to Phillipe that I'd been practicing my French language skills. As a former Parisian, he would have cringed at my atrocious pronunciation. Also, I was afraid that such an admission

The Culinary Caper

might jinx my chances of conversing with my son in his native language.

"Pity. Well, if she ever moves back—" The intercom buzzed, and Phillipe punched the door button. A couple of minutes later, Arthur wheeled a handcart piled high with his drum kit into the living room.

"I bet your neighbors are going to love us," I said, stepping out of Arthur's way.

"I'm on the top floor, and my downstairs neighbors are out of town." Phillipe placed a tray loaded with meats and pungent cheeses on the kitchen island, then fanned out an array of organic rice crackers.

After Arthur set up his drums, Fredo plugged in his gear, and Kiko tuned her violin, we spent the next hour playing through our favorite tunes, all the while stuffing our faces with a squadron of cheeses, smoked sardines, and Iberian ham—and of course, a steady flow of wine and shots of tequila.

Rocking out on accordion, I felt lighter and freer than I had in weeks. Every squeeze of the instrument seemed to expel some of the negative energy that had been building up inside of me. However, thoughts of the three yet-to-be-stolen paintings and the Picasso sculpture still hovered above my head like stubborn rain clouds.

Next to slinging food and playing music, hanging out with fellow cooks was my third favorite thing to do. Probably because of that unique sense of camaraderie that evolves out of the insanity of kitchen life. Maybe it was that lingering surge of adrenaline that came from having survived another night in the trenches. Rollie and I used to hang out like this. Was it my fault we'd grown apart? Given the mounting distractions in my life, probably.

Halfway through "Crazy," Phillipe waved us to a stop. "Anton. "What are you doing?"

"Uh . . . playing accordion." I ran my hand up the keyboard.

"You skipped the augmented chord." Phillipe strummed the last few bars of the tune. "Did you forget the changes?"

"I don't think so . . . Umm . . ." I tried to remember the chord progression but drew a total blank.

"Phillipe's right," Kiko said. "You've been a bit off tonight."

"Sorry guys. I've just had a lot . . ." There was no way to finish the sentence that didn't include larceny, child support, or my growing sense of impending doom.

"Hey guys." Arthur adjusted his hi-hat and then tapped it with a drumstick. "Before we play another tune, can we discuss business for a second?"

A collective groan spewed from the pride of chefs. We were here to drink and play music. Arthur, however—an unrepentant obsessive/neurotic—was famous for his "business talks." Drummers!

Hoping it might be a useful distraction, I tipped some añejo into a highball glass and handed it to him. "Have another shot."

"Thanks." Arthur tossed it back. "I spoke to several clubs about hiring us. They love the idea of celebrity chefs playing in a band."

Excluding his humble beginnings, cooking at Bob Evans back in high school, Arthur had spent his entire career working for one man—the owner of Cincinnati's premier steak house empire. And, like most of us, Arthur was not famous. Phillipe, with his French accent, nimbus of gray hair, and gastronomic realm, was the only true celebrity in the crew.

As much as I liked the idea of gigging more, I knew it couldn't work. We were too busy. And the chances of all of us being free on any given night were only slightly better than those of winning the lottery.

When catering jobs conflicted with the food truck, I always sent a sub. Lately, Rollie was rarely pleased with even the most experienced ones. If he found out I'd chosen a Remoulade gig over the truck, he would blow a gasket.

Phillipe, however, had an army of minions that did most of the actual cooking, and Kiko rarely stayed in the kitchen past nine, trusting her small but well-trained staff to serve up the best ramen and sushi in town. I struggled to imagine what it would be like to have minions or staff.

"Also," Arthur continued, "and you're not going to believe this, but I talked to this booking agent, and he thinks we should go on this tour he's putting together."

Kiko jabbed the tip of her bow at Arthur. "What the fuck are you talking about? Some of us have restaurants to run. We can't just up and leave."

"I don't know," Phillipe said, topping off his wine glass. "Sounds like fun."

"Are you crazy?" Kiko glared at the French chef. "Unless you're traveling with the symphony or are a major act, tours don't pay for shit."

Kiko would know. She'd done both of those things. I, on the other hand, burglary aside, had led a relatively uneventful life.

"So, is that a hard no?" Arthur asked. "You don't want to gig more or go on tour?"

"Definitely not," Kiko said emphatically, eyeing Phillipe.

"Phillipe?" Arthur pressed.

Phillipe glanced at Kiko, then examined his nails. "No."

Arthur shook his head in disgust. "Anton?"

Deep down, I loved the idea of putting my knives down, walking away from the truck and everything else. Immersing myself in music. Sounded amazing. At least until reality inevitably took hold: playing for peanuts, traveling hundreds of miles in a beat-up van and sleeping in shitty motels or on friends' couches. Suddenly not so glamorous. "Now's not a good time." Would it ever be?

"Very disappointed in you, Anton," Arthur said. "Always thought of you as the guy who wasn't afraid of anything."

I could handle disappointment, had been for years. But, as far as "afraid" . . . if he only knew what I got up to in my off-hours.

Arthur pointed a drumstick at Fredo. "Down to you, Frodo. You in?"

"Artie," I interrupted, "our bassist might be short, but he's not a hobbit. He's Italian."

"Shut up, Ant Boy," Arthur growled. "And, by the way, you sucked ass tonight."

"That's enough, Arthur," Kiko warned.

Rollie telling me I sucked, and now Arthur? Was it time to hang up both of my hats? But if I couldn't cook or play music, who the hell was I?

"Uh . . . guys. Now might not be the best time to tell you this, but . . ." Fredo paused, looking at each of us. "I'm moving to Florence."

"Kentucky?" Arthur asked.

"No," Fredo said. "Italy."

This unexpected declaration was met with cosmic silence.

Fredo, after several beers, had often talked about moving back to Florence, where he was born, where most of his family still lived. He'd left at seventeen to see the world and never returned. And recently, even sober, he'd begun to wax nostalgic about the Old Country, making me wonder what it was like to have a clear dream of the future.

"When?" I ventured.

Everyone continued glaring at Fredo.

He studied his shoes. "Next week."

The Culinary Caper

"And when the fuck were you going to tell us?" Arthur barked. "You do realize that we have a gig at the end of the month?"

My phone chimed. I slipped it out of my pocket and read the message from Trina.

If you're done early come over. I'll be up.

Without replying, I slid the phone back in my pocket.

"I know. I was planning on telling you tonight. Sorry." Fredo poured each of us a shot of añejo, finishing the bottle. "I'll find someone to cover the gig."

Phillipe, Kiko, Fredo, and I downed our shots in unison.

Arthur threw a drumstick against the wall, denting the drywall and nearly dislodging a picture of Chef Phillipe posing with Sarah Jessica Parker.

"Kind of figured that's what you'd all say. Wimpy motherfuckers." Arthur glared at me and Fredo. "That's why, as of now, I'm quitting the band. Knife Rack is going on tour in ten days and asked me to—no, begged me to join them."

Phillipe, unflappable as always, straightened out the photo. "What is this Knife Rack?"

"A metal band," Fredo said. "Mostly a bunch of dishwashers."

"Just because they're not cooks doesn't mean they're not good musicians." Arthur began dismantling his drum kit. "And they're definitely not a bunch of snobs, like you assholes."

Great. The one non-stress-inducing aspect of my life was about to go the way of the dinosaurs. Was the universe trying to tell me something? We'd had a good run, and it'd been gratifying exploring my musical inclinations, but maybe it was time to either double down on the food truck or dive back into a legit kitchen. I was still light-years away from having the capital to open my own place. Probably always would be.

At least I still had the gig with Trina coming up. A gig I was starting to feel more comfortable about, but not comfortable enough to tell my band, or now possibly former band, about. Playing for other musicians is always stressful, even if it's not their day job.

At the moment, though, I just wanted to be free from the tension-filled room.

"Uh . . . does that mean we're done for the evening?" I glanced at the time. Just past midnight. Maybe I'd take Trina up on her invitation.

Phillipe raised a hand.

Kiko pointed at him. "Phillipe?"

"I know a bassist who could replace Fredo."

"Who?" Kiko asked.

"Danny Pasko." Phillipe replied.

My turn to ask. "Who?"

"He's not a chef, though," Phillipe conceded. "He's a real musician, and very talented."

Leave it to Phillipe, who had decades of dealing with staff turnover, to immediately start thinking about a new bassist. Maybe we were all replaceable. Would Rollie replace me? Would Trina? Julia certainly had.

"If he's a 'real musician,'" Kiko air-quoted, "why the hell would he want to slum it with a bunch of chefs? Not to mention, our gigs usually don't pay shit."

Phillipe, ignoring Kiko's question, topped off my glass. "Anton, Danny's the truffle guy I was talking about earlier."

Chapter Fifty-Three

Never Underestimate a Russian's Predilection for Their National Beverage

"You're finally awake." Trina was perched on the edge of the bed.

I pried my eyes open, only for a merciless shaft of sunlight to bore holes through both my retinas.

"Mrph," I muttered, pulling a pillow over my face.

After a quick analysis, I deduced that the bed I was in was Trina's. I had a vague memory of bourbon shakes—heavy on the bourbon—but was unable to calculate exactly how many I'd consumed. Or remember what ensued after finishing the tasty but lethal drinks. Wait a second. That memory was coming back to me. And it was worth remembering.

"You should get up." Trina pulled back the covers. "Rollie is on his way over. Coffee's ready."

"What?" I had other questions, too, but that was the extent of my verbal capabilities.

After shifting to the far side of the bed to avoid the sun's unforgiving laser beam, I detached the drool-covered pillow from my face. Trina was dressed in black jeans and a pink T-shirt with a sketch of a guy in a bow tie and the words *Awake, Jarred Awake* in a thought bubble. Appropriate, but way too ironic or existential for me to fully comprehend, pre-caffeine.

"Your phone chimed earlier." Trina rose from the bed and headed out of the room, pausing in the doorway. "Rollie wanted to know where you were and if you had time to meet up."

"Why?" I asked, calling up yet another classic monosyllabic inquiry.

I probably should have been upset that she'd read my text. Massively hung over, though, I couldn't dial up that emotion. Instead, I dragged myself out of bed and threw on the previous night's clothes, wondering why Rollie couldn't have unleashed his usual bombardment of texts instead of having to make an actual appearance.

After splashing water on my face and finger-brushing my teeth, I felt slightly revived. As I shuffled into the kitchen, Trina pointed at the mug of coffee waiting for me on the counter.

"Last night—" I began, but Trina kissed me hard on the lips, preventing me from finishing the sentence. Not that I had any idea how I would have completed it.

"Last night was wonderful," Trina said. "But I was sorry to hear about the demise of your band."

"Me too." I sampled the coffee. It was strong and hot—exactly what I needed. "But Phillipe knows another bass player, and drummers are a dime a dozen, so maybe there's still a future for Remoulade."

Speaking of the future, standing in Trina's Northside house, I realized I had no idea what the future held for me in my occupational, financial, or emotional pursuits. Did anyone?

Trina put her hands around my waist. "You okay? You look a little woozy."

Woozy didn't begin to describe how I felt. "I'll be fine. Just going to need a couple of gallons of this." I tapped the rim of the mug. I omitted the other thing I probably needed. An epiphany? Without the assistance of magic mushrooms, it was probably too early in the day for that.

The doorbell rang, vaporizing my pseudo-existential musings. Trina, leaving me to my coffee, went to the door and ushered Rollie inside.

"Hey, kids," Rollie beamed. "Hope I'm not interrupting."

"Course not," Trina said. "Can I get you some coffee?"

"That'd be most excellent." Unlike me, Rollie looked freshly scrubbed, cheerful, and fully caffeinated.

While Trina fetched another mug, Rollie took in my dishevelment. "Late night?"

"Kind of." I'd never been good at early-morning small talk. Or small talk in general.

"How was band practice?" His tone was slightly prickly.

Trina handed Rollie the mug. "Anton probably doesn't want to talk about that."

Rollie gave me a look. "Oh?"

Trina was right—I didn't want to discuss the band situation. Contrary to what I'd just told her, I didn't have high hopes for the future of Remoulade. "What was so important it couldn't wait?"

"It's not that important," Rollie said. "Just wanted to tell you in person, so you wouldn't get mad."

Not liking the sound of his prologue, I studied my mug of coffee, waiting for him to disappear. He didn't. In the ensuing silence, the antique wall clock ticked ominously. "Why would I get mad?"

"Remember that party we catered last week?"

"Yeah." Whatever this was about, I knew I wasn't going to like it. I just hoped it had nothing to do with stolen paintings.

"Walter Owens, the dude whose party it was, called me and asked if it was okay if he passed my contact information on to some guy named Trevor Anderson—plays for the Bengals. I told Walter that was fine. A couple of days later, this Anderson guy calls, wanting to hire the truck for an event next Friday. We weren't working, so I said yes."

"You just booked us a private party, which pays way better than flinging pierogi to a bunch of drunks at a brewery. Why would I be mad? You did quote him our usual rate, right?"

"Of course. Just thought, since you got the Owens job, you'd be pissed off because they called me instead of you."

I drank more coffee, considering what he'd told me. It was a bit odd that Walter hadn't called me; I mean, I was the one who'd booked the job. Although my attentions at the party had been focused elsewhere, while Rollie had spent time schmoozing the host. If anything, I should have been mad at myself for not being more proactive. But then again, my skill set ran more toward the culinary game than the commerce game. Did that mean I'd never open an eatery of my own? Or was I still gun-shy from my unfortunate experience with the least imaginative group of restaurant investors ever? A group that thought Cracker Barrel constituted fine dining.

"So, we're good, then?" Rollie asked.

"Yeah man, s'all good." I didn't know if the previous evening's vast alcohol consumption had mellowed my grumpy vibe, but I meant it.

"Cool," Rollie said. "There is one other thing."

Had Rollie seen us steal the Duveneck? Was he now going to want a slice of the action, or possibly start blackmailing us? Maybe he'd read my mind and discovered I was growing increasingly disillusioned by the food truck. In anticipation of the "one other thing," pinpricks of anxiety began crawling up my spine like a brigade of ants on their way to a picnic.

Rollie turned toward Trina. "Could you give us the room?"

She glared at Rollie, then glanced around the small living room. "Sure. But if you do anything to upset Anton, I will break you in half."

"Uh . . . of course. I mean . . . I won't . . ."

"Just kidding." Trina smiled mischievously. "But make it quick, I have things to do. Anton, I'll be in the bedroom if you need me."

Rollie and I stood, mouths agape, as she vacated the premises.

The Culinary Caper

"I should go." Rollie set his mug on the counter.

I grabbed his arm. "Don't leave. She's a kidder. I never know what's she's going to say next." This was true. And sometimes scary. "Just tell me what you need to tell me. I'm a big boy. I can take it."

Rollie glanced nervously down the hall. "Okay, but don't take this personally."

"Naturally." Anytime someone says that, I guarantee you it's going to be personal.

"The subs you've been sending for the truck suck. I mean big-time suck. Like destroy-our-business kind of suck." Rollie scanned the hallway before continuing. "So, the next time you get asked to do some cushy catering gig, either decline or let me hire the sub."

There was nothing cushy about catering jobs. Sure, they paid well, but they always challenged not just your culinary skills, but your interpersonal and logistical skills as well. This, however, probably wasn't the time to explain that to him. "Dude, I'm sorry. I had no idea. Why didn't you tell me?"

"Because you kept sending different guys." Rollie gritted his teeth, almost as if trying to keep the words he really wanted to say from jumping out. "And I always figured the next one would be better. But they weren't."

"Damn! So sorry about that." The truth was that those subs had been my last resort. I hired them because they were the only ones available. Maybe there was a reason for that. To hide my tell, I used both hands to pick up the mug "Those guys came highly recommended."

"By who?" Rollie demanded. "Doesn't matter. The point is, going forward, let me do the hiring."

"You got it, bro."

The food truck world existed in a relatively small universe, and Rollie had probably already gotten the lowdown on these undesirables.

"Also," Rollie continued, "speaking of terrible cooks, I hope you never have a shift like last night again. And to be honest, it wasn't just last night. This has been going on for weeks."

"Rollie, did you forget what I said?" Trina, standing in the hallway with arms crossed, shot him a glare that could have melted the remaining polar ice caps.

I'd hoped the recent decline in my kitchen skills had gone unnoticed. But, given Prudence's tiny square footage, clearly I'd been deluding myself.

"I b-b-better go," Rollie stuttered, then pulled me into an awkward embrace. "You know I love you man, but you got to get your head back in the game."

"I will. I promise. Things'll change."

Rollie patted my back, apparently satisfied by my promise. Which reminded me about the previous promise I'd made about hiring him if I ever needed help on one of my catering jobs.

"Hey, Rollie, I keep forgetting to ask—would you be available for a catering gig next Wednesday? A former pitcher for the Reds is doing some kind of charity auction. It's two days before the Bengals food truck gig, but I'd make it worth your while."

Rollie's eyes widened. "For real?"

"You bet. The party's way too big for me to handle by myself. Having you there would make things so much easier."

He continued staring at me.

"If you'd rather just take Prudence out, I'd certainly understand."

"Are you kidding? Of course I want to do it. What's on the menu?"

"Still working that out with the client," I said. "Nothing too complicated. Maybe you could help me with it."

"That would be fantastic."

"Cool."

"And Anton?"

"Yeah, Rollie?"

"Thanks, brother."

The doorbell rang, ending our bro heart-to-heart. Trina, registering that all was well, went to answer the door.

"Papa," Trina said, hugging her father. "This is an unexpected surprise."

"I brought rugelach." Peter Danielovitch handed Trina a small white box. "Your favorite."

Her father's arrival brought more than pastries. It brought feelings of doom. If Danielovitch had shown up earlier, when I was still half-naked in Trina's bed, who knew what he would have done?

Trina opened the box and peeked inside. "Yum! Anton, you've met my father?" she asked.

I nodded at Papa Danielovitch.

Apparently, that wasn't a proper Russian greeting, because her father clasped his arms around me like a long-lost relative. "Antonovich, my friend, good to see you again."

I didn't say the same to him, but he didn't seem to notice. I just hoped he wouldn't say anything in front of Rollie about the Rockwell and its pending abduction.

"Papa, this is Roland." Trina led her father into the living room. "Anton's business partner."

Roland? Nobody ever called him that. This, I would be teasing him about.

"Roland, this is my dad."

Peter extended a beefy hand to my partner. "Very good to meet you, Chef. I can't wait to try your pierogi."

"Nice to meet you, too," Rollie said. "Stop by the truck sometime and I'll whip you up a plate of our best." Rollie excelled at the niceties of commerce. Me, not so much. That was why he would always be the mission specialist.

Peter's face lit up at Rollie's offer.

"You guys gotta try these." Trina held out the box to Rollie. Inside were a dozen or so small, croissant-like pastries, dark filling oozing out from the folds.

Rollie popped a whole one into his mouth. "These are freaking amazing."

Trina shoved the box toward me. "Anton?"

I grabbed a rugelach, studying its composition before taking a bite. The pastry dough was remarkably light, and the filling was some type of chopped nut mixed with raspberry jam. Delicious! I wanted another, even before finishing the one in my mouth.

"Have you boys ever eaten one of these before?" Danielovitch probed.

Rollie shook his head.

"I've heard of them, but I've never had one." I eyed the open box. "Mind if I have another?"

Danielovitch grinned. "You better ask Katrina. She doesn't like to share."

"Papa!" Trina reached into the box and handed me a second one. "It's the cream cheese in the dough. That was Mama's secret."

Trina and her father exchanged a look that I imagined had something to do with her deceased mother.

"Well kids, gotta run," Rollie said, helping himself to another couple of rugelach. "Anton, talk later?"

In a nodding mood, I nodded. Noticing my mug was nearly empty, I strode into the kitchen and re-upped.

Apparently unhappy with my antisocial tendencies, Trina glared at me. "Would you like some coffee or tea, Papa?"

The Culinary Caper

"No, I am good." Danielovitch followed me into the kitchen. "But I am glad you're both here. We need to discuss the Rockwell situation."

"Hang on a sec, Papa," Trina said. "Anton, do you mind making us some breakfast?"

"Sure." I was more than happy to delay discussion of the Rockwell. "What would you like?"

"I don't know. Surprise me."

Despite her father's unsettling presence, I suddenly realized I was starving. After surveying Trina's dismal fridge and pantry offerings, I managed to scrounge the ingredients for huevos rancheros.

Trina climbed onto one of the kitchen stools and began swiveling back and forth. "Papa, you should join us."

"Nyet." Danielovitch shook his head. "I have eaten."

I tipped some olive oil into a sauté pan, turned a burner on to medium-low, and began mincing some garlic.

Trina, abruptly dismounting the stool, went to the fridge and studied its contents. "Should I make Bloody Marys?"

"Not for me, *Myshka*," Danielovitch said. "I have much work to do."

"I'll pass." The coffee was doing its job, and vodka wasn't a horse I was ready to remount. After draining and rinsing a can of black beans, I added them to the pan.

"Poor thing. I'll make you a virgin one." Trina grabbed V-8 juice, Worcestershire sauce, lemon juice, hot sauce, and celery, and lined them up on the counter.

"Next Friday," Danielovitch said.

Trina and I looked at her father, waiting for an explanation.

"That is when you will steal my Rockwell."

His Rockwell? Wow, talk about visualization. Maybe that was something I should practice. Picturing my dream restaurant. A postmodern bistro in a hip neighborhood with plenty of natural light and a spacious, open kitchen. Nah, scratch that. I didn't want a bunch of rubbernecking foodies watching me while I cooked. Open kitchens were more about theater than quality of product. But a well-equipped bar with a knowledgeable mixologist, absolutely essential.

Trina, unaware of my culinary reveries, set about making the mocktails.

"Don't you have people that could do a better job of stealing your . . . *the* Rockwell than me?" As the capo, he must have had a stable of petty thieves at his beck and call.

"'Stealing' is such a vulgar word. I prefer to think of it as simply retrieving what should have been mine." Danielovitch leaned against the kitchen island, watching me cook. "Of course I have such men. But I want you to do it."

Had he said next Friday? That was the day Rollie had just booked a food truck party.

Danielovitch's request was most likely the equivalent of a royal decree, but perhaps I could use the food truck event as a valid excuse to decline. "Unfortunately, Rollie and I are catering a party that evening. So, I guess *retrieving* the Rockwell will have to wait."

I added cumin, salt and pepper, and a dash of cayenne to the beans. After sniffing a somewhat suspect jar of salsa, I scooped a tablespoon into the pan.

Danielovitch folded his thick arms across his broad chest, grinning at me.

"I know."

How the hell could he know about the party? I only just found out. Were he and Rollie in cahoots? They'd just met. Or had they?

Trina handed me a Bloody Mary and then clinked my glass. "Vashe zdorov'ye."

The Culinary Caper

The Bloody Mary was bold and spicy. Just like her. "That is so tasty." I took another sip. "Wait, did you put vodka in this?"

Trina swirled a celery stalk around her glass and smiled. "Maybe . . . a little."

Her father hooked an arm around her shoulder, giving her an affectionate squeeze. "My little Myshka."

I shot a barrage of ocular daggers at them, but realizing I should never underestimate a Russian's predilection for their national beverage, I revisited the zesty cocktail.

After counting out four tortillas, I pulled another pan out of the cupboard and threw in a couple of tablespoons of butter. While I waited for it to melt, I pressed the black beans with a potato masher.

"Do you mind if I ask how you knew about the party?" If Rollie was somehow complicit, I needed to know. Whether Danielovitch would answer truthfully was another matter.

"I don't know what Trina has told you about me," Danielovitch said. "But Antonovich, I am just a simple businessman."

So was Al Capone.

"As such," Danielovitch continued, "I have many connections. One of whom keeps me informed about certain social activities. I'm not at liberty to give you his name, but I will tell you that he is a former athlete, and that we share an interest in art. He is the one who told me that your pierogi truck would be providing the food."

Danielovitch pulled a folded piece of paper out of his shirt pocket and handed it to me. "Here is everything you need to know about your little task."

Feeling rebellious, I slipped the note into the pocket of my jeans without reading it.

"If you have any questions, ask Trina. It's best for both of us if we no longer have direct contact. I will leave you kids to enjoy your breakfast." He gestured at the beans, eggs, and tortillas. "Whatever the hell that is."

"*Do svidaniya*, papa." Trina set her drink down, hugged her father, and accompanied him to the front door.

As he reached for the knob, Danielovitch paused, turning toward me. "Don't disappoint me, Anton. That would make me most unhappy."

I'd disappointed Julia, Rollie, and Arthur the drummer. Why not add one more person to the list? Although Trina's father, given his antisocial tendencies, might prove to be the most hazardous.

When Danielovitch pulled open the door, Ricky was standing on the front porch, his hand mid-knock.

"Oh, yeah," Trina said. "Forgot to tell you. Ricky also texted earlier."

"Freaking Grand Central Station," I muttered.

Danielovitch nodded curtly at Ricky, then continued down the porch steps.

"Who was that?" Ricky asked.

"My father," Trina said.

He raised an eyebrow, giving me a look that probably meant *so, this is a real-life Russian mob boss*.

Trina batted him on the shoulder. "I saw that."

Ricky shrugged.

"You coming in or not?" She gestured toward the living room.

"I need to have a word with Anton first."

"Fine," Trina said. "You boys go ahead and have your little secrets. But Anton . . ."

I braced myself for some sort of ultimatum. "Yes?"

"Huevos rancheros?"

"Oh yeah, I'm on it." Food ultimatums were something I could deal with. "Could you turn the burners down? I'll be in in a second."

After Trina headed back to the kitchen, I stepped out onto the porch, shutting the door behind me. Trina had recently applied a fresh coat of white paint to the railings and had also restained the beadboard ceiling. I loved sitting out here with her on a warm evening, sipping a glass of something, and chatting up the neighbors. It almost made me feel like a normal human being.

"What's up?" I pointed toward the pair of chocolate-brown wicker chairs at the end of the porch. Ricky declined.

"Vincent," Ricky whispered.

I glanced up the street, worried that at that very moment the errant gangster was hurdling up the sidewalk. "What do you mean?"

"He called last night. Apologized, and said he wants back in."

"What. The. Actual. Fuck?"

"I know," Ricky said. "I asked him if he was insane."

I continued my survey of the street. "I think we already know the answer to that."

Ricky followed my gaze. "He explained that he'd just broken up with his girlfriend, his landlord had raised his rent, and work had been really stressful lately. That, he said, was what set him off."

"Sounds like a country song. But I imagine that burglary, breaking legs, and general racketeering must wreak havoc on one's day-to-day." Having only done one of those, I could imagine the pressures of a triple-header. "What should we do?"

"We should stay the hell away from him," Ricky said. "We certainly don't need him."

"Maybe you should call . . . what's his name . . . James, the PI. See what he suggests. I mean, presumably he knows Vincent better than we do."

Ricky leaned back against the porch railing. "I did. James says there's nothing he can do unless Vincent goes postal again."

"Great." It was bad enough that there were still three more works of art to repatriate, without dealing with Vincent and his volatile personal issues.

"I know."

"Should we tell Trina?" I asked.

"Your call."

"There's something else." Ricky studied his shoes for a minute, rubbing his forehead.

I gave his left toe a little kick. "I'm not going to like this, am I?"

Ricky continued examining his footwear. "Mannie Ortega's Vermeer, the painting I told you that was going up for auction?"

"Please don't tell me," I begged.

"When he took it to get appraised, they discovered that it wasn't real."

I had a feeling this was only the tip of the iceberg. "And . . ."

"And now . . ." Ricky finally met my gaze. "A lot of his teammates are getting their pieces evaluated."

"Fuck."

"I know," Ricky said. "But that shouldn't affect us. Unless they had them authenticated before they bought them. Which I doubt they did, since they all purchased the pieces from the crazy cousin of one of the pitchers."

Maybe Ricky was right. Besides, why would the ballplayers think we were involved with the forgeries? We were just there to cater. "And what about the three remaining pieces?"

"They're still real. So, all's good."

After weighing all the possible Armageddon-like scenarios, I shook my head and then ushered Ricky inside.

"Want some breakfast?" I asked.

"Already ate. But I wouldn't mind one of those." Ricky pointed at my sadly depleted Bloody Mary.

"I got ya," Trina said.

When the butter was sufficiently melted, I gave the pan a shake, cracked four eggs, and eased them in. As the eggs cooked, I warmed the tortillas over a gas burner and then flipped them onto the plates.

"So why are you here, Ricky?" I scooped beans onto the tortillas, spatula-ed the eggs on top and then garnished them with salsa and cilantro.

"Because we need to discuss the final painting." he said. "Do you want to know who the final *artiste* is, and when we're going to steal it?"

"No, and no." I hauled the plates over to the kitchen island and set them next to the fresh round of Bloodys. In no hurry to hear what Ricky was about to tell me, I sampled my drink. Stronger than the last one.

"Sit." I jabbed a finger at the empty stools.

Ricky remained standing. "I can tell you're dying to know."

I sighed. "Okay, who?"

"Jasper Johns." Ricky clinked his glass to the two unraised Bloody Marys on the counter, then settled on a stool.

Johns was one of Ricky's favorite artists. As a whole, the man's work didn't speak to me in the way the impressionists and realists did. But if I admitted that, Ricky would probably say my taste in art was too provincial. Maybe it was. Maybe that was why I didn't fit in at art school.

"So, when?" I seemed to have descended into two-word responses, probably because my stomach was empty, and I was drinking before noon.

"Friday."

I stared at Ricky. "Wait. Next Friday?"

"The Friday as in eight days from now. The night you and Rollie are catering a party."

"How do you know about that?" Why was I always the last one to know stuff?

"Same way I did about all of our ventures. Through William. Why? What's so important about Friday?"

I took turns glaring at Trina and Ricky. "Because—"

"Anton, no," Trina barked. "You can't—"

I pointed my fork at her. "He has a right to know."

"Know what?" Ricky asked.

Danielovitch had insisted that I not tell Ricky about the Rockwell. But feeling rebellious, or perhaps just emboldened by the vodka, I pushed his demand aside. "Her father requested I steal a Rockwell on that same evening. And he doesn't want you to be part of it." The mere mention of the upcoming theft gave me the heebie-jeebies.

Ricky eyed me skeptically. "A Rockwell? Really?"

Most people would have been shocked to learn that their pal's girlfriend's father had issued such a request, but Ricky seemed more shocked by the artist in question. He raised a finger. "First off, it hurts my feelings that I'm being excluded." He added a digit. "Secondly, and more importantly, why does her father want a painting stolen?"

"It's complicated," Trina said.

"It's not even close to complicated," I protested. "Her father wants me to steal a painting because he's a stone-cold gangsta. What's complicated is stealing a Norman Rockwell and a Jasper Johns at the same time. By myself."

Trina glared at me. "Anton . . ."

Maybe it was the strong coffee followed by the Bloody Marys, but the more I talked about the pending heist, the more agitated I became.

The Culinary Caper

"Take it easy, Anton." Setting her fork down, Trina wrapped her arms around me. "I'm going to be at the party as a guest, with my father. I can help you."

"Wait." I pushed her away. "Your father's going to be there, too?"

"That doesn't matter." Trina squeezed my hand. "What matters is that I'll be there."

"Yeah, be cool, dude," Ricky said. "We'll figure this out."

Chapter Fifty-Four

Said the Fiddler to the Devil

The last thing I wanted to admit was that I actually enjoyed working on the Picasso sculpture. Did the fact that it was going to be difficult to switch mine with the real one scare the hell out of me? Yes. But digging my hands into the clay had triggered some sort of latent art school predisposition. A predisposition that had a rather calming effect.

The flip side of that rekindled Zen-ness was the Friday event where I would be flying solo, stealing a Norman Rockwell and a Jasper Johns, which was a mere two days after the Picasso/de Kooning repossession.

If that wasn't stressful enough, on the day in between those two super-fun heists—yay—was the duo gig with Trina at Ghost Baby. A gig that, as each day grew closer, caused my blood pressure to soar to new heights. If I managed to fend off a full-blown panic-attack, it would be some sort of miracle—something I definitely didn't believe in.

But, and this was a big but, this would be my last foray into the underworld. After which, my life, such as it was, would be a gleaming example of the straight and narrow—or so I hoped. There was also some degree of irony that Ghost Baby was a subterranean club built in a former beer-lagering tunnel. Maybe I was better suited to life in the shadows.

I added another clump of clay to the bull's shoulder—did bulls have shoulders?—and then smoothed it back to the neckline. Satisfied that it looked sufficiently Picasso-esque, I took a few steps back to appraise my work.

Overall, not bad for my second sculpture in twenty years. Was it genius? No. Would it pass muster amongst the non-art crowd? With a few more modifications, probably.

As with the Rodin maquette that I'd done several months back, exhuming my long-buried artistic skills had been, alternately, frustrating and rewarding. Now, with the bulk of the work behind me, I felt a sense of accomplishment that I hadn't experienced in some time. I did still have to create a mold and cast the bronze, however—two tasks I was not looking forward to.

Still, with a couple of fingers of bourbon, and Miles Davis riffing on Spotify, the time seemed to fly by. Maybe that was all that mattered.

After topping off my glass, and switching out Miles for Coltrane, I pulled off my clay-encrusted smock and collapsed onto the couch. Hopefully Ricky wouldn't show up and judge me for early-afternoon drinking.

A knock on the door pulled me from the soothing allure of the sofa's pillows. Before turning the lock, I peered through the peephole. William. I'd been looking forward to a nap, or at least some quality me-time, but I opened the door anyway.

I'd met William a handful of times, but his sheer height and level of fitness continued to impress me. Maybe it was because I was lacking in both of those areas. Following each interaction with this impressive specimen, I swore I'd start working out. Somehow, the motivation never seemed to reach the launch phase.

"Ricky told me you'd be here. Mind if I come in?"

I waved him in and then dialed Trane back a few decibels. William clocked the highball glass on the coffee table but didn't say anything.

"Would you like some?" I asked.

William glanced at his watch and shook his head. "We need to talk about Peter Danielovitch and the Rockwell."

His words stopped me in my tracks, and I hadn't even been moving. "How do you know Danielovitch?"

William settled into a chair next to the coffee table. "It's complicated."

I assumed his response meant he didn't want to talk about something or didn't have a decent answer. Or both.

"You're going to have to do better than that," I said.

"Ricky told me about the Rockwell." William shook his head. "No accounting for taste. But I've been acquainted with Danielovitch for some time."

Needing fortification for whatever he was about to tell me, I dropped onto the sofa and took a swig of bourbon. "I'm listening."

William sighed, then pointed at my glass. "Maybe I will have one."

In the kitchen, I topped off my own drink, tossed a couple of ice cubes in a mostly clean glass, and poured William a healthy serving. After handing William the glass, I returned to the kitchen and grabbed the bottle. Good to be prepared.

William took a long pull. "Around a year and a half ago, I was thinking about opening a restaurant. Thought it might be fun. I didn't have enough money, so I was looking for investors. But no one was interested. A few months went by, and I was ready to give up on the idea when, out of the blue, Danielovitch shows up at my office. Said he'd heard about me and what I was trying to do. Turns out he was looking for a similar project."

Anyone who thought that opening a restaurant would be "fun" needed to have their head examined. Especially if it meant partnering with the Russian mob. But that was a conversation for another day. "So, did you actually open this money laundering . . . I mean restaurant?"

"Not funny, but yes. We just had our one-year anniversary."

The Culinary Caper

"Congrats." More than half of all restaurants failed within the first year, so that was a worthy milestone. Then again, not to be overly pessimistic, but the next four years often knocked out another twenty to thirty percent. I knew this all too well. I'd worked in a number of restaurants that had folded quicker than Kenny Rogers with a pair of twos. Seeing first-hand the incredible stress the owners had gone through, as well as my own wretched foray into a partnership, had left me with persistent fears about opening my own place.

"What kind of place is it? A Russian tearoom?"

William glared at me. "Are you always this sarcastic?"

"Pretty much, yeah." If I'd become Captain Sarcasm, did that mean I was a bitter thirty-something, afraid to reveal his true emotions? Or was it just a defense mechanism to cope with the everyday bullshit of an imperfect world? The only way to discover the real answer to this perplexing question was probably years of therapy. Since I wasn't looking for answers, I'd pass.

"To answer your question, no, my restaurant is not a teahouse. It's an upscale, locally sourced, organic steak house, but we do serve tea."

Great, another overpriced meat palace. Just what Cincinnati needed. Typical former pro athlete. However, instead of scooping up another helping of sarcasm, I opted for polite conversation. "So, what do you call this eco-friendly establishment?"

"Tiller and Meadow."

"Wait, that's you?" I'd heard good things about the place but, for budgetary reasons, had never been. I also thought the name sounded more like a has-been night-club act than a high-end steak house. Why hadn't Ricky told me that William owned a restaurant? "Who's your chef?"

"Jeremy Pilot."

"Damn, dude!" No wonder the restaurant had gotten such great reviews. "How'd you swing that?"

Jeremy, one of Phillipe's former sous chefs, was a much-talked-about up-and-coming talent. He'd recently been voted, *Chef most likely to open their own restaurant and succeed.*

William smiled. "I've got connections."

Perhaps if I'd taken Chef Phillipe up on one of his many job offers, I might have eventually been offered the helm at one of Cincinnati's latest, hippest bistros. But no, always the rebel, I'd bailed on the fine-dining concept and gone rogue with a food truck. And now, even food trucks had become mainstream. Given my track record of poor decisions, what would I screw up next?

"Congratulations, you did your research on kitchen staff. But what did you know about Danielovitch?"

"Not a thing," William said. "He told me that he'd always wanted to partner in a restaurant. I assumed that meant he had deep pockets."

I swirled the ice cubes around my glass. "Oh, his pockets are plenty deep. And so are the pockets he has his hands in."

"Yeah, well, I didn't find that out until much later." William sipped his drink. "Anyway, he was willing to invest a pretty big chunk of cash. More than enough to make up for what I was short. So, how could I turn that down?"

"Said the fiddler to the devil." I regained my position on the couch.

William chuckled. "You're one to talk."

I was tempted to remind him that it was he—abetted by Ricky's persuasive skills—who'd started me on this life of crime. Instead, I chose to sit back and enjoy the warm embrace of the bourbon, letting Coltrane's music wash over me.

The Culinary Caper

"And, since I know you're going to ask, I do own the majority share of the restaurant." William set his glass on the coffee table. "Danielovitch said up front that he just wanted to be a silent partner."

"I bet he did." Silent, but deadly. Like a tofu fart.

"Anyway," William said, "I came here to tell you that I can help."

"Help? How?"

"Whatever you need to make the final heists successful." William downed some more bourbon. "Did you wonder why Danielovitch didn't want Ricky to be part of this?"

"Not really. Those were just my instructions. Figured they weren't up for negotiation."

Coltrane was tearing through "My Favorite Things." Making me wonder, if I had to make a list of my favorite things, what would I include? Four things that would definitely be absent from the list: Borrowing money from a loan shark. Stealing art. Working for a Russian gangster. Sending most of what I earned to Julia.

Coming up with favorites, however, left my mind a total blank.

"Do you want to know why?" William asked.

"I assumed it was because Danielovitch didn't want anyone else involved."

"Partly," William said. "But the real reason is that Danielovitch is a major homophobe."

My jaw dropped. "But you're in business with the guy."

"Before we jumped in bed together, commercially speaking, he didn't know about me, and I didn't know that about him."

Raising my jaw, I brought it to the rim of the glass and sipped some bourbon. "So, why would you want to help?"

"Not to help Danielovitch. Obviously. Mainly to keep you and Ricky safe until we recover the final pieces of art. Ricky's already working on a Rockwell forgery."

"What are you talking about? How would he know which Rockwell painting?"

"Same way as the others. I took a picture and sent it to him."

"Danielovitch doesn't want a reproduction." I swallowed some bourbon and then struggled to take a couple of deep breaths. Maybe I needed a yoga refresher course. "He wants this Anderson guy to know that the Rockwell is stolen."

"Yeah, well, talk to Ricky about that. Anyway, I'm going to be at the party. And don't forget, aside from the Rockwell, you also have a Jasper Johns to steal. So, you'll probably also need help with that."

If only I could forget about the upcoming double-header. Especially if I was going to have to switch out two paintings with forgeries. I drank more of the amber liquid, considering William's offer. Would it hurt to have additional help? Probably not. But would William be more of a hindrance?

He lifted his glass toward the bull sculpture at the far end of the studio, splashing a few drops of bourbon on the floor. "Is that the Picasso?"

"If you can't tell, then we're both in big trouble." I noticed that the bull's tail wasn't quite right. "I still have to make the mold and cast the bronze."

"I played baseball. I didn't go to art school," William said, testily. After downing the rest of his drink, he set the glass on the table and stood. "I gotta go. Let's circle back in a few days and go over the plan."

I was tired of circling. I needed to move onward. But in what direction, I didn't know.

Chapter Fifty-Five

Do Six-year-olds Experience *Hate?*

Finally, after nearly two years of intermittent woodshedding, the accordion was starting to feel almost as comfortable as the piano. Would I ever reach virtuoso status? No. But I'd been playing piano since I was five, and I never would on that instrument either. Music, for me, was more about creative output than fame and fortune, so I'd probably just stick to the kitchen as a source of income.

After extending the squeeze box to its fully open position, I launched into "For Once in My Life." I couldn't quite match Stevie Wonder's groove—who could—but, from somewhere deep inside of me, I managed to conjure up a tiny fraction of the heartfelt emotion that always infused Stevie's music. The songs that spoke to me, not just Stevie's, were the ones where you could feel and almost touch the soul of the artist.

I wasn't sure why I chose that particular tune—it certainly wasn't directed at anyone in particular. Or was it?

My phone, perhaps programmed to interrupt such enigmatic musings, rang. I finished the last few bars of the song and then reached for the meddlesome device. After seeing that the call was from Julia, I hit decline. Immediately, a text chimed. I read it.

Answer your damn phone. I know you're not working.

How did she know? I glanced out the window, wondering if Julia was in the apartment building across the street with a pair of binoculars. Although since the food truck rarely went out in the morning and early catering jobs were just as scarce, it didn't take Sherlock Holmes to deduce my whereabouts.

The phone rang again. This time I answered. "Hey, Julia."

"Hope I didn't wake you." She didn't sound like she meant it.

"Been up for hours." First lie of the day. With luck, it'd be the last, or at least for the duration of this phone call. "Rockin' out on accordion."

She laughed. "Seriously?"

"Would I lie about that?"

"Fair point."

This sounded more like the Julia from days of yore, reminding me that we hadn't had a real conversation in years. When she first moved to Paris, we talked every week, excited about our new careers. Gradually, that morphed into once a month, eventually fading to two or three calls a year. Lately, our communications had disintegrated into texts and voicemails.

Had something changed? I was almost afraid to say another word, lest I disturb the current repartee. But it was my turn. "What's up?"

"How'd you like to meet your son?"

Her question left me completely speechless. Whatever I'd been expecting, it certainly wasn't this. "Uh . . . what?"

"You heard me. I'm coming to Cincy next week for my sister's wedding. Thought maybe it was time for you and Francois to meet."

When the room began to spin, I unstrapped the accordion, set it on the couch, and leaned back with my eyes closed. Was this really happening? Could the very thing that I'd been hoping for for almost six years actually become a reality? Was I dreaming?

"Of course. That would be . . . I mean how . . . or when . . . I . . ." Now I was just babbling.

"Take a breath, Anton."

I did as instructed, rearranging my words into a coherent train of thought. "What day are you coming?"

The Culinary Caper

"I was going to arrive on Monday. But I have to change my flight because of a work thing. Still trying to figure that out."

There were a million questions swirling around my brain. Afraid I'd scare her off if I launched the whole barrage at once, I chose two. "How long are you staying? Where are you staying?"

She laughed again. "What is this, twenty questions? I'll let you know later. Just wanted to give you a heads-up."

I took several deep breaths, still trying to corral my thoughts. "I'll be available any day. Or every day."

"Aren't you working?"

Shit. Between the food truck, catering jobs and the gig at Ghost Baby, I was working almost every night. But my days were mostly free. If I had to, I could probably trade a couple of prep days with Rollie or maybe talk Trina into rescheduling Ghost Baby. That was a terrible idea, given how pumped she was about our first duo gig.

"I'll figure something out. Can I—"

"You do that. I gotta go. I'll text you when I know my travel plans."

She hung up before I could ask her the remaining 999,998 questions.

I tried slowing the frantic thoughts racing around my head. Should I take Francois to the zoo? Would he want to stay with me? Did he like sushi? Were six-year-olds allowed to eat sushi? Would he hate me? Did six-year-olds experience hate?

Chapter Fifty-Six

I'd Rather Be Making Pierogi

Ricky and Trina agreed to meet me for lunch at Findlay Market. I hadn't told them why they'd been summoned, but since they were both free, and loved the bustle of the market's food stalls, they were happy to oblige.

Trina had gone off to grab barbeque from Eli's. Ricky and I were waiting for our arepas. My phone chimed and then chimed again. Texts from Rollie, the usual prework checklist. I ignored them.

"Why didn't you tell me William owned a restaurant?" The pleasing aroma of spices wafting from the kitchen should have been inspiring, but since I'd skipped breakfast, the long wait was making me cranky.

Ricky shook his head. "Because you always get mad when you hear about someone else opening a new restaurant."

"Do not."

"Do too."

"Nuh-uh."

Ricky glared at me. "What are you, five?"

"Did you know that Danielovitch was backing him?"

"Not at first," Ricky said. "But, yeah."

I folded my arms across my chest. "And you didn't think that might be something I needed to know?"

Why was the kitchen so slow? Were they short staffed, or was stuffing cornmeal with savory fillings more complicated than it sounded?

"Does it really matter now?" Ricky asked.

"Well . . . no. But that's not the point."

The Culinary Caper

"What is the point?"

"The point is . . ." I glanced out the front window at the array of food carts bordering the market, trying to decipher my thoughts. "What if this whole art recovery scheme wasn't about William exacting revenge from his teammates? What if it was Danielovitch masterminding the whole operation for his own nefarious purposes?"

"Nefarious? That's insane," Ricky said. "We 'recover' the art and give it to the insurance company. The insurance company returns the painting to the true owner, and we get the reward money. What would Danielovitch get out of any of this?"

"Maybe the insurance company is just a ruse."

"You're delusional." Ricky tapped my stomach. "You should eat something."

My stomach groaned in assent.

"Did you tell Trina about Vincent?" Ricky asked.

"Not yet. Why?"

"Because he called again this morning."

"Fuck." Having other things to worry about—stealing four pieces of art, Julia's upcoming visit, the gig with Trina—I'd mostly managed to put Vincent out of my mind. "What did he want?"

"I told you. He wants back in," Ricky said. "But now he's getting more belligerent."

As long as Vincent stayed in New Jersey, I didn't care if he got belligerent. But what if, at this very moment, he was motoring westward? "Should I let Trina know?"

"Might be a good idea." Ricky tapped out a couple of texts and then stuffed his phone into a pocket. "You going to the studio today?"

"Possibly." I had several truck-related errands to run, plus kitchen prep, plus a rehearsal with Trina. "Why? Do you think the Picasso still needs work?"

I'd just gotten the sculpture back from Ricky's friend, who worked at the Verdin Bell Company. Casting bronze required superhot temperatures—temperatures that were usually only available in foundries. Since this was a much smaller project than Verdin's usual output, Ricky's friend was able to do it after hours.

Two dings signaled more texts from Rollie. I ignored them.

"No, the sculpture looks great. Almost there. Just wanted to let you know I won't be at the studio today, so the place will be all yours. The way you like it."

Ricky knew I worked best in solitude. Being alone also meant I got to choose the music. "What do you mean 'almost there'?"

"Color's not quite right."

"I know." I'd been fooling myself that he wouldn't notice. But Ricky, a true artist, noticed everything. Any free time I might have had would now be spent with a blow torch, trying to match the patina of the original Picasso.

"Do you remember that painting Trina stole while we were repossessing the Duveneck?" Ricky asked.

"Uh . . . sort of." I scratched my chin. "Local artist?"

"Yeah, Charlie Goering."

"What about it?" I knew I wasn't going to like the answer.

"Walter Owens finally noticed it's missing."

"Seriously? How long has it been?" Not the most observant person, I shouldn't be one to judge. "Are we worried?"

"Probably don't need to be. Just thought you should know."

Knowledge—according to some famous dude—was power. But for me, knowledge just meant worry. "What if Owens thinks it's tied in with the forgeries?"

"Who cares," Ricky said. "As long as he doesn't link the Goering to us, it doesn't matter."

I never understood how Ricky, or anyone for that matter, could be so optimistic. My phone chimed again. Looking for distraction from knowledge and worry, I read the text.

Did you get my texts?

If I didn't acknowledge soon, Rollie would continue pestering me. I replied with a thumbs-up emoji.

"Rollie?" Ricky asked.

"You guessed it."

Ricky shook his head. "So, what's up? What are we doing here?"

"I'll explain when we sit down." I pointed at an unoccupied table. "Our order should be almost ready. Why don't you grab that?"

A few minutes later, with arepas in hand, I joined Ricky and Trina. In my absence, Ricky had outfitted each of us with a beer.

After handing Ricky his arepa, I peered at Trina's sandwich. "What'd ya get?"

"Brisket," Trina replied. "I always have trouble deciding between that and the pulled pork."

"I love the brisket. Although their ribs are pretty damn good too."

"So, what's with all the intrigue?" Trina asked.

"Yeah?" Ricky seconded.

"No intrigue." I wiped off a chin full of cheese. "Can't I just have lunch with a couple of friends?"

They stopped eating and stared at me.

"Okay, fine." I took a bite of the tasty arepa—filled with chorizo, black beans, and fried plantains—and then returned their stares. "The Rockwell."

"What about it?" Trina asked.

"Ricky, do you want to tell her?"

He volleyed back a stare. "What's to tell?"

"Really?" If I'd known this was going to be like pulling teeth, I would have brought a drill and a syringe of Novocain. "Trina, Ricky's been working on a Rockwell reproduction."

Trina's turn to stare, this time at Ricky. "What the fuck, dude? Didn't Anton tell you that my father didn't want a forgery? He wants the guy to know his painting was stolen. Teach him a lesson."

"I started working on the painting after William sent me pictures of the Rockwell and the Jasper Johns, before Anton told me." Ricky dug back into his arepa. "Don't you see? It's better for everyone if I replace both paintings."

"And why is that?" Trina leaned back in her chair and folded her arms.

"Because they're both important works of art. If something happens to one of them, the other one is likely to get scrutinized. I've seen this happen before."

Trina turned to me. "What do you think, Chef?"

"Me?" I'd rather be making pierogi than stealing art, but that probably wasn't the question. "As much as I hate to admit it, especially since I'll have to switch out two paintings during one party, I think Ricky's right."

"Hmm. I guess." Trina took several bites of her sandwich, following them with a swig of beer. "But I'll have to convince Papa. Which won't be easy."

Sensing we'd accomplished my mission—ratting out Ricky and getting Trina to broker an agreement with her father—I went all in on the arepa. A task that required several more napkins.

"So, Ricky," I said, once I'd vanquished my food. "What are you going to do when this is all over?"

Ricky looked up from his now-empty plate. "You mean lunch?"

"No, you idiot. I mean after we've stolen our last painting."

The Culinary Caper

Ricky raised his beer but then set it down without taking a sip. "Not sure. Maybe move back to New York. My sister is getting tired of me staying at her place."

"What time's she going to be here?" Trina asked.

"As soon as I text her." Ricky glanced at me. "Forgot to tell you, Anton. Isabella is meeting up with Trina and me. We're going shopping. Wanna join us?"

When Trina dug back into her sandwich, I glowered at Ricky. Isabella and I had dated briefly, and the breakup—as Ricky was well aware—had been borderline apocalyptic. Spending time with Isabella and Trina at the same time was definitely not a wise move.

"I'll pass. I've got my own shopping to do." Aside from food-truck errands, I was planning on buying a present for Francois, but I had no idea what.

Trina nudged me. "You're no fun."

"I know." I used to be.

"You should totally meet Isabella," Trina said. "She is such a cutey. You'd like her."

Trina liked to bait me with comments about other women. But, after a precipitous learning curve, I'd deemed it best not to weigh in on such matters.

"How about you, Anton?" Ricky said. "What are your plans once you've retired from the burglary game?"

I was grateful to Ricky for the change of topic, although the new subject matter was no less thorny. I downed the remainder of my beer. "Well, hopefully I'll be set financially. At least until the food-truck season starts up again. So, I can relax a bit and try and figure out a long-term plan."

"What do you mean by long-term?" Trina asked.

"Yeah, dude," Ricky said. "Time to spill the beans."

"What if we don't quit?" I asked.

Ricky gave me an odd look. "Quit what?"

"Our little art swap business." I wasn't remotely serious about this.

Ricky shot me an icy stare, but Trina's usual sixty-watt twinkle swiftly dialed up to about one twenty, which was a tad worrisome.

He continued glaring at me. "Your long-term plan is to dedicate your life to crime? Seriously? You get stressed out just talking about art, never mind stealing it."

He was right. Every time we'd repossessed a piece of art, I experienced an incredible high knowing that a painting by one of the masters was rolled up in a PVC tube in the back of my catering van. Maybe that, too, was worrisome.

"Just messing with you," I finally admitted. "I have no clue what my long-term plans are."

Trina pecked me on the cheek. "So, Ricky, did Anton tell you about our gig at Ghost Baby?"

Chapter Fifty-Seven

Status Quo is My Favorite Subject

With my crime career nearing retirement, it was time to start thinking about the future. The future, however, was my least favorite subject. Mostly because it meant doing something more than maintaining the status quo. The status quo was my favorite subject.

Sprawled out on the couch, I glanced around at the disheveled state of my apartment, a clear reflection of my mental state.

Prior to signing a lease on this one-bedroom, third floor walk-up, I'd shared a place with Julia in Clifton. Six months after she flew off to Paris, I realized I could no longer afford the rent. My new apartment on Orchard Street, in the OTR neighborhood, was supposed to be temporary. But here I was five years later.

Orchard Street was a great location, walking distance to tons of bars and restaurants, not to mention less than a ten-minute drive to Prudence's off-duty parking spot. And, during those five years, the neighborhood had definitely improved. Also, every time I found myself around the corner on Fourteenth Street, I would peer in the windows of a building that had briefly housed a tiny North African-inspired restaurant. If I closed my eyes, I could almost picture how I'd remodel the layout and design the kitchen.

It was possible that a change in my living situation might lead to a transformation in the other aspects of my life, similarly mired in existential quagmire. Maybe even for the better. But where to move? Back to Clifton? Too many memories. Portland, Oregon? Great restaurant scene, but too expensive. Like with most major life decisions, I had no idea where to go or what to do.

My phone chimed. Rollie. On the off chance he might have some worldly advice, I read the text. He didn't.

Procrastinating from my food truck chores, I moseyed over to the piano. Well, not exactly a piano—an electronic keyboard. None of my friends had been willing to help haul a real piano up three flights of stairs.

I played through several scales and arpeggios, loosening up my fingers. The Ghost Baby gig was six days off, and I was starting to feel pretty good about the tunes. I had most of them memorized, but I still needed to lock down a couple more.

After waking up my iPad, I pulled up one of Trina's originals and worked my way through the first verse into the chorus. The chord progression was a bit unusual, so it took several repetitions before muscle memory began to take hold.

My phone chimed again, but I played through the tune a few more times before reading the text.

Did you buy groceries yet?

He would have to remind me that I was slacking off. Feeling marginally guilty, I tapped out a response. *En route. Whatcha need?*

Sending a revised list, Rollie responded.

As tempting as it was to reply with an eye-roll emoji, I instead opted to send a thumbs-up. He out-emoji-ed me with two right back at me.

Returning my attention to the iPad, I played through Trina's tune one more time and then scrolled to the next song on the set list, an original I'd written five or six years ago, a song Trina had uncovered on my music stand a few nights back and insisted on including in the show.

I hadn't told Trina, when she first sang through the piece, that I'd written it shortly after Julia left. The lyrics were the usual mix of love and heartbreak. Cliché, I know, but some of the best songs arise out of the depths of these intense emotions.

The Culinary Caper

Confident that the tune was solid, I went back to the beginning of the first set and played through each song one more time, making sure I remembered all the intros and outros.

Rollie texted again. *Don't be late. Lot to do. Long drive*

"For fuck's sake, Rollie, leave me the hell alone!" I shouted at the walls. They didn't respond.

After taking several deep breaths, I closed my eyes and tried to find my happy place. When that failed, I set my hands back on the keys and played through every upbeat song I knew. An hour later, I realized that in spite of Rollie's warning, I was going to be late. When my phone rang, I assumed it was him and was relieved to see that it was Ricky.

"Hey, what's up?" I asked. Maybe he was going to tell me he'd shelved his Rockwell forgery.

"So, you remember I told you that Vincent's been calling."

I didn't like where this was going. "Yeah?"

"Well, I think he might have followed me home." There was a slight quaver in his voice.

"Are you sure?" Ricky's house was miles away, but I couldn't stop myself from going to the front window and peering out.

"No, I'm not sure. I don't really know cars, but it was red and sporty and American."

I would never forget our last encounter with Vincent. And, unlike Ricky, I knew enough about cars to know that Vincent had been driving a cherry-red Dodge Charger. But lots of people drove cars like that. Right?

"You're probably just paranoid because he's been pestering you." I was trying to sound reassuring, but that didn't stop a crop of goose bumps from popping up on both of my arms.

"Yeah, but what if it was Vincent?" Ricky asked. "What's he doing here?"

"Well, you did say that he apologized and wants back in and—"

"And I also told him to fuck off," Ricky interrupted.

"Telling a gangster to 'fuck off' probably wasn't the wisest choice of words." Not that I was an expert on how to converse with "wise guys." Then again, I had been getting a bit of practice dealing with Trina's father.

"Obviously, I didn't literally say that. I don't have a death wish."

"Obviously." I left my post by the window, gathered up my wallet and keys, and headed downstairs to my car.

"What should we do?" Ricky asked.

"Let's go with the assumption that it wasn't him." I dropped into the driver's seat, opened the window and started the engine. "I mean, we don't have anything going on until next Wednesday, so why would he be here now?"

"Think about it," Ricky said. "If he knows what we're going to steal—although I'm not sure how he would—but he doesn't know where or when, the best way to find out is to follow one of us until we lead him to it."

"You think he wants to grab the painting before we hand it off to the courier?" I paused, processing Vincent's motives. "Well . . . if he bypasses us and the private investigator, he could keep all of the reward money for himself. Greedy bastard."

"High marks for the food truck chef."

"Fuck that," I said. "I need that money. Rollie and I probably only have another month or so before we shut down for the season. My cut for the Picasso and the two paintings is crucial to tide me over until spring."

The food truck season usually slowed to a crawl as temperatures dropped. At a certain point, it made more sense to close up shop than feed a handful of diehard customers. The hope was that you'd banked enough during peak season to carry you over until Reds Opening Day.

"Let's just make sure Vincent doesn't get anywhere near these works of art," Ricky said.

I put the car in gear and headed west toward Main. "And how exactly do we do that?"

"Don't know yet."

"Well, I've got errands to run—why don't you figure that out?"

"On it, boss man," Ricky said.

Chapter Fifty-Eight

Anxiety and I Were No Strangers

The last couple of nights had been a tempest of tossing and turning. Sure, anxiety and I were no strangers, but I hadn't been this stressed since final exams at culinary school.

Even after eight-plus years, the memory of the chef certification exam still evoked a mild sense of terror. The cooking portion of the test, thanks to the intense repetition of skills I'd been drilling for the prior two years, was something I probably could have done with my eyes closed. But the written stuff—fundamentals of nutrition, food costing, and financial management—still made my head spin.

Standing in the kitchen with a mug of coffee, I went through a mental list of the week's stress-worthy items.

1) Steal a Norman Rockwell – Trina's father
2) Steal a Jasper Johns – Greater good (GG)
3) Steal a Picasso – GG
4) Steal a de Kooning – GG
5) Duo gig with Trina
6) MEET MY SON

Note to self: The order of these items doesn't necessarily reflect the timeline or level of anxiety produced.

The intercom squawked.

"Just me," Trina crackled through the tinny speaker.

I buzzed her in, set my coffee down, and waited by the open door.

"Mornin'." Trina drew me into a hearty Russian hug, then handed me a small pastry bag. "I brought you rugelach. I saw how much you liked them."

"Wow, thanks!" I peeked inside at the lovely pastries, their beauty calling for a kiss of gratitude, which I produced. "Coffee?"

She held up her thermos. "Nah, I'll stick to water. Better for my throat."

This morning was the final rehearsal for the Ghost Baby gig. At the previous rehearsal, we'd worked out the remaining kinks. Trina had sounded fantastic. I'd even begun to relax into the music. Today, the plan was to run the show—assuming I'd be able to shelve my litany of anxieties and dial up a serviceable rendition of a pianist.

Trina dropped her purse on the couch, then set the thermos on the table next to the piano. "I talked to Papa about Ricky's Rockwell forgery."

After topping off my coffee, I dug into one of the rugelach. It was every bit as tasty as I remembered. "And?"

"It took a while to convince him. Greater good, yada, yada . . . but, in the end, he came around." Trina unscrewed the thermos cap, took a sip, and then sang a couple of arpeggios. "You might owe him a favor, though."

"Wait, now I owe Don Corleone a favor?" My pulse took off like an odds-favored thoroughbred at the Kentucky Derby. Another item to add to my aforementioned list?

"Probably something minor, like smuggling in opium-filled balloons from Afghanistan." Trina laughed.

Not remotely amused, I scowled at her.

Trina stopped chuckling. "But seriously, there is one thing Papa wants."

Here we go. Maybe not opium. My soul, perhaps. "And what might that be?"

"He wants to leave a note on the back of the Rockwell, maybe tucked into the frame, saying something like *Trevor Anderson is a loser.*"

"What, is he thirteen?" Were all sixty-something gangsters this petty, or was this some kind of a Russian macho thing?

"This is nonnegotiable."

"Fine, but he's writing the note." I had to draw the line somewhere.

I finished the rugelach and then washed my hands at the kitchen sink. After setting my cup on the window ledge, I powered up the keyboard. "What do you want to start with?"

"Let's do your two tunes first."

My phone rang before I could start the intro. Julia. "Uh . . . Trina, I kind of need to take this."

Julia had texted when she arrived late last night. She was spending today with family but had promised we could meet up later in the week.

Trina put her hands on her hips and glared at me. "Is that your other girlfriend?"

"No. I mean . . . I don't have another girlfriend." I could barely manage one relationship. "I'll explain after."

"Go ahead," Trina said, her frown softening into a smile. "I'll sing through a couple of tunes while you're getting your life sorted out."

"Thanks." I headed into the bedroom, closed the door, and hit accept. "Hey, Julia."

"Thought you weren't going to pick up."

"Sorry, rehearsing for a gig." I hadn't played a note yet, but she didn't need to know. Perched on the edge of the bed, I wiggled the fingers of my free hand, warming up those soon-to-be-played notes.

"You're still playing with Phillipe's band?" Julia asked. "I never thought that would last."

"Nor I." I could have argued that Remoulade was, in theory, a democratic entity. But, given the French chef's indomitable prestige, I'd only be fooling myself. As far as the longevity of the band, it was probably due to the infrequency of our gigs. Less chance for egos to clash. "But this rehearsal is for a duo gig with a singer."

"Oh? Your latest girlfriend?"

I could hear Trina singing through our opening number, an Adele tune. Even muted through the closed door, her voice came through clear and powerful.

"As a matter of fact, yes. She's very talented. Studied opera at the Cincinnati Conservatory of Music." Why did I feel like I had to defend Trina? She, of all people, didn't need protection from a not-quite-gallant knight.

"Well, goody for her."

Did I detect a note of snark? Time to change the subject. "So, when can I meet Francois?"

"You sure you want to do this? Once you open that door, there's no turning back."

Was she handing the kid over to me? Tag, you're it? "What's that supposed to mean?"

"When Francois meets you, he'll finally be able to put a face to this mythological father figure he's been pondering over. And once that happens, if you don't completely scare him off, he will have a billion questions for you. Questions that can't be answered in one brief get-together. He gets a bit obsessive about things. I wonder where he gets that from."

"You think I get obsessive?" I asked. "I don't think I do. Do I?"

Julia ignored my queries. "But if you're okay with all that, we can do this either tomorrow afternoon or Thursday morning. My sister has a ton of pre-wedding stuff arranged, so I don't have a lot of free time."

"I can't do tomorrow—got a lot of prep to do for the food truck. Thursday morning is good, though."

"Thursday, then," Julia said. "Where? Scratch that, you don't know what kids like. I'll pick a place and text you."

This was really happening. I was about to meet my son. Francois. Could I call him Frankie? I lay back on the bed, trying to imagine my first glimpse of this miniature human being. Would he look more like me or Julia, or would he be a collage of the two of us?

But what if this whole child support thing had just been a scam, and there was no Francois? Julia had just cooked up the scheme to bilk me out of my hard-earned cash, and to fund the Parisian love nest she shared with a French butcher named Maurice. And, after murdering me, Maurice was going to hack me into a dozen pieces with his favorite cleaver and dump me in the Ohio River. Was I obsessing again?

"We need to discuss a game plan," Julia said.

I shook off my paranoid ramblings. "Game plan?"

I checked the time on my phone. Was this going to involve charts, diagrams, and a rule book? Ugh, final exams all over again.

"This is going to be a lot for Francois to process. I don't want him freaking out."

Him freaking out? What about me? My first encounter with the kid was likely to induce one of my epic panic attacks. "We'll take it slow. I promise. Everything will be fine." Never having spent time with small humans, I didn't believe a word of this. "What have you told him about me?"

"Nothing."

"Nothing?" Julia always knew how to hurt me.

"Well, not nothing," she conceded. "He's not an idiot—he knows he has a father."

"Glad to hear that. And?"

"And, I might have mentioned that you were a chef."

Making progress. "And . . ."

"And nothing. You don't usually come up in conversation."

"But I do come up?" Getting answers from Julia was harder than making the perfect soufflé. At least my soufflés were light and airy, unlike this conversation.

"Six-year-olds are always bubbling over with questions. Mostly they're about dinosaurs and poop, but, occasionally, he asks about you. He's also very interested in food."

My musician friends often debated the significance of genetics vs. environment. Hearing about Francois's interest in food made me wonder if he'd inherited this culinary predilection from Julia and me. Better that than burglary and panic attacks.

"Ever since he started walking, Francois has been hanging out in kitchens," Julia said.

"That's awesome." I mentally scrolled through a list of recipes I would share with him.

"Awesome would be you not trying to cram six years of fatherhood into one hour."

I was thrilled to hear she was allowing me a full sixty minutes with my son. But she was spot-on about me wanting to stuff a mini-lifetime into a single hour. "I'll dial up my best Buddha-like repose."

"Does that mean you've become obese?"

"Buddha was only heavy later in his career, like Elvis," I said.

Julia was probably right about having a game plan. But where to start? Were there scripts for this sort of thing?

The bedroom door opened a crack. Trina stuck her head in. "Almost done in there?"

"Be right there," I whispered. "Julia, I got to go. Text me where and when, and I'll be there."

"Yeah, you better get back to work," Julia said. "You don't want to piss off an opera singer. And Anton, wear something nice. You only get one first impression."

Chapter Fifty-Nine

If You're Seeing Someone Else, Just Tell Me

"This oughta be interesting," Trina said, when I returned to the living room. She was stretched out on the couch, working on a half-finished crossword puzzle.

I retrieved my mug, also half-finished, from the windowsill and warmed its contents in the microwave. When it beeped, I grabbed the mug and joined Trina on the couch. Sipping the scalding coffee, I tried to find the words that would best explain the nature of the phone call, and my life. None came.

"Well?" Trina prompted. "If you're seeing someone else, just tell me."

"It's not that. But . . ." Maybe this was like yanking off a Band-Aid. Okay, fuck it. "I have a kid. Thursday, I'm meeting him for the first time."

This declaration was met with silence. Not the polite librarian-shushing silence, but the absolute deep-space kind.

When Trina dropped her pencil, the almost eerie stillness shattered into a thousand tiny shards. "Holy shit, Anton!"

"Right?" Except for the "Anton" part, those were the exact words I'd used when I'd found out.

More silence.

"I have a feeling that you didn't *just* find out. Am I right?"

Unsure how to answer, I stared at the floor.

"And when were you going to share this minor detail with me?"

"Trina, I—"

"So, this is the deep, dark secret you've been keeping from me? Why didn't you just tell me?"

"I haven't told anybody. Didn't know what to say."

Trina eyed me skeptically. "Nobody, really?"

I sighed. "Well, I did tell Rollie, but only because he answered my phone when Julia called."

"And Ricky, does he know?"

I shook my head.

"Should I assume you're paying some kind of child support and that's why you're so in debt?"

There was slightly more to it than that, but I nodded anyway. "Yes, and yes."

"Who's the mama?"

Telling Trina about the existence of Francois was one thing, but deep diving into my relationship with Julia was a whole new level of complicated. "Just an old girlfriend."

"Obviously." Trina tossed the crossword puzzle at me. "I didn't think she was some pay-by-the-hour skank."

Realizing that I needed to give Trina more than just a cursory explanation, I added, "Julia and I went to culinary school together. After we graduated, we came back here and got restaurant jobs. She worked for Phillipe Rameau as a pastry chef."

"This girl must be very talented if Phillipe hired her right out of school," Trina said.

"She was. I mean is," I agreed. "That's why she jumped at the chance to move to Paris and work in her grandparents' bistro."

"Apparently this amazing talent didn't prevent her from getting knocked up and running off to work in a Paris diner."

"It's a bistro, not a diner. And she didn't get pregnant on her own." I took a breath. "Also, Paris or not, she lived with her grandparents in their apartment above the restaurant. Didn't even have her own room; had to sleep on the couch." Just minutes ago, I was defending Trina from Julia.

"Boo-hoo for her." Trina wiped a pretend tear from the corner of her eye. "So, how old is this creature of yours?"

I assumed she wasn't referring to Julia. "Six."

"Boy or girl?"

"Boy. Francois."

"Ooh-la-la. Tres Francais." Trina's accent was impeccable. Then again, she did speak three languages. "So, this chick never let you meet your own son? What the hell did you do to her?"

"Nothing. It's just . . . complicated." I didn't feel like explaining the reasons Julia hadn't wanted me to meet him. Especially since those reasons had always been somewhat vague.

"Oh, it's not complicated," Trina said. "Bitch is bleeding you dry."

"It's not like that." I sprang from the couch and went to the window. Below, street traffic seemed to move in slow motion. A couple with a small black-and-white dog waited to cross Main Street. Pat, the mailman, his bag slung low across his shoulder, was working his way up the street, one shop at a time. After a minute, I turned back toward Trina.

"Shortly after Francois was born, he developed a serious heart issue." I stared at the floor, swallowing back tears. "The doctors weren't sure whether it was a condition he was born with, or due to some kind of infection. The point is, he was very sick, almost died, and getting him, and keeping him stable was, and is, very expensive. National health care didn't cover all the specialists, so her grandparents helped a bit, but their bistro was doing poorly. So, naturally, I stepped up."

Trina got up from the couch and pulled me into a hug. "I'm sorry. You're a good man, Anton. Don't listen to me—I can be a bitch, too."

I kissed her on the forehead. "It's a lot to process. I'm still processing."

"Don't get mad at me for asking, but are you sure it's your kid?"

"Yep. We did a paternity test."

"So, how's Francois doing now? And how are you dealing with all of this?"

"According to Julia, Francois is doing okay. There's still a lot of expensive doctor's visits, but overall, he's able to live a pretty normal life." The jury was still out on how I was dealing with things.

Trina stepped back and studied me for a minute. "Do you trust her?"

Did I trust anyone? "What do you mean?"

"I mean, are you sure the kid is still sick? What if he got better?"

I glared at Trina. "Obviously she would have told me."

"Are you sure? Think about it. Here you are, this cash cow sending her beaucoup bucks every month. It's not exactly cheap living in Paris."

Her questions were making me uneasy. "Can we change the subject?"

"Okay, what should we talk about?"

"How about instead of talking about kids and ex-girlfriends, we start rehearsing?"

Trina raised an eyebrow. "Kids? Plural?"

Chapter Sixty

We Are All Created to Be Miserable

"This is so great," Rollie said. "Working in a legit kitchen with my main man. Just like the old days."

As per my agreement with Harold the Cheesemonger, the Creamery's owner, Rollie and I had usurped a corner of the kitchen to prep for the evening's non-food-truck event. The job I'd booked and hired Rollie to assist. The cheese shop part of the Creamery opened in the morning, but the café part was only open for dinner. So, as long as I prepped early for my catering jobs, there were rarely conflicts with kitchen space.

Unlike me, Rollie had been here since the wee hours, making desserts for the evening's event. I had planned to outsource dessert to one of my favorite bakeries, but Rollie insisted on tackling the job himself. Turned out he had mad baking skills. The things you don't know about a person.

"Glad you were willing to help out." I opened the oven and stuck a thermometer into several of the racks of lamb. Satisfied that they were nearly done, I began cutting the stem-ends off a pile of Brussel sprouts.

Bringing Rollie in on the job had been an attempt to ease the tension building between us. Or should I say, an apology for my as-of-late poor performance on the truck. "How are the pigs-in-blankets coming?"

"One more batch." Rollie slid a completed tray down the counter and began rolling out dough for the next round of mini-sausages. "These are freaking genius, dude. I mean who thinks of stuffing merguez and andouille into puffed pastry? And you're making all these sausages in-house, that's insane!"

"Actually, I kind of borrowed the idea from Bob Facci." I often told myself that "borrowing" was really just a compliment. Besides, can you really own a recipe?

"Behind you," shouted one of the Creamery staff, lugging a massive wheel of white cheddar.

"Facci, as in the guy who owns Roberto's?" Rollie asked after the curd carrier had safely passed.

"Yep." I set my knife down and sampled a spoonful of the cassoulet simmering on the stove. I added a pinch more salt, dialed back the burner, and then checked it off the to-do list. We were ahead of schedule, but that didn't mean we could slow our pace.

"You're like a totally different person today," Rollie said. "I mean, last night you could barely stuff a taco, and today you're doing like six things at once, and crushing it."

"Isn't that the job?" I asked.

Rollie was right, though. The tasks I could normally do in my sleep went to shit the second I stepped on the truck. Not wishing to dwell on the significance of this culinary conundrum, I finished trimming the Brussel sprouts, drizzled on olive oil, balsamic vinegar, and lemon juice, and then tossed them with salt and pepper.

"It's supposed to be the job." Rollie stopped wrapping dough around the sausages and studied me for a minute. "But maybe you've given up on the truck."

I hadn't yet admitted it to myself, but Rollie was right again; I'd mentally hung up my food truck apron. If I was "crushing it" as a caterer, did that mean I'd chosen that as my future career path? Thus far, I'd failed as a fortune teller, so maybe it was best just to get through this week before choosing any paths, career-wise.

Harold sidled up between Rollie and me. "Hey guys, almost done?"

"Just about," I said. "We'll be out of your hair shortly."

The Culinary Caper

"No worries," Harold said. "Though, if you don't get those racks of lamb out of here soon, I'm going to grab a knife and fork and dive into one of them. They smell incredible."

"I'll bring you the leftovers," I said. "If there are any."

"Works for me." Harold patted my shoulder, then headed back to the aging room where his finest cheeses, like future debutantes, lay in waiting.

"Rollie, what you said about giving up on the truck? That's not true." I wiped my hands on a dish towel and then took a swig of water. "It's just lately, I've been a bit distracted. Life's gotten somewhat—"

"Complicated?"

I set the water bottle on the counter and exhaled sharply. "Julia is in town. Tomorrow I'm meeting my son for the first time."

"Holy shit, Anton!"

"That's exactly what Trina said."

"Dude, that is so great!"

Not the word I would have used. "To be honest, I'm terrified."

Rollie pulled me into an embrace. "Don't be ridiculous, bro. You got this. It'll be amazing."

"I hope so." I patted his back.

"You should buy the kid a bunch of presents," Rollie said, releasing me. "Maybe a big teddy bear, or a puppy."

"Yeah, I probably should." I would definitely be googling *What do six-year-olds like?*

"When do I get to meet the little whippersnapper?"

I had to hand it to Rollie; he was not one to shy away from new and possibly awkward situations. It was, perhaps, this trait that enticed me to join him on the food truck venture. When he wasn't around, I made a point of steering clear of "new" and "awkward."

"We'll see how tomorrow goes," I said. "I might screw it up and get banished from seeing him again."

"Well, if you need a wingman, I'm your guy."

"Thanks, dude."

Rollie finished the last tray of pigs-in-blankets and then perused the to-do list. "Just need to ice the cupcakes."

"Cool. I'm going to start loading the van." I grabbed the crate containing the silverware and serving utensils.

"Need some help?" Rollie asked.

"Nah, do what you need to do." I needed him occupied while I transferred the Picasso sculpture from my car to the catering van.

"Anton?"

"Yeah?"

"I really appreciate you bringing me in on this job. Means a lot to me."

"Of course, Rollie." Before he could instigate another bro-hug, I began stacking handfuls of table linens on top of the silverware crate. Then I carried the crate out to the van.

After checking that Rollie was still in the kitchen, I popped the trunk of my car and peered at the case containing the Picasso "El Toro" replica. I was about to lift it out of the trunk, but wanting to examine it one last time, I opened the case.

The sculpture looked pretty damn authentic, right down to the slight dent on the left rear haunch and the patina of the bronze. Maybe my artistic skills were surfacing from the depths like an oxygen-starved whale. Or possibly, it was just because I'd copied this sculpture back in art school. Either way, I felt way better about this piece than I had the Rodin maquette.

After closing the case, I removed the linens and false bottom of the silverware crate and set the Picasso inside. Satisfied that Rollie would never discover the sculpture, I placed the linens on top and slid the crate into the back of the van.

Pulling out my phone, I checked the time and then texted Ricky: *About to head out. Everything good?*

All's well, he wrote back. *Picking up Trina now.*

It didn't feel like all was well, but I replied with a thumbs-up.

"Anton."

The voice startled me. I turned around. Ilya was leaning against one of the Creamery's delivery trucks. I wondered how long he'd been there, and what he'd seen.

Ilya wasn't a large man, but what he lacked in size, he made up for in the quiet intensity simmering just below the surface. Kind of like a cobra waiting to strike.

"Hey, Ilya," I said striving for cool and collected, and failing miserably. His presence here was definitely not a social call.

"Which one?" he growled.

I looked around, confused. "Excuse me?"

"Which one?"

"Which one, what?"

"Which limb would you like me to break?"

Every atom in my body shot into hyperdrive, and yet, at the same time, my muscles seemed to be encased in ice.

"You missed your last two payments. And the two payments before that were light." Ilya reached into his shirt pocket, pulled out a pack of cigarettes, and lit one up.

"I . . . I can explain," I stuttered. "We have a big catering job tonight. I can pay you everything I owe tomorrow."

He took several puffs, then moved a couple of steps toward me. "That doesn't really work for me." After taking a deep drag of his cigarette, he blew out a perfect smoke ring. "Are you a reader?"

"Am I what?"

"Do you read? Not comic books or Facebook posts, but serious literature?"

What was this, a college entrance exam? "Sure, I guess."

"Have you read *Anna Karenina*? That's Tolstoy, if you didn't know."

"Actually, I have." I'd read the book a million years ago but couldn't remember a single thing about it, other than that I'd made it all the way through and still hadn't grasped Tolstoy's philosophical takeaway. Talking about books, however, was much preferable to having my bones broken.

"Well, good for you," Ilya said. "Anyway, there is a line in the book that might apply to your situation. I can't remember who said it—maybe the guy on the train with Anna—but it goes something like this: 'We are all created to be miserable, and that we all know it, and all invent means of deceiving each other. And when one sees the truth, what is one to do?'"

I wanted to scream, *What the hell was that supposed to mean?* But he seemed so impressed with his literary prowess that I was afraid he might break an extra limb just for my ignorance. Instead, I took a minute to ponder my "miserableness," my "deceit" and my "search for the truth." Which only added to the tentacles of dread that were tightening around me.

I considered making a run for it, but since he knew where I lived, it would only delay the inevitable. "Tell me how much you want, and I'll find a way to get it for you."

He inched closer. "You're making me look bad. I don't like that."

Just then, two of the Creamery's staff came out the back door, one of them pushing a dolly, the other carrying several boxes of cheese, heading toward the delivery truck.

The Culinary Caper

Before disappearing into the shadows, Ilya shaped his hand into a pistol and pointed it at me. "Be seeing you soon."

Grateful that all my limbs were still intact, I collapsed onto the rear bumper of the catering van, taking in huge lungfuls of air, attempting to slow my pile-driving heart.

"You okay?" asked one of the apprentice cheese mongers.

Unable to speak, I nodded. Then, closing my eyes, I tried to picture myself on a sandy beach, sun caressing my skin, and the rhythmic crash of waves matching that of my breaths. A few minutes later, I no longer felt like Mount Etna seconds before erupting.

"How's it coming?" I asked when I returned to the kitchen.

Rollie was piping out sea-foam swirls of icing on a sheet pan of cupcakes. "Perfect. This is the last batch."

I turned off the burner under the cassoulet, then studied the to-do list. Everything had been checked off. "I'm going to load up the hot carts. When you're done, give me a hand carrying stuff out."

"You all right?" Rollie asked. "You look kind of pale."

"I'm fine. Just tired."

"I hear you, brother." Rollie waved a spatula at me. "Have you thought about what you're going to do when we close for the season?"

Move to Montana and change my name. "Still thinking about it."

"Are you going to keep doing the catering thing?"

On good years, we could bank enough from the food truck to make it through the winter. That meant busting our asses the rest of the year, which we were happy to do. With my catering business ramping up, I could probably get by without working the odd shift at one of my friend's restaurants. Unless, of course, Julia started asking for more money.

"I don't have much booked yet," I said. "How about you? What do you have planned?"

"I may go down to Florida for a bit. A buddy of mine is opening a restaurant in St. Pete and needs some help."

My turn to get jealous. "Are you going to come back?"

"Relax, brah. It's just a couple of months. I would never leave you hanging."

If I'd said that, I wouldn't believe it for a minute. Coming from Rollie, however, those words were as good as a sworn oath. I guess that made him a better human being than me. Or at least not a criminal.

"We better get going," I said. Better to be working than questioning the strength of my rapidly declining character.

Chapter Sixty-One

The Painting's Hanging Upside-down

"That is one huge-ass tent," Rollie said as we pulled to a stop in front of an imposing, ultramodern house.

A mammoth tent was set up in the grass, off to the left of the asymmetrical structure that seemed to tilt forward, as if ready to collapse onto uninvited guests.

A Lamborghini, two Ferraris, and several other high-end cars were parked in front of the precarious dwelling. To one side, a team of valets were setting up shop on the edge of the textured cement driveway.

"The auction will be in the tent, after dinner," I said. "They'll be eating out there, but the food will be inside, in the dining room. And we have full access to the kitchen."

Rollie gave me a thumbs-up. "Awesome!"

Having the majority of the party outdoors would make switching out the Picasso and the de Kooning with the imposters a tad easier, especially if we could do it during the auction, when no one would be inside loading up plates.

I steered the van around the right side of the house, then backed up next to the kitchen door, a spot that would make it more convenient to offload the Picasso. Ricky would be bringing the de Kooning forgery in the usual PVC packing tube. And he would, if all went well, be taking the real Picasso and de Kooning home with him. If all went well.

"I am so psyched about this," Rollie said.

He was psyched. But, because of the pending dual heist, I was borderline psychotic. After climbing out of the van, I opened the side door and surveyed the contents. "Let's scope out the layout before we start bringing stuff in."

"Right behind you, boss," Rollie said.

Inside, we were waylaid by a slender man in a purple shirt and a light gray linen jacket. "You the caterers?"

This was no doubt the event planner—they were known to materialize out of thin air. I just hoped he wasn't the high-strung, autocratic type.

"That's us," I replied.

The man held out his hand. "I'm Roger. With Exquisite Events."

I shook the offered hand. "I'm Anton, and this is Rollie."

"Nice to meet you, Anton. Tables are set up for you in the dining room. Please let me know if you need anything else." Roger pointed out the window at the tent. "I may be outside, but I'll be floating around."

After Roger drifted off, Rollie and I passed through several rooms before ending up in a ballroom-sized space—probably the dining room. Several tables were lined up in the middle. On one end, next to a huge stone fireplace, was a single table, set slightly away from the wall. The carving station.

"All righty, then," I said. "Let's go find Ricky and Trina."

Rollie followed me down a short hallway into a kitchen splashed with technicolor accents, mid-century-modern cabinets, and a swooping, continent-sized Formica island. The appliances, almost unrecognizable at first, would have made Mrs. Jetson swoon.

Trina and Ricky were at the far end, tying on aprons and admiring the cartoon-inspired design.

"Wondered where you were," Ricky said. "What do you want us to do first?"

"Where's Astro?" I asked.

Trina adjusted the collar of my chef's jacket. "Astro was my favorite Jetson. Who was yours?"

I'd never really considered the question before. "I always had a thing for Jane, his wife."

Trina batted me on the chest. "You bad boy."

"Rollie, Trina, get the van unloaded," I said. "Ricky, come out to the tent with me."

"Yes, Chef," the three of them said in unison.

Once we were out of the kitchen, I motioned toward the far end of the house. "Let's take a little detour."

"I know where they are," Ricky said, heading purposely down the hallway.

We were just about to enter a well-lit, teak-furnished room when someone shouted my name.

"Oh hey, Devon," I said, turning to face Devon Snoot, former Reds pitcher and the evening's host.

"Can't wait to eat your food." Devon covered the length of the hallway in just a few strides.

Like most pitchers, he was a big man. I'd forgotten how big.

"Going to check out my art?" Devon asked. "I love to show it off."

Having grown accustomed to pro athletes flaunting their priceless works of art, I quickly shook off any fears I might have had. "That'd be great."

Devon put a powerful arm around each of our shoulders and steered us into the room.

"Isn't that just incredible?" Devon said, pointing at the painting hanging behind a post-modern Danish desk. "I mean, the way de Kooning captures color in such playful ways, and yet at the same time, you feel his angst bursting off the canvas. I find it almost overwhelming. Don't you?"

"Yeah." In my case, the overwhelm had more to do with the twofer thievery we were about to engage in. Although knowing that there was only one more criminal outing after tonight did slightly ease that anxiety.

"The painting's hanging upside down," Ricky whispered in my ear.

I jabbed him in the ribs.

"What?" Devon asked.

"Ricky was just commenting on how this piece is an excellent representation of the intangible contradictions you often find in de Kooning's works."

Devon looked momentarily baffled by my poor imitation of an art critic.

"Then, there's the Picasso." Devon jabbed a cigar-sized index finger in the direction of the "El Toro" sculpture, sitting atop a slender teak pedestal. "Who would have thought I'd ever own one of those. I mean, dang."

Certainly not me, and by Ricky's smirk, clearly not him either. However, being in the presence of the great artist's work, unencumbered by thick glass or a gaggle of security guards, I was drawn toward the sculpture.

"Stunning, isn't it?" Devon asked.

I bent over "El Toro," taking in Picasso's workmanship. The piece was relatively simple, not in his later cubist style. Still, there was so much going on in every swipe of his chisel. No wonder this dude had become famous.

"Don't get too close," Devon warned. "If you bump it, the alarm might go off. I just hope they're real. A buddy of mine recently found out that his Vermeer was a forgery." His phone buzzed. "Got to take this. Enjoy the art, but please don't steal anything."

Devon strode out of the room, not registering the panic on our faces.

"Fuck." I glared at Ricky. "Did you know about the alarm?"

"William didn't mention it."

"Do you think the de Kooning is wired too?" I asked.

"No idea. But you'd think if the idiot had bothered to memorize that trite bullshit about 'angst' and 'capturing color,' he'd at least hang the picture right side up."

"If that's how he likes it," I said. "I mean, eye of the beholder and all that."

Ricky studied the pedestal under the sculpture. "I'll figure something out."

"Should we be worried that Devon knows about the Vermeer?" I was a card-carrying worrier.

"Doesn't matter."

I was inclined to disagree, but instead glanced at the de Kooning, the Picasso, and then back at Ricky. "If you say so. By the way," I said, "I'll be flying solo tonight."

"On both pieces? Are you crazy? Why?"

"Because I need you and Trina in the tent making sure no one comes inside." I peered around the edge of the de Kooning's frame, looking for suspicious wires.

"Remember what happened the last time we switched jobs?"

I wiggled the finger I'd punctured during that unfortunate debacle. "Yes. Thank you very much for reminding me. But, if you can figure a way around the alarm system, I got this."

"I'll call William."

"You do that." I took a deep breath and rolled my neck. "I've got to check out the tent."

Chapter Sixty-Two

Event Planners Aren't Typically Sticklers for Syntax

The open sides of the football field-sized tent revealed a wooden floor with a circular bar in the middle, surrounded by dozens of tables and chairs, as well as several cozy sitting areas with comfy couches. Above, chandeliers twinkled like disco balls.

At the far end of the tent, a sax player, pianist, and bassist were getting situated. As I stepped closer, I realized the bassist was Fredo, the about-to-be former member of my band.

Since Fredo was in the process of tuning his instrument, and I needed to take a tally of chairs and tables before scurrying back to the kitchen, I let work take precedence over socializing. There'd be time to say hello later.

On my way back to the kitchen, I stopped in the dining room, where Rollie was setting up the carving station and Trina was lighting cans of sterno under the flotilla of chafing pans lined up on the long table.

"Where you been?" Rollie asked. "We were wondering how you want the food laid out."

"I ran into Devon and then had to check out the tent." I handed Trina the scrap of paper on which I'd jotted down the number of place settings. "Can you see to this? Everything should be in the crates. There's a hand cart in the back of the van."

"You are so organized." Trina kissed me on the cheek. "How're you feeling about tomorrow? Ready to meet your son?"

I shook my head. "I can't stop thinking about it. But right now, there's too much to do, and I need to focus on tonight."

She winked at me. "There is, isn't there?"

I glanced surreptitiously at Rollie, then nodded. "Before you start with the place settings, can you check in with Ricky first, see if he needs help with anything?"

Another wink. "Better get to it, then."

"Hey Rollie, all good?"

"Everything's terrific." Rollie gave me a hearty two thumbs up. "Let me know if anything else needs doing."

I couldn't recall ever having used the word "terrific." Did the use, or lack thereof, define each of our outlooks on life? "Once you get your station set up, come back to the kitchen. I could use some help prepping. And Rollie . . . glad you're here."

"Thanks, bro. Should just be a few minutes."

In the kitchen, I pulled steam pans out of the hot boxes and checked the temperatures of their contents. After unwrapping the trays of cold apps, I started spreading the various offerings out on the serving platters. I was adding the final garnishes on the mini-bruschetta's when Ricky came into the kitchen.

"Just talked to William," he said. "There's no alarm on the de Kooning, and we've figured out a way to swap out the Picassos."

"Wonderful," I said, feigning enthusiasm. "Now let's get to work."

"Yes, Chef." Instead of dashing out of the kitchen like the meticulous, hardworking server he usually was, Ricky folded his arms in front of his chest and gave me the stink eye.

I mirrored his posture. "What?"

"Trina told me."

"Come on, Ricky. I don't have time for mind reading?"

"Julia? Francois?"

I sighed. Now the whole world knew. "Look, the reason I didn't tell you was . . ." I stared at the ceiling, trying to think of a good reason.

"I always assumed your cash-flow issues were from gambling debts. Rollie mentioned you liked to bet on the ponies. But never in a million years would I have pictured you as a father."

That made two of us. "Ricky—"

"Doesn't matter," Ricky said, his stink eye mellowing. "I hear tomorrow is a big day for you."

I nodded. "I wish everyone would stop reminding me of that."

"Well, I'll leave you to it, then." Ricky departed the kitchen with a chuckle and a head shake.

Roger, the purple-shirted event planner, manifested himself in Ricky's place. "How soon are you going to be ready?"

"Ten minutes?"

He narrowed his eyes at me. "Is that a question or a statement?"

Event planners weren't typically such sticklers for syntax. "Both?"

Roger eyed his watch and then glanced around the kitchen as if doubting my grammatical aptitude. "Guests should be here any minute."

"We'll be ready."

After Roger vanished from the kitchen in a self-important wisp of smoke, Rollie, manning the carving station, and I, holding down the kitchen like a four-star general, launched into full-steam-ahead mode. And then, for the next ninety minutes, we tended to the gastronomic whims of the rich and semi-famous.

Dabbing a bead of sweat from his forehead, Rollie ambled into the kitchen with a bottle of water. "They're about to start the auction."

"Finally." I wiped off the counter and checked the time. "The auction's supposed to last about thirty minutes. While they're throwing outrageous sums of cash at baskets of wine and gourmet gift certificates, we need to start striking the buffet and carving station and reset for dessert. It'll probably take a while to corral everyone out to the tent,

The Culinary Caper

so we don't have to kill ourselves. Also, let's load any equipment we're done using back into the van."

"Sounds good."

"And Rollie." I squeezed his shoulder. "There's no way I could have done this without you."

"Thanks, bro," Rollie said. "Any time."

"I'm going to find Ricky and Trina and have them start clearing the tent tables." I paused at the kitchen door. "I promised the band we'd save them some food. Do you mind making up three plates for them?"

"Gotcha."

Trina was coming in from the tent when I found her. "Ready?"

"You bet. The 'cream' and 'sugar' are under the couch in the study. But I hear there's some kind of alarm on the 'sugar.'"

"Yeah, really sucks," I muttered. Why was there always a fly in the soup? Just once, couldn't things be as easy as pie? Okay, enough food-based analogies. "Anyway, as soon as everyone's in the tent, and Rollie is otherwise engaged, I'll get to it. So, the quicker you can herd them out, the quicker this will be over."

Then, I thought, on Friday, there'd be one final criminal escapade. After that, this cook planned on living a life of virtue and integrity. Or at least one of those two.

"You're really doing this by yourself?" Trina asked.

"I couldn't think of another way," I said. "It'll be fine." If only I believed that.

Trina threw her arms around me. "I'm sure it will be."

I would have been happy to linger in the warmth of her embrace, but the molten lava of adrenaline surging through my body would not cease until the two pieces of stolen art were safely stowed in the trunk of Ricky's car and dessert was being served. "Not to be a whip-cracker, but can you also help Ricky clear off the serving tables?"

"On it." Trina kissed me on the cheek and then moseyed off.

It took almost twenty minutes to coax the rest of the guests outside. We had broken down the carving station and removed all the food from the serving tables, but Roger had insisted we wait until everyone was in the tent before putting out dessert. He didn't want guests stuffing their faces with sweets when they were supposed to be outside bidding on the auction items. And neither did I.

I'd just loaded one of the hot boxes into the back of the catering van when my phone rang. I didn't recognize the number, but not ready to deal with what lay ahead, I answered.

"Hey, Anton, it's William. Ricky told me about your problem."

Being the proud owner of a plethora of problems, I was going to need a bit more to go on. "Which one?"

William laughed. "The Picasso one."

"Do you have good news for me?" Good news meant putting the kibosh on the evening's illegal activities.

"So, here's the deal," William said. "The alarm on the pedestal is triggered by weight."

"Okay, and . . ."

"The Picasso supposedly weighs four pounds, three ounces."

"And?"

"And, when you made your replica, you matched the specifications of the original, right? Including the weight?"

"Uh . . . yeah." Google, Ricky, and I had all done our homework.

"Great. Then you should be fine."

"Fine? Care to elaborate?"

"There's a three-second timer on the alarm. As long as you make the switch quickly enough, it shouldn't go off." William paused. "Unless . . ."

I hated unfinished sentences almost as much as I did unfinished cocktails. "Unless what?"

"Unless you got the weight wrong."

"Thanks for the pep talk, coach. I feel so much better now."

"I trust you," William said. "Gotta run. Good luck."

He hung up before I could explain to him that "good luck" and I had not been getting along for quite some time.

Rollie, Trina, Ricky, and I were loitering on the far end of the dining room, close to the kitchen, when Roger finally dragged the last couple of stragglers out to the tent.

"All right," I said. "Ricky, you and Trina head outside. Make sure the guests have what they need so they don't have to come back in here. I'll text you if I need you."

Ricky saluted. "Aye, aye, captain."

"Rollie, did you make the plates up for the band?"

"They're on the kitchen island, ready to go."

"Cool. Thanks," I said. "Why don't you head back to the kitchen and take a break? I'm going to go find the trio and send them this way. I also need to call Julia about tomorrow morning. So you might not see me for a bit. Text if something comes up."

"No worries, dude."

Chapter Sixty-Three

Hope You Find Your Mouse

I peered into several rooms, pausing at the doorway to the empty dining room, listening for voices. The house appeared to be deserted. To be certain, I strode down the hall to the side door that led out to the tent. The guests, mostly seated, a few at the bar, were focused on the auctioneer standing at the far end, near where the trio had been playing.

Aware that this was my narrow window of opportunity, I made my way to the Scandinavian-themed study. After taking another gander at the de Kooning and the Picasso, I knelt down and peeked under the couch to confirm that Ricky had stashed the surrogates.

"Lose something?"

Scrambling to my feet, I found Fredo and the other two members of his trio standing at the doorway. They were holding plates piled precariously with medium-rare lamb popsicles and generous helpings of the other buffet offerings.

"Hey, Fredo," I said, striving to keep the terror out of my voice. "I heard a noise. Thought it might be a mouse."

"Do rich people have rodent problems, too?" Fredo asked.

"I didn't see anything. But I imagine they do."

"Your food is the freakin' bomb." Fredo beamed at me, then thrust an elbow toward the pair of couches huddled around a coffee table. "Do you think we can eat in here?"

"Nah. Sorry. Devon was adamant about only having food in the tent or the dining room." My lying skills had been improving, but when I caught myself rubbing my left thumb and index finger together, I

The Culinary Caper

realized I'd forgotten to hide my tell. Hopefully the starving musicians wouldn't notice.

With the strict timetable, I needed these guys out of here ASAP. "The dining room would be your best bet. But there might not be any chairs there."

"We're used to that," Fredo said. "Well, we better hustle. We're supposed to start playing again as soon as the auction is over. Great to see you. Let's get together before I leave town."

"Definitely. By the way, you guys sounded fantastic."

"Cool painting." The goateed, beanie-wearing pianist was pointing at the de Kooning I was about to steal. He strode further into the study. "Isn't that a Jackson Pollock?"

It wasn't, but Pollock had been a fair guess. Lately, it seemed like the general populace had been picking up artsy tidbits from the History Channel.

"Don't know much about art," I lied. I needed these guys gone. Now.

"We better go," Fredo said. "Hope you find your mouse."

After they departed, I checked the hallway for other wayward guests, then grabbed the PVC tube from under the couch. Since swapping the de Koonings was going to take the longest, I started with that.

I took several deep breaths, slipped on a pair of disposable gloves, and then removed the painting from the wall, laying it face down on the floor. No alarms went off. In the distance, I could hear the oddly reassuring, staccato call of the auctioneer.

Unlike last time, I made sure to take my time untacking the canvas. Maybe it was the hypnotic accompaniment of the auctioneer, but as I worked my way around the stretcher bar, removing staples, the rhythmic undulations of his voice calmed the anxiety that had been building since the minute I'd walked into the room.

Once the canvas was freed from the bar, I draped it over the back of the sofa and pulled out the reproduction. I then loosely rolled up the original and slid it into the PVC tube. I wasn't taking any chances on mixing up the paintings.

Stapling the forgery back onto the stretcher bar took way less time than the removal. Pausing before rehanging the painting, I fought the urge to position the de Kooning with the correct side facing up. Even though it'd been in short supply lately, common sense prevailed.

After sliding the poster tube back under the couch, I grabbed the case with the faux Picasso and placed it on the floor next to the pedestal holding the real one. In theory, replacing one sculpture for another should have been a piece of cake. Theories, however, like leaky boats, were often filled with holes. Or, in this case, an alarm system with a three-second timer.

Closing my eyes, I employed several of the deep-cleansing breaths I'd learned during my brief dalliance with yoga. The results, like my fling with yoga, were only mildly successful. But since the clock was mercilessly ticking away, I opened my eyes, and then the case.

My right hand shook as I held the reproduction inches away from the authentic sculpture. The plan, if you could call it that, was to grab the real one with my left hand and then set down the duplicate as quickly as possible. Not very scientific, but neither am I. Unfortunately, I had no way to judge three seconds without having a third hand and a stopwatch.

After taking in one final deep breath, and holding it, I slipped my fingers around the sculpture, careful not to put weight on it, and then counted to three. As I lifted the Picasso from its perch, a loud chirp rang out from somewhere inside the base of the pedestal. Panicked, I dropped the copy in its place. The chirping ceased.

"What the hell are you doing?" Rollie, a silver serving platter tucked under his arm, stood just inside the study door.

Chapter Sixty-Four

It's Not How It Looks

Stunned by Rollie's unexpected presence, I nearly dropped the Picasso back onto the pedestal.

"Are you stealing that statue?" Rollie's eyes were nearly as wide as his gaping mouth.

"I'm . . . um . . . it's not how it looks." How many serial killers had used that same defense?

"The fuck, dude. If you needed money that badly, you could have come to me."

"Rollie . . ." As tempting as it was to spin some extravagant yarn about reuniting the long-lost twin Picasso Toros, I just couldn't summon the energy.

Wielding the platter like a silver shield, Rollie glared at me. "Don't 'Rollie' me! The last thing I want to hear is another one of your bullshit excuses."

I tried arranging words into some kind of intelligible order, but they stubbornly refused to obey. I needn't have worried, because Rollie had already retreated from the scene of the crime. "Fuck!"

After placing the authentic Picasso into the padded case, I slid it under the couch next to the de Kooning. Ricky would retrieve it later. I needed to get the desserts on the table, but how was I going to face my partner?

Was this who I'd become? A thief? A liar? Had these nouns come to define me more than cook or musician?

If this was going to be my last night as a free man, then I was at least going to cater the shit out of the remainder of this party. Maybe that would be my epitaph. *Here lies Anton Cherny. He may have been a thief, but he catered the shit out of your special event.*

To roust myself from my torpor, I pulled off the gloves, slapped myself on both cheeks, and headed out of the study. Only to run into Roger.

"Why aren't the desserts out yet?" Roger barked. "The auction's almost over."

"The . . . um . . . I . . ." Apparently, I'd lost the ability to speak. Aware that Roger was still glaring at me, I dug deep. "We didn't want the desserts sitting out longer than necessary." Complete nonsense, but it only needed to sound plausible enough to fool an event planner.

"Well, do it now." After issuing the thou-shalt-obey edict, he turned on his heels and scampered off.

Rollie—always the consummate professional—had taken the initiative, with Ricky and Trina's assistance, and started laying out desserts in the dining room. They were, after all, his creations. He avoided making eye contact as he brushed past me with a pan of cupcakes. Ricky and Trina shot me inquisitive looks as I slunk into the room. I responded with a discreet thumbs-up.

"Trina tells me the two of you are playing at Ghost Baby tomorrow night," Ricky said. "Should I come?"

I shrugged. "Up to you. Trina sounds fantastic."

"So does Anton," Trina added.

"If you're done chitchatting, do you mind getting back to work," Rollie snarled.

Skirting the elephant in the room, I headed to the kitchen, hoping I could think of a way to explain my actions to Rollie that didn't leave me in handcuffs and with ten years in the state pen.

Back in the kitchen, a blanket of tranquility settled over me. I didn't know whether it was because this was the one room where I felt comfortable, or because I'd successfully exchanged the two pieces of art without setting off any alarms. Well, except for Rollie's. And maybe, just maybe, I was ready to accept whatever course of action Rollie felt obliged to take.

Since the three of them were tackling the desserts, I began cleaning and putting away the equipment we no longer needed.

"What's up with you and Rollie?" Ricky asked as he grabbed another tray of cupcakes off the kitchen island.

"I got busted."

"What?"

"Rollie came in as I was swapping Picassos." Maybe that was what I'd name my prison band: Swapping Picassos.

"Fuck."

"Yeah."

Ricky set the tray back on the counter. "What's he going to do?"

"Don't know," I said. I did know, however, that Rollie had an unfailing moral sense and a deep respect for those who enforced the prescribed social parameters. My senses, moral and otherwise, on the other hand, were definitely failing.

Rollie stormed into the kitchen like a power-walker into a mall juice bar. "Ricky, I need those cupcakes out there now. And make sure you don't crowd the eclairs."

"Yes, Chef." Ricky lifted the tray, tossed me a sympathetic look, and hustled out of the room.

"Well?" Rollie folded his arms across his chest and stared at me. "And please don't say, 'It's complicated.'"

I almost laughed, but sensing this was not the time for levity, refrained. "Can we do this later?"

"No." Rollie jabbed a finger at me. "I need to know what this is all about. Was this your first time?"

"First time?"

"Stealing art."

Might as well lay my cards on the table. "No."

"Kind of figured." Rollie opened the fridge and grabbed a bottle of water. "Okay, start talking."

"First off, all the art we've taken was previously stolen."

"Wait. We?"

Oh shit. Did I say *we*? "Doesn't matter. The point is—"

"It does matter." Rollie swigged some water. "And, by the way, whatever you're about to tell me, doesn't excuse any of it. So, does the *we* include Ricky?"

I sighed, which no doubt threw Ricky under the bus.

"We're actually working for an insurance company." Only partly a lie. He didn't need to know how many degrees of separation existed between us and the final destination of the recovered art. But I hoped—since he was always going on about "mission statements"—that if I employed the right words, Rollie might appreciate the legitimacy of our art-rescue operation.

"Our mission is to return the art to their rightful owners—for a reward, of course."

"Of course," Rollie echoed. "Why not just let the police confiscate the stuff?"

"Because . . ." I was reluctant to throw anyone else under the inexorable wheels of public transportation. Namely, William. "We're the only ones who know that the art is stolen, and we know where they are."

"There's something else you're not telling me."

"Look, Rollie. We *steal* the art, replace them with reproductions, and then give the real ones to the insurance company, who returns them to the true owner. And, if it helps, we're only doing this one more time. Then we're calling it quits. I promise."

"Hmm." Rollie scratched his chin, mulling over the veracity of my promise. "Calling it a reproduction doesn't lessen the fact that they're not real. What you're doing is still burglary. Plain and simple."

Was anything, really, plain and simple? Okay, maybe meatloaf and mashed potatoes. "Do what you got to do, Rollie. Ricky and I made the decision to do this. And we both sleep well at night, knowing we're doing the right thing."

I was shoveling the shit a little deep here, but I was trying to appeal to Rollie's clearly defined sense of right and wrong.

Rollie, revisiting his chin, stared at me. Having nothing more to say, I stared back.

"If this is your way of tanking tomorrow's meeting with your son, you're an even bigger idiot than I thought."

He was right, I was an idiot. But I would never purposely screw up a chance to get to know Francois. Especially if it was my only chance.

"So, what was that little sculpture you were stealing? Is it valuable?"

"It's a Picasso. So, yeah, kind of." I wasn't about to mention the de Kooning.

Rollie's eye widened. "Damn! Did Ricky make the reproduction?"

"No, I did." I probably shouldn't have told him that, but pride, that much-maligned construct, was rearing its head. "Did I ever tell you I'd gone to art school? Or more like dropped out of art school."

"Yeah, a hundred times. That's where you met Ricky, right?"

"Yep. Only unlike me, Ricky didn't drop out. He's the real artist."

"Hey guys, sorry to interrupt," Trina said. "Are there any more of those truffles?"

Rollie popped open one of the coolers and pulled out four covered cake pans, each one containing a different flavored truffle: Bourbon, margarita, raspberry, almond joy. While he snapped off the plastic tops, I set a couple of serving trays on the counter. It seemed, for both of us, that work took precedence over everything else. Even if that everything else included felony larceny.

As Rollie loaded up the trays with an assortment of truffles, Trina and I exchanged a series of head tilts, eyebrow raises, and shoulder lifts. An intense, yet soundless workout.

"Thanks," Trina said, palming the trays and, after shooting me one final muted missive, whisking them out of the kitchen.

Washing his hands at the sink, his back to me, Rollie said, "I wish I hadn't seen what I'd seen. But unfortunately, I can't unsee it. And knowing what I now know is going to be very difficult for me."

I had to admire Rollie's infallible moral compass. Perhaps, going forward, he could act as my surrogate compass. I exhaled the breath that I didn't realize I'd been holding. "I understand."

"You said you were going to do this one more time. When?"

Did I have anything more to lose by telling him? He already knew I was a thief. I studied my shoes, trying to decide what to do.

"At this point, after what you've already told me, it doesn't change anything," Rollie said.

"Friday. The food truck gig you booked."

Rollie glowered at me. "You better not fucking implicate me or Prudence in any of this. I have no intentions of going to jail because of your poor decision-making skills."

"Of course not. I would never drag you into any of this." I wasn't about to tell him about the previous crimes committed with Prudence as the getaway vehicle.

The Culinary Caper

He dried his hands on a dish towel, then turned toward me. "I'm going to need some time to process all of this."

"I understand." Coming around the island, I stood next to Rollie. "When this all started, I was not in a great place. Money problems, Julia problems, existential life problems. I was a fucking mess. So, when the opportunity arose to solve some of those problems, and justify it with Robin Hood-type rationalizations, I jumped on it." I raised a palm, preemptively. "I know, quick fixes are rarely the wisest choice, and usually end poorly, but . . . just so you know, whatever happens, I take full responsibility for my actions."

Roger, out of breath, burst into the kitchen like Sir Edmund Hillary summiting Mt. Everest. "Devon Snoot wants to see you in the tent. Now!"

"Everything okay?" I glanced nervously at Rollie, wondering whether he'd already sold me out.

"I don't know." Roger eyed his watch impatiently. "Devon just told me to fetch you."

Rollie, an unreadable expression on his face, stared at me as I followed Roger out of the kitchen, my head lowered like a naughty puppy.

When we arrived at the tent, Roger did his vanishing trick. Devon Snoot, talking to an elderly couple next to where the auctioneer had been belting out his siren call, waved me over. The trio, just to the left of the dais, was swinging hard on the old standard, "It Had to Be You." Was the song an accusation of my recent crimes?

Putting the arm—that used to propel hundred-mile-per-hour pitches toward unsuspecting batters—around me, Devon ushered me forward, then signaled for the band to stop playing.

Had the stroll to the tent been a march to the scaffold? I glanced at Fredo, wondering if he would think less of me for my crimes. Then, I thought of Julia. If I ended up in jail tonight, I wouldn't be able to meet

Francois the next morning. Another disappointment by his deadbeat dad. For Julia, this would only confirm my lack of qualifications for fatherhood.

Devon tapped the microphone. "Hey everybody. Just wanted to thank you again for coming out tonight and digging deeply into those gold-filled pockets of yours. I've been told to give you all an A plus."

The laughter and applause did little to appease the feeling of the noose around my neck.

"Except for you, Bill." Devon pointed at a rotund, bow-tied man at one of the front tables. "It was supposed to be a bourbon tasting, not a bourbon guzzling."

More laughter.

"And lastly," Devon continued. "Before you all leave, I'd like you to give a huge round of applause for Chef Anton Cherny and his amazing food. Without him, this evening would have been worse than a double-header rain delay."

Instead of the "off with his head" shouts I'd expected, I was showered with cheers, ear-splitting whistles, and "bravos." Even the band joined in.

Chapter Sixty-Five

I Even Shaved

After setting my coffee cup on a nearby table, I checked the front of my shirt one more time for stains. I was sitting in the children's section of Joseph-Beth Booksellers, anxious as a teenager at his first prom. Dressed in a blue button-down and sport coat, maybe I was a tad overdressed, but I wasn't taking any chances. I'd even shaved.

Last night, after declining separate offers from Ricky and Trina to go for drinks—no invitation from Rollie—I'd gotten to bed at a reasonable hour. But, due to the pending rendezvous with Julia and Francois, I'd barely slept.

Even now, lines of script were racing through my sleep-deprived brain faster than an amphetamine-popping actor cramming for a last-minute performance of *Macbeth*—or should I say, The Scottish Play. *Julia, you're looking well. How was your flight? What's it like living in Paris? Francois, what kind of ice cream do you like? Do you want to go to the zoo?* Then, dialing up my best James Earl Jones impression: *I am your father.*

Before I could sort these random questions into any kind of logical order, I spotted a woman leading a small boy by his hand. The boy, with his straight blond hair and roundish face, clearly took after his mother.

It took me several seconds to realize that this slender woman, in the tight, knee-length dress, complicated braid, and floral scarf was Julia. In contrast to the jeans and casual tops she'd worn in days of yore, she couldn't have looked more Parisian. I was glad I'd rejected the jeans and brewery T-shirt that were my go-to ensemble.

More conflicting than wardrobe choices, however, was that I was floored by her beauty. A beauty that still left me speechless. Aware that relationships, ours at least, were not defined solely by attraction, I shook off these confusing thoughts and painted a smile on my face.

"Anton." Julia stopped a few feet away, Francois clinging to her dress, half-hidden behind her leg.

I'd given up on the idea of buying Francois a present, mostly because I couldn't make a decision—decisions were my nemeses. Also, because I didn't want to endure Julia's wrath if I purchased the wrong item. I took a final sip of coffee—to bolster my courage—set it back down on the table and rose to greet them.

"Julia." I took a couple of tentative steps toward them. I was used to awkward, but this was some next-level shit.

Francois pointed a chubby finger at me. "C'est mon père?"

"Oui, c'est lui," Julia replied.

Thanks to Duolingo, I understood what they'd said, but hearing Francois's voice for the first time was slightly surreal. Standing before me was an actual human being, a direct result of the commingling of Julia's and my DNA. I'd seen pictures of him, but I hadn't anticipated the full impact of his physical manifestation. *What creature hast thou wrought?*

"Bonjour, Francois." I inched forward; my eyes riveted on the blond child in front of me.

"Speak English," Julia commanded. "He needs the practice."

Francois, a hand still holding tightly to Julia's dress, eyed me suspiciously.

"Can I get you guys something? Coffee, maybe?" I asked. "There's a café on the other end of the store."

Julia shook her head. "Six-year-olds don't drink coffee."

The Culinary Caper

Shit. Two minutes in, and I'd already screwed up. "Of course . . . I meant . . . whatever you want."

"We're fine," Julia said. Her expression hovered in the middle ground between actually being fine and 'you're an idiot.' "How 'bout you just get to know your son."

Francois took a cautious step away from his mother. "I can make spinach soufflé."

"Wow dude, that's amazing!" I exclaimed. "Spinach soufflés are the best."

"Want to see my friend?" He reached into his pocket and pulled out a plastic yellow dinosaur.

I knelt in front of him. "I love dinosaurs." There was a possibility that this wasn't going to be a total disaster.

"Maybe I *will* grab a coffee," Julia said. "While I'm gone, try to remember that he's six."

"I got this." That was a slight exaggeration, but not as much as it had been a minute ago.

Francois handed me the dinosaur. "His name is Henri. He is a stego . . . saurus. But my favorite dinosaur is Lucas. He is a triceratops. But Lucas does not like to leave Paris."

"I can dig that." Francois's English was very good. Julia must have him enrolled in a bilingual school.

Francois gave me an odd look, possibly wondering if I might be a paleontologist. I examined Henri, then returned him to Francois's outstretched palm. "Is this your first time in the United States?"

"I think so."

My knees were beginning to cramp, so I pointed at the sitting area, where my coffee was growing cold. "Should we go over there?"

Francois shrugged and looked down at the floor.

"So, little man, what do you like to do?" Sober, I wasn't much of a conversationalist; I was much better at internal dialog. Even those thoughts had a tendency to spiral downward.

"I like to help *maman* in the kitchen." Francois stuffed Henri back in his pocket. "I also like to play futbol. But I'm not very good at it."

"Maybe we should cook something together. Would you like that?"

He shrugged again.

"Have you ever been inside a food truck?" I was running out of material.

"What's a food truck?"

Ah, to be a Parisian, with a plethora of nonmobile dining options.

Francois started wiggling his foot. I wondered if he needed to use the bathroom. Would Julia freak out if we weren't here when she returned? How quickly would she call the cops on me?

"A food truck is kind of like a tiny kitchen on wheels." I seemed to recall that the younger set was fond of all things mobile. "It's very cool, because we can go just about anywhere."

For the next ten minutes, I fielded questions about food trucks: Could the truck go to the moon? Did I ever have sleepovers on it? Was there a bathroom?

Julia returned, holding a small cup of coffee, a slight smile twitching at the corner of her mouth. "How you boys getting along?"

Francois tugged on her skirt. "May . . . I go . . . *regarder les livres*?"

"Of course, Cherie. But first tell me what you think of your father. In English, please."

I held my breath, waiting for him to recite my encyclopedic list of faults.

"He has a kitchen bus. That is so cool."

Bullet dodged.

"Can I go now?"

"*Oui* but stay where I can see you." Julia set her cup on the table, and after making sure Francois didn't wander off, sat down beside me.

"So, how are you?" I asked. This was our first face-to-face conversation in almost four years. I figured it was best to start off with softball questions.

"This pre-wedding stuff is a nightmare. If my sister doesn't have a coronary before the big day, it's going to be a miracle."

I nodded as if I had clue about what she was talking about. Which I didn't. I pointed at Francois. "Seems like a good kid."

"He's the best." Julia glanced at her son, her gaze softening. "What about you? How are things going?"

Given that all of our recent interactions had been contentious, I couldn't tell whether she genuinely wanted to know or was just making a valiant attempt at civil discourse. However, since it might be another four years before I saw her again, I decided not to hold anything back.

"I'm thinking about quitting the food truck, my band is breaking up, and I can barely pay the rent. So . . . not great."

She eyed her coffee, steam rising from the lid, but didn't pick it up. "You play in a band?"

"Really? That's all you got?" I stood up, anxious to be anywhere else.

"Sit down, Anton." She patted the chair I'd just vacated. "I was kidding."

I glanced at Francois, head buried in a picture book, and then at the front door. My first instinct was to flee. But if I did, would that sabotage any future I might have had with my son?

"Please, don't go." Julia reached for my hand. "Tell me what's going on."

"Like you don't know." I took several deep breaths, trying to quell the anger heating up inside me, and then returned to my seat. "Francois's monthly medical bills are eating up almost every cent I earn."

The daily stress from my financial troubles felt like a living, breathing entity, one that grabbed me by the throat every time I thought about it, much less articulated its presence. Evoking Francois's severe congenital heart issues usually helped relax its death-grip.

Julia opened her mouth, as if ready to say something, but instead studied me for a minute. "The way you go on about your food truck and how successful it is, I figured you owned a whole fleet of them."

"Just the one," I muttered.

Julia pushed a strand of hair out of her eyes and then sipped her coffee. "You're always bragging about these celebrity parties you've been catering. And, before that, just after I left for Paris, you'd gotten that sweet gig as a sous chef at Roberto's. I thought you were crushing it."

These days, we only spoke two or three times a year, but damn, she was right. I'd been painting this picture of myself as a kitchen crusader. In culinary school, there'd been so many talented students with oversized egos that the only way I could fit in was by dialing up an equal level of arrogance. I'd even told my classmates that, after graduating, I was moving to NYC and going to work my way up the ladder at some Michelin-starred restaurant. Then, I'd beat Bobby Flay at Iron Chef and open my own place in the West Village.

Instead, too scared to face the fierce competition in Manhattan, I'd taken the safer path and moved back to Cincinnati. Fearless Julia, however, after two short years, had fled Cincinnati to Food Central.

Even before she'd flown off to France, I'd been jealous of Julia's kitchen skills and career opportunities. Maybe it was this plateful of insecurities that had driven her away.

The Culinary Caper

Unlike the misrepresented status of my career, however, my money issues were quite legit.

"You were always such an incredible cook," Julia said. "So intuitive."

"Thanks for saying that. But my budgeting skills, on the other hand, are the polar opposite of intuitive." Was "tuitive" a word? Her compliment took a bit of the edge off my fury, but I still felt the need to explain my fiscal woes.

Julie set her cup down, waiting for me to continue.

"When Rollie and I bought Prudence, we had to totally gut her." The image of the truck's interior stripped down to the frame still induced a sense of terror. "I didn't have enough cash to cover my share. Rollie, Mr. Financially Prudent, had to put up the bigger share. So, not only do I owe the bank, I also owe Rollie. And, of course, this is aside from helping out with Francois's medical problems." I was not about to mention the money I owed Ilya.

"I'm assuming Prudence is your food truck and not some geriatric English sex worker?"

Had it not been for the lather I'd worked myself into, I might have laughed. "Yeah."

"Anton," she said, her tone now more somber, "you should have said something."

Francois trotted over and leaned into his mother's ear. "*Je dois faire pipi.*"

"Okay, sweetie," Julia said, getting up. "I've got to take Francois to the bathroom."

The store's armada of bookshelves suddenly felt like they were marching toward me, like soldiers into battle. Desperately needing fresh air, and perhaps a fresh start, I hoisted myself out of the chair.

"Francois, it was very nice to meet you. Would you like to see the truck sometime?"

He nodded enthusiastically. I ruffled his hair and then started walking away, but Julia grabbed my hand. "Can we talk more, later?"

I nodded. I wasn't sure I had anything more to say to her, but I definitely wanted to spend more time with Francois.

"Where's your truck . . . I mean, Prudence, going to be tonight?" Julia asked. "Maybe we could stop by and get a bite to eat."

"Rollie and I are taking the night off." I was sorry to disappoint Francois, but I was also anxious to flee the bookstore. "Rollie's going to Louisville to visit his parents, and I have a gig."

"A catering gig?"

Why couldn't she just say goodbye? "No, a music gig, with a singer.'"

"The one you were rehearsing with? Your girlfriend?"

I tried, and failed, to stifle a sigh. "Yeah."

Julia either didn't register the sigh or chose to ignore it. "Where?"

"Ghost Baby. It's just a small club. You don't need to come."

"Of course not," Julia said.

Chapter Sixty-Six

Time To Give Up My Vow of Stoicism?

Unbeknownst to Trina, sitting beside me at the bar, the flock of butterflies that had taken up residence in my stomach seemed to be planning some sort of coup d'etat.

It didn't help matters that Ghost Baby, a cozy subterranean club—not a good fit for claustrophobics—was packed, and the quartet playing before us was groovin' hard, the audience rapt. Also making me anxious was having to reset the stage as soon as the quartet finished their set. All I had to do was haul my keyboard from one side of the stage to the middle, and reposition the microphone for Trina, but even that minimal effort—in my current state—seemed a Sisyphean task.

I'd considered getting a medley of prescription drugs to offset the anxiety that had been building all week, but that required a doctor's appointment. And a doctor. Which I didn't have. Again, too much effort. Instead, I'd opted for a couple fingers of Woodford Reserve.

The upside to the gig, since the club was several stories below ground, was that if World War III began, and Cincinnati got nuked, we'd probably survive. That, and the bar was well-stocked.

"You, okay, Anton?" Unlike me, Trina was drinking club soda with a twist. "You look a bit pale."

"What? No, I'm fine. It's just the lighting."

She cupped my face in her hands. "You. Have. Got. This."

"Hey, kids." Ricky appeared behind us, holding hands with a reedy man in a mauve shirt and teal sport coat. "This is Jad. He's from Dubai."

I shook the extended hand. "Nice to meet you, Jad."

"The pleasure is all mine," Jad said, his accent slightly British.

Ricky clasped his arms around Trina and me. "You guys ready to rock and roll?"

"Absolutely," Trina said. "But you know we're not really rocking out, right? Our set is more of a mellow vibe."

"Sure, it is." Ricky squeezed my shoulder. "How about you, Anton? You going to dazzle us with your keyboard stylings?"

"Hey, everybody." Rollie sidled up next to Ricky, a buxom brunette in tow.

"You made it!" I said, somewhat unnecessarily. Given that the jury was still out on Rollie's acceptance of the previous evening's burglary, my surprise was well-founded.

"Wouldn't miss this for anything, bro." Rollie pushed his date forward. "This is Jocelyn. She's a fireman. I mean, woman."

Rollie's previous girlfriends had been named Helga, followed by Iris. With Jocelyn, he was staying true to his alphabetical dating plan.

"Hi, Jocelyn." I couldn't help picturing her in tight-fitting firefighter's garb, aiming a python-like fire hose at a burning building, a pair of overzealous dalmatians at her side.

"Nice to meet y'all." Jocelyn beamed, like she truly meant it. "Can't wait to hear your music."

"Hey guys, thanks for coming out." Trina gestured at the band, packing up their gear. "Looks like we're up, Anton."

"Can I grab Anton for a second?" Rollie asked.

Trina glanced back at the stage. The quartet seemed in no hurry to vacate. "Okay. But make it quick."

After escorting Jocelyn to a table, Rollie led me out of the main room to a far corner in the back bar.

"I've been thinking a lot about what happened at the party—kept me up half the night. But this morning, it occurred to me that what you and Ricky are doing is kind of like *Monuments Men* meets *Ocean Eleven*. In fact, maybe, after you've recovered the final painting, you could make a movie about this."

I was happy that he'd said "recovered" instead of "stolen." Although I couldn't quite comprehend the cinema mashup he'd referenced.

"Anyway, after much soul-searching," Rollie continued, "I've decided that I'm okay with you completing your final top-secret mission. But, if I find out you're bullshitting me, I will personally deliver you to the gulag."

"Fair. Thanks, Rollie." Being an inexperienced soul-searcher and equally inept mission specialist, I was grateful for any amount of validation. And not having to worry about Rollie, and his unimpeachable conscience, was a great weight lifted off my shoulders. That didn't, however, stop the specter of Ilya from lurking in the shadows. "I better go get set up."

The moment my fingers touched the keys, the stress of the last few days evaporated, and the countless hours spent practicing kicked in. When Trina started singing, I was transported to another planet. A planet where all that existed was her and me. A planet where there were no stolen paintings, no food trucks, and no ex-girlfriends with unexpected children.

The first tune was an original I'd written several years ago, about a former girlfriend— a botanist who communicated better with her plants than with me. When the song ended, the explosion of applause brought me back to Earth. Trina, a wide smile on her face, blew me a kiss.

"Thank you, everybody." Trina tapped the edge of the keyboard. "That tune was written by my talented pianist, Anton Cherny. We'd like to continue with a little song called 'Moskva,' that I wrote about growing up in Russia. Maestro . . ."

I try not to pay attention to the audience when I perform, don't want to get distracted. This time, for some reason, the blonde woman seated at the end of the bar caught my eye. It took me several seconds to realize that it was Julia. And another minute, thanks to her unexpected presence, to become aware that I'd started the tune in G Major rather than A minor. Fortunately, I was able to disguise the mistake by extending the introduction and working my way back to the intended key. The audience was none the wiser, but my convoluted intro induced a look of sheer panic on Trina's face.

Fifty minutes and eight songs later, after the echo of Trina's final high note faded away, the audience, clapping riotously, leapt to their feet. Gazing out at the sea of smiling faces, I experienced a puzzling sense of relief and disappointment. Relief that it was over. Disappointment that we couldn't have played a second set, which, given how much I'd worried about making it through a single song without melting down, surprised me.

Trina pulled me off the piano bench and led us in a theatrical bow. As the crowd dropped back into their seats and began settling their bills, Julia was nowhere to be seen.

"That was pretty damn good. Wasn't it, Anton?" Wrapping her arms around me, Trina kissed both of my cheeks.

"It was." At that moment, I experienced something I hadn't felt in a long time. Tranquility. A long-lost sensation, and one I'd missed.

Releasing me, Trina guzzled the rest of her bottled water. "A couple of notes, though."

Here we go. Burst my blissful bubble. At least I was used to short-lived happiness.

"'Rehab' started off kind of slow, but we managed to bring it back up to tempo. And what the hell were you doing at the beginning of 'Moskva'? I thought you were having a stroke or something."

"Sorry about that." I disconnected the sustain pedal and pulled out the cable to the amp.

"Don't be sorry," Trina said. "It was freakin' genius."

My eyebrows arched in alarm. Maybe *she* was the one having a stroke. "I don't know about genius."

Sometimes, the best ideas did evolve out of major screw-ups. More than a few times, I'd added the wrong ingredient or mixed up a recipe, and the result had been delicious. Occasionally, I even remembered what I'd done wrong.

Rollie and Ricky, abandoning their dates, stormed the stage.

"Dude!" Rollie pulled me into a bone-crushing embrace. "I had no idea. I mean I've heard you play with Remoulade, but this was . . . I don't know, so much . . . so awesome."

"Thanks, bro. Appreciate that."

Maybe it would be best to take a page from Rollie's heart-on-the sleeve approach to life. Was it time to give up my vow of stoicism?

"Rollie's right. You guys are ready to conquer Cincinnati," Ricky said, slightly less ebullient but no less heartfelt. "I mean, after tomorrow night."

I glared at Ricky. He would have to mention the one thing guaranteed to kill my buzz.

The club's manager, a Johnny Depp clone, pushed his way through the crowd of well-wishers. "Hey Trina, you guys sounded great. We absolutely must get you back on the calendar. But right now, I need you to clear the stage as quickly as possible."

Chapter Sixty-Seven

What the Fuck?

Trina nudged me. "You going to answer that?"

I thought the calypso music was coming from the Caribbean band playing on the beach while I sipped a Mai Tai. Turned out that was a dream. Disappointed, I fumbled for the dream-crushing device. "Hello."

"Anton, sorry to wake you," Julia said. "I need to tell you something."

I sat up in bed, trying to shake off the fog of sleep. "Is everything okay? Is Francois okay?"

"Francois is fine. Everything's fine."

"Okay, so can we talk later, then?" The post-gig hang with Rollie and Ricky, and their plus-ones, had turned into a full-on pub crawl. Gallons of strong coffee would be required before I'd be capable of an actual conversation.

"No," Julia paused. "This is important."

I sighed, climbed out of bed, and slipped on some sweats. "Fine."

"Who is it?" whispered Trina.

I considered not telling her but knew she'd get it out of me later. "Julia."

She pulled the pillow over her head.

"What's so important it couldn't wait?" In the kitchen, I started the kettle and then scooped coffee beans into the grinder.

"I was at Ghost Baby last night."

"I know." I started the grinder, then walked to the far end of the living room to distance myself from the ratcheting noise.

"Trina is a very beautiful woman."

I sensed it was safer to stare out the window than to respond.

"You looked so happy playing piano with her. I don't remember you ever looking that happy when you were with me."

I was too hung over to enjoy a leisurely cruise across Nostalgia Lake. Especially if it meant conjuring up faulty memories. "Julia—"

"Please. Hear me out."

"Fine." When the grinder stopped, I returned to the kitchen and emptied the ground beans into the French press.

"The day Francois was born, the doctors discovered he had a serious heart condition. If he hadn't gotten the treatment right away, they didn't think he would live."

"I know all that," I said testily.

"Anton, I'm trying to tell you something."

"Really? Then tell me already?" Anger was doing a better job sobering me up than the coffee ever would. "I told you. You'll get your money."

"Just listen, will you?"

I exhaled sharply, releasing the rising frustration. "Okay, but get to the point."

"I'm trying." She paused. "Aside from Francois's life-threatening issues, my grandparents—who I was living with at the time—were not in the greatest health, and the café was struggling. And then, a few months after I arrived in Paris, Grandfather, who'd run the business for almost sixty years, passed away. My grandmother was devastated, but she's a very stubborn woman, and insisted on keeping the café open, even though she no longer had the stamina to put in the long hours."

Speaking of stamina. "Julia—"

"Let me finish."

When the kettle chimed, I poured the water into the press, set the timer on the stove, and sprawled out on the couch.

"That's when I came up with the idea of turning the café into a bakery. At first, Grandmother hated the idea, but she eventually came around. Especially when I told her I would do all the baking. However, since that was going to require tons of hours in the kitchen, I needed help with Francois." Julia paused again. "Grandmother loved Francois to pieces, but taking care of him was wearing her out. So, once she saw the bakery was doing well, she decided to move in with her younger sister in Lyon. That meant figuring out day care for Francois." Pause. "Don't worry, I'm getting to the point."

"I think I got it," I said. "Bakery, Grandma, day care."

She ignored my interruption. "Here I was in Paris, a single mother with a sick child, doing my best to keep the bakery afloat. And there you were in Cincinnati, bragging about your food truck and your awesome catering gigs. Not a care in the world."

Wow, when she put it that way, I sounded like a total tool. Had my arrogance, the unfortunate trait I'd acquired in culinary school, been my own downfall? "You're forgetting that I was sending you tons of cash every month, which was sucking me into the Black Hole of Debt."

"That's why I called," Julia said.

The timer beeped. I dragged myself off the couch, pushed down the plunger, and tipped the hot coffee into a ceramic mug. "And why is that? To remind me of what an asshole I am?"

My question was met with silence. During the lull, Trina shuffled into the kitchen, hair disheveled, eyes glazed and poured herself a cup of coffee. She gave me an inquisitive look. I shrugged.

"No," Julia finally said. "I called to tell you that I no longer need your financial assistance."

My mouth nearly hit the floor.

"What's going on?" Trina whispered. "What does she want?"

My brain, still resonating from Julia's proclamation, barely registered Trina's queries. Shaking my head in disbelief, I turned my attention back to the phone. "What did you just say?"

"I have a lot going on right now," Julia said. "And not just my sister's wedding. The day before I left Paris, someone put a bid on the bakery. The location is in a very desirable area, but the taxes are extremely high. So, when this guy, out of the blue, offered me an insane amount, I told him I'd consider it."

I sipped some coffee, wondering where this was going. "And?"

"And I just accepted the offer. So, I don't need you to give me any more money." There was a long pause before she continued. "There's something else I need to tell you. And I hope you can forgive me for what I'm about to say."

I tried to imagine what she was going to tell me. In spite of the tension between us, mostly due to my monetary tardiness, I understood that these issues were largely a result of my own actions. I accepted that. What could she possibly need to ask forgiveness for?

"I was so accustomed to the extra money coming in, even after Francois got better and the bakery took off. And, since you seemed to be so incredibly successful, it never occurred to me that you couldn't afford it."

Somewhere in the back of my brain, a bass drum began pounding out a heavy beat. "What exactly are you saying?"

"Francois is perfectly healthy. His heart problems are gone."

The bass drum had now been joined by the entire percussion section. "How long has he been *perfectly healthy*?"

The gap between Julia's responses was growing exponentially. "About three years."

Her answer hit me like a slap in the face. "What the fuck, Julia! Child support is one thing, but this is straight-up . . . extortion."

Trina, leaning against the kitchen counter, froze, cup halfway to her lips. Then, a sly grin played across her face. "Told you so."

I glared at her.

I'd been sending Julia money for six years, since just after Francois was born. But it was exactly three years ago when my debt to the loan shark had come due, and when my financial problems began spiraling downward. Staring into the dark-roasted abyss of my cup, I tried to calculate how much money I'd sent her during those thirty-six months. I'd always been terrible with math, but I did know that whatever that number was, it had negatively impacted the amount I owed Ilya.

"I'm truly sorry. I don't know what else to say. You must hate me right now."

That wasn't a strong enough word to describe what I was feeling. But then, something happened. Something I couldn't quite describe. It was almost like a giant arm had extended from above—no, not that dude—and lifted a great weight from my shoulders. And for the first time in years—three, to be exact—I felt like I could stand upright.

Maybe it was the newfound freedom, financial and metaphysical, or maybe it was the residual serenity from the Ghost Baby gig, but the hate that had almost flared into a full-on firestorm vanished—to continue the metaphor—in a wisp of smoke.

"Anton," Julia said, almost in a whisper. "Say something."

I exhaled a long breath, and then Planet Earth—which had momentarily quit spinning—resumed its stubborn orbit. "I'm confused and pissed off . . . but I don't hate you."

It suddenly occurred to me that Rollie had probably felt the same way when he'd caught me in the act of swapping Picassos. Maybe, like him, I could come to accept deceit. Somewhere, I'd read that "forgiveness liberates the soul."

I took another deep breath. "For now . . . I think I'd rather just move on."

What "moving on" meant, I had no idea. But I did know that if I dwelt on her deception, it would bore into my brain like a bloodthirsty earwig.

"I completely understand," Julia said. Another long pause. I thought she might have hung up. "When you're ready, let's talk about what selling the bakery might mean."

I had no desire to talk to her about anything, much less her post-bakery plans, but I agreed anyway, and ended the call.

Chapter Sixty-Eight

Mum's the Word

"So, what are we stealing tonight?" Rollie asked after I parked Prudence in front of another McMansion.

"First off, there is no *we*. And secondly, you and I are just serving food. There are no extracurricular activities."

"Of course. Mum's the word." Rollie gave me a conspiratorial wink.

Almost eight hours had passed since Julia's early-morning phone call, during which time I'd attempted to digest the full ramifications of what she'd told me. The headspace that the sudden cancellation of my financial obligations occupied almost eclipsed the pending thefts of the Rockwell and the Jasper Johns—the final heists for the League of Pilfering Purveyors. This time, however, it was a single purveyor, because Ricky had been benched for the season closer.

I shut off the engine, stretching noisily. It was only five o'clock, and I was already exhausted.

"I've told you this like a hundred times," Rollie said, "but your show last night was killer. Can't wait to hear your next one. You're going to do more, right?"

"Don't know. Trina's in charge of all that." The days leading up to the Ghost Baby gig had been incredibly stressful. Since the performance had been a success, I was looking forward to dipping my toes back into the duo collaboration.

"Chill for a minute," Rollie said. "I'll touch base with Trevor."

"Thanks." I was glad Rollie was the point-man tonight—I had enough going on.

My phone rang. "Hey, Trina."

After Julia's shocking revelation, I'd filled Trina in on the gist of the phone call. Gloating over her correct guess about Julia's extortion, Trina had grabbed my hand and danced me around the apartment singing. "Freedom."

"How you feeling?" Trina asked.

"Tired."

"I know. Me too. But I still can't believe what Julia did. What a bitch."

Strangely, I wanted to defend Julia. Explain to Trina that she was just a struggling single mom who had gotten overwhelmed with life and made some poor decisions. Much like me, minus the single-mom part. At the moment, however, I didn't have the time or energy to dive into life's capricious whims. "I wish I had time for a nap."

"Guess we shouldn't have stayed up until three," Trina said. "Technically, that last hour was . . . anyway, I'm in the car with Papa. We should be there in about twenty minutes. I have both . . . uh . . . items. Oh, and Papa wants me to remind you not to disappoint him this evening."

The last thing I needed was a reminder about the binary burglary, the very thing that had been giving me nightmares for the past week. Also, I wished she would refrain from sharing the details of our late-night trysts with her father. "I'll try my best."

Seconds after hanging up, I dozed off. I wasn't sure how long I was out, but when I awoke, my phone was ringing, and there was still no sign of Rollie.

"Just wanted to let you know," Ricky said when I picked up, "I handed the two 'books' over to Trina a couple of hours ago. Wish I could be there to help. But if you're as good at 'returning items to the library' as you are playing piano, then you'll absolutely crush it."

"Thanks, dude. I wish you were here, too."

"One more thing." Ricky paused. "You sure Rollie is okay with our little art project?"

"Hundred percent." Seventy-five was probably a more realistic number.

A sudden banging rattled the side of the truck, and seconds later, two bald, beefy men, with tattoos creeping up their necks like some species of insidious ivy, appeared at the bottom of the steps. Given their prodigious girth and ink-proclivity, I figured they were ravenous Bengals anxious to get a fistful of perogi.

"I gotta go." I ended the call.

"You Antonovich?" asked Neck Tattoo Number One in a thick Russian accent. So much for members of the local team. I considered bolting out of the driver's-side door and making a mad dash for the bushes, but the only time I'd dashed anywhere in the last couple of decades was to the liquor store.

When Neck Tattoo Number Two, pushing past his comrade, reached a hand inside his black leather jacket, I braced myself for the burst of gunfire from a vintage Kalashnikov, or at the least the snap of my arm like a week-old baguette. Instead, he held out two PVC poster tubes. "You take. From Katrina."

Trina never mentioned having her own pair of Russian pit bulls. Then I remembered she was at the party as a guest with her father.

After I accepted the delivery—half-expecting to sign for the forgeries in the PVC tubes—the Russians trudged off, chuckling, most likely about the wimpy little American who almost shat his pants.

Relieved that I was still alive, with all my limbs intact, I stashed the tubes in a lower cabinet, behind several bags of flour. I was still attempting to lower my blood pressure when Rollie climbed aboard Prudence.

Noting that I hadn't lifted a finger since he left, he gave me a worried look and clasped a hand on my shoulder. "All good, bro?"

Chapter Sixty-Nine

Not On My Watch

Most of the events we catered on Prudence had a bell curve. They started slowly, customers trickling in, either famished and wanting to beat the crowds, or octogenarians accustomed to early-bird specials. Then came the general stampede, people talking loudly and taking forever to decide what they want. Finally, having taken full advantage of the open bar, there were the late arrivals, moseying up to the window and eyeing the menu like a pack of hungry wolves—or in this case, a streak of tigers.

Rollie and I served up several heaping plates of tacos and pierogi to a trio of inebriated Bengals, so enormous they blocked the sun better than a total solar eclipse. After Rollie and I shooed them back to the house with their bounty, I wiped the sweat off my forehead with a dish towel and downed half a bottle of water. We'd been hitting it hard for the last couple of hours, and the heat was taking its toll. "I'm going to get some air."

As I stepped off the truck, Trina came jogging out of the house and grabbed my arm.

"What's up?" I could see Rollie watching us from the service window.

"Slight problem," Trina said. "Both the Rockwell and the Johns are in the same room."

"Actually, that's quite convenient."

Trina shook her head. "Not exactly."

I stared at her, waiting for her to elaborate.

"The paintings are in the room with the guests."

"Shit!" Then, a glimmer of hope caught my eye. "Guess that means we'll have to abort."

"That's not an option. Papa still wants his Rockwell."

"You know it's not actually *his* Rockwell, right?"

"You don't know my father. Anyway, he's going to have one of his guys create some sort of diversion. Get everyone out of the room."

"Or," I arched an eyebrow, "we could just go back to your place and pick up where we left off last night."

"You mean, with you passed out on my couch? Sorry, but no. This is happening."

So much for my persuasive charms. "Remind me again, why is your father here?"

Trina glared at me. "Why shouldn't he be?"

"I thought these people were mostly Bengals and Reds and their hangers-on."

"See that man over there?" Trina pointed at a pudgy guy in a sky-blue sport coat. "He's the sports anchor on one of the local TV stations. And the guy next to him, he's a Kroger VP. Over there, the tall blonde, she's some high-powered attorney. So, no, not just a bunch of jocks and sycophants."

"Got it." I was impressed by Trina's familiarity with local celebrities. Maybe I needed to get out more or do a better job of keeping up on Cincinnati's movers and shakers. Or not.

"Anyway, Papa says it will be obvious when the time is right." Trina tilted her head toward the house. "I better get back. Good luck."

She kissed me, then dashed up the front steps and through the open door.

Not ready to return to Prudence's tropical heat, and since there were no customers in sight, I decided to circle the truck a couple of times, hoping to calm my nerves. As I came around the back side of the truck, I ran head-on into my former business associate.

Vincent grinned at me. "Bon soir, motherfucker."

"Vincent?" My brain was having trouble processing this unexpected reunion.

"In the flesh," Vincent purred, as if in anticipation of slicing off a pound of mine.

"What are you doing here?" Instead of making polite conversation, I should have high-tailed it out of there. But when I tried to skedaddle, my feet felt like they were encased in cement.

"I've come for your soul." Vincent cackled like a B-movie villain. "Just kidding. Fuck your soul, I want your head."

"Wait." I extended an arm, palm out. "Let's talk about this."

"Too late for that shit. You bastards cut me out of thousands of dollars and forced me to go on the run. Now your skull is going to meet my little friend."

From behind his back, Vincent produced a not-so-gently-used gym sock filled with coinage from the US Mint. Before I could protest further, he swung the smelly hosiery toward the center of my forehead.

"You all right?" Rollie, at least I think it was Rollie, was standing over me, frowning.

My eyes were having difficulty focusing, my head pounding more intensely than a bass drum in a metal band. Instead of worrying about whether Vincent might still be lurking in the shrubbery, an image of Trina's father, towering over me and shaking his head, popped into my muddled brain. He kept repeating, *"Don't disappoint me, Antonovich."*

Rollie bent down and patted my cheek. "Anton, you okay buddy?" When I didn't reply, he eased me up to a sitting position. "Who was that guy?"

The ability to form words seemed to be eluding me, but that didn't stop me from wondering why Vincent had chosen tonight to exact his revenge. Regardless of Vincent's presence, Danielovitch would still be expecting to leave the party with a Norman Rockwell tucked under his arm. "I got to go."

"Dude, you're in no shape to go anywhere."

"I just need to walk it off." I hauled myself to an upright position.

"Let's see if you can stand first." Rollie, leaning me against him, walked us several feet away from the truck.

"I'm good, really," I lied, my head spinning like a drunken top.

Rollie tightened his grip around me. "No. You're not. Let's walk a bit."

We'd gone about ten feet when there was an insanely loud pop, and Prudence leapt off the ground like a startled frog, shrouded in a cloud of smoke. The ensuing shockwave knocked us flat, a shower of debris raining down on top of us.

"Prudence!" Rollie, dragging himself to his feet and wailing at the top of his lungs, ran toward the truck, but the heat from the fire stopped him in his tracks. "No!"

Lying on the ground, I felt an odd sense of relief, like I'd just finished the final chapter of a hard-to-read novel. *Infinite Jest*, perhaps. Then, Danielovitch's visage popped back into my head, and I realized that the two reproductions were still rolled up in the PVC tubes. Inside Prudence.

Seconds later, the parking area in front of the house was teeming with the hundred-plus party guests, swirling cocktails and chatting loudly. Trina broke away from the pack, running toward me.

"Oh my God, Anton! Are you okay?"

Unable to speak, I stared in horror at the flames shooting out of Prudence's shattered windows. Trina, pushing the hair back on my forehead, examined the knot that was rapidly forming, a byproduct of Vincent's sock attack.

"Vincent," I croaked.

Trina glanced nervously around. "Here?"

I nodded, which only exasperated my throbbing head.

Danielovitch, making a beeline toward us, hoisted me to my feet. "Retrieve my Rockwell. Now!"

"Papa, let him be. Can't you see he's hurt?"

"Stay out of this, Trina," Danielovitch warned.

I wanted to say, *Are you fucking kidding*? But the severe look on Danielovitch's face suggested he wasn't. So, I went with the most logical reason to abort. "The reproductions were inside the truck. Guess we'll have to call it off."

"Not a chance. I told you before that I don't care if Trevor Anderson knows the painting has been stolen."

Maybe Danielovitch was right. Maybe, since this was the final heist, I didn't need to worry about replacing the Jasper Johns and the Rockwell with forgeries. I could just blame the thefts on Vincent.

A dark thought flitted through my addled brain: Earlier, Trina had told me her father was going to have his men create a distraction to get everyone out of the house. Had he blown up Prudence for one lousy painting?

Danielovitch patted me on the shoulder. "There's a good boy. Let Trina know when it's done." Not waiting for a response, he vanished into the sea of fire-watchers. In the distance, the warble of a siren grew louder.

Rollie, on his knees and covered in ash, was staring at the flames, moaning quietly. I knelt down beside him, and he turned toward me, his gaze focused in the middle distance. I pulled him into an awkward hug.

"We'll get through this." It seemed like the kind of thing you were supposed to say after a tragic event, but I had no idea what it actually meant.

Rollie nodded absently.

"I gotta pee." I climbed to my feet. "Back in a minute."

He grabbed my arm. "Was it the guy who hit you that did this?"

"I don't know. Probably." I didn't want to think that it was Danielovitch.

He tightened his grip. "Does this have anything to do with your art heists?"

"I don't see how blowing up Prudence could have anything to do with recovering stolen paintings." Which should have been true, if it weren't for the unpredictability of Vincent. Or Danielovitch. "We can talk more when I get back. Right now, I really need to pee."

After he released my arm, I scurried off toward the house, circumventing the guests enjoying Prudence's cremation. William, at one end of the crowd, appeared to be engaged in serious conversation with Danielovitch.

In the foyer, a bartender was doling out drinks quicker than a Vegas blackjack dealer. Once fortified, the thirsty revelers doubled back outside to watch the rest of the fireworks show. Leaving the rest of the house to me.

Following the directions Trina had given me, I made my way inland, past more rooms than I could count, eventually reaching the aptly named Great Room. Fortunately, I was still wearing the apron with the secret inner lining.

Pausing at the threshold of the cathedral-like chamber, I peeked around the corner. Vincent, at the far end, was dislodging a bold geometric painting—the Jasper Johns—from the wall. The Rockwell, a nostalgic portrait of a very American family seated around a table at a diner, was still in its frame, leaning up against the back of a couch.

"Not on my watch, asshole," I muttered, sotto voce.

I didn't know whether it was getting cold-cocked with a smelly gym sock full of quarters, watching Prudence get blown to smithereens, or the culmination of the general pissed-off-ness I'd been living with for the past six months, but seeing Vincent in the process of appropriating the paintings on *my* to-do list triggered something in me that had been waiting a long time to surface.

Just inside the room, on the top of a bookshelf, was a bronze statue of a helmeted dude, one hand extended, palm out, the other grasping a football to his chest. In the absence of an actual plan, I grabbed the statue—a Heisman trophy—and charged Vincent like a bull who'd just been stuck by one of those colorful doohickeys they used in bullfights. Which, for the record, I am decidedly against.

What I lacked in stealth and skill, I made up for in enthusiasm. Vincent, having removed the Jasper Johns from the wall, had just placed it on the floor when he registered the demented food truck cook, sculpture raised above his head, charging toward him like Braveheart heading into battle.

Unlike Mel Gibson, I had little else going on aside from momentum. Vincent, on the other hand, must have had some experience dealing with frenzied food truck cooks, because he deftly knocked the bronze trophy out of my hand.

I tried to summon the Tai Kwon Do skills I'd learned in ninth grade, but they stubbornly refused to surface. So, I went all Tasmanian Devil on his gangsta ass. Sadly, lacking any real pugilistic skills, few of my punches landed, and I quickly found myself running out of steam.

I eventually connected with a couple of successful blows, but Vincent got lucky with a solid fist to my chin, whiplashing my head and knocking me off my feet.

Straddling me, he shook his head and smirked. "You know what you are?" He didn't wait for me to reply. "You are nothing but a stinking piece of shit. And your stupid little food truck? Nothing gave me greater pleasure than seeing that bitch up blow up."

As I mentioned before, I was mad. But these words—unimaginative as they were—pushed me over an emotional precipice. From some place deep inside of me, a cauldron of rage boiled over, and I began pummeling his face with every ounce of remaining strength.

Vincent managed to block the first few punches, but they were coming too quickly. And then, somehow, he was on top off me and the Heisman was in his hand, speeding toward my head.

Only, the trophy never reached its intended destination. Instead, Mr. Heisman smashed into the floor inches away from my left ear and Vincent, a confused look plastered on his face, collapsed on top of me, unconscious. Behind him, Rollie, grinning madly, stood with both hands clenched around an iron fireplace poker as if he'd just hit a three-hundred-foot drive down the fairway.

"That's for Prudence, motherfucker." Rollie, relaxing his stance, held the poker out in front of him and let it drop on the tile floor, instantly qualifying for the best mic-drop of all time.

Chapter Seventy

Now What?

Rollie tapped the front of my apron. "That hidden lining is pretty nifty."

We were outside, sipping high-end bourbon cocktails, watching a posse of firemen soak Prudence's charred remains. Flanking the shiny red fire truck were two police cruisers.

A parade of well-wishers had come and gone, offering their deepest condolences, including the hosts, Bengal's offensive tackle Trevor Anderson and his wife. So far, no one had volunteered to start a GoFundMe account to rebuild Prudence.

Content with the knowledge that the Rockwell and the Johns were safely stashed inside my apron, I sipped the whiskey, letting the warmth work its magic. "Why'd you come looking for me?"

"You'd been acting squirrelly all evening," Rollie said. "When you didn't come back from your bathroom trip—which I knew was bullshit—I got worried that the dude who blew up the truck might do something even worse to you."

"Do you really mean that?" I dodged a blast of water coming from one of the thick fire hoses.

"Mean what?"

"That me getting beat up was worse than Prudence being torched?" I was touched and surprised by this possibility. Rollie had always treated the truck like a princess, or at the very least, a kid sister. I'd always been more like the bratty sibling.

Rollie glared at me. "Are you glad the truck blew up?"

"What the hell are you talking about?"

"You know exactly what I'm talking about. For the last couple of months, you've barely been there. I mean physically, yes, but mentally, you've been a million miles away."

"I know. Sorry, dude." I'd tried to hide my growing ennui, but as my screw-ups multiplied, there was no denying my mental nonattendance. "The last thing I ever wanted was for anything to happen to Prudence."

"Hmm. So, now what?"

"I have absolutely no idea." Somehow, the thought of not knowing was oddly comforting. "What about you?"

"You know the guy I told you about? Who was opening a restaurant in Florida?"

"Uh . . . yeah." I had a vague memory of this conversation.

"Well, originally, he asked me to partner up with him. But we had Prudence . . ." He gazed wistfully at her carcass. "But now . . ." Rollie shrugged.

I nodded sympathetically. "I feel ya. A change of scenery might be the right move."

"Yeah, I dunno." Rollie brushed some of Prudence's ashes out of his hair. "Anyway, I'm supposed to go talk to the cops about what happened."

"Want me to go with you?"

"Nah, I got this."

After Rollie trotted off, Danielovitch approached with his neck-tattooed bodyguards. "Finally, I catch you alone. Do you have my Rockwell?"

"Do you know who did this to me?" I pointed at my bruised face, which had begun to take on more colors than a Rothko.

The three stared at me impassively.

The Culinary Caper

"Did you blow up Prudence?"

"Who is this Prudence?" Danielovitch asked.

I gestured toward the barbequed food truck.

Danielovitch shook his head. "My guess? Probably your gangster."

My gangster? Vincent? Trina was gangster-adjacent enough for me.

"Where is my painting?" Danielovitch repeated, this time with an edge to his voice.

I patted my apron. "It's safe. I'll give it to Trina later."

"Excellent!" Danielovitch exclaimed. "I told you I would pay you well for your troubles. Do you remember that?" We hadn't discussed an amount, but I'd hoped it would be similar to the insurance company's reward money. He placed a beefy hand on my shoulder. "Consider your debt paid."

What the hell did that mean? Was he not going to give me anything? "What debt?"

"I forget." Danielovitch laughed. "You are a man with many debts. The one I am referring to is the one you owe me."

Now I was really confused.

"You are acquainted with Ilya Skolnik, are you not?"

"Ilya?" What was happening here?

"The money you borrowed for that restaurant—terrible investment, by the way. That was mine. Ilya was just my . . . representative."

Peter Danielovitch was the loan shark? How was that even possible? Did this mean that Danielovitch was the one who'd issued instructions to break one of my limbs? Or was Ilya, striving for employee-of-the-month, simply showing initiative? And did Trina know about this? "Wait, are you telling me, since I stole the Rockwell, you're canceling what I owe Ilya . . . I mean . . . you?"

"Please don't say 'stole.' Such a vulgar word. I'd much prefer 'liberated.' But yes, that is exactly what I mean." Danielovitch reached into his jacket and handed me an envelope stuffed with cash. "Here's a little something extra. For Prudence."

Danielovitch tilted his head toward one of the neck-tattooed minions. I wasn't sure whether it was Number One or Number Two. "Would you like Vladimir to stay with you? In case your friend comes back."

Vladimir scrunched his nose at me like I was something he'd accidently stepped in. The feeling was mutual. He scared me more than Vincent. And the last thing I wanted was a pissed-off Russian chaperone. "I think I'll be okay."

"Hey, boys." Trina arrived with fresh drinks for Rollie and me. "Playing nice?"

With Rollie still off chatting with the cops, maybe I'd get to consume both cocktails. Trina, having other plans, only handed me one, which I swiftly sampled. "I was just telling your father that, aside from getting my ass kicked by Vincent and having my place of business reduced to charcoal briquettes, the mission was a success."

Danielovitch gave my shoulder a nerve-numbing squeeze.

"This one has potential, Myshka." After kissing Trina on both cheeks, and saying something in Russian to his two enforcers, he sauntered back to the party with the men.

Trina, seeing that Rollie was occupied, commandeered the remaining cocktail for herself.

"Oh shit!" I exclaimed, mid-sip. "I need to let Ricky know what happened. He's going to have a coronary when I tell him his reproductions went up in smoke."

"Chill," Trina said. "I already told him everything. He understands. He's going to meet us later for drinks. Unless you'd rather go to the emergency room."

I did a quick tally of my injuries—two black eyes, swollen cheek, bruises from neck to chest—and then revisited my cocktail. "Drinks sound like way more fun."

Rollie, walking toward us, held out a hand. "I believe that's my cocktail?"

"Sorry." Trina took another sip and relinquished the glass to him.

"Just had an interesting conversation with Cincinnati's Finest," Rollie said.

I raised an eyebrow. "Oh?"

"When they went to the Great Room to nab your buddy, he was gone."

"Vincent?"

"Vamoosed." Rollie clasped my shoulder with his un-cocktailed hand. "However, I'm pretty sure I convinced the cops Vincent was the one who absconded with the two paintings. So, Anton Cherny"—Rollie lowered his voice— "it looks like you're free and clear. You're welcome."

I wasn't sure whether my eyes widened before my jaw dropped. Either way, I was pleasantly surprised by yet another rescue by my pierogi partner. Turning a blind eye toward my thievery was one thing, but concocting a thoroughly believable alternate version of events went above and beyond.

"Thanks, bro." I clinked my glass to his. "Here's to the conclusion of my criminal capers."

"Cheers," Rollie said. "Now we just need to figure out how we're getting home."

"You can ride with Papa and me," Trina suggested.

Before Rollie could accept Trina's offer, I pulled out my phone and beckoned a Lyft.

Chapter Seventy-One

Who Was I Now?

Maybe it was the sun streaming unapologetically through the bedroom window. Maybe it was Trina, naked under the sheets. Or maybe it was that I had absolutely nothing on my plate. No obligations. No places to be. No art to steal. Whatever the cause, this was the first time in a long while that I'd woken up with a smile on my face. Not a creepy serial-killer smile, but a full-on shit-eating grin.

This was surprising for many reasons. First and foremost, I was seriously hung over. To commiserate Prudence's demise, and celebrate the end of our crime spree, Ricky, Trina, and I had met for drinks—emphasis on the plural—at Longfellow and stayed until last call.

Second, there was the matter of Prudence—into whom I'd put countless hours of blood, sweat, and tears—being blown to bits before my very eyes.

Lastly, but definitely not least, were the still-tender bruises, thanks to Vincent, that seemed to inhabit every square inch of my body.

All of those negatives combined still couldn't wipe the smile off my face.

Trina stirred but didn't wake. I watched her for a minute, jealous of her ability to sleep through anything: sirens blaring outside the window, screaming neighbors, barking dogs. Staring at the ceiling, I returned my attentions to the previous evening's events, and what they meant for the future.

Peter Danielovitch had wiped the slate clean on my failed restaurant debt in exchange for stealing the Rockwell—or, as he kept putting it, *his* Rockwell. There would also be insurance money coming in from

Prudence's passing. Rollie would get the larger share, but I would still pocket a decent amount. Then there was the reward coming from the Jasper Johns. Johns's paintings often sold for millions, so my cut would be a healthy five-figure number.

Perhaps more significantly, there was the cancellation of my monthly obligation to Julia. I'd promised to continue child support for Francois, but it would be a fraction of the previous amount.

All told, this newfound financial freedom would be enough to sustain me until I figured things out. Although given my usual inability to come up with a plan, that might take some time.

So, who was I now? A chef without a kitchen? A piano player without a band? A sculptor without a studio? Or simply . . . Francois's father?

Maybe I needed a gap year—can adults have gap years? —to discover the true Anton Cherny.

My phone, clearly programmed to discourage such idle ramblings, chimed. I picked it up and glanced at the sender: Bob Facci, chef/owner of *Roberto's*.

Heard about your truck. Horrible news!!!

Gossip traveled fast in the Cincinnati food world.

How'd you hear?

Local food blog. A link to the article followed. When I clicked on it, I was greeted by a photo of Prudence, flames jutting skyward like a campfire marshmallow.

Damn!!!! I texted back.

I assumed the picture must have been taken by one of the guests, but then I remembered the photographer floating around, snapping candid shots. The event, after all, had been touted as a "celebrity auction," which I later discovered didn't mean the celebrities themselves were up for auction.

And, speaking of celebrities, did Peter Danielovitch's presence suggest that he was one? Since when did mob bosses qualify for celebrity status?

Just before I closed the link to Prudence's obituary, I noticed a recent posting about Chef Phillipe Rameau hiring a new baker. Not surprising—Phillipe's kitchen staff was constantly on the move.

Bob texted again. *Maybe this is too soon, but I'm opening a new place in OTR. And since Fredo is moving to Italy, I'm going to need a chef de cuisine. Interested?*

I nearly dropped the phone. Every single day I'd worked for Facci had been a revelation. I'd only left because Rollie had convinced me that food trucks were the next big thing. I still couldn't believe Fredo was walking away from that job. Family, as I was beginning to learn, could be a bigger draw.

My fingers hovered over the keys, unsure how to respond to Bob's job offer. Minutes earlier, I'd been a free spirit, able to do anything, go anywhere. Was I ready to jump back into the roller coaster of kitchen life? Would Rollie think me a traitor? Perhaps I should explore the possibility of expanding my catering business before returning to work under someone else's culinary umbrella. Even if that someone was the esteemed Chef Roberto Facci.

Or, since I was about to have a bank account with a bunch of zeroes after the first number, maybe it was time to open my own restaurant. I know, classic Anton, blow the whole kit and caboodle—whatever the hell that meant—on a whim. But what if this wasn't a whim? What if this was kismet?

Who was I kidding? There was that place on Fourteenth, the small storefront restaurant that had been closed for two years. Every time I walked by, I tried to imagine how I'd reinvent the place to reflect my own culinary vision.

The Culinary Caper

When my phone rang, I assumed it was Bob wanting an immediate response. I was wrong. It was Phillipe. I hit decline.

Bob texted right as I did. *You still there?*

You do know this is Anton, right? I asked.

Lol. You don't have to decide today. Come in and we'll discuss.

I took a deep breath and then slowly exhaled. I was in no rush to make any decisions, but he did say "discuss." Which didn't imply any sort of immediate commitment. Right?

Sounds great! I responded.

Did Bob's offer mean it was time to start calling myself a chef instead of a *cook*? And did that mean I'd become a different person? A better person? Anton 2.0?

"Who were you texting?" Trina stretched and yawned.

"Roberto Facci."

"*The* Roberto Facci?" She sat up abruptly, the sheet falling away. "No way!"

"Way."

"Did he just offer you a job?"

"Yep." My phone rang again, but I was too distracted by the beautiful, naked woman in bed next to me to pick up.

Ignoring my brazen stare, Trina tapped the phone. "You should answer that. Maybe Bob's telling you the salary."

Reluctantly, I shifted my focus back to the device. There was another missed call from Phillipe. And, seconds later, a text. *Answer your damn phone!!!*

When he called again, I answered. "What?"

"My condolences," he replied.

"For what?"

"Prudence. Saw the story on my newsfeed. So sorry to hear that."

"Merci, Phillipe. I appreciate that."

"Also, wanted to give you a heads-up . . ." Phillipe paused.

I waited, stealing glances at Trina.

"Just hired Julia as my new head baker."

My morning smile vaporized—the smile, which just seconds ago, I'd thought nothing could erase. "What the actual fuck, Phillipe!"

"We met for coffee yesterday. She told me she was moving back to Cincy. Obviously, I offered her a job."

Traitorous bastard! "Not to repeat myself, but what the fuck?" I punched the "end call" button.

Julia, in her confessional call, had mentioned selling her Parisian bakery. But never in a million years would I have guessed she would move back to Cincinnati.

"Was that Bob?" Trina asked, pulling the sheet up to her shoulders.

"No. Phillipe."

"Aren't you Mr. Popular," Trina said. "Did he offer you a job, too?"

"Not exactly."

Why was I pissed at Phillipe? I should have been pissed at Julia for not telling me about her plans to relocate. Or maybe I shouldn't have been pissed at all. In spite of what I thought about Julia's money-grubbing deception, didn't I want to spend more time with Francois?

"What's going on?" Trina asked.

When I told her, she raised an eyebrow. "Well now. This is an unexpected twist. Should I be worried?"

I considered the question. Aside from the incredible opportunity to get to know my son, Julia moving back here didn't change a thing. I would take Chef Bob up on his job offer, or I wouldn't.

More importantly, now that the dark cloud that had been hovering above my head for years had finally dissipated, there was no rush to make major life decisions. There was, however, one thing I had decided: The woman in bed next to me—Russian mobsters notwithstanding—was someone I wanted in my life.

"Maybe this'll answer your question." Relieving Trina of the phone, I tossed it on the bedside table and planted a noisy kiss on her lips. She responded by kicking the sheet aside and pulling me closer.

About the Author

Nick Greenberg, a professional bassist and composer, has played a wide variety of musical styles: Classical, jazz, rock, Broadway musicals, and even the occasional polka gig. His performances have included concerts at Carnegie Hall, the Kennedy Center, and in such distant locales as Taiwan.

Nick's first job was as a busboy but he quickly climbed the ladder to dishwasher. Later, he worked for a caterer in Minneapolis and then did a stint as a prep cook at his uncle's restaurant. His brief career in the food industry, however, convinced him he'd much rather be playing and composing music, writing fiction, and eating his way through the world's restaurants. Nick is a former chocolatier, a current winemaker, and an award-winning home brewer.

Filled with humor, food and music, Nick's writing draws on the colorful and eccentric characters he has encountered in the music business, as well as from the vast chronicles of his culinary quests.

Nick lives in Cincinnati with his wife and golden retriever.

Upcoming New Release!

NICK GREENBERG

THE CATERER
By Cook or By Crook
Book 2

Prudence, Anton's food truck, has been reduced to a pile of ashes. His former partner, Rollie, has fled to Florida, and Ricky is pursuing the artist's life in New York City. As a result, Anton doubles down on his catering jobs. However, not by choice, he continues to steal valuable works of art. Unlike his previous scheme of returning the stolen pieces to the insurance company, Anton is now blackmailed into delivering the stolen items into the coffers of Pyotr Danielovitch, the Russian mob boss.

Danielovitch informs Anton, a former sculptor, that his next heist will target a collection of Russian jewels on display at the Art Institute of Chicago. Anton is expected to create copies of each of the pieces. During a reconnaissance mission to the museum, Vladimir, one of the mob bosses' henchmen, spots a pair of Russian FSB agents…

**For more information
visit: SpeakingVolumes.us**

Now Available!
RANDY SHAMLIAN

A Murder in the Kitchen
Books 1 – 3

For more information
visit: SpeakingVolumes.us

Now Available!
AWARD-WINNING AUTHOR
JODY WEINER

The Krafters: Partner in Time
Book One

"***Raise Your Other Right Hand*** is funny, wry, and so thrilling you can't stop turning the pages." —Frances Dinkelspiel: Award-Winning Author of *Tangled Vines: Greed, Murder, Obsession, and an Arsonist in the Vineyards of California*

For more information
visit: SpeakingVolumes.us

www.ingramcontent.com/pod-product-compliance
Lightning Source LLC
LaVergne TN
LVHW091618070526
838199LV00044B/848